P9-BYC-530

DECLAN'S GAZE WAS DRAWN TO HER EXHAUSTED EXPRESSION.

Libby looked ready to drop and she still had an evening of waiting tables ahead of her, never mind taking care of her son and grandfather . . . and his own demand that she come to his cabin tonight after she was through with work.

Suddenly, the need to comfort her overcame the wanderlust in his heart. The anticipation of taking her to his bed evoked an emotion as compelling as sailing the seas. Libby was an amazing woman made up of beauty, brains and an admirable work ethic. A woman a man could be proud to call his own . . .

Quickly, Declan shook off his unwanted feelings and sparked to action. The sooner the fair was up and running, the sooner he could find his loot, procure a boat and leave this place. No matter the century in which he now lived, he was a man with a roving eye, not one to settle down and make a home on dry land. The treasure had been his goal two hundred years ago, as it was now and always would be.

Books by Judi McCoy

YOU'RE THE ONE

I DREAM OF YOU

SAY YOU'RE MINE

Published by Zebra Books

Free Public Library of Monroe Township
306 S. Main Street
NJ 08094-1727

SAY YOU'RE MINE

Judi McCoy

ZEBRA BOOKS
KENSINGTON PUBLISHING CORP.

http://www.kensingtonbooks.com

Free Public Library of Monroe Township
306 S. Main Street
Williamstown, NJ 08094-1727

ZEBRA BOOKS are published by

Kensington Publishing Corp.
850 Third Avenue
New York, NY 10022

Copyright © 2002 by Judi McCoy

All rights reserved. No part of this book may be reproduced in any form or by any means without the prior written consent of the Publisher, excepting brief quotes used in reviews.

If you purchased this book without a cover you should be aware that this book is stolen property. It was reported as "unsold and destroyed" to the Publisher and neither the Author nor the Publisher has received any payment for this "stripped book."

All Kensington titles, imprints and distributed lines are available at special quantity discounts for bulk purchases for sales promotion, premiums, fund-raising, educational or institutional use.

Special book excerpts or customized printings can also be created to fit specific needs. For details, write or phone the office of the Kensington Special Sales Manager: Kensington Publishing Corp., 850 Third Avenue, New York, NY 10022. Attn. Special Sales Department. Phone: 1-800-221-2647.

Zebra and the Z logo Reg. U.S. Pat. & TM Off.

First Printing: September 2002
10 9 8 7 6 5 4 3 2 1

Printed in the United States of America

To my husband, Dennis.
Inside each of my heroes beats the heart
of a wonderful man.
This one's for you, honey,
today, tomorrow and always.

Prologue

Declan O'Shae strutted the dock. He could see the tip of the *Lady Liberty*'s mast as it rocked at anchor in the harbor, rising tall and straight against the brilliant blue sky. His crew stood ready to accompany him, for he'd promised each man a share of his treasure. Determined to set sail on the evening tide, he strode past the food stalls, ignoring the vendors hawking their wares. He was almost to the end of the dock when he heard the subtle hiss.

"Psst, Captain O'Shae. Come this way."

Declan turned and perused a pile of crates.

"Here. Over here," the reedy voice singsonged. "For you've need of me this day."

He squinted at a pyramid of barrels waiting to be loaded onto a merchant ship bound for England. There, between the waning sunlight and the start of the evening shadows, stood a stoop-shouldered woman, waggling her fingers at him in a decidedly come-hither manner.

Being a gentleman above all else, he stepped toward her. "Good day, madam," he said, well aware of the gypsies who made their living on the wharf. Some offered themselves to the sailors and dock workers; others sold charms or magic potions. Judging by her age, this woman could only make a living at the latter.

"Come closer, O'Shae," she said more boldly.

Though positive they had never met, Declan thought her harmless enough. Feeling magnanimous, he searched the pouch at his belt and pulled out a token. "I've no time to hear a fortune, old woman, but I'll gladly give you something for your purse."

He tossed her the coin and she snatched it in midair. Tucking it beneath the ruffle of her blouse, she flashed a smile through surprisingly white teeth. "I thank ye kindly, but 'tis not yer fortune I'm selling. This journey ye'll be needin' something a bit more special."

Impressed by her lightning-swift hands, Declan strode closer, his mood still patient. He'd waited out a war to reclaim the booty he'd hidden on one of the small islands off the tip of southern Florida. A few more minutes couldn't hurt. "What do you want, if not to foretell my future?"

She winked as she shook her mane of gray-streaked hair. "'Tis something much better, Captain. And much more powerful."

Declan frowned as he stared into her strangely mismatched eyes, one an amber brown, the other a cat's eye of yellowish green. "Do I know you?"

The gypsy rubbed the side of her sharp-bladed nose with a grimy knuckle. "Nay, we've never met, but I've had me eye on you. The time to meet yer destiny has come."

Which eye, he wondered, holding back a laugh, *the green or the brown?* "I've no time for games, woman, for I've a ship to sail. How is it you know my name, and what do you want of me?"

She chuckled softly, and he thought he heard the chiming of bells. Bending down, she reached into the basket at her feet, pulled out a tangle of metal and leather, and began sorting through the mess.

Ready to go, Declan spun on his heel, but strong fingers clamped his shoulder and held him in place. A tremor ran through him and he shrugged off her hand. "Leave me be," he said. "You have nothing I need."

Quick as the wind, the gypsy scampered to face him. "Ah, but I do." Sticking out a palm, she displayed a cluster of trinkets. "Now choose, O'Shae, and choose wisely. Yer life may well depend on it."

"I've no need for baubles," he pronounced, tired of the game she played. "So if you will excuse me—"

"Yer going to retrieve yer treasure, I'll wager."

He blinked in shock. If Black Pete or Jonas or any of his crew had bragged of this journey, he'd skin them alive and hang them from the yardarm. "And what do you know of my treasure? Which of my men spread tales on the dock?"

" 'Twas not yer men who talked, Captain. 'Twas the stars that told me what you were about." She thrust her overladen hand under his nose. "Choose carefully, for only one will do."

Declan stared at the odd assortment. Some of the amulets resembled ancient coins, while others bore strange designs hammered into burnished metal. Raising a brow, he sneered. "None are to my liking. Find another hapless mark to beguile and leave me to my task."

She smacked the geegaws against his chest and he felt a prick against his skin. Growing wary and, dare he admit it, a bit muddled in his brain, he batted at her palm. His fingers tangled in a length of leather and he pulled back his hand, dragging one of the medallions along with it.

"Yer smarter than I gave ye credit for," the gypsy said with a cackle, nodding at the golden disk. "You've made the perfect choice."

He unwrapped the thin leather from his fingers and shoved the medallion toward her. Instead of taking it, she jumped back, and it fell to the ground. "Nay, O'Shae, it belongs to you now. Beside protecting you, it will lead you to your destiny.''

Declan bent over and picked up the amulet. When he stood, the woman was gone. Gooseflesh rose on his skin as he scanned the spaces between the barrels and crates, then walked around and back again. Dumbfounded, he gazed at the circle of metal and saw that it was etched with the profile of a woman . . . a beautiful woman.

Stomping toward his longboat, he raised his hand to toss the thing into the water. Then he felt it, a warm steady pulsing that heated his palm. He stared at the delicately carved face, and a shaft of anticipation shot from the pit of his stomach. Not sure what to make of it, he slipped the leather thong over his head and let the medallion nestle in the center of his chest.

A feeling of calm washed over him and he heaved a sigh. He wasn't a superstitious man, but he wasn't a stupid one either. What harm could it do?

The sky turned an ugly greenish black, like something purged from the bowels of the damned. As he had for the past few days, Declan clutched the amulet hanging around his neck. A moaning wind whipped his shoulder-length hair from its leather tie and shoved him toward the wheel. The ocean crested and heaved, swirling the ship in a vortex of wind and water.

He looked to the small island in the distance, then scanned the roiling mass of clouds building in the southeast. Two days ago, Black Pete had sensed a mammoth gale was approaching, but Declan'd felt in his bones that they could make their destination. Once they arrived in the protected inlet, they would be sheltered from the storm.

Some of his crew had lashed themselves to the guardrails, while the bravest were lowering the sails, readying the vessel for its battle with the elements. Declan called to his first mate, who was tying down the hatch, but the roaring wind snatched his voice and tossed it away.

A wall of water twice the height of the ship loomed toward the bow, its destination clear. He shouted a fruitless warning to his men, then braced for the blow. Wrapping one hand around a sturdy rope, he grabbed at the pendant with the other. Inhaling a lungful of damp sea air, he prepared to meet his fate.

Seconds later, the world turned black.

Chapter One

Libby Grayson rested her head in her hands. After rubbing the heels of her palms into her eyes, she stared again at the worn notebook. Since she'd begun her profession as a bookkeeper, she'd seen dozens—maybe hundreds—of screwed-up accounting systems. The one she was inspecting now had them all beat . . . by a country mile and then some.

Unfortunately, the yellowed ledger, with its ink-stained pages and scratched-out tallies, belonged to someone with whom she was well acquainted. Someone she cared about. Someone she loved. The ledger for the Pink Pelican Bar and Grill belonged to her grandfather.

"Mom?" A small hand tugged at her faded T-shirt.

"Hmm?" Libby asked, still gazing at the muddle of figures. If she stared long enough, maybe she'd be able to make heads or tails of John Patrick Grayson's convoluted idea of keeping books and find the outrageous amount of money she calculated they would need to modernize the bar and pull it out from under.

"Mo-om. Can I have some cookies? I'm starvin'."

Libby realized her son was back from his morning excursion and pushed herself away from the table. "Hey, sport, did you have a good time?" She walked to the counter, opened a cabinet, and took down a fresh bag of J.P.'s favorite chocolate cookies. "Where's Grandpa Jack? I thought the two of you were spending the day together."

J.P. climbed onto a rickety chair and began swinging his sturdy legs under the scarred farm-size table. "He's coming, just as soon as he ties up the boat. We caught lots'a fish this morning. Grandpa Jack says Uncle T's gonna make fish cakes and mush puppies for dinner."

She set a napkin and three cookies on the table along with a glass of cold milk. "I think you mean hush puppies, honey, and Uncle Tito's are the best."

"But Grandpa Jack says the fish have to die first, before they get cooked. He says my grandma died. She was your mom, right? But she's dead now. Grandpa was her fathering law."

"Yes, Grandpa Jack was her father-in-law. That means my mother was married to his son."

"And he's dead, too, right?"

Libby rolled her eyes as she prayed for patience. On the morning Brett Ritter, the man with whom she'd shared her life for seven years, had moved out of their apartment and headed off for parts unknown, their son had returned from day care to find his pet goldfish Humphrey belly up in his bowl. For some reason, he'd equated the two episodes and become obsessed with death. And as many times as she'd tried to explain that the incidents had no relation to one another, it just wasn't sinking in to his five-year-old brain.

"Yes, sweetie, both my parents, who were your grandparents, are dead. But I'm alive and well, and so is Grandpa Jack."

"But Grandpa Jack is really old, isn't he? And old people

die faster than young ones.'' J.P. twisted apart the two chocolate cookies filled with icing and began to lick at the snowy middle, a trick he'd been taught by Brett one rainy afternoon while Libby had been working overtime.

"That's true,'' she said matter-of-factly. She'd never lied to her son and she wasn't about to start now. "But Grandpa Jack is in good health and he's really not that old. I'm betting he'll be around for a long, long time.''

"Damned straight I will,'' came a rusty voice from the back porch. Seconds later, Jack Grayson, looking fit and tan for his seventy-five years, pushed open the screen door and entered the kitchen. Swinging a string of grouper from both hands, he walked to the sink and unloaded his catch, then turned and gave his granddaughter a wink. "J.P. did fine today, Libby. Caught three fish all by himself, didn't you, boy?''

"Uh-huh,'' said J.P., still working on the icing. "It's lots more fun here than in New York. When can we call Dad and ask him to come?''

Libby walked to the table and set a hand on his shoulder. "I wouldn't count on seeing Daddy anytime soon, honey. Like I told you, it's just you and me now, and Grandpa Jack. We have to learn to take care of ourselves.''

"Your Mom's right, J.P. I've been waiting for another little boy to coddle. Now that you're here to stay, we can go fishing every day if you like.''

"Can we look for more buried treasure?'' asked J.P., rubbing a knuckle under his nose.

Libby stiffened when she heard the question. Before she'd realized it, her grandfather had lifted the boy from the chair and set him on his feet. "Say now, isn't it about time you walked to the marina and collected our mail? I bet Hazel has it banded up and waiting.''

J.P. grabbed the last cookie off the napkin. "Can I, Mom? Sometimes Hazel lets me stick my hand in the 'quarium and pet the sea horses if I promise to be gentle.''

"Okay, but don't be a pest," she warned. "If Hazel is busy, get the mail and come right back."

Calling a "Yes, ma'am," from over his shoulder, J.P. raced out the door. Libby took a calming breath before she rounded on her grandfather. "Jack, how could you?"

Looking properly chastised, the old man ambled to a chair and sat. "We didn't do any real looking, Libby girl. I just let him hold the metal detector while we walked along the beach. We weren't actually hunting for buried treasure."

Scrambling for a way to make Jack understand, Libby went to the dingy gray refrigerator and took out a pitcher of tea. After loading the glasses with ice, she poured the tea and carried it to the table. Setting down the drinks, she took a seat across from him.

"I thought I made my request pretty clear. We're not to discuss Brett, the reason he left, or the possibility of his return in front of J.P. And we're not going to talk about anything else that will build up his hopes. Right now, it's important he be grounded in reality. It's bad enough he's got all those abnormal fears about death rolling around in his brain. If John Patrick keeps thinking his father is going to up and reappear some day, or that life is just one big round of treasure hunting, he's only going to be disappointed."

Jack took a long swallow of tea before he answered. "Disappointment is just as much a part of life as the fairy tales, Libby. A kid needs a little fantasy, something special to believe in as he grows to be a man."

Try as she might, Libby couldn't hold back a snort. "There is no such thing as a fairy tale. There's only reality. Life is tough, and you have to be tougher to survive."

Her grandfather wrinkled his brow, clearly irritated. "What the hell happened up in that fancy city you been livin' in? When you were little, you used to love it when we went huntin' for treasure. The two of us used to dream of all the things we'd do when we found our pirate's booty. Don't you remember?"

Libby refused to be drawn into the past. Life in New York

with a man who wouldn't grow up, who'd left her alone to care for their son with nothing more than a note of explanation, was all she needed to prove fairy tales didn't exist.

"I don't have time to remember. And here's a reality check for you: Brett Ritter didn't want me, and he didn't want our child. In the seven years we lived together, he couldn't even find it in his heart to make a legal commitment to our family." She rested an elbow on the table and toyed with her pen. "I now realize marrying him would have been a disaster. The good news is, he's out of our lives and can't hurt us anymore. The less we talk about him, the sooner J.P. will forget. Right now, I think that's for the best."

Jack folded his arms on the table. "Don't tell me you've given up on finding happiness for yourself? Surely you can't deny that love makes the world go round?"

She ran a finger over the condensation coating her glass. "That's *money,* Gramps. Money makes the world go round. Love just makes it complicated. My parents and you and Grandma may have experienced true love, but that kind of commitment and devotion is not the norm, believe me."

"It could be, if you wanted it bad enough," Jack responded, picking at the cookie crumbs on J.P.'s napkin.

Libby sat up in the chair and turned the ledger to face him, swallowing the words she'd almost uttered out loud. No way would she have the chance to find true love in this city of senior citizens. It was bad enough she was hurting inside; she didn't need to make her grandfather feel guilty because he'd called her home.

"You want a fairy tale, I'll show you one." She tapped a finger on one of the book's most unreadable pages. "This accounting system is the biggest load of hoo-ha since Sleeping Beauty. I can't tell which of your suppliers has been paid or who owes you an order. And what were you thinking, not paying the IRS for so long? It's a wonder they haven't closed this place down."

He peered at the scratched-out, barely legible figures from

across the table. "What's the problem? Can't you read my writing? What'd you learn at that fancy college, anyway?"

"Jack," she said through gritted teeth, "this is supposed to be a set of books for a business. The Pink Pelican has been in the family for close to fifty years. Grandma Martha kept decent-enough records. Why can't you?"

Looking suddenly deflated, he raised a shoulder. "How in the heck should I know? Martha never bothered me about that kind'a thing. After she died, I muddled along fine enough. Things just sort'a got away from me . . ."

Libby didn't have the heart to lecture further. It was bad enough her grandfather had to face the fact that he would lose his livelihood if things didn't change. There was no use beating a dead conch.

"I'm sorry. I don't mean to nag. I know it was hard when I left. I'll always be grateful for the money you sent, and the payments you made toward my tuition while I was at school. I—"

"That's not up for discussion, young lady. I don't want to hear another word about what I did to help you get through college. You had the smarts and the drive to make something of your life. And you're here now, aren't you? Came as soon as I called."

"By the time you phoned, I'd already decided the city was no place to raise a child. The apartment was in Brett's name, as was most of the furniture. All I had to do was pack and change my mailing address. We would have been here in a few days, even if you hadn't reached us."

He leaned across the table and patted her hand. "You know, in an odd sort of way, I'm grateful to the sonofabitch. If not for Brett Ritter, you wouldn't have J.P., and you wouldn't be here right now."

Libby folded her arms and made the offer she knew he would take as an insult. "I managed to save some money. It's only a couple of thousand, but I think we should use it to—"

Jack's hazel eyes flashed with indignation as he jabbed

a knobby finger on the tabletop. "Stow it, girl. Charity isn't an option. And besides, somewhere down the line you and J.P. might need the cash. If that happened, I couldn't live with myself, knowing I took what was rightly yours."

She rubbed at a knot of nerves throbbing at the bridge of her nose. Her grandfather reached across the table and took her hand. "Tell you what, why don't you go for a walk and give some thought to finding another way out of this mess. Tide's real low. You could stroll that cove you like so much and have a good cry. Get it all sorted out, like you used to do when you were little."

Holding back a sigh, Libby pushed up from her chair. "You know, you might be right. All I've done since Brett left is stomp and curse and act mean. Maybe a good cry is exactly what I need. Think you can take care of J.P. until I get back?"

"Hell, yes. Like you said, I still got a lot of years left in me. And I aim to enjoy each and every one of 'em with my first great-grandson. Now git. It's a supper night at the bar. I got to help Tito make a bushel basket of hush puppies to go along with his fish cakes."

Libby squinted against the setting sun, a huge fiery disk that looked so hot she was certain it would sizzle when it finally slipped into the ocean. Walking this cove held so many memories. Her mother had brought her to this spot more times than she could count to collect shells or share a picnic. After her parents died, she'd come here to read or think or just stare at the sunset. When things had gotten her down in the city, she'd retreated here in her mind, to this wonderful stretch of pure white sand and quiet water.

Once at the lip of the ocean, she realized Jack had been correct: The tide was lower than she'd ever seen it. Using her toes, she turned over a few bits of colored glass, worn smooth by the roll of the water. Picking up a starfish, she gazed at its delicate beauty. The sea gifted the world with so many precious things. If only it could wash up a miracle, a way to rescue the business and her grandfather from almost certain financial ruin.

Striding to a familiar outcropping of rocks, memories overwhelmed her. As a child, she'd climbed this miniature mountain a thousand times or more. It had been her private place to read or dream . . . or grieve.

Just as she made up her mind to scale the heights again, Libby realized the entire pile of boulders was exposed, something she couldn't ever remember seeing before. Walking around to the ocean side, she was even more surprised to find a small rounded archway at the very bottom that looked big enough for a person to crawl through.

She knew the movement of the tide fairly well and was certain she had a while before the water would return to hide the opening. Wouldn't it be amazing if, after all this time, her pile of rocks had guarded a hidden cave?

Squatting, she stuck her head through the hole and peeked inside. A glint of gold caught her eye and she dropped to her knees. Digging at a small grouping of stones tucked behind the archway, she uncovered what looked to be half of a metal disk. Etched with a profile, it was smooth and rounded on one side but jagged down the other, as if it had been snapped in two.

For no reason other than its uniqueness, she tucked the find into the breast pocket of her T-shirt and inched farther into the opening, waddling ducklike until she could stand. She was a tall woman, close to five-nine, and when she rose to her feet there were still several inches of space above her.

Glancing around, she grew accustomed to the eerie half light seeping in from a spidering of nearly invisible cracks in the ceiling. The cavern was almost squared on the top and sides and held a smattering of seaweed and ocean life. Hesitantly, she walked forward, until she bumped into a rocky shelf just a little higher than her waist. Grabbing at

Free Public Library of Monroe Township
306 S. M...
...iamstown, NJ 08094

the ledge to steady herself, she felt something damp and yielding under her palms.

Scuttling backward, she gasped at the pile of rags—no, not rags—clothes—arranged over what looked to be a lifeless body. With her hand to her throat, she scoured the cave from top to bottom, then looked back at the man—yes, it was definitely a man—lying on the ledge.

Was he dead? Recently drowned and washed up with the tide? Given the way the body was arranged, perfectly flat with arms straight down at his sides, it seemed unlikely. Though his clothes were tattered, he looked too well preserved to be dead.

She spied a good-sized piece of driftwood on the cavern floor and picked it up. If she were still in New York, she wouldn't dare touch the guy, but this wasn't the Big Apple. This was the very tip of southern Florida, light years away from the sometimes crazy, sometimes dangerous citizens of Manhattan.

Tentatively, she poked at his thigh, then poked again, but he showed no reaction to her jabbing. She swallowed down a lump of fear. If she had half a brain, she'd just turn around and crawl back out into the sunshine.

"Hey, mister," she called softly, giving him another firm poke. "Are you okay?"

The body didn't stir.

Rueing the fact that she'd had only one quick course on CPR in college, she took a few steps closer, trying to decide whether or not to interact with the guy. When he continued to lie statue-still, she set the driftwood at her feet. Stepping nearer, she placed two fingers on his neck where, to her great relief, she found a slow, steady pulse.

Still, the figure didn't move.

Hesitantly, she placed her hands on his chest . . . his very muscular chest. Her palms touched smooth, slightly moist skin, then felt the strong even beat of his heart. Her own heart performed a sprightly tap dance and she jerked away.

"Mister?" She prodded his corded biceps with a shaking finger. "Hey, mister, wake up."

Nothing. Not a move or a blink, not even a change in the tempo of his breathing. The ocean lapped at her feet and she knew there was no time to call for help. She leaned forward until the ledge met her waist. "Hey!" she shouted in his ear. "You need to get out of here. If the tide comes in, you'll drown."

She glanced at the walls and saw that the waterline came to the very bottom of the shelf. So much for that stellar idea. Still, she couldn't just walk away and leave him lying here . . .

She peered down intently, just in case the guy was running some kind of con. Scouring his face, she took in his wide forehead, his square jaw shadowed with just a trace of a beard. Straight brows framed eyelids graced with a starburst of dark spiky lashes. A slightly hooked nose sat above firm lips. A small scar bisected one eyebrow, adding an aura of mystery to his severe yet serene-looking face.

She sighed. If she didn't know better, she'd swear he was a movie extra, the kind who played a desert sheikh, or maybe a western desperado . . . or a pirate.

Lord, Libby, where is your common sense? Brett looked like a choir boy, and remember what a jerk he turned out to be.

Inhaling a breath, she set both hands on his cheeks. None too gently, she rocked his face up and down and back and forth until she heard a clinking sound. Staring, she saw that the chunk of metal she'd found in the doorway had worked its way out of her pocket and landed square in the middle of the hulk's well-defined chest.

And it rested on top of what looked to be an identical half of broken medallion.

She dropped his head, giving no notice to the thunk it made when it hit the rocky bed. Carefully, she moved her piece of the metal disk with one finger until it aligned with the section tied to a strip of leather around his neck. She maneuvered the halves together and found they were a perfect fit.

"Jaysus, Mary, and all the saints," the man muttered, jerking his head.

Libby jumped a foot. Bending down, she scooped up the hunk of driftwood and held it like a baseball bat.

Declan O'Shae licked at his lower lip. His brain felt like an iron pellet rolling in a pie plate. His mouth tasted like the bottom of a bilge pump. If he didn't know better, he'd swear he'd been trampled by a platoon of foot soldiers. What the hell had happened to him?

He lifted his eyelids in stages, first gazing down the bridge of his nose, then glancing straight up at some kind of strangely lit ceiling. Finally, he focused on the shadow at his side—a buxom, half-naked woman with a fall of dark curly hair. Unfortunately, her lips were screwed into a frown and she was brandishing a chunk of wood like a hatchet.

Dressed so scantily, she could only be a prostitute, more than likely a going-away present from his men. Which meant he and the woman had probably spent the night together, though he couldn't recall a moment of pleasure. Ignoring her warrior's stance, he hoisted himself up on his elbows and moaned. Surely she could tell by his pained expression that he was in no condition to cause her any harm.

"Tell me, darlin', was it a fine time we had last night? Am I owing you any coin, or have you already been paid for your services?"

"Paid for my services!"

Declan closed his eyes as the sound of her shriek bounced off the walls and echoed in his ears. "For God's sake, woman, calm yourself. I'm in no state to listen to a banshee."

The hunk of wood hit the ground with a thud. "If you think this is some sort of game, I'm here to tell you the fun's over. Any second now the tide's going to rush in and we're both going to end up sitting on that ledge . . . and does offering me *coin for my services* mean what I think it means?"

"The tide?" he parroted, ignoring her question. Rubbing a hand over his jaw, he sat up and whacked his forehead on what felt like solid rock. He stared at the cracks of light and stifled a curse. One thing was certain, he wasn't reclining in an upper berth on his ship.

Placing a hand on his battered head, he swung his legs over the side and dropped to a shaky stand. Sweet Mary and all the saints, his joints were rusty as the bottom of a tin box. Struggling to his full height, he banged his head on the ceiling and saw an explosion of stars.

He held a hand to the top of his battered head and groaned. If his skull were a melon, his brains would be splattered like seeds in a garden right about now. Hearing a noise that sounded suspiciously like a snort, he raised his gaze to find the woman chortling gaily, her hands clamped over her mouth and a wicked gleam in her eyes.

" 'Tis good to know you find this predicament so amusing," he said with a scowl. "Would you mind telling me where I am?"

Squaring her shoulders, her lips thinned in disapproval. "Look around, fella. We're in a cave."

Declan squinted into the darkness. A cave. Hell's bells, how had he come to be here, with a scantily dressed woman who could only be a—

Frantically, he made a grab at the waist of his breeches. Slapping at his pockets, he gave a heavy sigh, then held out his hand palm up. "I'll take my money pouch, if you don't mind."

The doxie's eyes grew round as portholes. Her magnificent breasts rose with the force of her indrawn breath. "I beg your pardon?"

Folding his arms across his chest, Declan glared. Once, as a youth, he'd been taken in by a lightskirt. Since then he'd learned to be firm. "If you thought to lure me here with your charms in the hopes of robbing me, it was a foolish move. I've run men through for less."

Her enticing mouth opened and closed. With an indignant

huff, she set her hands on lushly rounded hips covered by a mere swath of fabric. "Lure you in here? Rob you?" Her shocked gaze shifted to fury. "You have some nerve. First you call me a prostitute; at least I think that's what you meant by that 'paid for my services' crack. Now you're accusing me of stealing. If I had to make an educated guess, I'd say you don't have a nickel to your name. I'm the one who should worry about being robbed."

She took another quick look at the water rushing up toward her ankles. "You're choice, buddy—either stay or crawl out into the sunlight, it's all the same to me—but I'm outta here."

With that, she turned and ducked through the opening in the bottom of the wall.

Determined to follow her, Declan took a step, but his knees buckled from under him and he fell to the ground. Resting his backside on his heels, he gazed at the lichen-covered walls and seaweed-strewn floor. The sharp-tongued wench had been right: Somehow, he'd managed to get himself mired in a cave. Unless he wanted to be trapped by the tide, he had to get out—now.

As he rose, he spotted a shiny object nestled in a mound of seaweed. Thinking it might be the last of his coins, he scooped it up in his hand. Crawling toward the light, he managed to slide his shoulders, then the rest of his bulk through the opening. Once outside, he grabbed at the boulders and raised himself up. God's blood! Were those his bones he heard, screaming with the effort to come to a stand?

Turning, he saw the woman march over a distant sand dune. He shook his head to clear the cobwebs. At least things were coming back to him, even if they looked like scenes from a book with pages missing. The dock in Charleston; a gypsy woman accosting him, giving him an amulet; howling wind and churning water, then terror as a huge wave swamped his ship . . .

But the island they'd been sailing to was deserted. Or at least it had been the last time he'd landed and buried his treasure. Had people colonized this area to escape the war? If so, this was the first he'd heard of it.

Running a hand through his hair, he tried to remember. When last he'd seen Black Pete, the man had been tying down the hatch on the *Lady Liberty,* while Declan had been holding on for dear life.

He staggered to the side of the rocks, hauled himself to the top and squinted at the horizon. For as far as he could see in three directions there was nothing but cresting waves of blue-green water. No ship, no long boats, no men—just a myriad of small islands and the endless swell of the ocean.

Something stabbed at his palm and he gazed down at the piece of metal still in his hand, then the jagged disk hanging around his neck. Just his luck, the medallion he'd come to regard as a talisman had split apart during the storm. But how had both halves managed to end up in the cave? Unless the woman had tried to steal that, too.

He sighed as he slipped the broken half into a pocket and eased his way down from the rocks. Stumbling toward the ocean side of the boulders, he saw that the incoming tide had already obscured the entrance. There was no way he could go back inside and search for a clue to his predicament, damn and blast it.

Arms folded across his chest, he studied the land behind him. This stretch of beach looked familiar, but he couldn't be certain with his brain in such a scramble. Somehow, he'd been saved from a watery grave. But what of his crew? Had anyone else survived the gale? If so, where were they?

He glanced down at his tattered breeches and ripped shirt, little more than rags hanging from his body. If nothing else, he had to finagle clothing and a few nights' shelter. Then he needed to find the wench and demand his money pouch. Once he figured out exactly where he was, he could hunt down his treasure.

He had no choice but to follow the woman.

Chapter Two

Libby charged over the dune and down the rise, still fuming at the way she'd let herself be spoken to. The way her luck had been going lately, it figured she'd try to be humane and help someone, and the wacko would accuse her of a crime. He'd acted just like another man she knew. Brett had often tried to blame her whenever one of his schemes went awry or he got hopelessly tangled in a predicament of his own making.

Why should it be any different with this bozo, trying to make her believe he was some kind of zombie rising from the dead? Just how many fools did he think would crawl into that cave in those few minutes when the tide was low and try to rob him?

Well, she certainly didn't care enough to waste another minute's thought on the guy. She had more serious things to worry about. The idiot could rot in that cave until Christmas as far as she was concerned.

After stopping to catch her breath, she started down the path that led to the cluster of shops that made up Sunset Key. On the ocean side, Frank and Mary Spitzer's combination gas station/grocery store was the first business one met coming into town. Besides auto repairs and gas, the store carried a smattering of everything: groceries, hardware, office supplies and a bank of washers and dryers available to the public. Mary even sold homemade cookies and bread to tourists on the weekends. Looking comfortably tacky, the Sunset Gas and Go resembled an old-fashioned dry goods store straight out of a Hemingway novel.

Hewitt's Marina came next. The most modern building in town, the marina ran a daily fishing tour, sold bait and tackle, and housed the locals' boats. Hazel tried to keep the place painted and polished but, due to a lack of able-bodied workers, found the chore difficult.

On the far side of the marina, across from the town square, stood the weather-worn Pink Pelican. A dilapidated porch wrapped around all four sides. Shingles hung like drunken monkeys off its faded gray walls. Patches of thatch were missing from the roof, while drooping hurricane shutters, most fastened by a single hinge—or was it Crazy Glue?— framed the windows. The Grayson family manor, a large two-story of dubious charm, came next. Before she'd left for college, Libby had thought about running a bed-and-breakfast from the house, but there'd been little money for the major renovations the home needed. One thing was certain, Grandpa Jack hadn't spent any of his hard-earned profits on the upkeep of either place.

On the other side of the street stood the Queen of the Keys, a cleverly named restaurant run by Phil and Don, two men who were partners in business as well as their personal lives. Phil cooked, Don managed, and their combined efforts made the restaurant the most prosperous in town. Customers were happy to drive over the causeway to sample perfectly prepared food served amid the quirky chatter of two elderly gays who entertained with easy banter and relaxing ambience.

To the right of Phil and Don's was Olivia Martinez's craft and T-shirt shop, Sunset Gifts. In need of a serious face-lift, the store carried a varied inventory from artists around the Keys, as well as bathing suits and clothing. Olivia had a knack for finding the most interesting and unusual items, both in art and apparel, but she did a poor job of showcasing them.

Nestled between and behind the restaurant and gift shop stood six identical cottages, owned by Olivia and rented to tourists adventuresome enough to stay in Sunset overnight. Each had a kitchen, bath, sitting area and bedroom, plus the added bonus of a sagging front porch with an ocean view.

Scattered on the far edge of town were a few novelty and surf shops that seemed to change hands every few years. Farther down the road were an array of bungalows, homes to many of the locals. The problem was, most of the young people who'd grown up here had left for school and not bothered to return, just as Libby had done. The kids on the main drag didn't want to work in Sunset, mainly because it was off the beaten path, which meant fewer tourists and less tip money.

She sighed, thinking of the unfortunate way in which her hometown had aged. During college and her time in New York, she'd remembered Sunset as quaint, an eccentricity loaded with charm. Now it simply looked battered and weary. Just about everyone who lived here was rundown, exactly like the buildings.

Today was Friday, so the town was busy. The Pink Pelican would soon be visited by hungry tourists. Monday through Thursday the bar served drinks and a limited lunch menu, but on the weekends Uncle Tito cooked a variety of specials for dinner, along with his signature dish, fish cakes and hush puppies.

Libby hurried along the street. She was supposed to be at the bar right now, helping Jack with the drinks and food. In between, she needed to keep an eye on J.P. and make sure he stayed out of mischief until she tucked him in for the night.

She ran through the kitchen door and spoke to the large

black man hovering over the six-burner stove. "Sorry I'm
late, Uncle T." She grabbed a clean apron off the rack.
"Just give me a minute to make myself presentable, okay?"

In the half-bath, she pulled up the sides of her unruly hair
with white plastic clips, swiped a tube of cherry-colored
lipstick across her mouth and brushed mascara on her lashes.
After stepping out of her cut-off jeans, she slipped into a
pair of clean white slacks, tied the apron around her waist
and gave herself a final once-over in the tarnished mirror
over the sink. This was one of the things she liked most
about Sunset—all she needed were casual clothes and
enough makeup to guarantee she wouldn't frighten small
children, and she was ready for work.

Libby hurried into the kitchen, straight to J.P., who was
drawing on a roll of butcher paper they used as tablecloths
in the bar. "That's very . . . um . . . interesting, sweetie,"
she said, unable to find the words to describe his portrait of
a yellow-colored fish swimming belly up in a bowl.

"It's Humphrey," J.P. said in somber tones. "Do you
think he's in heaven?"

Libby dropped a kiss on her son's curly head. Was there
such a place as fish heaven? Maybe if she pretended it was
a perfectly normal picture for a five-year-old, he would move
on to sketching things with a pulse. "I'm sure he is. Now,
be good for Uncle T. I'll be back in a second."

She checked the ticket attached to a string over the warming lights, picked up three platters of food and raced through
the double doors that led into the bar. Without losing a beat,
she sized up the interior of the lounge. Each of the twelve
tables was filled, a line had formed at the front door and
Jack was taking an order. As usual, he looked in his element
as he made small talk with the customers. Some things never
changed, she thought with a shaft of guilt. Most men her
grandfather's age were retired by now, not standing on their
feet fifty hours a week, serving drinks and waiting on people.

Though Jack had made it clear he wouldn't touch the few
thousand she'd squirreled away, there had to be some way

to use the money to refurbish the place. If she'd been able to save more while she lived in the city, she might have returned with a nest egg big enough to hire someone to do repairs around the bar. But the cost of living was high in New York. And she'd paid all the bills for the last six months, while Brett had been off on another junket to "find himself." She'd been so foolish . . .

She set the plates in front of a family—a husband, a wife, and a daughter. "Sorry for the wait. Give me a second and I'll be back to see if you need anything else, okay?"

Jack met her behind the hand-carved oak bar. "Here you go," he said, handing her his pad. "Before you take the next order, how about tellin' them folks at the door to come find a seat. Drinks are half-price while they're waiting for a table. Got to woo the customers if we want 'em to come back."

"I'm sorry I'm late, Gramps. I was—"

He put a hand on her shoulder. "Nothing to be sorry for. Now get a move on. Looks like it's gonna be a busy night."

Declan made it over the rise in time to see the woman disappear through a thicket of trees. Strange, he thought, taking in the packed earth path and its trodden foliage; this walkway looked old and well used, as if it had been around for over a decade. To the best of his recollection the area was only intermittently visited by smugglers and privateers like himself. How long had the woman, had anyone, been living on this island? Had the British turned it into some kind of secret settlement?

He trudged carefully for a few minutes, pleased to find his limbs loosening and his steps more steady. Even his head had cleared enough to allow him a bit of logical thinking. He had to be wrong about the British. The woman's voice didn't have the proper accent, and this place was too remote, too far from the mainland to be of any use in their war efforts.

He couldn't have been in the cave long. Most probably,

his men had given up looking for him and made their way to the strumpet's camp. He hadn't seen his ship because they'd sailed it nearer to where they'd taken refuge. Once the woman mentioned she'd found a man stranded in a cavern, his loyal crew would know immediately it was him. They would be overjoyed to see their captain, knowing he would do as he'd promised and give them a share of the bounty.

He climbed another low hill. The sun had finally slipped into the sea, but he could still make out shapes and outlines in the light cast by the moon. He stopped at the crest and stared down . . . onto a shocking sight.

A true village with buildings and a road lay before him, waiting to welcome him.

He scanned the town and the area around it until a smile feathered his lips. There, jutting into the sea at the eastern tip, was a familiar outcropping of land. He *was* on the right island, for he'd used that particular mass as a marker when he'd buried his booty. His treasure was down there somewhere, and once he got his bearings he would find it.

He approached the town at a trot. His feet hit the road and he stopped short. What manner of dirt was this, packed hard and black and separated down the center by a bright yellow line? Stepping more cautiously, he made his way farther onto the road and bent to inspect its surface.

A noise blared and he jumped, spinning to the other side of the street. Sweet Jesus, he'd almost been run down. But by what manner of carriage? It had whizzed by so quickly the tatters of his shirt were still flapping in the breeze. He watched the odd conveyance disappear into the dusk, the lights on its backside glowing like the eyes of a devil. Where were the horses? What propelled such a demonic vehicle?

Perplexed, he ran a hand through his hair. Looking up, he spied a wooden sign printed with the words WELCOME TO SUNSET, ESTABLISHED 1936. He shook his head, wondering why the town's founders had allowed the sign painter to make such an error in the date. Still, the idea that they had named the town showed prosperity . . . and permanence.

But the closer Declan got to town, the more confused he became. Dozens of vehicles similar to the one that had almost flattened him were lined up neatly in front of the shops. Bright light shined from glass globes balanced on the tops of tall metal poles, and he had a suspicion their glow did not come from candles or whale oil. People strolled the walkway, all speaking the King's English, but their words were tinged with accents he couldn't quite place.

"This town sucks! When can we get ice cream?" a lad pleaded to a flustered-looking woman Declan suspected was the child's mother. Wearing pants that looked three sizes too large, his shirt bore the drawing of a goggle-eyed, yellow-haired boy. The words on the shirt, written in colorful letters below the picture, read, BART SIMPSON, PROUD TO BE AN UNDERACHIEVER.

The woman, who was dressed very much like the doxie from the cave, carried a screaming tot on her hip and dragged another along behind as she called to her son, "Hey, cool the trashy language, and tie those sneakers before you trip."

Declan watched Bart Simpson fumble with the laces on his oddly shaped green and purple shoes, then race after his mother and siblings. He had heard of *iced* cream, but he'd never tasted any. And how could a town "suck"?

His stomach rumbled, and Declan realized he couldn't recall what or when he'd eaten last. Dismayed that he had no coin, he moved slowly, taking in the astounding sights as he pondered his next move. Horseless carriages ran freely over the road. People trod the streets dressed in clothing that looked completely different from what he remembered. He opened, then quickly closed his mouth at the sight of a young woman wearing nothing more than two pieces of black fabric across her bosom and bottom.

"Take a picture, it'll last longer," the girl snapped. She raised the middle finger of one hand as she walked away.

He spotted a wooden bench in front of the store window

and sat down with a thud. His stomach growled again, but he paid it no heed. What manner of place was this? What kind of people lived here? Where were his men and his ship? What in blue blazes had happened to the world?

Before he could make sense of the situation, a woman came out of the shop and began to sweep the walkway. She wore a faded blue dress, more familiar to him than anything he'd seen on the other ladies roaming the street. She smiled, and he raised his feet to allow her broom access under the bench.

"Thanks," the woman said, giving him a nod.

Declan grinned in return. His stomach growled more insistently, and he grew bold. "I'd gladly do the chore for you, good woman, in exchange for a bite of whatever is creating the wonderful aroma coming from your fine establishment."

She stopped sweeping and sized him up through piercing gray eyes set under heavy brows. After a few seconds, she held out the broom. "I'm guessin' it's the homemade bread you're smelling. I suppose I could spare a sandwich and some cookies. Didn't have time to unload and stack the canned goods today, either. You interested?"

Declan had been the fourth son of a modestly successful ship builder from Dublin. The only legacy he'd received from his father, a small frigate, had been so storm-damaged that he'd had to repair the vessel on his own before he could sail to the colonies. Ever since he'd left Ireland to make his fortune, he'd worked for his keep. From the looks of it, he'd need money to make his way in this strange place, at least until he found his treasure. He stood, gave a bow and took the broom.

The woman clucked her approval. "You're a flirt, if ever I saw one," she said with a shake of her head. "Come on inside and meet my husband Frank. He'll show you what needs doin'."

* * *

For Libby, Saturday morning arrived all too soon. Her job in New York had been mentally taxing, but she'd spent most of her time at a desk, studying ledgers or tapping at a computer keyboard. Standing on her feet for eight to ten hours a day was going to take some getting used to.

She rolled out of bed and tiptoed down the hall straight to J.P.'s room, one of five bedrooms in the house. Jack and Martha Grayson had built the huge two-story as a vacation home. They'd hoped for a big family, but soon after Libby's father was born, Martha had been diagnosed with cancer. Medical science treated the condition differently back then, and Martha had undergone a hysterectomy as well as the removal of a breast. After her chemotherapy treatments, they decided a life with less stress would be better for her health, so the Graysons sold their bar in Miami and moved to Sunset, where they opened the Pink Pelican Bar and Grill.

J.P. was fast asleep, but Libby couldn't help noticing the picture of Humphrey he'd drawn in the restaurant last night, tucked under his pillow. She rested her forehead on the door frame as another wave of guilt swept through her. She'd been so absorbed in her problems with Brett and Grandpa Jack, she'd been ignoring her little boy's fears. Why hadn't she figured it out sooner? J.P. needed a pet, something alive to focus on instead of something dead.

She'd have to speak to Mary. Last she'd heard, the gray tabby that lived in the gas station repair bays had birthed a litter of kittens. When they were old enough, J.P. could choose one for his very own. Heck, he could pick one out this morning and visit it every day until it was ready to leave its mother. Waiting for the kitten to mature would give him something to look forward to. She could use the birth to help him understand the normal progression of life and death and get him to accept the big picture.

Libby smiled smugly as she sat on the edge of his bed. She was brilliant, a paragon of mommyhood. Score one for guilt-ridden single mother's everywhere.

J.P. turned and blinked open his sleepy hazel eyes. "Good

morning." She pushed the curls from his brow. "You sleep okay?"

He grinned. "Uh-huh. And I'm starvin'. Are you making breakfast this morning?"

Libby stood, went to his dresser and pulled out shorts and a T-shirt. "You bet. Brush your teeth and wash your face, then get downstairs on the double. Soon as you finish eating, we're going to Mary and Frank's."

J.P. shot from the bed. "I met them before, didn't I? They own the gas station, and they're all alone, 'cause their son and daughter left and moved to nilli-noise, right?"

"Jeff and Cheryl moved to *Illinois*. Jeff is a professor at Northwestern and Cheryl married a doctor and lives in Chicago. Sweetheart, they're both fine. They come back to visit every once in a while."

J.P. padded out the door, but not before saying, "That's good, 'cause I thought they might be dead."

Declan jolted straight up in his cot and blinked at the sunlight streaming through the small window overhead. After taking a deep breath, he ran a shaking hand across his stubbled jaw and glanced warily around the room. Slowly blowing the air from his lungs, he swung his feet to the floor, then pinched his thigh hard through his ragged breeches.

No, he wasn't dreaming. He hadn't died and gone to hell, nor was he on his ship, or back in that cave. He was still in the storage room in which Mary Spitzer had allowed him to sleep overnight.

After what he'd discovered last evening, it was a miracle he'd been able to get any rest at all. He'd swept the store, emptied and stacked cases of something called canned goods, then unloaded two crates of fruit. In between the rigorous work, he'd listened and learned. But he still couldn't believe what he now knew to be true.

It wasn't 1783. It was the year 2002. Over two centuries had passed since he had last walked the earth.

He remembered the stand of newspapers he'd seen at the door of the shop. At first he'd thought them some kind of pamphlet made to entertain the customers. Until Mary saw him eyeing the papers and told him he was welcome to read one when he finished his chores.

Sweet Mother, what he'd discovered was still a shock. If it were true, he was totally and completely alone. His men were sleeping with the fishes, his ship was in Poseidon's graveyard, and his treasure had most likely been found and spent.

Declan shook his head, thinking to rearrange his muddled brain. He'd been knocked on the noggin so many times yesterday, perhaps he just didn't have it all straight. Bending down, he picked up the paper he'd studied before he finally drifted off to sleep. There it was, larger than life, the current date written clear as sunlight under the heading of the *Miami Herald*.

At least the paper had an explanation for so many of his questions. It either advertised or spoke of hundreds of things he couldn't begin to comprehend. The horseless carriages he'd found so amazing were called automobiles, and everyone in the country, the United States of America, owned one of the vehicles. Airplanes, enormous ships of the sky, carried cargo and passengers as they traversed the continents on a regular basis. The country had enlarged to fifty regions called states. He'd seen on a weather map how the colonies swept across the land from ocean to ocean. There was a president and a congress, an elected body of officials who governed the nation, very much like the patriots had foreseen in their fight for freedom.

He smiled as he imagined what Benjamin Franklin, one of the most vocal and intelligent statesmen of his time, would have done had he been the one in this predicament. The world and everything in it was bigger, more unbelievable, than anything man had ever dreamed.

Declan had no idea how he'd come to be in this situation, but he suspected the howling gale that destroyed his ship had something to do with it. The *Lady Liberty* had sunk and somehow, in the aftermath of the storm, he had found the cave, crawled inside, and heaved himself onto that ledge. Why he'd slept away the last two hundred years was the real mystery. How could he have done so and still be alive?

He ran a hand over his chest and found the only thing he had left to connect him to his past, half of the amulet he'd been given by the gypsy woman before he'd sailed. Standing, he slapped at his pocket and felt the other piece, exactly where he'd stowed it. Strange how even after being broken in two, it had survived the storm, just as he had.

Was it fate that he was in possession of both halves of the medallion? Was there divine magic at work here, some reason he should be in this place at this time? If so, what was it?

A knock on the door startled him from his musings.

"Mr. O'Shae? It's Mary Spitzer. Are you decent?"

"Aye, madam, I am. Please, come in."

The door inched forward as Mary poked her head into the room. "I . . . that is . . . Frank and I, we noticed your clothes were sort of . . . Well, we thought you might like a change. This stuff belonged to our son, but he moved away. I'm not sure anything will fit, you being such a big man and all, but you're welcome to borrow whatever."

Declan took the items she offered. "Thank you. I shall repay you as soon as I'm able."

Folding her arms across her generous bosom, Mary nodded. "That's another thing we wanted to speak to you about. Frank and me, we need help around here. Doesn't matter whether or not you're capable of working on cars, but we sure could use a hand with the type of chores you did last night."

Clutching the clothing to his chest, Declan grinned. "Are you offering me a position?"

"A position?" The woman worried her lower lip. "Well now, I guess we are. We can pay you minimum wage to start, though I can't guarantee there'll be enough to give you a forty-hour week, but I know there's plenty of work here in town, if you want it. Just depends on how handy you are.''

Declan didn't need to think for more than a few seconds. A position meant coin to obtain food, lodging, maybe even one of those automobiles. And a job would give him a reason to remain in town until he could find out what had happened to his treasure. He refused to give up on his life's work until he knew for certain it was gone.

"I accept," he said, holding out his hand. Women, it seemed, had much to say about business these days. And from the looks of it, Mary Spitzer ran this store equally with her husband. "May I stay here until I'm able to accumulate enough coin to find my own lodging?"

She shook his hand to seal their deal. "Lodging? Oh, you mean a place of your own." She ran her amiable gaze around the small storeroom. "Stands to reason a man of your size would want a little more space, but I don't think there'll be anything to rent until the season's over. Olivia lets her cottages go for a third of the price after that."

Declan wrinkled his nose. "Right now, I find myself more in need of a privy . . . and a bath. I fear it's been some time since I've had the luxury of a good washing."

Mary colored red as she rubbed at her nose, and they both chuckled. "Thank goodness you asked, because that was gonna be my next offer. Go outside and up the stairs, then follow the hall to the right until you find the bathroom. There should be a fresh toothbrush and disposable razors under the sink. There's coffee on the counter and bread and fruit on the kitchen table. You come on down when you're finished and I'll get you started on a few of those chores."

Chapter Three

"Hey, J.P., you settling in okay?" Mary Spitzer smiled a welcome from behind her cash register. "Libby, nice to see you again. Everything all right at the Pink Pelican?"

Placing a hand on her son's shoulder, Libby moved J.P. out of the way of a paying customer and rested an elbow on the counter. "About the same. You know Jack; he doesn't have a care in the world until it's too late. How's business been around here?"

Mary made change and handed it to an older man dressed in lime green shorts and a yellow-and-red-flowered shirt, then leaned forward and waited until the customer was out of earshot. "Fair to middlin'. Then again, it's almost summer. Trade's gonna drop to a trickle pretty soon."

"I know," Libby answered, well aware that once June rolled around, the hot humid months and hurricane season would hamper the town's earning potential. "I was just hoping things had picked up since I've been gone. Thought maybe someone had found a way to entice more tourists to Sunset in the summer."

"I hear ya. Still, we always seem to put by enough to

make it through November." Mary raised one bushy brow. "Isn't Jack showing a profit this year?"

"It seems Grandpa Jack hasn't made a profit for the past couple of years," Libby confided, feeling a need to talk to someone for the first time in a while. She'd known Mary her entire life, had grown up with the Spitzer children. Their apartment above the store had always been a second home, just like so many of the other businesses in town. "He hasn't kept the best of records. It's one of the reasons I came back."

The older woman nodded. "That man always did rely on Martha too much. Ever since she passed away—"

Libby sent a sideways glance toward J.P., who'd wandered down the candy aisle. "I know. He still keeps the daily take hidden in his underwear drawer, and I don't think he's written a check in years. He pays for everything in cash, when he has it." She lowered her voice a notch. "If I don't find a way to bring some money into the Pink Pelican, I'm afraid we might lose it."

Mary pursed her lips. "Now that just ain't gonna happen. Why, no one in Sunset would allow it. And what about Phil and Don? They'd never let Jack go under."

The bell above the door rang and a crowd of tourists sauntered in, fanning out in small groups to shop. "He wouldn't dream of taking charity, so I'd appreciate it if you'd keep what I said under your hat. I'm still working on the books." Libby waved to J.P., and he returned to her side. "We're here because I heard you had a special delivery in one of the bays last week."

Her eyes twinkling, the older woman nodded. "Sure did. Six little furballs in every color you could imagine. Think you know someone who might be interested in adoption proceedings, say in about six weeks or so?"

Libby winked as she smiled down at her son. "I might. Mind if we take a look?"

"You know the way," said Mary, her attention shifting to a woman with a basket full of supplies.

Libby clasped J.P.'s hand and led him through a side door, into the garage area of the building. Frank was nowhere in sight, so she assumed he was helping customers at the pumps or working in the rear of the store.

"Why are we in here?" J.P.'s voice echoed against the cinder-block walls.

Libby tilted her head, heard a faint mewling and tugged him forward. "Come on, you'll see." Threading through a display of tires, then a stand of tools, she followed the sound to the rear of the bay. The box she was searching for sat tucked in a corner next to a workbench.

Squatting down, she said, "Hello, Miss Betty. I've brought someone to see your babies." Libby grinned up at a gaping J.P. "Well, what do you think?"

The boy's eyes grew round as his lips slowly turned up at the corners. "Are they real?" he finally asked.

"Of course they are," she said, staring at the squirming mass of hungrily nursing kittens. "But they're little, so be careful. Don't move too fast or you'll frighten Betty."

J.P. nodded as he dropped to his knees. Tentatively, he raised a hand and set a finger on a white furred head. "Wow."

"I'll say," Libby whispered, pleased to see the boy so gentle. "Which one do you like best?"

J.P. still hadn't picked up on the idea that he was here to choose a kitten. "They're all nice. How come some of them are so pink?"

"Well," said Libby, "I'm not sure. But it takes a while for their fur to grow in. The pink ones will probably be light-colored, maybe white or gray like their mother. That black one and the one with the brown stripes are darker, so you can see the coloring better."

"Could I pick one up?"

Libby gave Miss Betty's head a scratch. Purring louder than a buzz saw, the cat rolled onto her back, popping the kittens from her belly like miniature fuzzy cannonballs. "I think that means yes, but go slow. Which one would you like to hold first?''

Almost reverently, J.P. reached into the box and placed his fingers on the black kitten's head.

Libby scooped up the baby, cradling it in her palm. ''Hold out your hands. Good, just like that.'' She set the cat in J.P.'s trembling fingers. ''Bring it close to your chest, but not too tight, okay?''

She heard footsteps from behind and thought it was Frank who had come into the bay. Turning to greet him, she looked up to follow a length of faded jeans stretched tight over muscular thighs, trim hips and a narrow waist. When she reached the cerulean blue T-shirt pulled taut over a flat, corded stomach and wide rippling—yes, rippling—shoulders, she knew for certain it wasn't Frank.

''Madam.''

''You?'' replied Libby. Closing her mouth, she scrambled to her feet. They spoke at the same time.

''What are you—?''

''How did you—?''

She took a protective step in front of her son. ''What . . . who let you in here?''

''I work here,'' the man from the cave answered, giving her a lazy grin. ''And you, my good woman, do not. I might ask the same of you.''

Libby couldn't believe it. The bozo had finagled a job from the Spitzers, two of the kindest, most naïve souls on the Key. She drew to her full height and still had to raise her chin to meet his eyes. ''Mary and Frank are old friends.'' She fisted her hands on her hips. ''How did you talk them into hiring you? Do they know where you came from?''

He folded his arms across his chest. ''They didn't ask. I worked in their establishment yesterday evening, and today they found enough charity in their hearts to offer me permanent employment.''

She tapped the toe of her sandal on the cement, grudgingly admitting that the Spitzers had aged. With Jeff gone, they

probably did need help, just like her grandfather did. One
of the reasons the town looked so ratty was because there
just weren't enough people living here with the energy and
enthusiasm needed to keep Sunset sparkling. But what kind
of friend would she be if she didn't clue them in on where
she'd found this guy?

"Well then, I guess someone needs to let the Spitzers
know you were living in a cave until yesterday."

His eyes, narrowed in challenge, matched the blue of his
shirt. "And you, I suppose, are that someone?"

"Darned right I am."

"Why?" he asked. "When I've done nothing to warrant
your distrust or theirs."

Libby bit her lower lip, annoyed at the way he made her
feel—like a butterfly pinned to a board just waiting for the
chloroform. His voice, a fascinating blend of Irish lilt and
old world charm, set her heart to thumping—giving her a
second reason to dislike him. The last thing she needed
was to find herself attracted to another irresponsible man.
Besides, there was something weird about this guy, something she couldn't quite put her finger on . . .

"Because . . . because you're a beach bum . . . and a . . .
a con man. You didn't fool me in that cave yesterday. You're
here to take advantage of my friends."

"And what about me, madam? I'm still wondering if you
did the same to me."

Libby glanced down at J.P., who was thoroughly
engrossed in the kittens, before she hissed out an answer.
"If you're still trying to accuse me of taking your money,
you can find a stick and sit on it. You're the stranger here,
so you're the one who can't be trusted."

"Listen, here, good woman. I'm—"

J.P. scrambled from behind Libby's legs, the cat cradled
against his chest. "Look what it's doing," he said, watching
the kitten curl into a sleepy ball.

The man squatted until he was level with the boy's face.

"They're a fine lot of fur, now aren't they? I've named that one Black Pete, in honor of a friend."

J.P.'s mouth puckered into a frown. "Then he's yours? You already picked him out for yourself?"

Libby watched the stranger's thick black hair, held at his nape with a rubber band, swing back and forth across his broad back as he shook his head. "Nay, not mine. He just reminds me of someone I once knew. Whoever claims him can rename him if they like."

"Honey," Libby chimed in, "maybe you should hold a different kitten for a while. You don't have to choose today."

J.P. whipped up his head, his little-boy face a mask of amazement. "You mean I can have one? For my very own?"

Ignoring the stranger, she guided her son back to the box. "Yes, that's why I brought you here. Now let's put this one—"

"Black Pete. That's his name."

"Um . . . all right . . . let's give Black Pete back to his mother and you can check out another one, okay?"

Carefully, J.P. did as he was told. Libby chose one of the pale gray kittens and set it in his hands.

He cuddled it close and took a step toward the stranger. "How about this one?"

"Bridget." A feathering of laugh lines appeared at the corner of his eyes, softening the man's severely carved features. "Because she has the temperament of a fair colleen I once knew."

J.P. nodded, as if he accepted every word, and went back to inspecting the litter. Ticked that this phony had the balls to still insist she was a thief, then look so engaging while he tried to con her son, just like he'd obviously done to Frank and Mary, Libby glared. "You have nerve."

Rising to his feet, the man offered his hand. "Declan O'Shae, at your service."

* * *

Declan watched the woman take the boy and fairly run from the building, her chestnut-colored curls cascading down her back like a waterfall. He shook his head, still enthralled with her long legs and pleasingly shaped backside. Now that he knew her style of dress was perfectly acceptable for women of today, he could afford to appreciate her superior form.

The way her honey-gold eyes flashed when she'd met him toe-to-toe told him that she had a temper. From the sound of her vehement denial, he'd been wrong about her thieving, so she had every right to be prickly. But what reason had she to be so distrustful of strangers? His courtly manner had forced her to shake his hand, and for that he was grateful. It gave him the opportunity to caress her smooth palm and slender fingers. The way she'd trembled under his touch had set his own heart to thrumming.

God's blood, she was a fine figure of a woman.

Last night, when he'd recalled their meeting in the cave, he'd thought her face familiar, but the light had been dim and he'd had an addled brain. Today, with the morning sun full overhead, he was certain he knew her from somewhere. The tilt of her upturned nose and the fullness of her lips called to some elemental yearning deep inside him. Though he knew it was impossible that they'd met before yesterday, he would remember how he knew her before the week was out.

He wiped the sweat from his brow and scanned the garage. Everything in this new time was a puzzle, each chore a game to be mastered. He'd learned how to operate the gasoline pumps, repair a flat tire, flush a toilet, make change of a twenty-dollar bill. Mary hadn't batted an eye when he'd asked to be shown the workings of an electric range and something called a Mix Master. And she'd agreed to lend him money so he could go to the shop across the street and purchase another set of clothes and essentials. She'd even talked of giving him a haircut, so he wouldn't look so *scruffy*.

His head was fair to aching with the things he'd had to

absorb, but he was beginning to enjoy it all. Though still not clear as to how this amazing transformation had taken place, he knew he had to adjust in order to find his treasure. If he was going to live in this time permanently—and so far nothing had happened to make him think otherwise— he at least needed to know where his past had gone.

Remembering he'd been sent to the garage for motor oil, he spied the carton he needed and took a can of the viscous stuff in each hand.

"See you found it," said Frank Spitzer, walking in through the open bay door. He scratched at the fluff of white hair standing straight up from the crown of his head. "Libby Grayson sashayed outta here a few seconds ago as if her tail was on fire. You two have a run-in or something?"

Declan had thought long and hard about how much he should reveal to these people, and decided to tell the truth whenever possible. He might have slept away two centuries, but he figured the human race had stayed pretty much the same when it came to accepting the unbelievable. If a man wasn't careful, a lie often came back to bite him, sometimes in the most embarrassing of places. With so many new things to ponder and store in his brain, he didn't think he could count on being clear-headed enough to keep up with the constant webbing needed to support a falsehood.

"We met yesterday, in the cove to the west."

"That would be Dream Cove," said Frank. "Libby never did like folks trespassin' in her special spot."

Well, that explained it, thought Declan. Libby Grayson had been wandering her private refuge when she'd come upon him in the cave. He'd surprised her, taken her off guard. But would that alone make her so suspicious and unbending? He filed the tidbit away for later and brought up another point of concern.

"She has a son," he said simply, waiting for Frank to fill in the details. As far as he could tell, the man was a bigger gossip than his wife and never minded discussing what he knew.

"Yep. He's named after Libby's grandpa, John Patrick, but I guess she decided it was too big a mouthful for such a little guy, so everybody calls him J.P."

"Where is the wen—ah, the woman's husband?" Declan asked, perplexed at the gut-wrenching way in which he felt compelled to learn more about her.

"Don't think there is one," muttered Frank. "John Grayson, we call him Jack, was proud as punch when he found out he was gonna be a great-grandfather, but he never did mention a wedding. Mary said it was none of our business."

Declan swallowed his surprise. He'd always tried to judge the mettle of people by their actions. In his day, any woman who birthed a bastard either gave the child away or left town in disgrace. If they had money and connections, they sometimes found a way to convince others they'd been widowed. He'd learned quite a bit about the morals of this time, just by listening to peoples' speech and observing the way they interacted with one another. Most children, it seemed, had little respect for their parents. Women flaunted their bodies and, if Libby Grayson was any example, lived a scandalous life.

Still, the boy was well mannered. And from the way the woman spoke of honesty and truth, she seemed to have changed her immoral ways. Perhaps he should withhold judgment until he had the chance to meet a few more of this century's citizens. Especially Jack Grayson, the man who had accepted his unmarried granddaughter and great-grandson so proudly.

Insulted and embarrassed, Libby hustled J.P. down the sidewalk. Why in the heck had she allowed the arrogant jerk to get her so worked up? All right, so he was a good-looking man with a better-than-average body. She was a normal woman with normal needs. Up until a month ago, she'd been involved in what she thought was a committed relationship with an attractive member of the opposite sex.

It was easy to accept the fact that Declan O'Shae sent her hormones zinging through her veins.

What she couldn't handle was the idea of this O'Shae guy thinking her a thief. If he knew how much money she'd handled in her last job and how easy it would have been for her to help herself, he never would have accused her of pocketing what had to have been a few paltry dollars.

But he didn't know her. And if he was telling the truth about not meaning anyone harm, then she had lost her temper and insulted him as well. Living in Manhattan for the past twelve years might have toughened her to the realities of the world, but she'd always felt a sense of pride in knowing she'd been able to keep her small-town manners intact.

What right did she have to say he was a con man or a fraud? Just because she'd found him unconscious or asleep or whatever he'd been in that cave didn't mean he was out to take advantage of the locals. Lots of people wound up down on their luck from time to time, so why not him? Feeling used and abused by Brett didn't mean every guy with whom she came into contact was the same.

Still, she was sick and tired of trying to relate to people who had their own selfish agendas. Brett had wasted seven years of her life, promising they'd get married as soon as he felt the time was right. He'd frittered away the last months of their relationship while she'd paid the bills and kept their family whole. She'd been a real chump.

But why would a man like Declan O'Shae, a man who seemed intelligent and looked so ... so ... competent, be dressed in rags and hiding in a cave?

Mildly comforted by the knowledge that he was now Frank and Mary's responsibility, she continued down the street. She didn't have to interact with the man at all if she didn't want to. If he was an opportunist, there'd be nothing to keep him in Sunset because there was no opportunity here. When he saw how things slowed down in the summer, he could go work the bigger tourist centers off the main

highway. Once the season ended, he'd be gone with the first
tropical storm.

"Mom?" said J.P., racing ahead of her to the bar. "Can
I go with Grandpa Jack?"

Still distracted, she swung her gaze to her grandfather,
who was walking toward them with an armload of fishing
poles.

"Got to catch us today's supper. You want to come
along?" he asked J.P.

"Can I, Mom? Please?"

Libby checked her watch and noted that it was ten-thirty.
In another hour they'd open for lunch, then there would be
a short lull and another crowd for dinner. She needed to
change her clothes and help Uncle T; having her son out
from underfoot would be a godsend.

"Fine with me." She gave Jack a pat on his whiskered
cheek. "I'll get cleaned up and give Tito a hand. Do we
have everything we need for lunch?"

"Special menu. I put it on the blackboard," Jack muttered,
not meeting her gaze. He took J.P.'s hand. "You talk to T
if you have a problem with it. We'll be back later."

Libby went into the house, made herself presentable, and
headed to the Pink Pelican, all the while wondering what
her grandfather had meant with that "special menu" crack.
Letting herself in through the kitchen's side door, she found
her surrogate uncle bent over the burners, shaking his head
as if he was crying.

"Hi. What's for lunch?" she asked, sniffing at the famil-
iar-but-out-of-place aroma filling the air.

Tito turned, his ebony bulk encased in a white apron, a
T-shirt and cook's pants splattered with crimson globs. His
black eyes gleamed fire as he waved a metal ladle in the
air. "Spaghetti and meatballs!"

"What?" Libby went to the stove and lifted the lid on a
huge bubbling pot. "You can't be serious!"

Tito heaved his massive shoulders. "I can and I am. That
man done this to me time and again. Forgets to pay the tab

with the suppliers, then has me makin' this white bread slop for lunch. Most of the time the customers read the menu and walk right outta the bar.''

"It smells wonderful," she said, hiding a confused frown. Tito had been the cook here since before Grandma Martha died. In all the years he'd been in charge of the kitchen, Libby couldn't remember the last time he'd made something so ordinary. To Tito, anything less than the Keys' specialties—conch fritters, Florida lobster, snapper, grouper, and Key lime pie—was a sin worthy of major repentance. If people wanted fancy steaks or trendy French food, they could go across the street to Queen of the Keys, or head farther south to Key West, where the tourists partied hearty. Not his restaurant.

"You're saying this has happened before?"

Tito shrugged, turned to the stove and stirred the vast quantity of meatballs simmering in a cast-iron fry pan. "Two, three times a month. An' he been catchin' the snapper and grouper himself. Says he enjoys fishin', but I knows better. He's just too poor to pay the men sellin' at Hewitt's Marina. Either that or he's bent on runnin' this place into the ground.''

His words sank in slowly, making Libby's head ache. From the sound of it, Jack hadn't been completely honest with her, and the subtle betrayal hurt. If her grandfather owed money to friends in Sunset, his financial problems were infinitely worse than he'd let on.

"Has he at least been paying you a salary? Does he owe people in town?''

"Not that I know of. And he's up to date with payin' me. I tell him time and again he should take care of the supplies and liquor first, but he just waves his hands an' says he be seein' to it.''

After he finished spooning the meatballs into the pot of bubbling sauce, Tito turned to her. "He's gettin' old, little girl. He can't keep goin' fishin' in the hot sun, or climbin' on the roof to fix the thatch. He's gonna get himself killed one day. Like the week before you got—''

His dark eyes darting to the clock on the wall, Tito smacked the heel of his hand to his forehead. "Lawdy, look at the time. I got to start salads if I'm gonna be ready for the lunch crowd, pitiful though it be.''

Libby's heart skipped a beat. *Grandpa Jack had been on the roof?* The man was seventy-five years old and he'd climbed a ladder in this tropical heat? "What aren't you telling me, Uncle T? What happened to Jack?''

The jumbo-sized islander carried a variety of salad fixings from the refrigerator to the counter and began to chop tomatoes. Libby laid a hand on his back and kept it there until he heaved a ragged breath and set down his knife.

"Nothin' happened. I got there just before he fell and kept him from hittin' the ground. Tol' him if I ever caught his bony white ass on the roof again, I was quittin'. That seemed to frighten some sense into him.''

Libby crumpled into a chair and laid her head in her hands. "Oh, God. Thank you for telling me. And thank you for being here.'' She looked up and caught the pity in his somber eyes. "What are we going to do, Uncle T? This place has been Grandpa Jack's whole world for so long . . . If he loses the Pink Pelican, he'll die.''

Tito pulled up a chair and straddled it. "Here now, there be none of that in my kitchen. You comin' back to make things right done been the best thing could'a happened. You be college-educated, smart, not like me or Jack. You're gonna think of somethin', I just knows it.'' He reached into the neckline of his T-shirt, pulled out a small leather pouch and upended it on his palm. Out tumbled a circle of bone surrounded by feathers and bits of cloth. "Besides, I got me a mojo workin'. I been prayin' to the goddess, and she's gonna be answerin' me any day now. She be sendin' us a magic man to get us outta this here mess.''

Libby stared at the folk charm, another of T's many home-made remedies for what ailed. When she was little and she'd caught a cold or the flu, he'd made her drink a variety of distasteful concoctions or fixed smelly poultices for her chest. When Grandma Martha had been ill, he'd brewed exotic broths and sprinkled suspicious-looking powders around her bed. She'd forgotten how much he depended on his spooky brand of island magic to help those he loved.

She smiled as she patted his hand. "I'm not sure your hocus-pocus is going to do anything to alleviate our problems this time. We need money ... or a miracle. As often as your charms made my colds better or helped Grandma sleep through the night, I've never seen either of those *m* words materialize."

Tito pushed from the table, a slash of white teeth lighting his polished ebony features. "Hmm-mm. So you think Uncle T don't know what he's talkin' about, do you, little girl? Well, you just wait an' see. Magic man, he be comin'. I can feel it in my bones."

Chapter Four

Libby checked her watch. It was close to ten P.M. and she still had tables to bus and a handful of customers to take care of. During the lunch hour the bar had resembled a morgue more than a thriving restaurant, which only proved Uncle T's point: Serving a conventional menu with lackluster specials was the kiss of death to an eating establishment. Tourists came to the Keys for imaginatively prepared seafood, not meals they cooked at home. Once they'd found out the noon fare was burgers, salads and spaghetti, a number of patrons had simply walked away.

Thank goodness the Pink Pelican had what the dinner crowd craved—flaky fish cakes and a few of Uncle T's other tasty specialties.

She carted a tray laden with dishes to the kitchen, set it down next to the double sink, and sighed. If her grandfather ever agreed to let her use her personal savings, the first thing she was going to do was install a professional-size dishwasher. The pile of dirty plates and flatware heaped in the chipped enamel sink was growing into a small mountain she and Uncle T were expected to tackle before leaving the restaurant tonight.

"Two more specials, T, and one broiled snapper, extra vegetables instead of potatoes," she said, dropping into a chair.

Tito shot her a grin over his shoulder. "We're outta snapper, but I still got a few of the lobsters and two or three of the fish cakes left. If they don't want that, offer 'em spaghetti and meatballs for free." He turned back to the stove and gave a satisfied snort. "Done a fine business tonight, we did."

If her exhausted body was any judge, Libby had to agree. Her shoes felt three sizes too small, her arms ached, and if she didn't know better, she'd swear someone had used her back for a pincushion. When she'd waitressed as a teenager, earning tips had been fun; at thirty years of age, the taxing profession took on a whole new meaning. Since she'd left for college, Grandpa Jack always managed to find some eager teen to do the legwork, but that hadn't been the case this season. How had he and T planned to tend bar, cook food, wait tables and clean up without extra help?

Rising from the rickety chair, she headed back into the restaurant to take care of the diner who'd ordered the snapper. Before she made it through the archway, she spotted another group entering the bar. She groaned silently, figuring the new guests would add at least sixty minutes to her evening, until she realized who the customers were.

Mary and Frank Spitzer, Olivia Martinez, and . . . Oh, hell, just what she needed, her nemesis from the cave.

From the look of it, Mary had taken Libby's concerns to heart and spilled the beans to Olivia and Frank, which had prompted the three neighbors to band together in a rescue mission. Well, shoot, it was no more than she deserved for blabbing their worries all over town. She should have remembered that Mary told her husband everything, and Frank was one of Sunset's biggest gossips.

The new guests called out a greeting to her grandfather and took their seats, then eagerly perused the menu. All except for the *caveman*, Declan O'Shae.

Instead of sitting down, he remained standing with his arms folded across his broad chest and his legs apart, as if bracing himself on the deck of a ship. He'd changed from his earlier work outfit to neatly pressed khakis and a yellow knit shirt, and someone—probably Mary—had given him a haircut. The new style was parted on the side, the top slightly longer than the back. With his raven hair, shadow of a beard and brilliant blue eyes, the man could have been a walking definition of the term *black Irish*. Worse, she noted, the shorter hair added a touch of sophistication to his already attractive face.

The guilt that had niggled throughout the day about how she might have misjudged him faded as she watched his open appraisal of the bar. For someone who less than forty-eight hours earlier had been wearing rags and sleeping in a cave, it was ridiculous to believe he possessed the funds to remodel the place or buy it. And he owed her an apology for that crack about stealing, too.

Straightening her apron, Libby spoke to the customer who needed to amend his order, then pulled out her pad and sauntered to her friends. Feigning nonchalance, she raised a brow. "Mary, Frank, Olivia. What a surprise. I thought you kept your stores open late on the weekend."

Mary and Olivia had the decency to avert their eyes, but Frank acted as pleased as a paper-trained puppy. "Evening, Libby. We decided to close early and celebrate with our new employee. I believe you met Declan this morning."

Before she could comment, the same disturbing butterfly-pinned-to-a-board feeling she'd had in the garage over-whelmed her, and she held back a shiver. Turning, she locked eyes with the caveman. His muscular arms were still crossed, but a bad-boy grin quirked up one corner of his generous mouth. She stood statue still as his blue eyes stroked her like a caress. Invisible fingers of heat touched her breasts, her waist, her hips and legs, then languidly worked their way back up to her face.

He was a *caveman*, all right, and not just because of where they'd first met.

She stiffened her shoulders and made a concerted effort to hold her temper. When she lived in New York, she'd made the singles scene and done her share of flirting; that was how she'd met Brett. She'd been scrutinized by plenty of guys, many better-looking and all more successful than this Neanderthal. Not one to resist a challenge, Libby knew that even the biggest womanizer would back down eventually—if a girl stood her ground.

Seconds passed before she realized she was wrong. The rakish glint in his eyes told her that he was enjoying their standoff, as if he knew damn well that he was turning her insides to oatmeal and there wasn't a thing she could do about it.

Good Lord, had she just used the word *rakish* in a sentence? And why didn't anyone else notice she was being ogled?

"Madam. It is a pleasure to see you again."

Hardly, Libby thought, finally coming to her senses. She ignored his offer of a handshake and the easy shrug of his shoulders. If he thought he could intimidate her, he was sadly mistaken. "What can I get for you?"

"Tito's fish cakes, what else," answered Frank. It figured he would pay attention once she mentioned food.

"Same here," chimed Mary and Olivia.

"What do you recommend?" asked the caveman, taking a seat.

Libby wrote down their orders, her mind churning. So he wanted a personal recommendation, did he? After arsenic, she had the next best thing. "Don't worry," she said sweetly. "I have something special, just for you."

Declan watched Libby stride away. Ah, but she was a lusty wench, with full rounded breasts and long shapely legs made to wrap tight around a man. He'd spent the day coming to terms with this odd new world but found that whenever his mind wandered to thoughts of Libby Grayson all he learned seemed to fade into oblivion. Sparring with her was even more intriguing than the study of his surroundings.

He'd just given the woman his best come-hither invitation and she'd met him look for look. If their relationship continued on such a positive path, he'd have her in his bed within a fortnight.

Still, he balked at her curious shift in attitude. This morning he would have bet his last gold coin the woman found him lacking. It was more than likely he owed her an apology for accusing her of thievery. And she didn't seem the type to be swayed by a haircut and mere change of garments. Surely a woman of her ilk had ample opportunity to find lovers. Why had she suddenly decided to choose him?

No matter, he thought, for it was obvious her suggestion of serving him *something special* for dinner was an olive branch, a way to make amends for her earlier rude behavior.

Her way of saying she would consider his invitation.

"Drinks are on the house," Jack called out, breaking into Declan's reverie. "What'll it be?"

Frank stood and Mary hissed up at him. "Frank Spitzer, don't you dare let that man give us free drinks. You pay for whatever we order. Olivia and I each want a glass of white wine. Declan, what about you?"

"A pint of ale, I think."

"Ale?" Frank parroted. " 'Fraid all you're gonna get at the Pink Pelican is beer on tap. I don't think Jack carries ale."

"Then beer it is," Declan said, giving the nearly empty room another once-over. Aside from a handsomely carved bar that ran the length of the far wall, the structure had seen better days. Creaking paddle fans anchored to joints in the ceiling twirled slowly in the warm spring air. Dusty sconces holding faintly glowing electric candles graced the shabby walls. Chairs that looked ready to collapse surrounded tables covered with white paper, while the weathered floor needed a polishing and the replacement of several boards.

The total effect, he supposed, was meant to give people

a feel of the tropics, maybe Jamaica or Barbados, both places he'd sailed to in his privateering days. But instead of being charming, the room simply looked tired and years older than Jack Grayson, the man tending bar.

Declan felt a hand on his arm.

"Mr. O'Shae? It doesn't sound as if you're from around these parts. Am I mistaken, or do I detect a touch of the Irish in your accent?"

"Ah, madam, you've found me out." Chuckling, he met Olivia Martinez's black-eyed gaze. "I hail from Dublin, though I've not been back since seven—ah, for several years. And please, call me Declan."

"All right—Declan," responded Olivia, her smile wide. "I thought it sounded as if you'd kissed the Blarney stone."

Though her skin was smooth and her features appealing, he suspected Olivia Martinez was close to Mary in age. Her blatant flirting seemed harmless enough, so he joined in the fun. "I'd imagine a woman of your great beauty has heard plenty of blarney in her life. How is it that a lady such as yourself has no husband to help manage such a fine shop?"

Mary shook open her napkin and placed it on her lap. "Hmmph. Sounds to me like what you know about modern women wouldn't fill a thimble. Women today don't necessarily need a man in their lives gumming up the works. Fact is, most smart women don't want one," she lectured. "I have my Frank, but if push came to shove I'd get along just fine without a husband. Olivia's been a widow for the past three years and she's doing well enough to get by."

Declan laid a hand over his heart and gave his best wounded grin. He had just learned an interesting fact about the females of this era, and from the chastisement in Mary's voice it was an important one. "I had no idea you were a widow, fair lady. I meant no disrespect. How is it no man has been clever enough to capture your attention after all this time?"

The women giggled girlishly, and Declan began to settle comfortably into the game, pleased to find he hadn't lost his touch. O'Shae men had charmed their way into women's hearts for centuries. His father and brothers would have been proud to find their masculine prowess still going strong two hundred years in the future.

After a few more nonsensical phrases, he sensed a presence at his side. Dishes brimming with a tempting array of food were set carefully on the table. He licked his lips in anticipation of his own meal, but before he could comment Libby slammed his supper in front of him so hard that it near to split the plate in half.

He gazed at the red sauce and balls of meat balanced atop a mound of string, then took in everyone else's food, which looked quite different from his own. "Pray tell, good woman, what is this dish?"

Red-faced, Mary and Olivia held napkins to their grinning mouths. Frank arrived at the table with their drinks and sat down. "What's so funny?" he asked. All Mary could do was point to Declan's dinner. "Jeez, Libby. What'd T do, run outta food? No one comes to the Pink Pelican to eat spaghetti."

Libby stood with her hands on her hips. A sly smile graced her lips as she said, "Sorry. It's all we had left."

Declan suspected he was being tested. Though he'd been prepared for fish, this pile of sauce and string looked tasty, and it certainly smelled appealing. If the wench was trying to get his goat, it would not be tonight. Gamely, he picked up his fork and dug into his meal. After all, it had been prepared especially for him.

Ready to wash the night's final load of dirty dishes, Libby tugged at her rubber gloves and gazed into the sink of steaming soapy water, berating herself the entire while. What she'd done had been childish and immature, but, darn it, the man had forced her hand.

"How you doin' there, missy?" T asked, peering over her shoulder. "You be careful now," he warned when she smacked a plate into the drying rack. "Ain't no money 'round here for new crockery."

She blew a curl off her forehead as she rinsed the next plate under hot running water. "Are you sure that was your most potent Tabasco sauce, Uncle T? You know the kind I mean—so hot it blisters your tongue before you can find the spit to swallow? Because that's what the customer asked for."

T propped a hip against the sink, picked up a dish and swiped it with a clean towel. "Trust me when I tell you it was the eye-watering, fire-spittin' kind, child. Where I come from, that concoction was known to make grown men beg for their mamas. The way you squirted that fire juice over those meatballs, I can't believe whoever ordered it didn't run screamin' from the building."

Libby bit the inside of her cheek to keep from telling T the truth. Declan O'Shae hadn't exactly requested that someone dump a bottle of hot sauce over his dinner, but that didn't mean he didn't deserve to have his tongue scalded. The way he'd been flirting and making eyes at Olivia Martinez, a woman at least twenty years his senior, was simply shameful.

Problem was, the contrary jerk had sucked down the pasta like a starving wolf, then practically licked the plate clean. Instead of dousing his mouth with a pitcher of ice water, he'd enjoyed the taste of T's hottest flavoring with manly gusto, and had the nerve to compliment the chef while doing so.

She placed the next dish in the drainer a bit more gently. "Okay, I was just making sure," she muttered. "Like you say, we have to give the customers what they want if we plan on staying in business."

"Ain't that the truth," T responded with a shake of his head. "Least ways, until we can figure out how to get a few more dollars into this town. You get any ideas today?"

Libby sighed, all memories of the caveman and his hot-as-Hades dinner forgotten. In between waiting tables and checking on J.P., she'd thought about nothing else. "How about if we call a town meeting to see if anyone else is as concerned as you and I are about the future of Sunset? Maybe if everybody put their heads together, we'd come up with something brilliant."

"Don' you be forgettin' 'bout my magic man," he said sagely, stacking the dry plates. "He be the one to save this town, but he's gonna need our help, for sure."

"T, please, this is serious," said Libby, knotting her hands on the edge of the sink. "If we want to make Sunset Key a viable tourist center instead of a quaint little pass-through kind of place, we're going to need concrete ideas, not hoo-doo magic. We have to convince a bank to install an ATM machine so people will have an easier time spending their money; even better if they opened a branch so the residents didn't have to drive the bridge to Marathon every week to do business. Once a bank moves in, it should be simple to convince a few basic retailers to locate here."

T arranged the plates on a shelf, then started on the cups, saucers and flatware, working methodically as he spoke. "You listen to me, Liberty Grayson, 'cause I ain't gonna say this again. I had me a vision. There's gonna be a real live magic man, come to save us any day now. He gonna be the one we need to listen to."

Uh-oh, thought Libby. When Uncle T used her given name, he was serious, and more than a little angry. "All right, let's say I believe in your prediction. What's this magic man supposed to do once he gets here? Give us a lecture on how to run businesses that have been in our families for generations? I doubt the townsfolk would want that. They're set in their ways. What makes you think Hazel, or Phil and Don, or the Spitzers would listen to some stranger, even if they believed in what you said about him?"

Tito heaved a sigh. "That's my point. Makin' the people listen is goin' to be a part of his magic."

Libby pulled the plug from the sink and watched the water eddy and swirl as it made its way down the drain. Wouldn't it be wonderful if their problems could be taken care of so easily? How she wished she could believe in T's fairy-tale prediction. But she knew better than most that magic simply didn't exist.

"So tell me, what will this guy look like? Is he going to be wearing a wizard's hat and waving a magic wand, or will he ride into town on a white horse, brandishing a sword and a fistful of cash?"

"Very funny, little girl." T folded the towel he'd been using and hung it over the back of a chair. "Let's just say I'll know him when I see him. Now you go on home to that boy of yours while I check on Jack, make sure he didn't do nothin' stupid, like give everybody in the bar a round of free drinks. He should'a closed up a half hour ago."

"Thanks. I don't know what we'd do without you," Libby said, kissing him on the cheek. She watched him leave the kitchen, then took off her apron, gathered the dirty linens, and went out the side door and around the front of the building to take the path to the house.

On her way across the porch, she heard a chorus of male voices coming from the bar. It sounded like T and Grandpa Jack were having a high old time, probably crowing over tonight's profits and planning how they would do it all over again tomorrow. A laugh boomed out, and she fought the urge to peek inside. The voice didn't belong to her grandfather or T; maybe Frank had stayed to join them in a nightcap.

Some men, Libby thought, never grew up. Grandpa Jack refused to admit his business was failing, and Uncle T thought a magic-wand-wielding white knight was on his way to town. Couple that with Brett Ritter and his search to "find himself" at age thirty-four and she was just about the unluckiest woman in the world when it came to the masculine gender.

Too exhausted to stop and find out who else besides Uncle T and Grandpa Jack were in the bar, she continued walking toward home and her son.

*   *   *

Declan squinted against the early morning sun. Stretching out his arm, he grabbed the stack of oblong slats Tito slapped against his palm and tucked them into the pocket of his apron. He bit down on the nails between his teeth and climbed farther up the ladder, then set a shingle in place, notched in a nail and began to pound. God's blood, it felt good to be useful again.

"I'm goin' to check on the potatoes," the huge black man said with a grin. "I'll send Jack out when breakfast is ready—say about ten minutes."

Declan nodded and continued to hammer against the side of the building. What good fortune that he'd decided to stay in the Pink Pelican last night for a final cup of ale—beer, he amended. Of course, after the fire-breathing supper he'd been forced to eat, he'd needed a pitcher of the frothy stuff to soothe his tingling tongue. Libby Grayson had tried to best him, but he'd not let her win.

He chuckled as he hammered the next shingle. She was quite a woman, clever as well as attractive. Her ploy to torture him would have been a good one if he had the senses of an ordinary man. Little did she know he liked his food spicy, the hotter the better. What she'd served him last night had gone a bit beyond his tolerance level, but not far enough to make him flee the table.

In a way, he owed her a debt. If she hadn't tried to scald his mouth with that supper, he wouldn't have remained in the bar to have a final drink. He wouldn't have become chummy with Jack or Tito, and he wouldn't have gotten a second offer of employment. The chores they'd hired him to do around the Pink Pelican were legion. This job, coupled with his position at the Spitzers', was the perfect stratagem. No one would question him when he began to search for his treasure, and he would soon have enough money to make his way in the world.

"You all right up there?" came a grizzled voice from below.

"Aye," said Declan, pounding at the last slat. "But I'm afraid this is just the beginning." He stepped lively down the ladder onto the porch and faced Jack Grayson. "From the look of it, I'll be replacing shingles for the next several days. Then I'll have to repair the shutters and rethatch the roof. And that's just what needs doing on the outside."

Jack clamped a hand on Declan's shoulder. "I know, and I have to be honest: When we struck up our deal, I should have told you it's my granddaughter who handles the money 'round here. I'm not sure how much she'll be willing to pay you. Fact is, if Tito hadn't looked so overjoyed at meeting you last night, I wouldn't have offered you the job at all. Don't know what got into him, but I respect his judgment. If he says you're the man we need to set this place to right, I believe him. Now we just have to convince Libby."

"Libby is your granddaughter?" Declan asked innocently. "She was the serving wen—ah, woman who brought me my supper, correct?"

"That'd be her," said Jack. "But I'd shy away from the word *serving,* if I were you, and refer to her as a waitress. These days, women are mighty particular about being labeled as servants. Libby is a CPA, and she's been supporting herself and her son for a while now. Had a job as a department manager in some big-time accounting firm in New York City until a few weeks ago. She's only waitressing until we can find someone else to do the job. I look at her as a full partner in this bar. When I die, it's all gonna belong to her and J.P. anyway."

Reminding himself that women had turned into a peculiar lot over the past two centuries, Declan filed away the warning. No wonder Libby was so bossy. From the sound of it, she'd overseen a cadre of people, just as he'd captained a ship. He'd suspected she was independent, but if she was used to being in control, it stood to reason she would expect more say-so in the way they handled their affairs. He would need to step carefully, perhaps do a bit of wooing to get her into his bed.

Not that he didn't look forward to it. The sweetest apples were usually found on the highest branches of the tree, and weren't the hardest fought victories the ones he was most proud of? Declan had worked for everything he'd ever achieved in his life, though most women hadn't made the job too difficult. Winning and bedding Libby Grayson would be a challenge he would accept willingly.

Tito poked his head out of the kitchen door. "Breakfast is served, you two. Come and get it."

"You go on inside and eat," said Jack. "I'll be along in a minute."

Somehow the sound of a drum banging, or maybe it was a jackhammer, had worked its way into Libby's early morning dream. Up until the racket started, she'd been sitting alone on a blanket in Dream Cove, meditating on the peaceful roll of the ocean. When a tall man dressed in polished armor rounded her favorite pile of boulders and marched across the sand, she was speechless.

Stopping directly in front of her, the knight stared down imposingly, his eyes flashing a brilliant blue through a slit in the visor of his helmet. Before she found the words to order him off her beach, a sword appeared in his long-fingered hand, while at the same moment a huge anvil popped into view at his feet. Grasping the hilt of the sword with both hands, he raised it above his head. It was then she realized the weapon had a curved blade that made it look more like a cutlass than a sword, but hey, who was she to make sense of weird things that happened in dreams?

With a mighty whack, the knight began to slam the cutlass onto the anvil over and over again, and instead of fearing each ringing blow, Libby applauded his prowess. Every piece of metal he chipped turned into a circle of gold, until he'd slivered the anvil into a huge mound of shining coins piled high in front of her.

When he was through, the knight broadened his stance and stabbed the tip of the cutlass into the sand. She heard his voice, a familiar mix of Irish brogue and hot buttered rum as he said, " 'Tis yours, Liberty Grayson. I give it to you freely, along with my heart."

Though she was asleep, Libby felt a sheen of tears form behind her eyelids. The knight placed a hand on his helmet, as if to reveal his face. The hammering grew louder, pulsing into her brain as he raised the visor. . . .

Poof! The knight, his cutlass and armor, along with the pile of gold, disappeared into the sunlight.

Rolling to her side, she groaned and opened one eye. Well, hell! She pulled the sheet over her face and dabbed at the wetness dampening her cheeks. The pounding noise grew more intense and she *tsked,* embarrassed that she'd let herself get so immersed in a silly dream. She'd been tired last night, and all that talk of Uncle T's about white knights and magic had seeped into her brain until she'd lost every cell of common sense.

The hammering continued. She swung her legs over the side of the bed, determined to ferret out the idiot who'd decided to do chores this early on a Sunday morning. Where was it written that people were allowed to be up at the crack of dawn making so much racket? More than impolite, it was downright rude!

Not bothering to tidy her hair or put on shoes, she dressed in shorts and a loose T-shirt and tiptoed into the hall to peek into J.P.'s room. Assured he was still asleep, she ran down the stairs and out the door to the back porch, where she focused on the pounding.

Her heart skipped a beat when she realized the noise was coming from the Pink Pelican. Good Lord, after all T had told her, she wouldn't be surprised to find her grandfather on a ladder . . . or worse.

She gazed at the restaurant but couldn't tell if Jack was

on the roof or not. The noise stopped and she began to run. Legs pumping, she hit the porch and raced around the corner to the side door. She skidded to a stop just in time to see her grandfather pat Declan O'Shae on the back as if they were the best of friends. Before she could huff out a protest, the caveman walked through the kitchen door.

Her grandfather turned and gave an embarrassed grin. Scratching at the last remaining tuft of white hair on his head, he said, "Libby. What's got you up and dressed so early?"

She sucked in a breath and blew it out slowly. "What is that man doing here?"

"What man?" he asked, looking around as if he'd been alone.

"You know perfectly well who I'm talking about, Jack Grayson. That . . . that man the Spitzers hired . . . that O'Shae person. What's he doing here at this hour of the morning?"

Jack's face turned pink. "Oh. Him."

"Grandpa," warned Libby, taking in the ladder, hammer and open package of shingles on the porch.

"No need to get yourself tied in a knot. I was gonna tell you later, after you fed J.P. and had a chance to wake up."

"Tell me what?" she said, though she feared she already knew the answer.

"I hired Declan O'Shae to work here. He's going to help us get the Pink Pelican back in shape."

Chapter Five

Jack had the good sense to mutter something about sweeping out the restaurant and walk quickly to the front of the building. With her mouth open, Libby watched him round a far corner of the porch. She couldn't have been more surprised if someone had doused her with a bucket of ice water. That sneaky beach bum . . . that conniving, cave-dwelling snake in the sand had taken advantage of her grandfather and charmed himself into a job here at the Pink Pelican.

She pressed her fingers to her temples. This was all her fault. If she'd whacked him over the head with that piece of driftwood instead of poking him until he'd woke up, none of this would be happening. Why hadn't she minded her own business and left him there to rot?

She took a deep breath and mentally ticked off excuses she could use to circumvent the unappealing situation. Declan O'Shae had no references. How did they know he was capable of doing a competent job? If he was employed by the Spitzers, when would he have the time to work here? And the most reasonable argument of all: Where were they supposed to find the money to pay him? She needed to organize her thoughts. Once her grandfather saw the light, he would agree.

Libby told herself that she had every right to eavesdrop as she peered around the side entrance to the kitchen. Declan sat at the table with his back to her. Uncle T was at his side, his gaze riveted on his guest, and there was a full plate of food in front of each man.

"Tell me again where it is you come from," she heard T ask.

"I lived in the Carolinas before I found my way to your fine island," Declan answered, lifting a coffee mug to his lips.

T picked up his fork and started on his breakfast. "And what made you come all the way down here to this tip of nowhere? Vacation? A job? Maybe a woman?"

"In all honesty, I'm not sure," Declan responded, his broad shoulders doing that impossible rippling thing as he shrugged. "Isn't it enough to know I plan to stay a while?"

"For now," said T. He sat back and folded his arms across his chest. "Tell me something, Declan O'Shae: Do you believe in magic?"

Libby thumped her forehead against the door frame. She didn't need to hear the caveman's response to know she'd better get her fanny inside before T revealed his outrageous magic man–to-the-rescue story and made a total fool of himself. Striving for casual, she finger-combed her hair as she sauntered through the door.

"Uncle T. I didn't expect to see you here this early, and you didn't have to make breakfast. Grandpa Jack could have eaten at the house with J.P."

Declan rose to his feet, but T stayed in his chair, his smile wide. "No trouble, little girl. This is the man I done tol' you about. Say a very fine good mornin' to Mr. Declan O'Shae."

"Miss Grayson." Declan nodded his head. " 'Tis a pleasure to see you again."

Determined to ignore his engaging manner and impressive physique, Libby screwed her mouth into a frown. Funny, but when she recalled Jeff Spitzer wearing this same worn T-shirt and pair of faded jeans, she remembered the clothing as completely ordinary. Why was it that on the caveman they looked sexily rumpled and perfect?

"Mr. O'Shae. Besides a free breakfast, what brings you to the Pink Pelican so early on a Sunday morning?"

Declan grinned as if he hadn't a care and sat back down. "The opportunity for employment, of course. Your grandfather has been kind enough to offer me a job refurbishing the place." Picking up his fork, he continued with his meal.

"I see." Libby went to the counter and helped herself to coffee. Turning, she rested her backside against the sink and blew across the steaming liquid. "That's a lot of work. What makes you think you're capable of the task?"

T shot her a disapproving glare. "Be nice, little girl. You ain't too big I still can't take you over my knee."

Declan's amused gaze focused on her puckered lips, then skimmed down her shabby T-shirt and ragged cutoffs, sending a shiver up Libby's spine. Shocked by the unwanted jolt of intimacy, she said, "There's no money to be earned here, Mr. O'Shae. Do you really think this is the place for you?"

The room pulsed with silence. Declan shoved back his plate; Tito drummed his fingers on the table. Jumping to his feet, he poured their guest a coffee refill, then collected the dirty dishes and walked to the sink. Nudging Libby aside, he dropped the plates in the water and whispered out of the side of his mouth. "Didn't you hear me? I said *this here is the man I was tellin' you about.* If I remember correctly, you promised to cooperate when he showed up."

Declan had no idea what Tito was blathering about. He only knew that from the moment they'd been introduced last night in the bar, the large black man had been congenial as well as curious. He'd met plenty of natives in his travels to the islands and knew them to be honest and hardworking. Men of color had crewed on his ship, and many had fought bravely during the war. Jack had agreed to hire him only after T gave his approval, and now the man was scolding Libby as if she were his daughter. From the look of it, the cook was held in high regard by both the Graysons.

He watched Libby flush an intriguing shade of pink. "Uncle T, let's talk about this in private."

Tito grunted as he grabbed her arm and hustled her into the bar. A scant second later Jack strolled through the side door. "Phew. I thought he'd never get that girl out of here." He picked up his plate from the warmer and brought it to the table. "Had enough to eat?"

Declan found himself grinning again. Jack reminded him of his first mate, Black Pete, in both his mannerisms and his physical appearance. For the second time since he'd crawled from that cave, he couldn't help but think there was a reason he'd survived the storm from hell and awakened in this century. At moments like this, he felt as if he belonged here more than he had in his own time. Surely, if he was patient, all would be revealed to him.

"Aye, the meal was a delight. Your Tito is quite the cook. A free man, is he?"

"Free man?" repeated Jack, scratching at his grizzled jaw. "He's free as a bird, far as I can tell. In all the years I've known him, Tito's never mentioned any relatives or a wife and children. He might have a few quirky notions about spirits and such, but he means well, and unless someone bad-mouths his cookin', he ain't got an evil bone in his body."

The answer wasn't exactly what Declan expected, but it told him what he needed to know. Black men were in control of their own lives in this century, and the fact pleased him.

Jack tucked into his breakfast. "The man's been with us so long he's family. Helped me to raise Libby and keep this place afloat after Martha died."

"Martha was your wife?"

Jack nodded. "Best woman I ever had the pleasure to know. It's been nigh on twenty years since I lost her, and

I still miss her something fierce. Don't get me wrong, my daughter-in-law was a good girl, but Martha was special. Libby takes after her grandmother, she does." He raised his cup in mock salute. "Gave me the first of my great-grandchildren and made me proud as a peacock when she did it."

Declan reined in the urge to question him further about that dubious accomplishment. He still didn't understand how everyone could accept a bastard child so easily, or think Libby Grayson wasn't a loose woman. From what he could tell, the people of Sunset respected her and the life she led. He'd better start doing the same if he wanted to stay in the townsfolk's good graces.

"I met her boy the other morning. He seemed a fine lad."

"Takes after his mother's side, real caring and sensitive, if you want to get into all that psychobabble crap. These days, it's okay for a man to be sensitive, ya know. Then again, you're a young fella. I guess you've read all them books."

Books! Declan wanted to shout with joy. Why hadn't he thought about books sooner? He'd seen a television show or two in the Spitzer home, which had confused him greatly. Mary had told him that he was free to read the paperlike publications she called magazines whenever he liked. There were bound to be books on history, modern customs, and the like he could borrow and peruse at his leisure. Books would hold the key to so many of his questions, and he could find his answers without arousing suspicion.

"A few," he said, telling the smallest of lies. After all, he intended to read them, just as soon as he figured out a way to locate them. "Which one did you like best?"

Jack fair to choked on his coffee. "Me? Heck no, I ain't read a one. But I heard about 'em. There was one . . . let's see now . . . *Men Are From Mars, Women From the Stars,* or somethin' like that. Anyhow, you know the one I mean."

Declan tucked the title into his brain. "So you don't own any of these books, you just know of their existence?"

"I know they're out there." He scooped up the last of his crabmeat omelet. "Martha and me, we never needed any books to be happy, but to each his own, I always say."

To each his own. Declan tried the phrase on for size, then added it to his list. Jack Grayson seemed to hold no prejudices, owned a business that had the potential for success and, along with his granddaughter, had respect in the community. From what he could tell, it might do him good to listen to the man in the future.

"Libby talk to you about a salary?" Jack asked, pouring himself a second cup of coffee.

Declan crossed his arms over his chest. "Not yet. I don't think your granddaughter holds me in high regard."

Jack sipped at his drink, his face wrinkled in thought. "Might as well tell you straight out, 'cause you're gonna hear it from someone sooner or later. Right now, Libby doesn't have one diddly-bop reason to think highly of any man. The fella she'd been living with in New York ran out on her and J.P. about a month ago. Left her high and dry with a mountain of bills and a bruised heart to boot."

Declan frowned. "I've heard some talk. They weren't married, if I understand it correctly."

"Lived together for seven years, with her always thinking marriage was right around the corner. Problem was, Brett Ritter always thought that corner was down the road and out of reach." He expelled a harsh breath. "Libby didn't want to force him into something they'd both regret, so she bided her time and let him set the pace. She gave their relationship everything she had and then some, but the idiot just kept on taking until she had nothing left to give."

"And the boy, does he know he's a—that his mother and father weren't—"

"Grandpa Jack," came a soft but severe-sounding voice from the doorway. "J.P. should be awake by now. Could you go to the house and make sure he's all right?"

Declan didn't miss the plea of silence Jack sent his way

as the old man pushed from the table. "Libby. We were just talkin' about . . . things."

Libby strode into the kitchen with her shoulders back and her head held high. Walking to her grandfather's side, she gave his cheek a peckish kiss. "Please take care of J.P. for me."

Declan watched their interaction with a keen eye. The man knew he was in danger of a tongue-lashing but thought he could manipulate his way free. From the peeved yet patient expression on his granddaughter's stern face, Jack would succeed, but it might take a while.

He finished his coffee as Jack ambled from the kitchen, waiting while Libby poured another cup for herself. Even with her back to him, he could sense her determination and pride. Her shoulders sagged, then lifted as she spun to face him.

Swinging a chair around, she straddled the seat as if she were a man. "Mr. O'Shae, I understand we have business to discuss."

Now, he wisely decided, was not the time to grin boyishly, or allow his gaze to wander over the length of shapely leg she displayed as she sat. If he wanted to work here, he needed to restart his dealings with the woman and get them back on an even keel.

"Before we talk business, I have something to say to you, Ms. Grayson."

She narrowed her golden eyes. "Oh, really?"

"Aye." He cleared his throat. "I believe I owe you an apology."

Sitting back in her chair, she raised a brow. "I'm listening."

Damn if she wasn't going to make him work for her approval, thought Declan, grinding his back molars. "I'm afraid I jumped to an erroneous conclusion in the cave the other day, when I accused you of stealing. I realize now that I was wrong and I'm sorry."

Libby sipped at her drink, then exhaled a sad-sounding

chuckle. "All right, apology accepted." She rubbed at the bridge of her nose. "Look, I realize that for the sake of keeping the peace around here, you and I have to come to some sort of amicable agreement, but from what I just overheard, I have the idea you think it's your right to ask personal questions about me. Since you'll be working here, I think I have the right to ask a few of my own."

Declan nodded, recalling the promise he'd made to himself to reveal only as much of the truth as he thought was safe. "Fair enough. What is it you need to know?"

Libby placed her cup on the table, then rested her arms on the top of the chair. "What were you doing in that cave?"

Though direct and to the point, it was the one question for which he truly had no answer. "Would you believe me if I told you I have no idea how I arrived on that ledge?"

Her lips thinned to a straight line. "Let's just say I'd have a difficult time with it."

"Yet it is the truth."

She sighed, and her weary shudder touched him from across the table. "You're not going to make this easy for me, are you?"

"I'm not trying to be difficult. I was as surprised as you when I first woke. Though I have no memory of how I got there, I've recalled a few things over the past two days . . . a tremendous storm . . . my ship torn to pieces . . . The only explanation I've managed to come up with is that I swam to shore, found shelter in the cave, and fell asleep until you happened upon me."

She picked up her coffee mug with both hands. "I'd be tempted to believe you if there'd been a storm in the area during the past week. But the weather's been a balmy ninety degrees with a cloudless blue sky and perfect humidity. Care to try again?"

It was Declan's turn to sigh. "I fear I don't have another answer. But let me ask you this—what do I have to gain by lying? And what is it you think I've done that is so heinous you refuse to trust me, or give me a chance to earn a living in your town?''

Her amber gaze pierced him with its intensity. "I don't like opportunists, O'Shae. I've lived off-island for more than a decade in one of the toughest cities in the world. I've met people from all walks of life, many of whom did not play fair. The residents of Sunset may be a little on the senior side, but they're not stupid. They know this town is dying, which makes them sitting ducks for any shyster clever enough to see the same. Unfortunately, they're also a bit naive. They'll say, do, or believe almost anything that's spouted with a silver tongue.

"I've talked to T, and for some inane reason he thinks you're the man we've been—the person we need to help out around here. I'll try to get along with you if you promise to stay out of my way, but if I catch you contemplating anything that might hurt one of the people I care about, I'm going to come at you with barrels blazing. Now, if you meant what you said about wanting work—''

Blown starboard by her tirade, Declan raised a hand. Her eyes sparked fire from their golden depths, while her cheeks flushed a brilliant pink. She was magnificent in her anger, her caring and her honesty, and because of it she intrigued him all the more.

"Truce," he interjected. Her luscious mouth snapped shut and he held back a grin, pleased he'd managed to suck the wind from her sails. "I understand and I agree. Now, about my wages ... I'll accept whatever you offer, but I warn you, woman, do not be niggardly.''

"Meals." She sat upright in the chair. "All we can offer are three squares a day. You can come to our home for breakfast between seven-thirty and eight; lunch and dinner will be here in the kitchen when we serve it at the restaurant, at the house when we don't. And you'll eat whatever I fix my son.''

Declan took his time considering the offer. Mary Spitzer was a decent enough cook, but he'd been eating his meals alone. Amassing money might be one of his goals, but sharing food meant sharing time and space with Libby, an idea that held strong appeal. He rose from the chair and stretched out his hand, knowing full well that this time she would have to touch him to seal their deal. She stood and rubbed a palm on her shirtfront. Her jaw clenched as she placed her hand in his.

He kept the handshake short and impersonal. "Provided you're as good a cook as Tito, we have a bargain. Now, if you will excuse me, I have work to do."

"We're goin' to see the kit-tens—kit-tens—kit-tens—" J.P. skipped ahead of Libby down the sidewalk, yodeling at the top of his lungs. The off-key tune sounded like nothing she'd heard before or wanted to hear again, and assured her the boy would never make his living singing at the Met. Oh, well; trash collectors earned a decent wage, as did computer programmers and veterinarians. Her son could be anything he wanted when he grew up, just as long as he grew into a happy, responsible adult.

She followed him into the bay and up to Miss Betty's cardboard box, where J.P. squatted and began to count aloud. "One, two, Black Pete and Bridget, three, four, Bilge Water and Posey-dan, five—"

Posey-dan? "What did you say?" Libby asked with a smile.

"Posey-dan. Declan says he's the god of the sea. He says it was Posey-dan who brung him here, so he named a kitten in his honor."

"Ah-ha," said Libby. It figured that besides all his other interesting attributes, the man would be a master of the tall tale. "I think he meant Poseidon, sweetie. And when did you talk to Mr. O'Shae?"

J.P. gingerly picked up Bridget—or was it Bilge Water?—and cuddled the squirming grayish-colored kitten to his chest. "While you were taking a shower. Grandpa Jack brought me to the bar and said I could draw on the back porch. Declan was hammering shingles, but he told me he'd named all the kittens. Once he hit his thumb really hard, and you know what he said?''

Libby rolled her eyes. ''Something I'm sure you shouldn't repeat.''

''He said 'jay-zus' really loud, then he stuck his thumb in his mouth and jumped up and down. What's that mean, Mom? The jay-zus part?''

Oh, great. Now the caveman was teaching her son to take the Lord's name in vain. ''It's a curse word, and you know they're not nice, right? Now promise me you won't pay attention to a word that comes out of that man's mouth, and stay out of his way. He has work to do around the Pink Pelican and you shouldn't be underfoot.''

J.P. gazed up at her, his expression puzzled. ''But I like Declan. He promised I could hand him nails and shingles after lunch, if I wanted. And tomorrow he's gonna climb the ladder and go on the roof and . . .''

Fall off and break his neck?

She gave herself a mental slap. *Shame on you, Libby Grayson, for wishing such a thing on any man.* But a frightening slide to the gutter, or a tidy yet bone-crunching drop and roll couldn't hurt. Just enough of an accident to scare the pompous boob into leaving town by sundown.

The talk Tito had strong-armed her into had netted her a big fat zero. Completely smitten with the overly charming, muscle-rippling jerk, he was convinced Declan O'Shae was the magic man Sunset had been waiting for. And from the sound of the conversation she'd overheard, her grandfather wasn't far behind.

She shook her head. There had to be a better way to save the town than rely on a homeless wanderer who had the lethal blue gaze of a laser, yet spoke with the lilt of a leprechaun. Declan O'Shae might look sincere, but so had Brett each and every time he'd promised to pay the bills or stay at his latest job. Or marry her and make their family legal.

Maybe it was time to call that town meeting she and T had talked about yesterday and . . .

"Morning, or should I say afternoon?" Mary suddenly appeared at Libby's side. "J.P. pick out a kitten yet?"

Libby gazed at her son, who had just set down Bridget and scooped up Poseidon, or was it Bilge Water? "I think he's in love with all of them, but he's got time. Five more weeks, I guess?"

"Just about," Mary answered, squinting at a calendar on the garage wall with a big red circle around a date. "Heard Declan was working at your place today. Glad to hear Jack still has a few brain cells firing."

Libby angled her head and walked out of earshot of her son, with the older woman following. "Mary, about Mr. O'Shae—"

"He's a looker, ain't he?" Mary cut in. "Real polite, too. And what an accent. I'll bet that man could charm a girl right outta her knickers, if you know what I mean."

Libby opened then quickly closed her mouth.

"Oh, say, I didn't mean nothin' by that, honey. I realize you're not like some of the young women out there, the ones who sleep with anything in pants. Everybody knows you were in a committed relationship with your fella when he upped and left." She patted at the cockeyed bun sitting on top of her head. "It's just that even Olivia thinks Declan's a Studly Do-Right, and thanks to that no-good alcoholic she was married to for twenty years, it's a rare day she sings the praises of any man."

Libby hoped to heaven she wasn't blushing. Never once while she'd been pregnant with J.P., or since he'd been born, had she regretted her decision to have him. But she'd fielded her share of questions and heard enough nasty whispers to know people judged. Hadn't she caught Declan O'Shae doing the very same thing just a few hours ago?

Brett had been out of town on one of his many weekend

junkets to investigate a new line of work when she'd gone into early labor. Annoyed he'd left her alone so close to her due date, she'd used her own name on the boy's birth certificate. Over the years, she'd come to realize it had been a smart move. Because of it, J.P. would never have to explain why his name and his mother's were different. If he were lucky, he would never have to answer to the fact that his father and mother hadn't married.

"Oops," Mary went on. "From the color in your cheeks I'm thinkin' I pinned the tail on the donkey. Even you're willing to admit that man is the best sight to hit town since my Jeff left."

Libby fluttered her hands, tucking a stray curl behind one ear. She'd always thought of Jeff as a sweet-faced, lost-puppy kind of guy, definitely not the words she would use to describe Declan O'Shae. From what she could remember, the only thing the two men had in common was their height. Since she'd learned as a teenager that very little escaped Mary's shrewd gray eyes, she tried to defray the woman's on-target observation.

"You didn't embarrass me. And yes, he's nice-looking. But I have too much on my mind right now to waste time mooning over a swaggering drifter. I was hoping you could back me in this, Mary. I'd like to call a town meeting."

Mary shuffled her feet a bit, then jutted her jaw. "I was wondering when you'd realize Jack isn't the only one in Sunset with problems. Frank and me were going to ask you to take a look at our books, and maybe help us figure out a way to cut a few corners. Hazel said she's gonna do the same, and so did Olivia. I wasn't exactly honest when we had that talk the other morning. People in this town need a miracle, and they need it yesterday."

Declan whistled as he cleaned out the craters left by the missing shingles and tacked new ones into place. His stomach rumbled, and he thought about his promised payment from Mistress Grayson. He'd warned her that she would need to be as good a cook as Tito to make this job worth his effort, but he'd been lying through his teeth when he'd done so. Her agreement to cater meals had been a mere enticement. The idea that he would be able to spend time with her in an intimate setting, at a table in her own kitchen, was the real draw.

Another empty rumbling made him scowl. The noon hour had come and gone. When Jack and T had offered him leftover spaghetti and meatballs he'd declined. The bar served only drinks on Sunday, not regular meals, which meant Libby owed him a lunch made by her own hands. From the hollow feeling in his belly, all the woman needed was the ability to boil an egg and he'd think her a master chef.

Standing back, he admired his handiwork. He'd completed two sides of the building. Two more, the worst of the lot, were left. Then there was the roof, bald to the rafters in patches, and after that the floorboards inside. The porch railings could use a good shoring up as well. Between his chores here and at the Spitzers' and trying to find books to read, he'd never have time to search for his treasure.

He walked to the far side of the porch and spied the tip of the familiar promontory he planned to use as a marker. Once he climbed onto the roof, he'd be able to see in all directions, get his bearings and learn the lay of the land. Surely then he would have a better idea of where he'd buried his coins.

In the distance he saw Libby and her son strolling the walkway. He could tell by the way the woman held her head that the boy had her undivided attention. Sunlight glinted off her flowing curls, changing the chestnut brown strands to a rainbow of russet and gold. Her long coltish legs moved in a lively rhythm as the boy skipped at her side. It was obvious the two shared a special bond.

She tussled J.P.'s darker hair and the boy laughed loudly, echoing Libby's own husky chuckle. Even though Jack had told him the woman had little to be happy about, she showed nothing but merriment with her son. What would it take, Declan wondered, to have her react to *him* in that same joyous manner? What did he need to say or do to make her smile?

Mother and son reached the porch and J.P. raced through the side door, leaving Declan to deal with Libby. Folding her arms across her generous bosom, she slowly walked past him as she inspected the new shingles.

"Finished so soon?" she finally asked, propping her backside against the porch rail.

"I'd consider tackling the other side of the building, if not for the fact that I'm fair to starving. You promised me lunch, if I remember correctly. Surely you're not about to renege on our agreement already?"

She set her hands on her hips, her expression perturbed. "Tito and Jack said they were eating here. Didn't they offer you lunch?"

"They did. But that was not a part of our arrangement. I distinctly remember you saying I could dine with you and your son at the house on the days the restaurant didn't serve to the public. There are no meals here today."

"Oh, for the . . ." She huffed out a sigh. "Well, I hope you like peanut butter and jelly, because that's all we've got, and you did agree to eat whatever I fed J.P."

As if on cue, the boy scampered around the corner and walked to Declan's side. "I told Mom you were going to let me help you this afternoon, and she said—"

"Maybe," Libby interrupted. "I said maybe. Now how about some lunch, sport? Peanut butter and jelly?"

"Can Declan eat with us?" J.P. was already off the porch and skipping in the direction of the house.

Surprised he'd won this first skirmish so easily, Declan grinned as he waved a hand, indicating that Libby should precede him down the steps. Quirking a dark brow, she shook her head as she took the path to her home.

Chapter Six

Libby brushed a damp curl off her forehead and slid around the end of the counter. Slouching against the wall next to the coffee machine, she surveyed the bar. The Queen of the Sea closed early on Sunday, encouraging its customers to walk across the street to the Pink Pelican for a nightcap. From the looks of the packed room, every one of Phil and Don's patrons had decided to take the hint.

Heaving a sigh, she walked to the sink and began to wash an assortment of glasses. Since their discussion about the caveman, she and Tito hadn't found a minute to talk. The entire day had held about as much appeal as a visit to the acupuncturist. And every needle had been wielded by Declan O'Shae.

After a lunchtime squabble over the rules and regulations of their agreement, Declan had surprised her by devouring two thick peanut butter and jelly sandwiches with childlike enthusiasm. If not for the fact that she knew he was joking, she could almost believe he'd never tasted the gooey concoction, especially after he and J.P. had giggled over the way the sticky stuff stuck to the roof of his mouth.

During the afternoon, she'd watched him on and off from the house windows while she washed and dried the restaurant's linens or worked on the tangle of Jack's accounting ledgers. Declan had tackled the shingles on another side of the Pink Pelican with J.P.'s limited assistance. Considering the type of questions her son usually asked, she had to believe he had the patience of a . . . Well, he had to be a patient man. Later, he'd joined them at the house for a simple dinner of burgers, baked potatoes and salad, during which he'd praised her so-so culinary expertise as if she were a twenty-first century version of Julia Child.

Since the caveman and Frank had arrived about thirty minutes earlier, Jack had served them beer and taken a seat at their table. Knowing Declan was here right now, following her with his perceptive navy blue eyes as she waited on tables scattered around the room, made her temper edgy and her nerves raw.

The CD player changed discs and she closed her eyes, hoping to lose herself in one of the delicate instrumentals Grandma Martha had chosen years ago and updated by Jack to compact disc. The simple folk tunes, a variety of old Irish and Scottish melodies, were played on flute or guitar or a comingling of both.

It never failed that at some point during the evening a customer would try to sing along. Most of the time the results were comical, but every once in a while a patron managed to entertain them with a fairly on-key rendition of one of the songs. Tonight someone was making an attempt to do the same—and not doing it well at all.

Libby concentrated on the music, wincing when the customer hit a series of sour notes. Thank goodness J.P. wasn't here to join in. The caterwauling would probably shatter her fillings.

The melody slipped neatly into an older tune and, just as quickly, the out-of-place droning changed from a flat nasal baritone to a tenor so seductively sweet it caused the entire bar to go quiet. Raising her gaze, she scanned the room, curious to see which man owned the marvelous voice.

In shock, she dropped a glass into the sink, soaking the front of her T-shirt in soapy water. *Declan O'Shae.*

Devoid of his usual swagger, the caveman sat in his chair, a pensive yet serene expression on his handsome face. Singing with true emotion in what she assumed was Gaelic, he lay the plaintive song before his listeners like a gift.

Seconds of muffled silence followed as the customers murmured among themselves. By the time he started his second number, she noticed more than a few tears glistening in the eyes of the enthralled crowd.

Still in disbelief, Libby dabbed at her cheeks to blot what she assured herself was perspiration. T sidled over, drying a glass with a towel. "What did I tell you?" he said smugly, his gaze locked on Declan. "The man oozes magic, pure and simple."

Secretly furious with the caveman for daring to sound like one of God's own angels, she sniffed as she blotted the front of her shirt. "All right, so the man can sing, just like plenty of other people. There's no magic in that and you know it."

Tito answered with a rude snort and a shake of his head. "Since when did you become such a hard-shelled woman? If I didn't know better, I'd think you turned into one of them spiny lobsters we got scouring the coastline down here. What happened to petrify your tender heart?"

She turned and raised a finger, resisting the urge to thump it against his chest. "What happened? I can't believe you'd ask me such a question, knowing what Brett Ritter did to me and J.P. I still have a soft heart, but I've learned how to build a nice big wall around it. Never again will I let myself or my son get hurt by a man. And certainly not one we know so little about."

T set the glass on the bar and folded his arms across his massive chest. "Well, I know all I need to. Declan O'Shae ain't like that no-account you got mixed up with. He might

not be what we expected, but he is who we've been waitin'
for, and you'd best believe it if you want to make changes
around here.''

Before Libby could answer, a round of applause broke
out and she swung her gaze to Declan's table. Grinning
boyishly, he accepted a pat on the back from her grandfather,
then Frank. Damn if he didn't have the entire restaurant
eating from the palm of his hand. *But not me,* she reminded
herself smartly.

T made polite small talk with a customer, then ran the
blender for two frozen margaritas. After making change, he
swirled a pair of stemmed glasses in salt, poured the drinks,
and passed them across the bar.

The CD player switched discs again, and Tito used the
quiet time to make an announcement. ''Last call, folks. Raise
a hand and Miss Grayson will come by to take your order.
The Pink Pelican closes in fifteen minutes.''

Grateful the day was almost over, Libby pasted a friendly
smile on her face and circled the room. Thank heaven she
would be out of here and asleep in her own bed soon—and
away from Declan O'Shae.

Declan swiped the foam from his upper lip while Libby
chatted with the few remaining customers. The hour was
late and he was tired. He'd put in a full day's work, eaten
two interesting meals, and enjoyed music from his homeland.
Now he had the opportunity to watch a fair colleen as she
finished her chores. Of course, it was his duty as a gentleman
to see her properly escorted home for the night.

He turned at the sound of Jack Grayson's rumbled snore.
Sometime during the last few minutes, the old man had
nodded off. With his mouth agape and his balding head
propped against the wall, he was oblivious to his surroundings, sleeping like a babe in its mother's arms. Tito walked
over as Declan was deciding whether or not to awaken Jack
and help him to his feet.

''I'll see to him,'' said the cook, his expression soft.
''Maybe you could give Libby a hand closin' up the place?''

Declan grinned his thanks at the ingenious suggestion. "Aye, that I can." He inclined his head toward the gently snoring man. "Must you do this often?"

The cook quirked up a corner of his mouth. "Not so much since Libby's here, but for a while Jack was so lonely some nights he'd sleep on a cot in the kitchen. The two of us even talked about me movin' into that big empty house of his. Now that his family's back, he's perked up. It's good to see him takin' an interest in life again."

Just then Libby walked over. Sporting a worried frown, she speared Declan with a glare. "What's wrong with my grandfather?"

T reached out and helped the old man to his feet. "What'sa matter?" Jack muttered groggily. "Can't a body get a little sleep 'round here?"

T grinned. "Sure you can. But it'd be smarter to do it in your own bed."

Jack rubbed his hands over his face, then looked sheepishly at Libby. "Sorry, I must'a dozed off. Just give me a minute to get my bearings and I'll be fine."

Flushing pink, Libby's expression turned embarrassed. "Are you all right? Did you have too much to drink?"

As if insulted, Jack threw back his bony shoulders. "The day's yet to come I can't keep my head after a few beers, young lady. You go take care of your son. T and I will close up here."

Declan laid a hand on his arm. "I would consider it a pleasure if you would let me see to it. Besides, there's something I need to discuss with your granddaughter . . . in private."

"In private?" Jack jerked his head from Declan to Libby and back again. "Oh." He flashed an ear-to-ear smile at Tito. "Well, in that case . . . Let's get outta here, T, and leave these youngsters to their um . . . business."

Declan waited until the men walked out the door, well aware of what was awaiting him. The heat of Libby's stare fair to burned a hole in his shirt. Sure enough, he turned to find her standing with her hands on her hips, her bosom heaving and her face scarlet.

"I don't know what you're trying to pull, but I will not condone it. Letting my grandfather and T think that you—that I—Well, you can just take yourself back to Mary and Frank's. I'll close up on my own."

"Mistress Grayson—Libby—"

She raised her chin a notch. "What's it going to take to convince you that we don't need you around here? Money? Well, guess what? We don't have any, and I doubt we ever will. Go find some other town to scam and leave Sunset Key and the people in it alone."

Declan tried to keep calm, but this newest insult was one he couldn't ignore. Since his arrival, he'd done nothing to give credence to her biting remarks. He'd had no idea why he'd slept away the last two hundred years, but he had to make the best of it. All he desired was to locate his treasure and find his place in this strange new world.

Taking a step toward her, he clenched his jaw as he spoke. "You go too far, woman. I've apologized for the incident in the cave, and I grow tired of your unfounded accusations."

"And I accepted. But that doesn't mean I have to like you."

He gave his best pirate's leer. Her eyes grew wide and she sidled backward, and Declan realized he had her full attention. "Then why is it I feel compelled to make you see otherwise?"

She squared her shoulders. "You don't scare me. I've been threatened by better men than you."

Declan pushed forward one step at a time, until he had her backed against the bar. "You mistake me as usual, good mistress, for I don't make idle threats. I'm asking you politely to cease your outbursts or I'll be forced to do something—"

Libby tried to edge away, but he moved like lightning, bracing his hands on the bar and caging her between his arms.

Her lower lip trembled, but she stood her ground. "Back off, before I—"

Declan twisted quickly to the right as her knee jammed his thigh. *The wench had tried to unman him!* He growled deep in his throat, "That was a low blow."

"Not low enough," she muttered, her scowl centered on his chest. "And stop calling me your mistress."

Incredible. He'd used his best stalking glare, then his mighty pirate's snarl, and still she gave him orders. Was there nothing the woman feared? "I meant no disrespect," he said with admiration. " 'Tis a courtesy where I come from."

The force of her stare might have withered a lesser man. "Why is it I get the feeling that *where you come from* men still lay their coats across puddles for fair damsels to walk over?"

He chuckled at her attempted humor and took a step back. "Nay, for I wouldn't ruin my cloak with such a foolish gesture. But I have carried my share of women across a muddied street."

She shook her head in disbelief. "That's cute. But I still don't like the word. Besides the obvious implication, a few of the nastier people I've come in contact with used it to describe—" She exhaled a breath. "Just don't say it, okay? It pushes all my hot buttons."

Declan bit back a groan. He was hot, all right, and so was she, if he read correctly the rapid rise and fall of her chest and the tempting way her nipples puckered under her damp shirt. A cruder man would use this opportunity to press his aching erection against her woman's mound and . . .

Think with your head and not with your rod, he warned himself. *Do not ruin this first attempt at wooing by being crass.* "I shall remove the word from my vocabulary immediately, sweet lady. Is there anything else?"

Her gaze rose a few inches to settle on his chin. "Stop

being so darned charming all the time. It gets really old after a while.''

Declan straightened, bringing their bodies close again, and though she tensed, she didn't try to slip away. ''My charm is but a memory. Henceforth, I shall make an effort to be as surly as possible at all times. This I swear on the graves of my . . . of my father. What more can I do to prove my sincerity?''

''You're impossible.'' She ran a hand through her glorious hair, then let it drop to her side. ''Where did you learn to sing like that?''

''From my mother, bless her soul. It's been a long time since I've heard those old tunes. Did my voice please you?''

Her shoulders rose and fell with a heavy sigh. ''It was . . . very nice.''

He grinned, thinking he would sing the night away if only she would smile. ''What else?''

Libby raised her gaze to his, and the look in her eyes, so sad yet so hopeful, sent a shaft of longing arrowing to his midsection. ''How about no more lies on how you came to be in that cave?''

Her womanly scent, fresh as a flower and filled with arousal, overpowered his senses. The pulse point throbbing at the base of her throat became a poignant reminder of her vulnerability. He moved his hands from the bar to her upper arms. ''No more talk about the cave.''

They stood inches apart for what seemed like an eternity while he ran his thumbs over her shoulders. The ceiling fans creaked rhythmically, fluttering the curls framing her face. The sound of the ocean lapping the shore and a bird trilling in the darkness faded until finally she found her voice.

''I've already had to deal with a man who told enough lies to last a lifetime. If you promise to be honest, I'll try not to be so . . . disbelieving.''

''Ah, Libby,'' he crooned, pulling her closer to his chest. ''All I can do is swear to tell you the truth from this moment forward. The believing will be up to you.''

Carefully, he cradled her jaw in his palms and bent his head until their lips met and parted, then came together again. When he detected no resistance, he deepened the kiss, overjoyed to feel her nestle in his arms. She moaned as she clenched her hands against his shirt, and Declan fought the urge to sweep her up and carry her to a place where no one would ever lie to her again. Teasing as he tasted, he sipped as if she were fine wine. Just as he expected, she was sweeter than honeyed ale, more potent than island rum.

Drawing back at the sound of her whimper, he gazed into amber eyes awash with tears. Damn him for a fool. Why hadn't he realized sooner that her shrewish tongue and bossy manner hid a delicate and fragile heart? He'd promised to tell her nothing but the truth from this point onward. Once he did, it was certain he would hurt her all over again.

He smiled as he brushed away the lone tear slipping down her cheek. "Let us finish closing this place, fair lady. Then I shall walk you to your door."

"Declan's in the kitchen and we're starvin'," J.P. loudly announced, rocking the bed like a boat on the water.

Libby rolled to her side and groaned. Monday was supposed to be her day off. She'd spent a lousy night tossing and turning until dawn, and now her son had the nerve to jostle her awake after what seemed like only fifteen minutes of decent sleep.

J.P. bounced again. "If you don't get downstairs and make us breakfast, he said to tell you he's gonna come up here and carry you down."

Just let him try, she thought smugly, focusing one eye on her alarm clock. It would serve the caveman right if he wound up with a herniated disc.

J.P. giggled when she peered at him from under the pillow. Hurtling from the room, he whooped at the top of his lungs, "She's up, Declan! Mom's up!"

Libby swung her legs over the side of the bed as last

evening's disturbing scenario came rushing back in a steamy haze. She'd done some dumb things in her lifetime, but letting Declan O'Shae get close enough to touch her was at the very top of her ten-most-stupid list. Licking her lips, she swore she could still taste the flavor of his kiss. When she tried to erase the memory, all she could envision were his muscle-corded arms caging her against the bar, his big, capable hands caressing her face while he kissed her with enough expertise to make her toes curl.

They'd tidied the restaurant without exchanging a word, and he'd walked her home like a perfect gentleman, but his heated gaze had stroked her right up until he'd said a polite good night at the front door. She'd watched him saunter off into the darkness, and it had taken every ounce of self-control and almost all of her pride not to demand he take her in his arms and kiss her again.

But worse than her primal reaction to his sexual come-on had been her response to the promises he'd made. *No more charm and no more lies.*

She had been such an idiot to let herself fall for his line. If not for telling Uncle T that she'd give the man a chance, she'd march downstairs right now and order him out of the house and out of her life. But that just wasn't possible.

Sighing, she ran a hand through her hair, dressed, and padded quickly to the kitchen. Thank goodness they only had to share meals. If she could manage not to be alone with him again, maybe she'd be able to forget the whole thing had ever happened.

"What are we doin' today, Declan?" she heard her son ask as she turned the corner into the hall. "Can I help you again?" His voice, a mixture of hero worship and little-boy hope, made her heart ache.

Please don't be nice, she pleaded silently. *Tell him to go fishing with his grandfather or play with the kittens. Don't let me—let J.P. think you're one of the good guys.*

"Are you up to working on the Pink Pelican, lad? I'll

need someone to hand me the nails and shingles, and you did a fine job of it yesterday."

"Uh-huh," J.P. answered brightly. "I'm a big boy."

Darn the man for being so agreeable—and hadn't he promised to can the charm? Libby walked to the refrigerator and took out eggs, bread and milk, then set her grandmother's cast-iron skillet on the range and turned up the heat. Ignoring Declan's inquisitive gaze, she cracked eggs into a bowl, added milk, and began to stir. "What about Grandpa Jack? Don't you want to go fishing with him today? He'll be lonely out on the boat all alone."

"I already asked, and Grandpa said I could stay here. He and Uncle T drove to the market for bed-jetables," said J.P., kneeling on his chair.

Libby dipped bread into the mixture and set it into the skillet. "I think you mean vegetables, honey. Do you know what time they left?"

When she didn't receive an answer, she turned to find two pairs of eyes gazing at her in hungry anticipation. J.P. shrugged and Declan answered, "I believe it was an hour ago, in Tito's vehicle."

"T's truck? What's wrong with Jack's?" She flipped the French toast, then walked to the coffeepot, where she measured grounds, added water, and started the brew.

"Grandpa said it's broken and he doesn't have the money to fix it."

Libby cringed. One more thing to add to their growing list of problems. Back at the stove, she slid slices of the fried bread onto plates and brought them to the table. After squeezing the syrup bottle until his toast drowned, J.P. passed Declan the golden liquid.

He stared at the boy's overflowing plate, then sniffed at the bottle. Finally, he poured syrup over his own food and began to eat. Chewing slowly, his blue eyes crinkled as he swallowed. "You, my good woman, are a master chef." He piled more of the toast on his fork.

"Mom's almost as good a cook as Uncle T." J.P. took a swig of milk

"Gee, fellas, thanks a bunch," Libby remarked wryly, secretly tucking away their approval. "I'll try not to let the compliments go to my head."

Declan met her teasing remark with a smile. "I promised not to lie, good woman. What do you call this wonderful dish?"

"It's French toast, silly. Mom puts sim-a-mum in the eggs, just for me."

Before she could correct the boy, Declan muttered under his breath, "Ah yes, the French. They always did have a way with eggs."

Less nervous than when she'd first come into the kitchen, Libby ignored his odd remark, poured two cups of coffee, and brought them to the table. So far, the caveman had been polite enough not to mention what had taken place between them in the bar last night, but she was sure it was only a matter of time before he brought up the indiscretion, just like any other man.

And when he did, she'd be ready for him.

J.P. downed his milk and wiped his mouth on his sleeve, then jumped to his feet and headed outside.

"Hold on, young man. Upstairs. Brush your teeth and wash the syrup off your hands and face. Then we'll talk about the rest of your day."

"Aw, Mom—"

"Obedience to the woman who cooks you such fine meals would be wise, lad. And I will return to Mary's to do the same. If she has no need of me today, I'll meet you at the Pink Pelican in thirty minutes."

"Okay," said J.P., stuffing his hands in his pockets.

The two adults watched him race from the kitchen and into the hall. Positive Declan would use this opportunity to make a smug comment or suggestive remark, Libby stared at the table as she pleated a paper napkin.

Instead, he finished his coffee. "Thank you again for the meal. I really could use the boy's help, you know."

Unable to believe he wasn't bringing up what had happened in the bar, she could only say, "If you're sure he won't be underfoot. I don't want him to be a pest."

The warmth of his smile started a skittering in her chest. He pushed back from the table and set his cup in the sink. "He's a fine boy, and you've done an admirable job raising him. Any man would be proud to have him for a son."

The screen door slammed. Libby heard his cheerful whistle as he went down the porch stairs and made his way to the gas station. A sinking sensation began in the pit of her stomach and edged its way north.

Damn the man, and damn his insufferable charm.

He'd just blown a hole square through her heart, in a way that was completely nonsexual and innocent. He'd said something Brett had never bothered to mention in all the years since J.P.'s birth. He'd told her that she was a good mother.

Declan trod the beaten path up the hill to the rise on the eastern side of town. He'd worked on the shingles with J.P. until Libby fed them their noon meal, then returned to the gas station to help Frank Spitzer with the unloading of crates. This was the first chance he'd had to spend a few moments by himself.

Mangrove trees and a tangle of vegetation covered the promontory, forming a sanctuary for pelicans and other colorful birds inhabiting the Keys. Snakes, too, abounded on these islands, as well as bugs, some smaller than a flea, others shiny black and as large as coins. Slapping at one of the buzzing insects attacking his neck, he wondered why modern science hadn't found a way to rid the place of the nasty beasties in over two centuries.

When he pushed past the tangle of leaves at the end of the path, he found himself at the very tip of the rise. Bracing his feet on the grass, he gazed onto Sunset Key. It was down there somewhere, he told himself, his reward for all the years he'd risked his life for the love of his new country. But time and human colonization had erased so much. Gone was the untouched inlet he'd sailed to with his men. Buildings now obliterated most of what he'd used to pace off the spot where he'd buried his treasure. In their place stood homes, roads, and ports—marinas, they were called—filled with all manner of ships.

The only thing familiar-looking was a pile of boulders situated on the grassy area between Hewitt's Marina and the Pink Pelican. But was it the first mound of boulders or the second from which he'd counted out his steps? How much of the land had been covered by pavement or buildings, how many of the trees had been removed since he'd paced off strides to his strongbox?

This side of the island was ringed by coral reef, like most of the Keys. He would have to walk the beach, guess where his longboat had landed, and retrace his steps from memory. A two-hundred-plus-year-old memory.

Declan fingered the jagged medallion he kept hidden under his shirt, his one link to the past. Since he'd awakened in the cave, the talisman had ceased its warm pulsing and turned icy cold. How, he wondered, had it managed to stay with him through the ravaging storm? And how had the broken half ended up on his chest?

He'd spent hours ruminating on his predicament and was fairly certain there was no way for him to reverse the passage of time. If magic had come into play here, he had no knowledge of it. For better or worse, he was stuck in the twenty-first century. But why?

He heard a rustling noise and leaped into a crouch. If someone had followed him . . .

"Declan, hey, Declan," J.P.'s voice hissed from the mangroves. "You up here?"

The branches parted as the boy struggled through the

vegetation. Breaking free, he stepped into the clearing. "What'cha doin'?"

"Boy," he acknowledged, relaxing his stance. "Are you following me?"

J.P. dragged the toe of his sneaker through the sandy grass. "Sort of. Mom told me to go to the gas station and tell you supper was almost ready. Mary said you walked this way and I just followed the path."

"Hmm." He folded his arms. "So your mother doesn't know you're here?"

J.P. shrugged. "Not exactly."

Declan raised a brow. "Perhaps next time you should ask her permission."

"Don't you want me here?"

The plaintive words hit his gut like a fist. "It's not whether I want you here that's the worry, lad. 'Tis your mother's disapproval I fear."

The boy grinned. "Mom's not so bad. Grandpa Jack says her bark is worse than her bite . . . and she never yells at me." J.P. walked to his side and stared out onto the ocean. "Wow, this is really high. What are you doing up here?"

"Looking for something I lost," Declan answered honestly.

"Did you lose it up here?"

"No, but I thought it might be a good place to start the search." He put his hands in his pockets. "What are we having for supper?"

"The last of the piz-ghetti, I think. It's one of my favorites."

"Mine, too." He stepped toward the path and held back a curtain of branches. "What say you lead the way home?"

They reached the bottom of the trail, and J.P. slipped a child-sized palm into his hand. A wave of caring washed over Declan and he warmed inside, noting how natural and right the innocent gesture felt.

"What did you lose?" J.P. asked after they'd walked a few minutes in companionable silence.

Declan heaved a sigh. "My treasure."

"Wow! A real treasure?" J.P. skipped ahead of him, turned, and began to walk backward. "When did you lose it?"

Realizing he'd said too much, he reached out and ruffled the boy's mop of curls. "A long time ago. And I'd be obliged if you wouldn't tell anyone. It needs to be our secret."

J.P. scanned the sidewalk, then took Declan's hand again and fell into step beside him. "Not even Grandpa Jack or Mom?"

"Especially not your mother. I fear she'd think me daft if she heard the entire story."

They stopped a few feet from the Pink Pelican. J.P. raced up the rear stairs, then jumped to the bottom with typical little-boy bravado. "You're prob'ly right. I heard her tellin' Grandpa Jack she doesn't believe in hunting for treasure. She said it was a fairy tale, and fairy tales aren't real."

Ah, Libby, Declan thought, *if only you knew . . .*

He scratched at his jaw as he stared out over the inlet onto the promontory, then swung his gaze to the roof of the bar. "What say tomorrow morning while it's cool we start on the roof? Knowing your mother, you won't be allowed up the ladder, but you could hand me thatch and a drink or two when I need it."

"Then could I help you look for your treasure?"

"We'll see, lad. We'll see."

Chapter Seven

The bar was closed on Monday, as were most of the shops in Sunset. That was the reason Libby called the meeting for tonight. Thanks to the Spitzers and Olivia, word had spread that the Graysons wanted to discuss with as many people as possible a topic they felt important to the entire town.

Today, in between ironing the restaurant's clean linen and spying on Declan as he and J.P. worked on the Pink Pelican, Libby practiced her speech. Though she didn't have a solution to their problem, she knew it needed to be addressed. She'd been home only a few weeks, and although she'd said a polite hello to many of the townsfolk, most of her time had been spent working in the bar or slogging her way through Jack's books. Now past the dinner hour, people were trickling in slowly, more interested, Libby suspected, in asking questions about her absence than finding out what she wanted to discuss.

J.P. sat perched on the bar beside her, while Jack and T stood behind it filling glasses with iced tea she'd made that afternoon. Mary set two plates of homemade chocolate chip cookies next to the tea, then encouraged everyone to help themselves as Libby made small talk with their guests.

"J.P., how you doing? Liberty, you look terrific." Hazel Hewitt nodded her approval. Though not the most motherly type, the marina owner had always been a friend. More importantly, she'd welcomed J.P. from their first day back and allowed him to hang out at the marina to study the many varieties of aquatic life she kept in several aquariums situated throughout the shop.

"Thanks, Hazel, so do you," said Libby, admiring the older woman's trim figure. Hazel was the only woman in town she'd ever needed to look up to when they spoke. With a classically oval face, attractive features and unlined skin, she always wondered why Hazel had hidden away in Sunset, when it was obvious she could have had a career as a New York fashion model.

"I keep meaning to stop by to tell you how grateful I am for letting J.P. spend time in the marina. There's just something about fish that intrigues him."

Hazel snagged a glass of tea and waited until Tito handed J.P. a cookie as a distraction. "The little guy 'bout broke my heart with that story about Humphrey's untimely death. When he told me his daddy had left him on the same day, I had to bite my lip to keep from crying. He's welcome anytime, and so are you."

Well, thought Libby, that answered the question as to how many of the people in town knew about what had happened between herself and Brett. If Sunset Key had a newspaper, her personal life wouldn't have received better coverage.

Hazel left to find a seat, and Libby waved to a group of fisherman who'd just sauntered in. They made their living supplying the Queen of the Sea and other restaurants on nearby Keys with a daily catch. Several people she'd yet to meet formally, newer residents whom she guessed had purchased either the antiques shop or ice-cream store down the street, walked through the door and she nodded hello.

Finally, Phil and Don arrived. Dressed in identical red

and yellow Hawaiian print shirts, white Bermuda shorts, and thong sandals, the two men shuffled over in double time.

"Libby, sweetheart," cooed Don, grabbing her hands and holding them out to the side. "You look divine. Doesn't she look divine, Phil?"

"Lord, yes," Phil agreed, eyeing her above-the-knee denim skirt and hot pink T-shirt. He kissed her on the cheek. "I simply adore a full-figured woman. And I love your hair. What do you use to keep those curls in check?"

Libby grinned at both men; Don, tall and handsome, with a full head of graying hair and a falsely officious manner, and Phil, rotund, balding, and so stereotypically gay it always made her laugh. When she was younger, her grandmother had explained in small doses all about the two men and their *peculiarities*. After visiting Key West and Miami as a teenager and ten years of living in the big city, she'd become more familiar with homosexuals and their habits. Phil and Don had been a devoted couple from as far back as she could remember. Her own track record should be so good.

"Phil. Don—"

"Uh-huh-huh. What happened to *Uncle* Phil and *Uncle* Don?" Phil asked, shaking his head. "And why haven't you been over to see us?"

"New York is what happened," countered Don. "And that spineless creep who jilted her." Quick as a blink, he sucked in a breath. "Sorry, sweetcakes, I didn't mean to bring up ugly memories. We're just being catty because we love you. We're absolutely thrilled to have you back."

Before Libby could muster a response, there was a commotion at the door. Frank walked in toting extra folding chairs, with Declan right behind him carrying twice the amount. She held back a frown at the sight of his broad shoulders and rippling—damn, there was that word again— muscles. So the caveman thought himself a part of Sunset, did he? Once this meeting was over, she'd set him straight on that little misconception.

"Well, well, well," muttered Phil. "If it isn't the hunky handyman in the flesh."

"*Flesh* being the operative word," added Don.

Phil winked at Libby as Don continued. "Quite an eyeful, isn't he? Do you think we could find something that needs fixing around the restaurant?"

"Behave yourselves," Libby managed to sputter, pulling her attention from the door. The last thing she needed was to agree with Phil and Don, even if Declan did look amazing in another one of Jeff's stretched-tight T-shirts and a pair of snug-fitting jeans.

Grinning, Phil gave her a hug, then Don did the same. "He's all yours, darling," whispered Phil. "We've already found our Mister Right."

Libby sighed her frustration as she watched them take seats behind Declan. Once settled, Phil waggled his fingers at her while Don patted his breastbone and fluttered his lashes. Both men were beyond outrageous, which was one of the reasons she liked them so much.

She surveyed the room and guessed there were about forty people in attendance, and aside from her, J.P., and the caveman, every one of them was sixty years of age or better. She'd have to choose her words carefully to make the night a success.

"Good evening," she began, pausing for their attention. "Thank you for taking the time to be here."

Several people spoke at once. "Hey, Libby."

"No trouble for you, Libby."

"Glad to have you back."

She smiled at the friendly faces and reminded herself that she was standing in front of her extended family—the people she trusted to help raise her son. The people she loved.

"It's good to be home. I asked you here because—"

"You back for good?" came a voice from the last row. Del Ferguson, one of the fishermen, raised his hand. "We missed you, you know."

"I'm back for good, Del. Had enough of the big city. Now if we could—"

"Who's the little fella sittin' on the bar?" asked a woman she thought might be the new owner of the antiques store.

Libby felt a rush of heat flare from her chest to her cheeks. After Hazel and Phil and Don's casual remarks, she was certain everyone in attendance knew of her failed relationship, which meant they all knew her son was illegitimate. She turned and smoothed J.P.'s hair, then moved her gaze back to the crowd. "This is my son, John Patrick," she said with a spurt of pride.

"Hey, John Patrick, how ya doing?"

J.P. giggled as he swung his feet, but Libby never missed a beat. "We're both happy to be home. I've been busy getting reacquainted with my grandfather, but I'd planned on stopping by to see each of you. After discussing things with Grandpa Jack and the Spitzers, I decided it might be better to call this meeting."

The room hummed with speculation, some folks mumbling to one another, others gazing at her as if she'd grown a second head. Realizing she had them worried, she raised a hand. "Sorry, I didn't mean to alarm anyone. But I think there are things we need to talk over . . . about the town."

"Sunset?" someone asked. "You called us here to talk about Sunset Key?"

Libby straightened her stance. "Please hear me out. If I'm wrong, you can go back home and no harm done." She looked over her shoulder at Jack and Tito, who nodded encouragement. "I assume you all know I've spent the past ten years up north, working as an accountant in the wild, wicked city?"

The room shimmered with subdued laughter.

Bolstered by their attitude, she went on. "Since I've been back, Grandpa Jack's had me studying his books, and I have to tell you I'm upset with what I've seen. Seems he's been having money problems for the past several seasons, and so have Olivia and the Spitzers. If the rest of you are in as much hot water as they are, we need to talk about it openly, because I don't think it's just their problem—it's everyone's.''

At the sound of the *m* word, the crowd settled down. Mary stepped to Libby's side and took the lead. ''Our business is barely in the black, and it's been that way for the past five years or so. I'd like you all to be honest. How many of you are in the same boat as Frank and me?''

After a few seconds hands began to rise, until eventually every person in the room was nodding.

''So it's true, then?'' Libby asked, stepping closer to the center of the room. ''You're all having trouble making ends meet? This year's profits are less than last year's and the year before that?''

Phil stood and rested a hand on Don's shoulder. ''I know the town thinks we're rolling in dough, but Don and I have noticed a definite downtrend over the past few years. With more and more of the big conglomerates opening exclusive resorts and upscale restaurants, our place is suffering as well. Not to mention the fact we can't find decent help.''

''All right,'' said Libby, waiting for Phil's words to sink in. ''So what do you propose we do about it?''

Declan leaned back in his chair, his gaze trained on Libby. By God, but the woman knew how to take command of a room. She'd hinted to him often enough that the townsfolk were an aging group. Assessing the crowd as soon as he'd entered the bar, he'd seen she was right. Besides himself, Libby, and her son, there wasn't a person in the room spry enough to trim a jib or man an oar, never mind refurbish a business.

Now that Libby had made her opening statement, people began to call out questions. Was she looking to start up her own accounting practice, or did she have something else in mind? And if she did, what was it? Just how much would they need to spend to get things back on track?

''I don't have the answers to all your concerns,'' Libby finally said after the hubbub died down. ''I just know we have to make a change. We need to draw more tourists here and give them better accommodations once they arrive. We need an ATM machine and a real grocery store, maybe a bakery and an aquarium or specialty exhibit, and somewhere for the children to go while their parents spend money."

"Spend money, that's the key," added Frank. "We need to think of a way to make Sunset so unique that people will want to lose their dollars here."

"How about advertising?" asked Hazel. "I already run an ad in several of those glossy tourist booklets. Maybe if we chipped in and did a full-page color promotion, or—"

Olivia interrupted, "You're missing the point, Hazel. We need something *to* promote; you know, a reason for them to come here. There are dozens of spit-sized towns dotting the Keys. The ones along Route One are prosperous because of location alone, but most of the smaller cities have a big resort or a surfing contest or a museum to lure the tourists."

A man in the rear stood up and cleared his throat. " 'Evening. Name's Bob Grisham. The wife and I just moved here from Ohio and bought the ice-cream parlor down the street."

Several people murmured a greeting as he continued. "One of the reasons we moved here was the peace and quiet. Louise and I are a few years short of retirement, but we hoped we could keep on working for the next twenty or so, have a simple life and still run a business. If what you're telling us is true, that we're not going to make a living in Sunset, I'll just sell the place and find a shop in Marathon."

Tito raised a brow. "Hang on, Mr. Grisham. That's why Libby done called this meetin'—to prevent folks from sellin' out and movin' to the strip. I been here thirty-five years and the last thing I want to see is a mass exodus because people are too scared or worn out to fight for this town and what they built here."

Jack walked out from behind the bar and the crowd grew quiet, their respect for the older man clear. "You all know me. My wife and I were two of the first to settle in Sunset. If I remember correctly, one of the reasons we decided to

drive across the causeway was to get away from the glitz
of the bigger hotels and tourist traps being built on the
highway. I didn't say anything sooner about my financial
state because I felt like a failure. Now that I see I'm not
alone, I have to agree with T. But I'd sure hate to give up
my privacy or quiet time just for the sake of making a buck.''

Several people began talking at once, most in agreement
with Jack and T's sentiments. Tito smacked an empty beer
mug onto the bar and Libby raised a hand. ''Okay, now that
we're all thinking alike, does anybody have any ideas on
what can we do about it?''

Up until now, Declan had listened in silence, but his
mind had been working double time. When he'd lived in
Charleston, the wharf had bustled with all manner of trade.
Cooks hawked tasty food and tempting sweets; seamstresses
sold scarves, shawls and unique items of apparel. Magicians,
puppeteers, and musicians walked the dock daily. Suddenly,
he remembered the gypsy who'd given him his medallion.
People were still interested in having their fortunes told;
he'd seen offers of card readings on the television.

Mary Spitzer did an admirable job with her baking. Olivia
had all manner of clothing in her shop. Tito cooked meals
fit for a king. Surely there were other people in town who
had a special talent or knew of someone who did?

He raised his hand, and the crowd grew silent. ''Mr.
O'Shae?'' said Libby, her acknowledgment just short of a
dismissal.

Declan rose from his chair and slipped his hands into his
pockets. ''Good evening. For those of you who don't know
me, my name is Declan O'Shae. I've been working in town
for a week now, doing odd jobs around the Spitzers' garage
and the Pink Pelican.''

''Are you here to stay?'' asked Phil. Don socked him on
the arm, and the crowd chuckled.

Declan gazed at Libby, recalling the promise he'd made
last night in this very room. *Be truthful, O'Shae, and admit
that once you find your treasure you'll be out of here.*

"I'm not sure," he responded. "But probably not."

She glared, and he made a little bow, which caused more laughter. "Your city is small and might need a bit of remodeling for what I have in mind, but I do have a suggestion."

"You're not a business owner, Mr. O'Shae," Libby tossed out. "I'm not certain you have a say in this matter."

Tito laid a hand on her shoulder. "Let the man speak, little girl. I'd like to hear what he thinks."

Declan flashed T a grin, then scanned the room until he had everyone's attention. "I propose we conduct a festival— a fair, you might call it. The docks at the marina and the free space between there and the Pink Pelican would hold dozens of booths. We could build a gazebo on the town square, hire entertainment, and sell goods. If we sent hand-bills—flyers—to the other islands and promoted it our-selves, the cost of advertising would be a pittance.

"When the event gets a favorable reputation, you'll only need to hold it once a season to bring in the extra revenue. That way the town is yours every day but one or two, while you carry on the same trade during the week. You would still have your solitude, yet be able to set aside the time for an influx of visitors."

At first there were only a few mumbled comments, and for a moment Declan thought the crowd would string him up in the town square. Then Tito began a slow, rhythmic clapping and everyone joined in. People stood and patted him on the back, all talking at once. He glanced toward Libby and saw a look of surprise on her face, then the barest glimmer of a smile.

And he felt as if he'd hung the moon.

Treading carefully on the path out of Sunset, Libby walked toward Dream Cove. Don and Phil had helped her close the bar while they'd caught up on old times. She'd left Jack and Tito home drinking coffee in the kitchen and J.P. in bed. Only seconds earlier, exhaustion had hit her like a lead blanket, smothering her where she stood. The thought of a peaceful night's sleep seemed positively perfect—and completely out of reach.

She'd changed into a pair of faded jeans, because the short denim skirt she'd worn earlier was inappropriate for what she planned to do. Silvery white moonlight reflected off the water, guiding her across the small stretch of sandy beach. The tide was low, but not low enough to reveal the entrance to the secret cave where she'd found Declan O'Shae. Strange, she thought, in all her years of coming here, she'd never seen the water at such a level. Had she just not been here on the days when the opening was clear?

She walked to the rear of the boulders and began to climb. Once on the flat surface at the very top, she shook out a homemade quilt that had belonged to her grandmother and sat down on it Indian-style. Exhaling a huge breath, she stared out onto the ocean. What in the heck was happening to her? she wondered, turning her attention to the stars twinkling from overhead. When had her life gotten so out of control?

When she'd first met Brett, fresh out of college, she'd known exactly what she wanted. A home and family, recognition for her business degree, and financial stability had sounded like the perfect recipe for success. When had all her hopes and dreams turned into a Happy Meal that had been left too long in the sun?

Brett had pursued her and offered her all those things. After a while, when none of his promises materialized, he begged her to give him time to sort out his life. She'd said of course because, like a fool, she'd believed his intentions were honorable. When she'd accidentally become pregnant with J.P., she thought he would finally keep his word, settle down and make them a family. Little did she know that he was looking for a mother, maid and bed partner, and not necessarily in that order.

Her grandmother would have been the first to tell Libby it was her own fault Brett had taken advantage of her. She

should have put her foot down the minute the snake shed
his skin. Martha had always said a woman needed to guide
her own life, because no man understood enough about what
a woman needed to guide it for her. Her grandparents had
formed a lifelong partnership, both in business and in love,
on that theory.

Libby had thought Brett wanted the same. It had taken
seven years to realize she'd misjudged him and the entire
relationship. Now here she was, drawn to someone she was
fairly certain was a drifter who, if she let him, would make
a fool of her all over again. At least the caveman hadn't
lied and claimed he would stay.

Declan O'Shae. The man's very name conjured up sweet
summer afternoons and romantic stories with fairy-tale end-
ings—the kind where brave knights rescued damsels in dis-
tress.

But she was no fair maiden, and he was no knight in
shining armor. They were real people living in a modern
world. A world filled with pitfalls and problems, where men
and women always seemed to want different things and
relationships rarely lasted more than a few months.

More importantly, she had a son who'd been wounded
enough times to have earned his own Purple Heart. He'd
just stopped talking about death and dying. When Declan
O'Shae left town—and she had no doubt he would—J.P.'s
heart would break all over again. And so would hers if she
continued to give in to the compelling ache of desire that
overwhelmed her whenever they were together.

He'd sounded so sincere tonight, setting his idea in front
of the town. It was a good idea, too, but why couldn't she
or T or Mary have been the one to think of it? Why had it
taken a stranger to lay out a program that could very well
rescue them all? Why did it have to be the caveman?

Waves tumbled to the shore, filling the tropical night with
their gentle lapping, almost drowning out the rustle she
heard on the rocks behind her. Starting, she glared over her

shoulder, annoyed she'd let herself get so caught up in her musings that she'd let someone sneak up on her.

"Madam." Declan's lilting voice hummed in her blood, vibrated through her veins. "I don't mean to intrude."

Yes, you do, Libby wanted to shout, fixing her gaze on the shoreline. *You've been intruding for a week now, in my mind, in my dreams, in my life.*

"I thought you went home with the Spitzers."

"I did." He sat down beside her as if she'd invited him. "But only to stretch my legs. I came back to the house, and Tito said you might be here."

Well, great. If T and her grandfather had suspected there was hanky-panky between she and the caveman before, this would certainly put the frosting on the cake.

"This is my spot, O'Shae. If you want to talk, we can do it tomorrow. You know where I live."

He stuck out his long muscular legs in front of himself and placed his palms at his sides, grazing her thigh with a hand. "What I had to say couldn't wait. It's about the meeting."

Refusing to inch away like a nervous teenager, she ignored the warmth of his touch. "Seems to me you said enough. The citizens of Sunset proclaimed you the chairman of their festival by unanimous vote. What more is there to talk about?"

"I take it you're not pleased with the outcome of the meeting?"

Not pleased? Now there was the understatement of the millennium. "I'm pleased someone came up with an idea everyone could approve of."

He huffed out a laugh. "But *dis*pleased the idea was mine."

"Bingo. As Mary would say, you've pinned the tail on the donkey."

He bent his knee and angled to face her. "I thought we'd worked through your distrust of me the other night. In the bar."

The bar. She wondered why it had taken him this long to throw that embarrassing moment in her face. "Let's just forget about last night, shall we? I'd like to pretend it never happened."

"Ah, but I don't think that's possible, fair lady, since our encounter in the Pink Pelican is all I've had on my mind for the past twenty-four hours."

He rose to his knees, and it took every ounce of restraint for Libby not to meet him face-to-face. "Think about something else," she advised, staring down at her hands clenched tight in her lap. "Snowboarding in the Catskills or maybe skydiving. Skydiving would definitely take your mind off—"

"Us?" he asked, sitting back on his heels.

"There isn't any *us*, O'Shae. And there never will be. Why don't you just go back to where you came from and—"

"I'm afraid that, too, is impossible."

Libby could see him out of the corner of her eye. She might have misread the sadness in his voice, but she couldn't ignore the expression of longing carved in his face, the look of pain radiating from his eyes. A new thought struck her, one she'd toyed with but had yet to voice out loud.

"Tell me something: Are you on the lam?"

He raised a black brow. "On the lamb? I didn't realize there were sheep on the island."

Cute. He was trying to be so darned cute, avoiding her very serious question. "You know what I mean—are you running from the police? Are you wanted for a crime?"

He folded his arms across his chest. "A crime?" His eyes did a playful dance in the moonlight. "Not exactly, though I have been accused of partaking in activities some might construe as illegal." Reaching out, he stroked a finger across her jaw. "Right now, my thoughts are far more wicked than my deeds, of this I can assure you."

A jolt of heat sizzled down her neck to her belly, sending her insides on a wild ride of sensation. Without thinking, she came to her knees and faced him. "Keep your hands to yourself. I never gave you permission to—"

Declan grasped her upper arms in a light but demanding grip. "Ah, but you did, sweet Libby. Last night, when I took you in my arms, your body told me it welcomed my attention."

She pushed at his chest and he smiled, his lips a curve of desire. He bent his head and her push became a frantic pull as she fisted her hands in his T-shirt. "Damn you, can't you see I don't want this? I can't give you what you're looking for. Not now, not ever."

"Ah, but you can, Libby mine, and your body knows it, even if it's yet to alert your brain." He bent his head, and she rose to meet him, her resolve melting like candle wax in a flame.

Declan sipped at her lips like a desert nomad quenching his thirst after a long arid journey. Sighing into her mouth, he teased, tasted, devoured. She felt his hands move to her back, then lower to cup her bottom. Pelvis to pelvis, they pressed against one another, and his arousal sent a shiver down her spine.

Shuddering, she leaned back and rested her forehead against his chin. "I can't fight you tonight. I'm just too worn out."

His chest rumbled with gentle laughter. "Fighting isn't exactly what I had in mind, sweet lady. 'Tis loving you that I'm after."

She raised her gaze to his navy blue eyes. "Don't use that word with me. Just say what you mean. You have the *hots* for me. We want each other. Pure animal lust is all we're feeling here."

"Though I'll admit to being warm in your presence, lust is a fair enough word to describe what I'm experiencing." He cradled her jaw, nibbled at her lips, sighed into her mouth. "But unlike the beasts of the field there are choices. I would never take you against your wishes, but I must warn you I was blessed with a powerful gift of persuasion."

She arched a brow in disbelief. "Gift of persuasion? Cut me a break. You're more like a runaway steamroller."

"Is that good, being a *steam roller?*"

She shrugged, wondering why he kept repeating her simple everyday phrases as if he came from another century. And darn it if that didn't make him sound even more romantic, more like a character from a Brontë novel. "I'm not sure. I'll have to think about it."

He ran his hands to her waist, then up her rib cage, until they rested under the swell of her breasts. Rubbing softly, he moved his thumbs over her peaked nipples. "Don't think too long, madam. My brain is fair to aching with the image of you lying beneath me, writhing in pleasure, our bodies joined and our desire sated."

She stiffened in his arms, and he tugged her back. "I'm merely voicing what I feel, as you asked. Tell me you don't want the same and I'll walk away from here and not bother you again. Though it may kill me to do so."

Libby sighed. Her breasts felt achy and swollen, her lower extremities moist and throbbing. And she'd always been a terrible liar.

Lifting her chin, she stood and rolled up the quilt, then tucked it under her arm. Taking the hint, Declan slipped down the boulders ahead of her and reached up to help her to the ground. Swinging her in his arms as if she were a child, he let her body ease over his as he set her lightly on her feet.

Singed by the erotic sensation, she stepped away from him. "I need time to think—about a lot of things. I'll see you at breakfast."

Declan ran a hand over his face as he watched Libby walk away, respecting her wish to be alone. God's toes but she set his blood to boiling. Her response to his kisses was more than he'd hoped for, her answer to his proposal like a life raft to a drowning man. If he understood her correctly, she was considering his offer and might actually welcome him in her bed.

After she disappeared from sight, he followed, just in case she needed him. The idea he'd offered the townsfolk tonight would help fill everyone's coffers, but it would also bring further progress to the area. Progress was often accompanied by ills. Greed, drunkenness, unsavory men who would enjoy taking advantage of the elderly and innocent—the people who inhabited this town.

The thought of anyone in Sunset wanting to hurt Libby Grayson was laughable, but he had a powerful urge to protect her all the same. He grinned. *Powerful* was the perfect word to describe every sensation he experienced while in her presence. His brain refused to think rationally, and the heat she'd mentioned seemed more an inferno raging low in his belly.

When he saw Libby slip up the steps to her house and close the door behind her, he headed back to the Spitzers. Stopping on the expansive grassy area between the bar and the marina, he glanced up and down the street, imagining it filled with booths, people, the sounds of a street fair. They'd given him a huge task, and he wasn't certain he could . . .

He dragged his hands through his hair. He had to ''get a grip,'' as he'd heard people remark on the television. From the look of it, he was stuck in this century for good. He'd yet to figure out the reason he was here, but he'd never been a man to wait for things to happen. He'd always taken charge.

The world had changed, become huge and wondrous, ripe with opportunity. There were places he'd like to visit— Charleston, Dublin—the Pacific Ocean. When he found his treasure, if it still existed, he'd buy a boat and sail the seas again, this time without fear of capture or retribution.

Aye, he'd work on the fair, but only because he owed the people of this town for their kindness. Once he unearthed his booty, he'd be gone from this place.

Scanning the square, he stared at the marina. If its con- struction had caused the removal of the first landmark, his treasure would be some hundred paces to the west, which would put it . . .

He sucked in a heavy breath. Sweet Christ and holy Christmas . . . his treasure would be buried directly under the Pink Pelican.

Chapter Eight

Libby woke to the sound of hearty male laughter and a high-pitched giggle, then the patter of running feet and a door slamming. Groaning, she turned to her side and checked the alarm. Okay, so she was late with breakfast. What else could she expect after two miserable nights of, at the most, twenty minutes sleep?

"Libby!" Her grandfather's voice hurtled up the stairs. "I'm goin' to Frank's to get the truck looked at and J.P.'s comin' with me."

The door banged a second time and she rolled to stare at the painted ceiling, dingy white and peeling in the humidity. One of these days, when she found a way to dig them out of debt, she was going to refurbish this house that had been so lovingly built by her grandparents' own hands. After he finished with the Pink Pelican, maybe Declan could start on the inside—

Nope. Nu-uh. No way was she going to let her mind travel down that dead-end road. Declan O'Shae was not the Graysons' personal handyman nor anyone else they wanted to count on. She was not going to give him a place in her future, no matter how hard he tried to insinuate himself in her present.

Libby swung her legs to the side of the bed and blew out a breath, unable to prevent the hot and heavy encounter they'd shared at Dream Cove from inching into her brain.

Lordy, the man could kiss. The memory of the way he'd held her in his arms and captured her mouth with his had her lips tingling all over again. And when he'd cupped her breasts in his big warm palms and run his thumbs over their aching peaks ... Good grief, her nipples grew hard just thinking about it.

She'd been intimate with only one man her entire life and had always thought their lovemaking adequate. Sex with Brett had been momentarily exciting but predictable and controlled, like riding an amusement park roller coaster. She couldn't remember being this edgy or unable to sleep, even when they'd first started dating.

After just two bouts of locking lips with the caveman, Libby knew for certain sex with Declan O'Shae wouldn't be controlled. And it would never be predictable. It would be more like soaring in a hot air balloon, rising higher and higher into the sky and never knowing when you might plummet recklessly to earth. The freedom of floating through the clouds and the thrill of free falling would turn the entire encounter into a mind- and body-shattering experience.

Sighing at the invigorating yet impossible thought, she padded to the bathroom, turned on the taps for her morning shower, and stepped into the tub. Hot water pelted her sensitized skin, running in rivulets over her breasts and stomach, automatically calling to mind the stroking heat of Declan's hands as they'd caressed her from top to bottom.

Libby shivered to her toenails as she lathered and rinsed her hair, then squirted gardenia scented gel onto a washcloth. Laving her prickling skin, she rubbed the terry cloth over herself slowly as she recalled the words he'd used to describe his idea of their lovemaking—her underneath him, pliant and panting while they were joined.

She closed her eyes, and there, imprinted on the back of her eyelids, was an erotic, sepia-toned movie with her as the star. She was nestled in Declan's arms, his hard body pinning her in place as he loomed over her, teasing, touching, tasting . . .

The thick nubby cloth became his warm rough palms gliding over her nipples, down her belly . . . Trembling in place, she fought the shock waves threatening to send her over the edge as she quivered down to her toes and back up again.

Jeez. And she'd thought showers were supposed to ease sexual tension.

She braced her hands against the tiles and waited until her heartbeat returned to normal. She was a healthy woman, used to having sex at regular intervals, but nothing like this had ever happened to her before. If the mere thought of being touched by Declan O'Shae could bring about such unexpected sensations, that hot air balloon ride idea was off base by a mile. If she decided to take him up on his offer, *which she wouldn't,* she might not even survive the experience.

She stepped out of the tub and dried off, then dressed in plain white panties and her bra. A feeling of femininity swept through her, and she decided to forego her usual shorts and T-shirt for a flowing, cotton-print dress. After glancing at her face in the mirror, she decided it was a good thing she'd be alone in the kitchen. One look at her befuddled expression and flushed cheeks and her grandfather would have been immediately suspicious of how she'd spent her lazy morning.

She slipped on her sandals and headed down the stairs on shaky legs, her nose twitching at the aroma of fresh coffee. Bless Grandpa Jack for thinking of her. A strong jolt of caffeine was sure to get her mind off the caveman and back to reality. Turning the corner from the hall, she froze in her tracks.

"It's about time you found your way to the galley."

Libby stared in shock at the sight of Declan O'Shae lounging in a kitchen chair as if he had every right to be there.

"What are you doing here?"

He grinned impishly as he saluted her with his coffee mug. "Breakfast, madam. Or did you forget our bargain?"

She rolled her eyes in aggravation, stared at the ceiling, and stomped to the sink, immediately rescinding her blessing. She was going to kill Jack for not warning her that she'd be alone with the man. "I heard my grandfather down here a while ago. Didn't he feed you?"

"He offered," Declan said wryly. "I simply couldn't imagine eating something called fruit loops, no matter how hard your son tried to convince me of their 'super-colossal' taste. When I saw those unappetizing bits of blue and orange floating in his bowl of milk, I knew I'd made a wise decision."

Libby turned away so he wouldn't see her smile. "I guess I have to agree with you. Cereal that looks and tastes like cotton candy isn't my idea of breakfast either. That's why J.P. only gets to eat it when I'm not around."

"I trust you had a restful night?"

The laughter she heard creeping its way into the question made it sound as if he knew darn well she hadn't slept a wink. If she looked at him now, he'd probably even guess about the shower thing.

Reaching for Martha's skillet, she resisted the urge to spin around and whack him on the head. "I had an excellent night's sleep. How about you?" she asked sweetly.

Declan had promised not to lie but couldn't find the words to admit he'd been up half the night pacing. He'd been having a difficult time coming to grips with the things this woman did to his brain and his body. Finally, sometime before dawn, he'd taken a swim in the ocean, just to cool his raging loins. "I slept like a babe."

Her answer was a noncommittal *"Hmmph."*

"Are you making that French dish again, the one with the eggs, bread, and cinnamon that J.P. enjoys so much?"

"If you want."

Libby walked from the refrigerator to the stove, her back stiff as a lightning rod. The pale pink flower-print dress she wore couldn't hide the roundness of her hips or the swell of her breasts when she reached into an upper cupboard for their plates. Imagining her as she'd been last night, soft and willing in his arms, stretched the metal-toothed contraption at the front of his trousers to the breaking point. To his dismay, she made no further comment until she set his food and a bottle of golden syrup in front of him.

"More coffee?"

"Yes, please. Are you going to join me?"

Instead of answering, she brought her own breakfast to the table and sat as far away from him as possible. He smothered a grin as he dug into his meal, letting the rich buttery taste of the syrup melt on his tongue, much the way Libby's kisses had done last night in the moonlight.

"What's that next to your plate?" she asked, eyeing the bottle Mary Spitzer had handed him this morning.

He picked it up and sounded out the words. " 'Coppertone-number-thirty. Gives skin max-i-mum protection from the sun's ultra vi-oh-let rays. Apply liberally over entire exposed area of the body.' " He quirked up a corner of his mouth. "It sounds rather interesting."

Libby's fork paused in midair. "Why do you need sunscreen? Are you spending the day at the beach?"

"I'm spending the day on the roof of the Pink Pelican. When Mary heard that Jack wanted me to take care of the thatch before I got too involved with the fair, she suggested I get you to help apply the lotion to my skin."

Libby rested her forehead on her palm and muttered what he thought might be a curse. Seconds passed; then she heaved a sigh. "I thought you'd be working with the planning committee. From the sound of it, there's a lot to do before Fourth of July weekend."

"We'll be congregating at the bar tonight, and every night

after it closes. Jack was kind enough to offer the place as
our headquarters.''

Was that a groan he heard escaping her thinned lips, or
perhaps another sigh? Was she pleased or perturbed that
they would be thrown together more often?

She pushed away from the table without comment and
took her plate to the sink, where she ran water for the dishes.
Declan tried but couldn't think of a thing to say. She'd
enjoyed last night's intimate encounter, of that he was certain. Yet face-to-face in the glare of morning, she acted as
if he were no more than a pesky dog begging for a bone.
She was leading him a merry chase, but two could play at
that game.

He walked to her back and set his empty plate in the
steaming water from behind. Her hands were covered in
garish yellow gloves, but her arms were bare, her hair slightly
damp and curling around her shoulders.

Boldly, he set his palms on her arms and ran them up to
slip into her tumbling mass of curls. Moving the heavy fall
aside, he leaned forward and placed a kiss on her delicate
nape, inhaling her exotic flowery scent. She trembled and
he smiled inside.

"Don't you have a roof to thatch . . . or something?" she
asked, her voice shaky and breathless.

"I do, but at the moment this seems a much better idea.''
He nibbled at her finely arched neck, then nuzzled his way
to her earlobe, where his tongue dipped and swirled along
the shell-like contours.

This time her moan was perfectly clear, and the sound of
it hit him low in his gut. Tracing her jaw with his mouth,
he skimmed his hands over her waist, then up to her breasts.
Her nipples beaded in his palms, pinpoints of fire that singed
him to his core. Still quivering, Libby set her hands on the
edge of the counter. When he turned her in his arms, her
full lips were moist and parted, and tiny tendrils of hair
framed her flushed face.

Dipping his head, Declan sipped at her lips. She opened

them willingly and he delved inside, tasting the succulent syrup on her tongue. Pulling her closer, he teased a nipple with his fingers while he slid a hand to her bottom and drew her to his straining rod.

"Feel how I ache for you, sweet Libby," he whispered, wooing her with his words. "I've not felt this randy since the war."

She tipped her chin, her expression questioning. "The war?"

"For independence," he replied without thinking.

Standing straight, she blinked and set her gloved hands on his chest. "Oh, my gosh . . . your accent . . . the covert attitude. How could I have been so dense? You're like Brad Pitt in that movie with Harrison Ford, the one where he played a rebel fighting for Ireland's independence. That's what you meant when you said you'd done things people might consider illegal, wasn't it? You are on the lam."

Ireland's independence? Were his blasted ancestors still fighting that bloody battle against the English? Who in blue blazes was Brad Pitt? And where were these damned sheep she kept blathering about? He had no idea to what her phrases referred, but if agreeing helped to explain his rash statement, then so be it. After all, it sounded as if independence was the same goal in both altercations.

"Pretend you didn't hear me say that," he muttered, keeping his promise not to lie.

She blew out a breath. "Are you wanted by the authorities in Ireland?"

"I don't think so," he answered honestly. England had put a price on his head for his privateering, but not his homeland.

She raised a brow. "You don't think so?"

"I'm certain of it."

When she set her forehead on his chin, he placed a kiss against her hair, letting her sweet smell surround him. Lifting her head, she furrowed her brow, her eyes glowing amber in the sunlight streaming through the kitchen window.

"Good Lord, O'Shae, I'm harboring a war criminal. What the heck am I going to do with you?"

Grinning, he shrugged. "Perhaps you should help me with that bottle of sunscreen? I have work to do, and if I dally with you any longer, it will never get done. You tempt me, woman, more than you can imagine."

Her shoulders lifted with the force of her sigh; then Libby gazed at him through too-bright eyes. Time seemed to stop for several seconds before she raised herself up and brushed her lips lightly across his own. In shock, Declan watched her expression shift to incredulous wonder as she placed her fingers on her lips. Obviously she'd surprised them both.

Stepping from his embrace, she tucked a strand of hair behind her ears and cleared her throat. She walked to the table, removed her gloves, and took the top off the Coppertone. "All right, let's get to it. I don't want Grandpa Jack to blame me if you don't get your work done."

Libby stood at her upstairs bedroom window and continued to gaze longingly at her grandfather's bar. To put it more precisely, she was staring at the roof. If she wanted to get specific, she was focused on the man working on the roof. What the heck, why not get right down to bare-bones picky and admit it. For most of the morning, she'd been ogling Declan O'Shae as he'd rethatched the roof of the Pink Pelican Bar and Grill.

Resting her forehead on the window frame, she willed herself to forget that she'd kissed the man. It had been a weak moment, one she couldn't afford to indulge in a second time. She needed to be the one in control of her hormones, not the other way around, even if the caveman had more sex appeal in his pinky finger than any man she'd ever met.

This morning in the kitchen, when he'd pulled his T-shirt over his head and revealed his bronzed, muscle-carved body, she'd suggested he didn't need to be slathered in sunscreen. But he'd just quirked up one side of his mouth and thrown her own thoughts right back at her. *It had been a long time since he'd worked in the sun. If he suffered heatstroke, rolled off the roof and cracked his head on the pavement, the blame would rest squarely with her.*

The memory of his big, hard body filling the room still set her to shivering. She'd smoothed her hands over his broad back, and it had taken all her self-control to resist leaning forward and kissing away the ugly white scars she'd found there, scars that looked as if they'd been made by a whip. Before she'd called up the words to ask about them, he'd turned and placed his lips on her palm, then grinned at her look of concern and squirted out more sunscreen.

God knows she'd tried to ignore his impressive shoulders when she'd applied the cooling lotion to his front. Tried and failed, she admitted grudgingly. His muscled chest, covered with a dusting of dark curly hair, only affirmed his potent masculinity. And when her hands took off in a direction of their own and worked the liquid into his corded abs and down farther . . .

A tremor rose from somewhere between her thighs as a flush of heat coursed through her veins. She'd spied his erection straining against the front of his jeans, but instead of acting embarrassed, the frustrating man had simply continued to grin that smugly confident smile as he slung his shirt over his shoulder and sauntered from the house.

She turned from the window and glanced at her watch, disgusted that she'd spent the morning mooning like some wide-eyed teenager. It was almost eleven; the lunch crowd usually started trickling in by eleven-thirty. She needed to gather the clean napkins and aprons and get ready for work.

In the bathroom, she tidied her hair and pulled it off her face with a ribbon, then applied lipstick and a brush of mascara. The one cosmetic she didn't need was blush, since she felt a blaze of color on her cheeks continually these days. After her steamy morning shower and the rubdown she'd given the caveman, she'd be surprised if she could ever face him again without turning tomato red.

Sighing, another thing she'd begun to do more often, she
headed downstairs, determined to avoid him. But Libby
knew in her heart that it was fruitless. She'd mulled it over
all morning and was finally coming to accept the fact that
she and Declan O'Shae had some kind of crazy chemistry
simmering between them.

Unfortunately, as she remembered from her high school
chem labs, most of the experiments flared brightly, then
fizzled, leaving nothing behind but a big smelly mess.

Declan stepped down from the ladder and took the ice
water J.P. held out to him. After downing the cooling liquid
in one long swallow, he handed the boy the empty glass.
"That hit the spot. Thank you."

J.P. jumped up and down, his exuberance clear. "Uncle
T told me to tell you lunch is ready."

"Is it, now?" Declan picked up his T-shirt from the railing
and used it to blot his face and brow, then his chest. "And
what are we having?"

"Some kind of salad, with tomatoes and chunks of green
stuff mixed in it. Oh, yeah, and mahmee-mahmee."

"I beg your pardon?"

"It's fish. Uncle T says it's fresh caught and really good.
He says we'll like it."

"If he says so, we probably will."

Still hopping in place, J.P. asked, "After lunch, can we
hunt for your treasure?"

His treasure. Declan frowned. How in God's blood could
he have worked the entire morning under the punishing sun
and not once thought about the treasure? Especially if he
was perched just forty feet above it?

He spied Libby coming out of the house and knew immediately the reason why. The mesmerizing woman had been
on his mind every second of every minute he'd spent on
the roof. When she'd applied that sunscreen, her quaking
hands had told him that he was winning the battle raging

between them, even if her words said differently. From the moment she'd stomped into the kitchen, her face flushed with the look of a wanton, to the surprising kiss she'd given him of her own accord, he could think of nothing else.

"Hey, Declan." J.P. tapped his arm. "Can we look for the treasure after lunch?"

He ruffled the boy's hair. "I don't think I'll find the time today, but we will, I promise. Now be a good lad and tell Tito I'll be there in a few minutes."

With his gaze locked firmly on the porch floor, J.P. kicked at an invisible speck. "Yes, sir."

I don't break promises, lad, he wanted to say, but J.P. was gone before he got out the words.

Settling a hip against the porch railing, Declan folded his arms across his bare chest and feasted his eyes on the object of his morning fantasy, walking with her usual no-nonsense stride toward the restaurant. Libby still wore the loose-fitting pink dress, but she'd tied a clean white apron around her waist, which showed off every curve of her generously formed body. He knew the moment she realized he was watching her, the current pulsing between them was that strong.

"Good day. Are you here to wait on the lunch crowd?"

She clutched the pile of clean linen to her chest, dropped her gaze to the steps, and began to climb. "It's after eleven. I have to get the tables ready."

He reached out a hand to assist her and she shrugged from his grip. "I'm a big girl, O'Shae. I don't need help with the stairs . . . or anything else, for that matter."

Keeping her eyes trained on her feet, Libby dodged to the right, and he followed. She feinted left, then right again, but he kept up with her dizzying efforts, blocking her path until she stopped dancing in place.

He pulled at the stack of clean laundry in her arms and she pulled back, drawing the linens tighter to her bosom. Grappling back and forth, the tug-of-war continued, until Declan gave one final jerk and sent the pile of neatly folded cotton flying. Squatting in unison, they bumped heads as they started to gather up the disheveled mess.

"Now look what you've done." She stood and rubbed at her forehead, then set her hands on her hips. "I have work to do. I don't have time for this."

Righting the stack, Declan offered her the linens. Finally, she accepted the napkins and towels. Balancing them against her chest, she continued to glower, until he rested his palms on her shoulders.

"There's always time for frivolity, Libby. You could use a bit more laughter in your life."

She straightened, and her mutinous gaze wandered to his chest, where she stared at the medallion—or rather, half of the medallion—hanging from around his neck. "Where did that come from?" she asked, her voice not quite a shout. "I mean . . . you weren't wearing it this morning when I helped you with the sunscreen."

"This?" He held the jagged half circle of metal in his hand. "It was in my pocket. I keep it with me at all times."

"You do?" Looking a bit subdued, she softened her tone. "Why?"

Because it's all I have left of my past.

"It's my one link to all I can remember of what I once had," he said instead. "Unfortunately, it snapped in the gale. I need to find a way to repair it."

"Then you still have the other half? I remember dropping it on your—on you when I found you."

So she *had* been the one who'd brought the broken piece into the cave. He'd often wondered how it had come to be on his person. "Where did you find the missing half?"

Slowly, she reached out and placed a finger on the amulet, tracing the partial portrait of the woman etched in the bronzed metal. "Wedged in a cluster of rocks just inside the archway. I saw it and tucked it in my shirt pocket. When I found you on the ledge and bent to wake you, it slipped out. I forgot about it until now."

He caught her hand in his. "You dropped it on my chest? And then what?"

"N-nothing," she stammered, tugging from his grasp. "I just moved it with my finger to make sure the pieces fit. When you opened your eyes, you startled me and . . . Well, you know the rest."

Shining like a lighthouse beacon, a pinpoint of clarity inched its way into Declan's brain. "And did you put the halves together, sweet Libby? Did you join them to one another?"

She jutted her chin. "Of course I did. They matched perfectly."

He frowned at this newest revelation, though it brought him a sweeping jolt of understanding. The gypsy hag had warned that the medallion would lead him to his destiny. Was the amulet the reason he'd been rescued from the storm? Did it possess magical powers that had kept him alive and waiting all these centuries? Was Libby, the woman who'd found the broken half and made the amulet whole, a part of it all?

He took a step back when he realized he was upsetting her and gave an apologetic smile. "I'm grateful that you did, as the medallion has come to mean a great deal to me. Another thing I have to thank you for, it seems."

Stiffening her spine, Libby pushed past him, but not before she said, "You don't owe me. I didn't do anything except walk into that cave and poke you awake. Don't go blowing what I did out of proportion, okay?"

She disappeared around the corner, and Declan ran a hand across his jaw. Knowing that Libby Grayson had found the broken piece of his medallion and set it in its proper place had him flummoxed. If the jagged bit of metal had been lying about on the rocks at the mouth of the cave, why, after all these years, had she been the one to find it? Even more puzzling, why had she been the one to discover the cave? What manner of magic had brought him to this time and place?

More importantly, what part did Libby Grayson play in that which the gypsy had decreed his destiny?

Chapter Nine

"Louise and I have four boys. The youngest is still in college, but the others are married. One or two of them were planning to come visit for the holidays. Maybe they can make it down sooner. We'll call and ask."

"It would be greatly appreciated," Declan said to Bob Grisham, a retired general contractor and the new owner of the town's only ice-cream parlor and coffee shop. The man had just offered to take command of the construction crew responsible for building the booths on the dock leading to the marina.

The first meeting of the Sunset Street Fair committee, the unofficial name of the festival, had been underway for an hour. With Frank Spitzer taking notes as Declan's assistant, the townsfolk had volunteered for a half dozen positions. Hazel Hewitt promised to handle the advertising, Tito the organization of the food stalls; Olivia would find tradesmen for the booths and arrange the fair's layout on the dock. Mary was in charge of obtaining workers for the day-to-day jobs, while Declan and Frank would oversee the entire affair. There was just one small thing that had yet to be addressed—finances.

Libby walked to the table with a pitcher of iced tea and began filling empty glasses. J.P. had gone home several hours earlier in the care of the owner of the new antiques store, a kindly woman named Ruth who'd offered to baby-sit so Libby could be free to help with the meeting. Though she hadn't said a word since they'd started, Declan suspected she'd been assessing his leadership capabilities, almost as if judging his worth.

"Well," he said, placing his hands on the table, "I believe we're off to a good start. There's just one problem, as far as I can see."

Hanging on his every word as they had most of the night, the older men and women sat at attention, and he cleared his throat, embarrassed by the unwarranted admiration he detected in their hope-filled eyes. "How were you planning on coming up with the coin to put the fair together?"

Phil and Don, two men Declan was still trying to figure out, said as one, "Do you mean money?"

"Aye, money. Where is it you'd thought to get the money to finance this endeavor?"

Wizened faces stared blankly. No one spoke as the air in the room stilled with the realization that seed money was necessary if they expected to make the project a success.

Del Ferguson folded his arms and leaned into the table. "The wife and I have some savings put by."

Frank tapped his pencil on his notepad and glanced at Mary. "Same for us. Guess this is the time to use it or lose it. If we don't spend it now, it'll just be wasted payin' in to a dying business."

Another one of the fishermen rubbed his palms on his thighs. "I don't have a family, so I managed to save a tidy sum. You can count me in."

"Well," said Phil, "it seems we're all in for a penny. And I know just the person to handle things." With a dramatic lift of an eyebrow, he looked at Don.

Don nodded and cleared his throat. "Libby, dear girl, Phil and I have managed to accrue a substantial nest egg. We'd be pleased if you would manage it and the rest of the festival's finances.''

Faded eyes brightened as the obvious dawned. Several old-timers spoke at once, all of them agreeing that Libby, with her accounting degree and business expertise, was the natural choice as the fair's treasurer. Who else could they trust to be in charge of their money?

Tito dragged over a chair and placed it next to Declan. "Hear ya go, little girl. Your turn to take a seat while I pour the tea.''

Libby's eyes grew round as the portholes on Declan's ship. "I—um . . . have to go to the kitchen for a second,'' she muttered. Before anyone could ask why, she disappeared through the double doors at the rear of the room.

Declan rose from his chair to follow her, but Tito placed a hand on his arm. "You got a meetin' to finish up, O'Shae. I'll see to Libby. We got a bit a'time before we need to collect the loot.''

Once in the kitchen, Libby set down the pitcher and walked to the sink. Leaning on her elbows, she hung her head and took a few deep breaths. Things just kept getting more and more complicated, and not only in her personal life. It was bad enough she had to eat her meals with the caveman as well as watch him make repairs on the bar. This morning he'd infiltrated her personal space in the shower. With Jack offering the Pink Pelican as the fair's headquarters, she was going to be with him practically twenty-four/ seven.

Now the townspeople had just agreed to trust her with their hard-earned savings. If the fair fizzled like a dud Fourth of July firecracker—and there was a very good chance that it could—she'd be the one who would have to explain how they'd lost all they had worked for.

Libby had been schooled to take responsibility for her actions her entire life. Grandma Martha had taught her to make the best of any situation, which was one of the reasons she'd worked for so long at salvaging her relationship with

Brett. In making the decision to continue her pregnancy, she'd committed 100 percent to him and their child. Once a person made a choice, even if it was a bad one, she lived with it. A responsible adult was expected to see things through to the end. Only cowards bailed.

When she'd made up her mind to leave New York, she'd talked herself into believing she was coming home to give her son a better life, but underneath her decision lay a colder, harsher reality. Not only had she gotten pregnant without benefit of marriage, which directly affected an innocent child, she'd failed at the relationship that had caused J.P. to be brought into the world. And by doing that, she'd failed her son.

Now it looked like she would be responsible for handling the money of dozens of people who'd helped to raise her. Senior citizens so naïve they trusted Declan O'Shae, a drifter she'd found in a cave who, if he was to be believed, had been awakened from some kind of weird hypnotic state. She didn't even want to give credence to the very real possibility that he might be a fugitive from the IRA. With her luck, he'd use the money to buy guns and ammo for the cause.

She'd already blown one important task in her life—giving her son a father. What would she do if she failed these people? What if Declan O'Shae was out to bilk them of their money and she became an unknowing accomplice? Could she ever look these trusting men and women in the eye again?

But if she didn't accept the job they'd assigned her, and the caveman did abscond with their funds, she'd never be able to forgive herself. And she could never continue to live here.

The swinging doors rasped at her back, sending a cool gust of air into the room. Expecting her grandfather, she spun around to meet Tito's serious, narrow-eyed gaze.

"Liberty."

She pivoted back to the sink, turned on the hot water and

picked up her rubber gloves. "Someone had to start washing the glasses. We were almost out of iced tea, and—"

Tito snorted softly as he walked to her side. "Don't try to fool me, missy. This here's Uncle T you be talkin' to."

Libby stared at the steaming water filling the sink as he wrapped an arm around her shoulder. "Why'd you leave us like that, child? Ain't you happy to be a part of the solution to our problems?"

Sighing, she turned to face him. "I sometimes wonder if I didn't create it all by bringing up the fact that something needed to be done. Did you see their eager faces, Uncle T? What if the fair isn't the answer? I don't think I could stand it, knowing I helped them to fail."

He hugged her close. "We got us a magic man, remember? With that kind'a good fortune, why you think we's gonna fail?"

"Magic man?" It was Libby's turn to snort. "It's time we faced facts, T. At best, we have a sweet-talking Irishman who appeared out of nowhere and was relegated to heading up this fair only because it was his idea. We don't know a blessed thing about the man. And we certainly don't know if he's the person your so-called goddess promised to send."

"I know what I seen so far." He let go of her shoulders and took a seat at the table. "Declan O'Shae is willin' to work for his supper. He's polite to the folks here and he's good to your boy. Besides the fact that his idea is sound, he's managed to get these people fired up. Believe me, that's somethin' hasn't been done in a long, long while."

Libby turned off the tap and rested her backside against the counter. "And if I'm right? If O'Shae manages to walk away from here with all their cash and I'm—we're left holding the bag? Then what? How do we go on?"

He sharpened his gaze, and every emotion Libby thought she'd successfully buried over the past two weeks seemed bared to his scrutiny. Tito had always managed to find just the right words to make her feel better. He'd been the one to comfort her when Martha died, knowing Jack was too devastated himself to counsel a ten-year-old girl who'd lost the second mother in her life. He'd also been the one to encourage her to leave the Key and get a better education. And now, for the third time, he was telling her that Declan O'Shae was the magic man they'd been waiting for, come to help save the town.

Over the years, she'd developed a knack for hiding her feelings from her grandfather, but she'd never been able to hide them from this man. Uncle T knew things other people didn't, knew how to cut to the heart of the matter when most folks saw through rose-colored glasses. It was one of the reasons she'd given credence to his mojo magic as she'd grown up. How she wished she could believe his predictions about Declan O'Shae!

"I'm so confused. I'm tired of pinning my hopes on people, then living through the disappointment. After what J.P. and I have been through, it's hard trusting again."

Tito crossed his arms over his spotless white apron and looked her up and down. "I know there's a war goin' on inside a'you, Libby. I know you're worried 'bout being a failure, like you think you was with J.P.'s father. But you got to believe me when I say Declan O'Shae is goin' to make everything right 'round here. Not only with the folks in this town, but with you, too."

The heated blush she'd been living with for the last few days crept upward from her chest to her cheeks to her hairline. "What the heck is that supposed to mean?"

"Hm-hm-hm. Living in the big city sure turned you into one hardheaded woman." He chuckled softly. "I see the way the man looks at you, little girl. And don't think I don't notice the moony eyes you be makin' whenever you look at him. There's a connection 'tween the two of you, and the sooner you admit to it the easier it'll be for you to get on with your life."

Oh, heck. Oh, jeez. Oh, great. Time to put on the old poker face and bluff big time. Libby saw his chuckle and raised him a laugh. "You are dead wrong, T. There is nothing going on between me and Declan O'Shae."

Tito just shook his head. "Uh-huh. And me, I'll be lily-white when I wake up tomorrow mornin'." He held up a hand before she could comment. "You just keep on denyin' fate, Liberty Elizabeth. Mark my word, the goddess'll find a way to set things to rights, with or without your approval. Now you leave them glasses and get on home to your boy. I'll finish cleanin' up in here. Go on, git."

Libby said good night to the last of the townspeople and finished wiping down the bar. In the end, she's appeased them all by accepting the position as treasurer of the fair, but she was still chewing over the responsibility. It only gave her more reason to spend time with the caveman, and that she didn't need.

She heard shouting from the kitchen and grinned. Jack and T were back there, washing up and squabbling like two characters from one of her favorite movies, *Grumpy Old Men.*

Tito insisted the glasses be dried by hand. Jack said the fresh air would do the job just fine.

Jack told T he'd be serving spaghetti and burgers for lunch tomorrow. Tito bellowed, "Over my dead body."

Where, she wondered, did the two of them get the energy to spar at close to midnight, when they had to be up and working so early in the morning?

"Good night," she called out over their bickering, fairly certain neither one was paying attention. Still pondering her discussion with T, she walked onto the porch.

"They're quite a pair, aren't they?"

The lilting dulcet tone stopped her in her tracks. "What are you doing, lurking out here in the dark?"

Declan stepped out from the shadows, a grin etched on his impossibly handsome face. "If there's one thing I do not do, my good woman, it is *lurk*. I've been waiting to escort you home.''

Silently wishing herself invisible, Libby ignored the current of awareness running between them and continued down the stairs. ''I don't need an escort to a house that's only a hundred yards away. And shouldn't you be in bed? If I remember correctly, you're supposed to be here early to finish the roof.''

The caveman fell into step beside her as if he had every right to be there. If it weren't for T's words still ringing in her ears, she might have taken off at a dead run. ''Stop following me, O'Shae.''

''I'm not following you, I'm walking beside you.''

She picked up the pace, but he didn't veer from her side. Frustrated, she stopped at the bottom of the steps to her home. ''Go away, before Ruth thinks there's something funny going on between us. She's new in town. I don't want her to know that I—you—''

The front door opened and the antiques dealer stepped onto the porch, tossing a cardigan over her stooped shoulders. ''I trust the meeting went well?''

''Um . . . yes, very well. I hope J.P. wasn't any trouble?''

Ruth shook her head as she made her way down the stairs. ''That boy is sweet as a sundae. Went to bed at nine, said his prayers, and fell right to sleep.'' She craned her neck to peer up at Declan. ''You should be gratified to know, Mr. O'Shae, that you've been blessed. J.P. asked the Lord to help you find whatever it is you're looking for, though he didn't mention it by name.''

She toddled down the walk, her blue-rinsed hair shining in the moonlight. ''I'll come by the Pink Pelican to pick him up tomorrow evening at eight. Good night.''

Libby watched Ruth hobble away, well aware that the caveman was standing by her side with an almost predatory expression on his face. She was going to give him a piece of her mind, but only after the woman was out of earshot. Skipping up the steps, she placed her hand on the front door and turned, bumping into his front. "This has got to stop. Please, just do the job you promised and stay out of my life."

The caveman had the nerve to grin as he removed her hand from the door. "I fear that is impossible, fair lady, for it's too late to stop what's between us."

He kissed the center of her palm, and the heat from his lips traveled straight to every nerve ending in her body. Angry her hormones were running at warp speed, she blew out a breath and tugged. "In your dreams, O'Shae. And why is it that my son has to pray for something you lost? Don't tell me you're not on speaking terms with God."

He frowned as he backed her into the door. "Since I've found myself mired in this place, the Almighty and I speak on a daily basis. The lad only wants to help."

Libby wrestled her hand free. Setting both palms on his rock-hard chest she pushed against him, but it was like trying to move a mountain with one of J.P.'s toy bulldozers. "So what did you lose?"

He grasped her hands and dragged them down to her sides, standing so close, she could smell the scent of the sea lingering on his body. "It doesn't matter." Inching his head nearer, he teased her jaw with his lips, then nuzzled a spot under her ear. "Nothing matters, except this."

The force of his kiss cut her off at her knees. Libby swayed in his arms, thinking she was going to free fall before she'd even taken that hot air balloon ride. Declan pinned her to the door with his hips as his fingers grazed the undersides of her breasts, then filled his hands with the soft mounds. She opened her lips to protest and he caught her words with his mouth. Taking, yet giving at the same time, the kiss made her quiver for more.

Declan's knee nestled between her legs, his arousal pressing hard and heavy against her thigh. When he found her throbbing nipples with his fingertips, she moaned low in her throat. "Please," she heard herself whisper, though she hadn't a clue what she begged for.

"Come to me, darling Libby. Tomorrow night, in the first cabin behind the Queen of the Sea. Olivia says it's empty and I can have it for as long as I stay here." Molding a swollen breast with one hand, he cupped the other hand between her legs, rocking the very center of her existence.

Her heart fluttered like a butterfly's wings as a slow but insistent tremor sizzled upward to her belly and breasts. Heat, all encompassing, threatened to set her on fire. She sucked in a breath, ready to dive into the flames. . . .

The sound of her grandfather's cheerful whistle shattered the quiet of the night and she lurched to a stand. A full second passed before Declan released her and took a step back.

"Go, please, before Jack finds us."

"Promise you'll come to me . . . tomorrow night after you close the bar." He teased the line of her jaw with a callused finger. "Please."

She fumbled behind herself for the doorknob. "No."

Declan swept her into another mind-drugging kiss, drawing her lower lip between his teeth and sucking slowly. "Yes."

"I can't. It's not right." She pulled away and pushed at the door.

He grabbed at the knob and held the door steady. "It's more than right, if you give me the chance to show you."

She slipped through the opening, but not before she met his sea blue gaze. "Yes. Now go."

Libby opened one eye and focused on her alarm clock, shocked to see that she'd slept for a full six hours. Narrow bands of pink and gold, the beginning of sunrise, peeked through a far window, bathing the shabby room in a wash of color and softening the dingy curtains and faded wallpaper.

Fully rested for the first time in a week, she swung her legs over the side of the bed. If she hurried, she could take a quick shower before Grandpa Jack and J.P. woke for breakfast, then whip up a batch of blueberry muffins, one of their favorites.

Once she'd settled into bed last night, she'd managed to come to grips with what she'd promised the caveman. After that, her sleep had been peaceful and deep. Amazing how the decision she'd made to go to his cabin and have sex with him had hit her like a double dose of Valium.

Hoping to avoid a repeat of yesterday morning's steamy shower scene, she washed and dressed quickly, then headed downstairs to start the coffee. All the while she measured ingredients for the muffins she told herself how uncomplicated it was going to be. No commitment, no strings, no muss or fuss. Just enough safe, basic sex to work off both her and Declan's frustrations; two adults entering into an agreement to satisfy one another until the itch was scratched.

Once they set a few ground rules and started to do the horizontal hula, her hormones would settle into a nice cozy rhythm, and so would she. If she kept those concepts in the forefront of her mind, everything would be just fine.

She heard the back door hinges creak and turned to find Declan standing in the doorway. *Or not!*

Sunlight gilded the droplets of water clinging to his raven hair and freshly shaved jaw. The cerulean blue T-shirt he wore matched the color of his eyes. Stretched tight across his broad, damp shoulders and corded abdomen, it contrasted perfectly with his tanned complexion. A corner of his chiseled mouth twitched upward as he lounged against the archway, appraising her with a heavy-lidded gaze.

"Good morning." He strode purposefully into the room and took her face in his hands. After gently brushing the stray curls from her cheeks, he framed her jaw in his palms and kissed her full on the lips.

Libby melted under his touch. Wrapping her fingers around his strong wrists, she fought to remember the conditions she'd only just recited. *Simple. Uncomplicated. No strings,* she reminded herself, resisting the urge to wreath her arms around his neck and mold herself to his steely chest.

He drew back and gazed deep into her eyes, his expression unreadable. She flicked her finger at a droplet of water dripping from one nicely shaped ear. He smelled of the open sea and the invigorating ocean breeze, scents she'd loved as a child. "It's customary to use a towel after you take a shower, O'Shae."

He grinned shamelessly. "Since I've met you, I've found the need for a morning swim, just to cool my senses. You drive me mad with wanting, sweet Libby."

She heard footsteps from above and stepped shakily from his embrace. "I'm glad you're here early. There are a few things we need to get straight . . . ground rules, you might call them. I thought we could discuss them before tonight."

He quirked a brow, as if amused by her serious tone. "And should I be sitting or standing for this discussion?"

The upstairs toilet flushed, and Libby realized there wasn't much time. Turning to the silverware drawer, she fished inside, grabbed a handful of cutlery, and walked to the table. "Look, for now just stay ten feet away from me at all times when we're in public, okay? No touching and none of that 'sweet Libby' stuff, either."

Staring at the tabletop, she laid out forks, knives, spoons and napkins. "And no more dopey looks." She raised her gaze to find his eyes crossed as he grinned full out.

"I mean it, O'Shae." Stifling a smile, she walked to the cupboard and took down mugs for the coffee. If she didn't take this seriously, neither would he. "No one, and I mean no one, can suspect that we're . . . that you and I are . . . um . . . you know. Especially J.P. and Jack, or Mary and Frank, or Olivia, or—"

Turning, she saw that his grin had faded to a disgruntled frown. "Are you ashamed of me, madam?"

Resting the cups against her waist, she sighed. "Of course not. It's just that I'm not used to flaunting my personal life. I also have a very astute and impressionable son, and I

142   *Judi McCoy*

wouldn't want to give him the wrong idea. Besides, the people in this town are psychic.''

"Psychic?"

"You know, mind readers." She poured coffee into a cup and set it in front of him on the table. "And they gossip."

Footsteps on the stairs had her whispering. "I can't say anymore right now. I—we have to change the subject until we're alone, all right?"

"Mornin'." Jack bounced sprightly into the room. Stopping at the stove, he turned and stared, first at Libby, then at Declan, then back to Libby. "What's got the two of you lookin' so all-fired gloomy? You arguing' again?"

"No, of course not," Libby answered a bit too brightly. She ran her palms down the front of her apron. "In fact, we've decided to declare a truce." Heat crept into her cheeks and she bit the inside of her mouth. "Right, Declan?"

Declan sipped at his coffee, grinding his back teeth in frustration. At least the wench had the decency to blush when she lied. To say that they'd declared a truce was like calling his privateering a mere bout of *borrowing* from the British. Still, she'd said they would talk later tonight. Since he'd yet to get her into his bed, it was best he agreed—for the moment.

"Aye. Seeing as we're bound to be working closely together, Libby and I decided to curtail our sparring."

Jack helped himself to coffee and sauntered to the table. "Well, it's about time. Got so's I hated to walk into a room while the two of you were in it; the electricity 'bout to curled my hair," he remarked with a snort.

Still rosy-cheeked, Libby busied herself opening the oven door. As if on cue, J.P. skipped into the room. "Mm-mmm. It smells great in here, Mom. Did you make muffins?"

Baking tin in hand, Libby swung from the stove, and the welcoming glow she flashed her son socked Declan straight in his midsection. Though she'd yet to smile at him in that same achingly sweet manner, she would, by God. Or he wasn't half the man he thought he was.

"Sure did. Blueberry, just for you and Grandpa Jack."
She set the tin on the stovetop and puttered with a breadbas-
ket and cloth napkin.

J.P. turned to Declan. "Do you like blueberries? I hope
so, 'cause my mom makes the best muffins from 'em."

"That she does, boy," chimed Jack. "Just like my Martha
used to make."

Jack knocked on the table and Declan tore his gaze from
Libby's backside. Damned if the old geezer wasn't grinning
like a fool.

"You got plans for the mornin'?" Jack asked, his voice
just short of a chuckle.

"I was hoping to finish the roof." Declan ruffled J.P.'s
hair, then picked up his coffee mug.

"Good idea," said Jack, licking his lips as Libby set a
basket of steaming muffins on the table. "Then what?"

"I hadn't thought much past the noon hour," he said
honestly. In truth, his every thought had been focused on
what he would do with Libby when he got her in his bed.
"I suppose I need to move a few things into the guest cottage
Olivia so generously offered me last night."

"Hey, that's right. You'll be livin' in a place of your own
soon," Jack taunted with a wink. "Means you can do a bit
of entertainin' in your spare time."

Ignoring the old man's pointed remark, Declan reached
for a muffin. J.P. grabbed at the same time and they made
swords from their index fingers, pretending to fight over the
basket until J.P. giggled and snagged one in his hand.

When Jack realized Declan wasn't going to rise to the
bait, he stood and tossed a set of keys on the table, then
took a wad of bills from the front pocket of his shirt. Like
a magician pulling scarves from a sleeve, he picked up his
shirtfront and removed two more stacks of bills, held together
by rubber bands, from the waistband of his pants.

"Jack." Staring, Libby set down the butter, orange juice,
and bowl of cut-up fruit she was juggling. "What in the
world . . . Where did you get all that money?"

"Oh, yeah," he muttered. "I almost forgot." Reaching around to his backside, he brought out a handful of ripped, overstuffed envelopes. After patting himself down, he counted silently on his fingers, then counted the stacks again, smiling from ear to ear.

"Last night, while T and I were cleaning up in the kitchen, a few folks came back and gave me these here envelopes. I think the two of you should go to the bank over in Marathon this afternoon and take care of it."

Chapter Ten

Libby kept one eye on the road and the other on Declan as she steered Jack's battered pickup over the causeway leading to Marathon Key. What kind of man didn't have a driver's license? And why was he hanging on to the door handle with that white-knuckled grip?

That afternoon after lunch, when Jack handed him the keys, Declan had taken one look at the more-rust-than-red, twenty-year-old Ford truck and set the key ring firmly in her hand. It had taken him a full minute to open the door, climb into the passenger side, and buckle his seat belt. If she didn't know better, she'd think he'd never ridden in a car or truck or any kind of motorized vehicle before today.

Downshifting into a curve, she hit a rough patch in the gravel, and Declan hissed out a breath. Libby couldn't help it. She giggled. "Sorry my automotive skills aren't up to par, but I've lived in New York for the past ten years. It's probably one of the few places in the country where it's not practical to own a car. Most of the people who live there don't drive."

Declan tugged at the open collar of his short-sleeved shirt. "They sound a sensible lot."

When Mary heard they were going to a bank, she'd insisted he dress in a manner befitting the chairman of their festival. She'd taken him to Olivia's, where he'd purchased a blue-and-white-striped cotton shirt to wear with a pair of Jeff's khaki slacks. Libby had to admit she'd noticed the new shirt was a perfect fit, and the pants were snug in all the right places.

"Guess they didn't have too many cars where you lived in Ireland, huh?" she said, hoping to find a logical reason for his illogical reaction to her driving. Once she turned onto the straighter stretch of highway leading south he seemed to relax a little, but he didn't answer her question.

"So, what part of Ireland are you from, anyway?"

"Dublin," he said tersely, releasing his death grip on the door handle.

"I've never been to Ireland," she said, in the way of polite conversation. If she was going to sleep with the guy, it might not be a bad idea to find out a bit more about him. Besides, her talking seemed to make him less tense. "Is it nice there?"

"I haven't been back in a long while," he muttered, whipping his head to follow a huge truck hauling a trio of flattened cars. He turned to the windshield and swiped a hand over his eyes. "Holy Mother and all the saints."

Ignoring his strained comment, Libby floored the truck to a rousing fifty miles per hour and passed a lumbering motor home. If she could just get him to talk about his past, maybe she could find a reason to justify trusting him the way Tito and the rest of Sunset did. "Guess the terrorist business is pretty risky, huh?"

From the corner of her eye, she saw him wince as he followed the fading motor home through his side-view mirror. "It couldn't be any more dangerous than riding in this unholy contraption. I'll take the roll of a solid ship's deck under my feet any day."

Just then they drove past Marathon Airport and its small flotilla of private planes lined up and ready to transport affluent visitors to Miami or Key West. "Did you fly here from Ireland?" she asked.

Are you in the United States legally? Do you have a passport or is your face posted on some bulletin board at the CIA?

Declan shuddered visibly as a small prop plane hit the runway in a series of bounces, then trundled smoothly to its berth. "If the Almighty had intended men to fly, He would have given us wings."

Now he was starting to sound cantankerous, just like her grandfather. "Then you sailed over? Where did you dock? Was it a steamer or a cruise ship that brought you here? I don't know which of the newer lines runs a cruise from Ireland these days."

His answer was an indrawn breath as they forged over a lovely expanse of ocean on one of the many bridges uniting the Keys. Pelicans and snowy egrets dotted the cement barrier or perched on the telephone wires anchored on tall metal poles that rose from the turquoise-colored water. Fishermen lined the barriers on both sides, casting their bait and hoping for the best, as motor-driven and sailboats made their way to and fro beneath them.

All right, so he was determined to keep quiet about his past and his present . . . and his activities with the IRA. Fine. But even the Unabomber had left a clue once in a while. This guy was as tight-lipped as a drum of toxic waste.

Libby spent the next ten minutes concentrating on the road, while she worked at forming a question he just might decide to answer. Declan fiddled with the radio, then rolled his window up and down a few times, his face lined in confusion. Folding his arms across his chest, he finally settled back to enjoy the scenery. When they passed the Lucky Buccaneer Resort and its impressive sign emblazoned with the image of a dastardly looking one-eyed pirate, he whipped his head around so fast, she almost rear-ended the SUV in front of her. She was so fascinated by his panicked actions, she forgot to continue her pop quiz.

They made it to the city proper, where she drove straight to the bank parking lot. Declan was out of his door and ten feet away from the truck before she'd turned off the wheezing engine. She climbed out and watched as he scanned the lot, walked to a bright yellow Porsche, and circled it slowly.

Didn't it just figure? He couldn't be bothered driving a rusty pickup, but the overpriced, testosterone-laden gas guzzler drew his attention like a bee to honey. For a fleeting second Libby wished she was the one with chrome alloy wheels and black leather bucket seats, just so she could be on the receiving end of his fascinated, almost reverent gaze.

"What is the name of this interesting vehicle?" he asked, ogling the flashy little convertible.

She wasn't impressed. "It's a Porsche Boxster and it costs a year's wages. Now come on; we have a lot to do this afternoon."

Declan gave the oddly named automobile a final lust-filled gaze and followed at Libby's heels. Out of sight of the expensive vehicle, he focused on the suggestive sway of her hips and was unable to decide which was more interesting—her amazing body or the activities of this newer, bigger city. Libby told him that she'd dressed for their visit to the bank exactly as she had when she'd worked in New York. She wore a dark blue jacket, some kind of flimsy, scoop-necked undershirt, and a short, snug-fitting skirt that showed off her long silk-clad legs. Balancing on shoes put together with mere scraps of leather and unbelievably high heels, she marched ahead of him in total control.

He stopped just inside the doorway and took in the official-looking business, with people writing at circular stands or waiting in line to speak with men and women stationed behind a counter that ran along the back of the room. In today's world, he'd learned, thin rounds of silver had replaced the gold coins he was used to, and paper had even more value than coins.

"You coming?" Libby stood at one of the circular counters and hoisted up her bag. He walked toward her and she began to dig, pulling out a slim leather folder and a variety of small printed cards, then the large brown envelope she'd used to carry the money she'd received from Jack.

After looking the papers over carefully, she tucked everything back into the carrier and raised her gaze. "I'm not saying this to be rude, but I'd feel a lot better if you'd let me take care of things here."

Declan leaned an elbow on the counter. "As I told you earlier, I have no desire to interfere in your handling of the fair's finances. If you have no further need of me, I'd like to take a walk. I have errands of my own to see to, and it's been a while since I had the opportunity to stroll a city."

"You're saying you don't want your name on the checking account I'm setting up for the festival?" she asked, surprise ringing in her voice.

He smiled smugly, knowing he'd just taken a bit of the wind from her sails. "Yes, that's exactly what I'm saying."

"Oh . . . well." Her expression changed from suspicious to puzzled, and she sighed. "In that case, sure. There's plenty to see here. If you go out the front door and to the left, there are all kinds of shops and restaurants. You could do me a favor and walk down to the Home Depot to place that order for lumber and supplies we got from Bob Grisham. Maybe talk to them about setting up an account and delivery schedule. I could meet you there in a little while."

"The Home Depot?"

Her eyes narrowed as she raised a brow. "You know, that big building we passed on the way into town. The one with the orange sign and overhang to match. The Home Depot."

He only vaguely remembered the mammoth, hideously colored eyesore and its huge parking lot filled with all manner of vehicles. "You'll need to come in and arrange for the account if you're the one in charge of the money," he reminded her.

"Oh, right." Libby glanced at her watch. "It shouldn't take long here. How about if we meet at their customer service desk in say, two hours?"

Declan figured it would be enough time to buy the items on his mental list and get to the store to place the order. The first thing he needed was something to hold the funds he'd earned at the gas station; then he wanted to purchase a few more articles of clothing. He held out his bare wrist. "Once I find a suitable timepiece and run my other errands, that will be my next stop." Giving her a jaunty salute, he headed for the exit.

An hour later, Libby pushed through the bank doors and into the humid afternoon sunshine. She'd toyed with the logistics of setting up the fair account all morning and still wasn't sure she'd done the right thing. Should the committee incorporate? File for a DBA or Federal tax ID number? Should she set it up so they needed one signature or two on the checks?

In the end, she'd decided to open a regular business checking account in her name. She'd added her savings to what Grandpa Jack had given her, which gave the committee a healthy chunk of change to begin their work. She was prepared to keep meticulous records, allotting a corresponding number of shares according to the percentage of money each resident contributed to the fair's costs. Declan O'Shae wouldn't get the opportunity to touch a single penny of their cash and, if the event fizzled, she'd be the only one who had to answer to the creditors.

Though he'd made it perfectly clear he wasn't interested in the townsfolk's money, his casual attitude left her wary. If he was trying to lull her into a false sense of security, he was doing a pretty good job. But she wasn't going to let it sway her from her original assessment—the caveman was still a drifter, a man with no roots or allegiance to anything in particular. From the looks of it, she'd bet the guy didn't even have a Social Security card or passport to prove who he was, never mind a driver's license.

No doubt about it, she'd been certifiable when she'd agreed to sleep with him. If she had a brain in her head, she'd tell him that she'd changed her mind. If he didn't like it, he'd just have to live with it, or learn to enjoy his dips in the ocean.

She sighed at the memory of Declan standing in her kitchen, still damp from his morning swim. If nothing else, the man was impressive to look at. While she'd always considered herself a solid seven, maybe a seven and a half on a good day, Brett had been a nine on the babe scale. If she were honest, she'd give Declan a ten . . . or an eleven.

Libby shaded her eyes and scanned the shops across the street until she spotted The Discount Bookstore. She hadn't found the time for a good read in ages, and with all the work needed on the festival she probably wouldn't for another several weeks. But she really missed her paperbacks. A romance by one of her favorite authors, or maybe the newest Janet Evanovich, was just what she needed to lighten her mood. If there was one thing she could count on in those books, it was a happy ending where the heroine always came out on top. She used to think it would be the same for *her* life, until she'd let things with Brett get so screwed up.

She entered the store and walked to the area that held the books she was looking for. Scanning the shelves, she found a few new titles and set them in her basket, then wandered to the children's section. She chose the latest Harry Potter for J.P., along with a book on the care and feeding of kittens, and one on the wonders of the ocean. Feeling productive, she turned to the register.

It was then that she spotted Declan, waiting his turn in the checkout line. No way could she mistake those quarterback-sized shoulders or long muscular legs and tight . . .

Libby ducked behind a bank of bookshelves as a wave of heat crept to her cheeks. The last thing she needed was to be caught blushing in his presence . . . again. The man had sexual radar where she was concerned, and it was just too darned embarrassing to have him think she'd been following him. She peeked around the corner and watched him make polite chitchat with the cashier. What in the heck had he bought? She squinted, barely making out the titles. Was that the John Gray relationship book he had in his hand, and some kind of book on history?

Feeling like a character from a spy novel, she rushed to the counter as he pushed his way through the door. "Could you hurry, please," she said to the cashier. "I'm late for an appointment."

By the time she got to the sidewalk, Declan had disappeared.

Libby hunched her shoulders and looked right, then left. She had enough time to find a drugstore, a very big, very impersonal drugstore, where no one would notice if she bought Tampax or toothpaste . . . or condoms.

Just in case she needed them, of course, because she was fairly certain she was going to tell the caveman she'd changed her mind about the bed thing. But it never hurt to be prepared. Even though she'd bet her last nickel Declan was the kind of guy who wouldn't want to use a condom. He would probably give her some stupid macho line like, "I want to feel myself inside you, babe," or, "Gee, honey, I hate rubbers. Besides, I thought you were using something to take care of it."

She crossed back to the bank parking lot, climbed into the truck, and headed for the nearest Eckerd. Once inside, she walked at a stroll, casually inspecting the makeup and cleaning supplies. At the end of the aisle nearest the pharmacy she found what she'd been searching for, a multitiered prophylactic display. She'd been on the pill when she'd lived with Brett, and J.P. was a testament to just how well that had worked. She'd never had to buy this kind of stuff.

Worrying a hangnail, she pondered sizes, shapes, colors and textures. Opaque, blue, Day-Glo pink, ribbed, lubricated, plain or extra-sensitive, regular, large or magnum-sized, the choices were endless. No wonder most men left the birth control issue up to women. There was simply too much latex to choose from.

She tapped at her chin, trying to remember what she'd heard about judging the size of a man. Declan was well over six feet tall and had rather large feet, so it was unlikely he'd be a small. Surely he wasn't a "magnum" kind of guy? Lubricated sounded good, as did the extra-sensitive, but which partner did that help?

She heard a cough and glanced up, straight into the eyes of a kindly-looking gray-haired pharmacist. "May I help you find something?"

Oh, boy. "Ah ... um ... nope, got it. Thanks." She grabbed three different-colored boxes and scuttled down the nearest aisle, only to find herself in front of the tampon display. *Could this shopping trip get any more embarrassing?*

Snagging a super-size box of tampons, she slithered to the checkout registers. The clerk, a mellow-looking seventeen-year-old girl with a silver hoop in her left eyebrow and a tattoo of Tweety Bird just below her collarbone, snapped her pale blue gum. "Wow, are you having a party or what?" she commented, price-scanning the boxes.

"Or what," answered Libby, cursing silently. Hadn't she read somewhere you could order condoms through the mail?

Clutching the plastic bag to her chest, she hurried to her car. Just her luck, she was late to meet O'Shae.

Declan made his way toward the Home Depot, his arms overladen with packages. The sign for the Lucky Buccaneer Resort loomed in the distance and he simply couldn't resist. He crossed the street and walked into the air-conditioned lobby. Unsure of what he might find, he only knew he had to investigate an establishment with such an intriguing and fanciful sign. When he saw the entry was clean and neat, with an empty counter running along a far wall, he relaxed and decided to look around.

Moving in a circle, he took in the cavernous room and its myriad artifacts, an array of items from a multitude of bygone seafaring eras. Ancient portholes, all buffed to their original gleaming brass, covered the glossy pine walls. Artfully arranged shells and spikes of multihued coral decorated an open cabinet and a large glass-topped table with legs made of mammoth pieces of driftwood. Sextants, chronometers, a beautifully preserved brass bell, and items he didn't recognize but knew instinctively had to do with navigating the seas, called to him from every corner of the room.

When he spotted the ship's wheel, a full yard in diameter and bolted to a shining burr of oak, standing in a far niche, he set his parcels on the tile. Walking to the circle of wood, he lost himself to its compelling lure. Hesitantly, he grasped the wheel. Swaying to the siren song of the ocean, he closed his eyes and rode the waves again, the tang of salt spray fresh in his nostrils. He missed it, he thought with a pang of sadness, that roving life he'd once led. The life he would lead no more. Oh, how he missed it.

"Gives a man a powerful yearning to raise sail, don't it?" echoed a grizzled voice from somewhere in the room.

Declan dropped his hands to his sides. His gaze darted around the lobby until he spied the owner of the quavering voice. There, tucked in a corner behind a cluster of potted plants, was a metal chair with spoked wheels. In it sat a man—or a gnome—he wasn't sure which, appraising him through storm-gray eyes.

"Miss the sea, do ya, young fella?" the gnarled man asked from withered lips. "I know how that is, I do."

Declan peered through the curtain of palm fronds. Libby had said the folks in Sunset were psychic, but this fellow lived in Marathon and had to be ninety if he was a day. "Aye, but how did you know?"

The old man chuckled dryly. "I seen it in yer walk the

second ya swaggered into the lobby. More important, I saw it in yer eyes.''

Stepping closer, Declan moved a branch so he could fully view the man. Harmless old fellow, he thought, ignoring the way the hairs on the back of his neck bristled. He held out his hand. ''The name's Declan O'Shae.''

The man's features reassembled into an expression of joy. He reached up and raised a knobby hand that Declan shook carefully, for the knotted fingers felt as fragile as the points of a starfish.

''Pleased to meet you,'' the man said. ''Folks in the Keys call me Pete.''

A chill of remembrance tripped up Declan's spine. He smiled at the name of his long-lost first mate, his mentor, and his best friend. '' 'Tis a fine name, and one to be proud of. Do you own this place?''

Pete wheezed out a cough along with a hearty grin. ''In a manner of speaking. I opened it right before the war, more'n sixty years ago. The land was deeded to me by my father, and his before that.'' He fisted his hands on the blanket covering his legs and pounded soundly. ''Used to take care of everything around here myself, until these dang things stopped workin'.''

Declan nodded, ready to pull up a chair and spend time with the old fellow, but a commotion at the front door stopped him. A man and his wife, with three squalling children in tow, walked into the lobby and rang a small bell on the counter. In a blink, a squinty-eyed middle-aged woman appeared from a back room and began the laborious process of welcoming her guests.

''That's my granddaughter,'' Pete croaked, shrinking into the chair. ''If she sees us talkin' there'll be hell to pay. Stand in front of me, now, and don't move a muscle,'' he hissed.

Declan complied, grinning the whole while. From her bossy attitude and imposing size, he didn't doubt for a moment the woman's ability to take command. There would be time enough to chat with Pete when the rowdy family and the granddaughter left.

Several minutes passed before the bedraggled couple and their ill-mannered offspring ambled out the rear of the inn. He breathed a sigh of relief just as the woman turned a sharp-eyed gaze his way. "May I help you?"

Declan cleared his throat, his feet planted firmly in front of his newfound friend. "No, thank you. I was just admiring your fine establishment."

The woman leaned forward into the counter, displaying a bountiful bosom and a snaggle-toothed smile. "Oh, really? Well, come on over here for a second so we can get better acquainted. Sure you don't need a room?"

"Um . . . not today, good mistress."

Before she spoke her next sentence, her narrow eyes seemed to bore straight through him. "Step aside, mister. The game's up and he knows it."

"I beg your pardon?"

Like a tidal wave, the woman surged from behind the counter and shoved Declan aside with a generous hip. Folding her arms, she stared down at Pete, who looked more like a naughty boy caught in the act than a man fully grown.

"Don't get your knickers in a twist, Nelda. I'm not tired and I—"

"This isn't the best of days to test my good nature, Grandpa," the woman chided. "It's time for your medicine and your nap. And you know you're not supposed to be in the lobby without a keeper. Now hush up and get rolling."

Pete shot her a mutinous glare. "I ain't goin' back to my room, and you can't make me."

"Oh, yeah?" Nelda stepped to the rear of the chair, grasped the handles in a death grip, and began pushing toward the opening behind the front desk. Just before she and the recalcitrant Pete disappeared, she called out a command. "If you want to talk to Pete, it'd be better if you came some morning next week, say between eight and eleven. And see yourself out."

* * *

Declan set his parcels on the floor and propped himself against the customer service counter of the Home Depot. His shoulders ached from craning his head so he could scan shelves that seemed as high as the masts of his ship. And there was still more of the store to see. He ran a palm across the back of his neck, overwhelmed by the number of inventions and gadgets and selections of the same that sat awaiting his inspection. He was so in awe, he could only stand and watch for Libby while he tried to figure out how some of the amazing products worked.

Though his provocative encounter with Pete and Nelda had been the highlight of his day, the rest of his travels through town had been enlightening. People were friendly and seemed happy to answer his questions, especially when they saw that he was prepared to spend money. He'd purchased books, a few new shirts, and a pair of jeans, but his catch of the day was the timepiece he'd found in a pawn shop. A watch that would, he'd been told by the proprietor, keep time under water. For his pleasure, he'd stopped in a liquor store where he'd bought ale and a bottle of red wine the clerk had assured him was nectar for the gods. He'd even found a store that sold chocolates and bought a box for Libby.

He'd learned to traverse the road that ran through the center of town by dodging those hellacious machines called automobiles, all the while eagerly taking in the scents and sounds of the sea. Ocean birds flew overhead, and statues of sea cows and dolphins adorned many of the buildings. Every side road and alley led to a wharf that docked all size and shape of ships, from mammoth to modest to barely larger than a bathtub. Some of the vessels had sails, but most had one of those modern contraptions called a motor attached to the stern, which he now knew was powered by gasoline, the liquid chemical sold at Frank and Mary's garage.

Shop after shop advertised charter boats for fishing tours or snorkeling and scuba diving, something he thought he might enjoy if he ever found the time. And interspersed among the various inns, food stores and eating establishments were businesses selling all manner of merchandise: cleverly decorated T-shirts, shells, dried sponges, jewelry and a variety of products advertised as made exclusively on the Keys. He'd been walking this building with its huge aisles and piled high displays for a half hour and it was still too much to comprehend.

At least things were clearer now than they had been when he'd first strolled the streets of Sunset. The Florida Keys was a minuscule part of the world. If such wondrous inventions could be found here, he could only imagine what he would find when he located his treasure and had real money to spend. The pang of sorrow he'd felt in the Lucky Buccaneer had been ill-conceived. There were plenty of ships available for purchase, if one had the right amount of coin. Though not as large or grand as the *Lady Liberty,* they would do admirably for a sail around the world.

He turned to scan the building's entryway doors. Libby was late and he was tired, not the ideal way to end their afternoon. There was still the order from Bob Grisham to be filled, and he'd yet to ask about an account, as Libby had requested.

"May I help you?"

Declan turned to find a gentleman wearing a bright orange apron imprinted with the name of the store standing behind the counter.

He pulled the list of supplies from his pocket and placed it in front of the man. "You may. We'll be needing these items shipped to Sunset Key as soon as you can manage it. And I'd like to do whatever is necessary to open an account."

The man read the paper carefully and set it aside. "This is a pretty big order. I assume you're wanting a business account?"

"Certainly," Declan answered, hoping that was the case.

"Cash on delivery, revolving, or due in thirty days?"

"Revolving," he guessed again, drumming his fingers on the counter.

The man handed him a paper and pen. "Start filling out this form and I'll see what I can do about taking care of your order."

Declan scratched at his jaw as he read the form. The name, address and phone number of the business, the name of the owner, and references both personal and professional were required. What had become of the world, he wondered, that a man's word and a hearty handshake were no longer good enough guarantees to repay a debt?

"Sorry I'm late." Libby's voice enveloped him from behind. "I hope I didn't keep you waiting too long."

Declan spun on his heel, relieved he wouldn't be the one to have to answer all these confusing questions. "I've only been here a short while. This is an interesting establishment."

Libby drew her brows together as she glanced around the bustling store. "Trust me, it's small potatoes after you've lived in a city the size of New York. You could put every person who lives on the Keys in the Village and still have room to spare."

"Truly," he muttered, not quite able to imagine what she was saying. Instead he pushed the paper and pen toward her. "I have no idea how to fill this out."

Libby took the form and hunched over the counter. "No problem. Applications for credit can be pretty daunting. I'll take care of it. Did you give them Bob's list?"

"I did. The clerk left with it a few minutes ago."

"Oh." She looked around the deserted station, then checked her watch. "Do you think you could find the guy and see what's up while I do this? I need to get back by five to start my shift."

Declan nodded, his gaze drawn to her exhausted expression and pursed lips. Libby looked ready to drop and she still had an evening of waiting tables ahead of her, never mind taking care of her son and grandfather . . . and his own demand that she come to his cabin tonight after she was through with work.

Suddenly, the need to comfort her overcame the wanderlust in his heart. The anticipation of taking her to his bed evoked an emotion as compelling as sailing the seas. Libby was an amazing woman made up of beauty, brains and an admirable work ethic. A woman a man could be proud to call his own . . .

Quickly, Declan shook off his unwanted feelings and sparked to action. The sooner the fair was up and running, the sooner he could find his loot, procure a boat and leave this place. No matter the century in which he now lived, he was a man with a roving eye, not one to settle down and make a home on dry land. The treasure had been his goal two hundred years ago, as it was now and always would be.

He tapped the counter with his knuckles. "I'll see what I can do."

Chapter Eleven

Libby stood behind the bar and focused on the chore of running a towel over the smooth dark wood. It was close to eleven. Declan had just walked in and taken a seat at a table with Bob Grisham and a few other committee members. Ruth was at the house baby-sitting J.P., Tito was cleaning the kitchen, and Jack was filling glasses with iced tea. Once the few tourists still occupying the restaurant left and they closed down the Pink Pelican, it would be time to start their first nightly meeting.

But it wasn't the meeting she was worried about. It was the *after* part that had her chewing her lower lip. Whatever had possessed her to promise Declan she would come to his bed?

Pheromones? The man had to be exuding some type of mind-altering pheromones. Why else would her knees buckle and her palms sweat whenever she got within ten feet of him? Then again, she felt weak and sweaty when she caught the flu. And everyone knew the best cure for the flu was a few days in bed.

Libby sighed. She was being ridiculous. More than likely,

it was simply the breadth of his shoulders and the way he fit into a pair of worn jeans that got her hormones racing and her heart to stuttering, a typical female reaction to any good-looking guy. Trouble was, she always thought she had more smarts than the women who were *typical.*

Rubbing at an invisible spot on the bar, she shrugged. She'd agonized most of the evening and pretty much decided sleeping with Declan wasn't going to work. But how was she supposed to find the right time to tell him so? Jack and Tito knew her every move. Aside from Dream Cove, she had no place to call her own, and the last time she and the caveman had met there things had gotten out of control, just like they did whenever she was alone with him.

Which called to mind another problem: His cabin was the first of six identical cottages tucked behind the Queen of the Sea. She would have to cross the main street and sneak past Phil and Don's Restaurant to get to it. The way people in town gossiped, she might as well shine a spotlight on herself, or maybe just hang a bright neon sign around her neck that said FALLEN WOMAN while she walked over there.

And what if J.P. woke in the middle of the night and needed her? Or her grandfather had some kind of emergency? Libby shook her head. No way could she carry on an affair under so much scrutiny. Obviously her thinking had been impaired when she'd given him her answer. How did other people manage to keep their private lives private? The logistics of finding five minutes of quiet time with the caveman staggered her, and their planned liaison wasn't even going to happen.

She would simply have to tell him that her hormones had been out of whack, or maybe that she'd been in the throes of a migraine. Better yet, she could always lie and say she had her period. It was one of the more embarrassing things a woman had to confess in her life, but not half as bad as making a fool of herself by sleeping with the wrong man.

"You look about as happy as a landed grouper," observed

Jack, ambling over with a tray of drinks. "I thought every-thing went okay at the bank today."

"It did," she assured him. "I'm just tired, that's all."

"You could always give your financial report first, collect the money folks brought over today, and go home. This meetin' is mostly to talk about the schedule for building the booths and such. Men's business," he added with a wink.

The idea of slipping away before Declan could corner her held appeal. But it wouldn't save her from the eventuality of having to give him her latest decision. She'd never been afraid of speaking her mind before and she wasn't about to start now, even if the topic made her tingle to her toenails.

"Thanks, but I think I'll stick it out. Besides, I have to talk to Declan about something. I'll be all right."

Jack raised a bushy brow and gave her a curious grin, almost as if he knew what she'd been thinking. "Suit your-self." He walked around the bar and picked up the tray. "Looks like the gang's all here. Come join us whenever you're ready."

Leaning forward, Libby propped herself on her elbows and waited for the meeting to begin. She listened to Declan go over the Home Depot's delivery schedule while Frank jotted notes. Hazel offered them an empty boathouse to use to store the materials, and they discussed a shift rotation for the building of the booths and the gazebo, which would be the focal point of the fair.

Bob's youngest son played in a start-up band that was more than happy to come down and entertain for the cost of airfare. Hazel had a sister and a niece who staged puppet shows at children's birthday parties up in New Jersey. They were thrilled at the idea of performing for a modest fee and the chance to spend some time in Florida. Ruth had sent word that her eldest daughter, the one who did chalk portraits and children's face painting in her spare time, was willing to fly down and split her profits fifty-fifty with the town. Everyone agreed the artists would be perfect for the fair's festivities.

"I guess it's your turn, Libby," Frank said, pulling out the empty chair next to him. It was then that a few people placed envelopes on the table. "Time to discuss finances."

In a heartbeat her spirits plummeted. So far, she'd managed to do a pretty good job of avoiding the caveman, but the chair Frank expected her to sit in was next to his. Right now, Declan seemed to be listening with only half an ear while the rest of the committee continued talking. His navy dark gaze followed her as she made her way around the counter.

Resisting the invitation to sit beside him, she leaned against the back of the chair and stared at the envelopes stuffed with bills and sitting on the table. Good grief, did everyone in town keep their savings in a dresser drawer like her grandfather did? If so, high finance was not something they would easily understand.

"Declan and I went to the bank this afternoon where I opened a business checking account. To keep things simple, I applied for a DBA and set up the account so only one signature is required on the checks. But I'd be happy to add another name to the account if one of you—"

"What about Declan? Why didn't you have him sign?" asked Hazel, whom Libby suspected was more savvy than the others. "He is our chairman, isn't he?"

"I declined the offer," Declan interjected smoothly. "I have no head for figures and there's too much for me to do without having to worry about money. I think we can trust Miss Grayson to handle our finances in an efficient and timely manner, don't you?"

" 'Course we can," said Tito, who'd just joined the group. "Don't want nobody doin' nothin' they ain't comfortable with, do we?"

Gray heads nodded in agreement as Del Ferguson stacked the envelopes and handed them to Libby. "Well, then, here you go. John Tulley, Red Smithers and Bill Olson said to count them in, and there's a few more folks who'll be contributing soon."

Libby recognized the names of the three men who operated a charter fishing service out of Hewitt's Marina. They'd attended the first meeting and volunteered for the building committee. Financing for the festival was adding up nicely, but she would have to make another trip to Marathon tomorrow to get the money to the bank.

"I think we should offer all of the performers a flat fee for airfare," she suggested. When she had given an out-of-state workshop on coping with inflation, that was how the company that hired her had handled her flight arrangements. "After all, once they arrive we'll be feeding and housing them. And I know it's early enough to get decent plane fares."

Frank jotted down Libby's suggestion, then looked up at her. "I was hopin' you might be able to take on another job."

Great, she thought, one more reason to put Declan off. She was going to be too darned busy to juggle an affair. "Sure. What do you need?"

Frank shoved his tablet and pen toward her. "I ain't so good with plotting things out, if you know what I mean. Mary always said I couldn't walk and chew gum at the same time. We need a timetable for the events happening on each day of the fair, and I figured the way you did twelve things at once around here, you might be the person to give me a hand."

Ignoring the caress of Declan's gaze, Libby folded her arms and concentrated on the best way to schedule the festival. "It's cooler in the morning, but starting that early would make for a really long day. How about we open at noon, do the children's crafts under the tents from one to four, take a break, and start the nighttime events at seven? That will give people plenty of time to wander the food booths for dinner. The evening breeze should be up about then, and the tourists will be ready for some entertainment."

"It's the Fourth of July, so we're gonna need to close with one mother of a fireworks display," a man said. "This thing is planned for the day before and the day of the holiday. I say we give 'em a show that'll light up the sky for miles on the first night; that way we'll draw a huge crowd for day number two.''

"Fourth of July?" Declan repeated, as if he'd never heard of the day before. "I've been meaning to ask why that date is so significant.''

"Hah! That's a good one, son.'' Del Ferguson slammed a meaty hand on the table and continued as if Declan hadn't asked his question. "I used to handle fireworks up in North Carolina when I was a volunteer fireman. I'd be happy to take on the task, if it's okay with everybody here.''

While the rest of the committee members patted Del's back and urged him to go for it, Libby watched Declan. At first she thought he was joking about the Fourth of July, but his expression had raced from confused to embarrassed to blustering in three seconds, almost as if he'd been caught with his pants down. He raised his eyes to hers and she grasped the chair back. There it was again, that plaintive, almost hollow look, as if he was adrift at sea without a paddle.

Before she knew it, he smiled thinly and shifted his gaze back to the table. "If we're done for the night, I suggest we meet again tomorrow at nine.''

Everyone agreed and headed out the door. Jack walked onto the porch, Tito went into the kitchen, and Libby stared at her hands still tightly gripping the chair. It was now or never—time to make her this-isn't-a-good-idea speech. But just before she opened her mouth, Declan startled her by standing up and quickly pushing away from the table.

What, Declan wondered, had he done to make the woman so nervous? Granted she'd ignored him most of the evening, but he thought it was part of her ridiculous request that they stay apart when they were in the same room.

Hoping to put her at ease, he said quietly, "I was not

planning to ravish you, madam. At least, not here in front
of Tito and your grandfather.''

With her amber eyes each the size of a gold coin, she
held a hand to her heart. "You're not? I mean, of course
you're not.'' She tucked a strand of hair behind her ear and
shuffled her feet. "So . . .''

Instead of acting on the urge to draw her into his arms,
Declan stuffed his hands into his pockets and rocked on his
heels. "I've been waiting for this evening. Are you ready?''

"Um . . . not exactly. We . . . uh . . . have to talk.''

He grinned at her. "Talking is not what I had in mind,
at least not until later. I've thought of nothing but this evening
since we returned from Marathon Key. Right now, there's
a powerful hunger for you gnawing at my vitals.''

She opened her mouth, as if gasping for air. "There is
. . . I mean, there isn't . . . there can't be. That's what we
need to talk about. I've changed my mind.''

Not sure he'd heard correctly, Declan took a step closer.
"Excuse me?''

Her grandfather took that moment to wander back into
the Pink Pelican. "Fine night for a stroll,'' he announced
to no one in particular. "Moon's full, breeze is warm, and
the air smells like them flowers we got growing in pots on
the porch.''

"I don't have time for a stroll,'' Libby snapped, heading
for the bar. "I'm tired and I'm crabby and I want to go to
bed. Besides, I have . . . cramps.''

The older man's eyes bulged. "Hey, hey, hey, none of
that woman talk now, you hear? I told Martha, and now I'm
tellin' you, female problems are best left to females. The
two of you just run along and leave me out of it. I'll send
Ruth home and make sure J.P.'s okay.''

Libby walked around the bar, grabbed her handbag, and
scurried for the exit. Declan resisted the impulse to hug Jack
and raced to intercept her. " 'Tis the best idea you've had

all night, my friend, and I thank you for it.'' Taking Libby
by the elbow, he led her out the door.

Libby set her handbag down on the front porch while
Declan unlocked the cottage door. She didn't have the cour-
age to follow him inside—not yet anyway—so she gazed
at the moonlight painting a golden path on the water. A gull
cried in the distance, a sharp counterpoint to the waves
gently lapping the shore.

All of the guest houses faced the gulf on this side of the
Key, offering a magnificent view of the sunset. She knew
exactly how they looked on the inside, because she'd worked
a few summers helping Olivia to clean and change the linens
here. The rooms had ceiling fans, knotty pine paneling,
ceramic tile floors and an eclectic collection of wicker furniture and throw rugs. The kitchens were fully equipped and
opened to screened living areas, with a closet and bathroom
to the left and a bedroom with a queen-sized bed at the
rear. The charming hideaways were perfect for couples who
wanted to escape the tourist traps on the larger Keys.

"Libby?"

She heard the squeak of a hinge. Declan's footsteps fell
softly behind her, until he was so close the warmth of his
breath fluttered her hair. The potent tangy scent that seemed
to trail after him like the tail of a kite enveloped her and
she sighed.

He set his hands on her shoulders. "You're trembling.
Are you afraid of me?"

"Of course not." She shrugged as she grasped the porch
railing with shaking hands. "Well, not exactly."

"All right," he murmured. "But you're worried about
something. Perhaps I could help, if you told me what it
was."

A sudden breeze billowed in from the bay, and Libby
clasped her arms around her chest. It was time to tell him

that he was the cause, not the solution of her latest worry, but she couldn't form the words with him standing so near.

"You're catching a chill. Come inside."

"People don't catch a chill in the Keys," she said, trying to keep the conversation light. "It's about eighty-five degrees right now and the humidity is the same. It can get a lot warmer than this."

"Will it hurt attendance at the fair?" he asked, running his hands down her arms to her elbows.

She tried to ignore his touch, but those damned pheromones just weren't cooperating. Her body wasn't cooperating either, she noted sadly. Her heart was hammering in her chest and she was having a hard time catching her breath. "I doubt it. This area always has plenty of tourists, unless it's hurricane season."

"And that would be when?" Slowly, his palms skimmed her forearms and met at her waist.

"August through November." She shivered again, but not because of the breeze. "Every once in a while we have a big storm in July, but it doesn't happen very often. How long were you in that cave, anyway?"

"Long enough," he said, moving his hands to her chest.

She tamped down the ripple of longing rising from inside and stared straight ahead. The man never gave her a straight answer. She'd been stupid to let him bring her here, to a place where they were so utterly alone. She had no resistance to his arms when they held her so close, his tongue when it tickled her ear, his palms as they cupped the undersides of her breasts.

Declan drew her back to his front and Libby felt the length and power of his erection. She'd stuffed the condoms in her bag right after dinner, before she'd decided not to sleep with him. From what she could tell, she'd done the right thing when she'd grabbed the box labeled MAGNUM.

"Come inside," he whispered, sending a gaggle of goose bumps marching up her arms. "You know you want to or you wouldn't be here."

Her nipples throbbed at the touch of his fingers. He fondled gently, moving his palms in languorous circles until her breasts ached and swelled. All her earlier resolve melted as he half turned her and lifted her in his arms. Rock-hard muscles bunched under her hands as she clutched his shirt in a death grip. No way could he carry her without getting that hernia she'd once wished on him.

She wrapped her arms around his neck, and Declan's teeth flashed white in the moonlight. The romantic gesture, like something from a fairy tale, literally swept her off her feet. It made her feel cherished and desired . . . and very ready to surrender to his charms.

She gave one last try at being sensible, even though her resolve seemed to have gone to bed for the night. "I'm no lightweight, O'Shae. Maybe you ought to put me down so we can talk about this."

"There will be time to talk later, Libby mine, after I've had the chance to prove you won't regret your decision. I'm going to make it good for you, and that's a promise."

She had no doubt it was a promise he could keep.

With Libby in his arms, Declan strode through the door and straight to the bedroom at the rear of the cottage. She was a curvaceous handful, and fit perfectly, as he knew she would. Once at the side of the bed, he put her down carefully and cradled her face in his palms. He needed to be sure her trembling was from desire and not a darker reason.

"I would never hurt you. You have to believe that."

She caught his wrists with her hands and met his gaze squarely, without a hint of trepidation in her eyes. "I can only do this if we agree to accept that we're consenting adults, two people who want to be with one another for the pleasure they might share. I'm just not sure it's the right time. There are complications, so many things that could go wrong. I've already made one mistake with my life; I don't want to make another."

Aye, and it was just what he wanted, too, a simple liaison for pleasure's sake alone. But the woman's continuous attempts at logical conversation were driving him insane. Pulling her T-shirt from the waistband of her trousers, he slid his hands down her back to cup her bottom. "This isn't a mistake, because we won't let it become one."

Moving himself into her hips, he pushed against her. "I want you so badly, the thought of bedding you has consumed my every waking moment. Tell me you've felt the same."

"I . . ." He nibbled at her ear. ". . . can't . . ."

Declan's fingers fumbled with the contraption around her breasts while he silenced her with a long, drawn-out kiss. Melding his lips to hers, he was determined to inhale all her words until she could think of nothing but the two of them, together at last.

Finally, he pulled back and gazed into her half closed eyes. "The time for talk is over. Let me show you how simple this can be."

He tugged off her shirt and tossed it over his shoulder. Setting his hands on the wispy scrap of satin wrapped around her bosom, he cursed his clumsy fingers until he heard her giggle.

"It's a front loader, O'Shae. Don't tell me the women in Ireland are still wearing the old-fashioned kind." She showed him mercy and undid the pesky clasp herself, letting the fabric fall to the floor.

He had no answer for her, but even if he had, the words would have turned to dust in his mouth. She was a goddess, Aphrodite by moonlight, carved in alabaster and his alone to adore. Deftly, he unzipped her pants and tugged them down and off her long, silky-smooth legs. She tore at his shirt and he threw it over his head. After shedding the rest of his clothing and shoes, he stepped toward her in the near darkness.

Hands at her sides, Libby stared with blatant approval. "Wow," she said on a breathy sigh. "I guess I was right."

"Right about us? I certainly hope so."

Her lips curved into a shy smile. "I . . . um . . . went to

the drugstore today, just in case we got this far, and I bought condoms.''

Declan had seen an advertisement for the distasteful sheaths on a huge sign outside Marathon this very afternoon. He'd worn the cumbersome things a time or two in his life and remembered them as more of a nuisance than a boon. He'd decided long ago that if he ever got a woman pregnant, he would do his duty and give her and the child his name, as would any decent man. From what he knew of Libby's past, that hadn't been the case with her blackguard of a lover.

But agreeing to wear one would be worth it, he decided, if it would get him inside her. "So where are they, then, these condoms?" he asked, matching her smile with one of his own.

She raised her chin and glanced toward the doorway. "In my bag. I guess I left it on the porch.''

Now it was his turn to sigh. "Then I'd better go get it.''

"But . . . but you don't have any clothes on.''

"And I plan to keep it that way.'' He slanted his head and gave her another drugging kiss. Damn but she was intoxicating. Delving inside, he stroked her tongue, inhaled her breath, sipped at her lips until she arched against him. Coming to his senses, he stepped back and laid a hand on her cheek. "Don't move. I'll be right back.''

Libby watched him walk away, admiring the little she could see of his bare backside and muscular legs. The man had no shame, and neither did she, it seemed. She was here and she was buck naked in his room. So far, Declan had acted as if he meant what he said. He was going to do everything in his power to make this a night to remember. She only hoped it wouldn't be a night to regret.

She pulled down the flowered coverlet and sat on the bed just as he strutted back inside. Dropping her bag on the mattress, he sat down beside her. Libby's face grew warm as she searched until she found the box and opened it. Then she handed him the foil packet.

Declan studied it, turning the small square in his palm and squinting as he tried to read the label in the dark. She couldn't help but think that for someone who claimed to be so eager, he was acting pretty strange. If wearing a condom was going to change his mind about sleeping with her, well, then, so be it.

Growing impatient, she finally said, "I think this is the part where you're supposed to open it and put it on."

Another second passed before he tore into the foil, took out the ring of latex and inspected it further. Finally, he set the condom in her hand. "I think, madam, this task should be yours."

Libby was positive her face was on fire. Where was it written that this was the woman's job? "Wait, let me guess. You've never worn a condom before, have you?" she asked wryly. When he didn't answer, she groaned. "Don't tell me they don't have these in Ireland, because I simply won't believe it."

Seconds passed before he whipped the condom from her fingers. "Just give me the blasted thing."

She heard his fumble, a hasty *tsk,* then a muttered curse as something smacked against the tile floor. "What happened?" she asked, pretty sure she didn't want to know.

Declan sighed, loud and long. "The cursed thing has a mind of its own. I almost had it right when it shot out of my hand like it was alive."

Libby couldn't help it. The expression in his voice, the implication of his words, and plain sheer nerves made her lose all control. Laughter bubbled up from her chest like a geyser. She put one hand over her mouth, then two, but it didn't help stifle the giggles. She was a thirty-year-old woman with a child, and she was failing miserably at having sex with only the second man in her life.

And the guy couldn't even put on a condom.

Suddenly, Declan's hearty laughter echoed with her own and she began to hoot all over again. He pulled her into his arms and they fell back onto the mattress like two exhausted children.

"I can explain," he said, giving a good impression of a man trying to be serious.

"Don't bother." She wiped the tears from her eyes. "The answer can't be as good as the reality."

He cleared his throat and reached for the open box. "I never thought I would say this, but I'm going to learn to wear one of these things if it takes all night."

Libby lay still on the bed, dabbing at her eyes while she heard foil tear, then Declan's determined grunt. Then he was looming over her, his grin just visible in the darkness. Scooping her up in his arms, he kissed her soundly, drinking the laughter from her lips.

His condom-covered erection lay heavy on her thigh and she felt a sudden stab of desire. She and Brett had never laughed like this in bed. The few times she'd tried to be playful, he'd gotten so flustered that he'd wilted like week-old asparagus. She returned Declan's kiss with fervor, relieved they'd moved past the awkward stage and on to the good stuff.

"Are you still laughing at me, madam?" he asked in an amused-sounding voice.

She reached between them and caught him in her hands, tracing the length and breadth of him with her fingers. "Does this feel like I'm laughing, O'Shae?"

He moaned as he nibbled at her jaw. "I'm not certain. Perhaps you need to do that again, so I can be sure."

Reverently, he ran a finger over one perfectly shaped breast. The pearly pink tip swelled, and he bent to take it in his mouth. She trembled in his arms and he raised her up. Feasting on the hardened nub, he reveled in the feel of Libby's body moving beneath him as he suckled at her breast. When she ran her hands through his hair to tug him closer, he bit down gently, branding her as surely as he'd marked his treasure box. She spread her legs and his fingers found her, damp and eager for his touch. Parting the moist folds, he touched her sweet spot, circling it until she quivered.

With his hands at her back, he settled himself between her legs and, like an arrow shot true from its bow, slid smoothly inside. She clutched at his shoulders and he ground his hips, trying to help her find her rhythm. In a heartbeat, Libby came alive in his embrace, fulfilling every dream, every fantasy, he'd ever imagined. Soon they were rocking in place, the sound of her breath matching his in perfect harmony.

Amazed at the way their bodies danced as one, he realized she had erased the lost yearning he'd felt since waking in this strange new place. Instead, she had became his rudder, his anchor in a sea of confusion and despair—his port of safety in a storm.

Free-falling, Libby thought with a shattering rush for completion. This is what it would be like to bungee-jump without a line. Declan whispered encouragement and she moved faster, meeting him stroke for stroke. His hands, his mouth, were everywhere, coaxing and caressing as she fell faster and faster into the void.

Stars magically brightened the room, at least in her eyes, then exploded as she plunged into space with him close by her side. He tensed above her and called out her name. She sobbed into his chest and rode the wave of pleasure until the room turned to darkness once more.

Chapter Twelve

Declan stroked his fingers through Libby's unbound hair, a tangled mass of curls fanning the pillow. After more than two hundred years of celibacy, this one night had been well worth the wait. God's blood, but the woman hadn't let him down. She'd been as lusty and impetuous as he'd hoped, a perfect complement to his own desire.

Still breathless from the force of his climax, he rose up on his elbows and caught the glimmer of her smile in the moonlight. With her eyes closed, Libby raised her arms overhead. Arching like a pampered cat, she gave a purr of contentment, making him want her all over again.

He continued to stare, admiring the fullness of her rosy lips, the tilt of her nose, the look of wonder in her now wide-open golden eyes—

Her dreamy expression turned to shock as she pushed weakly at his shoulders. "I have to get home before Jack starts to worry about me."

Guessing her intent, Declan held fast. Though confident of his powers of persuasion, he knew full well that Libby had a mind of her own and the resolve to use it. At this moment, he could tell the contrary woman was wishing she was anywhere but here, in his arms and in his bed. A wish he fervently hoped to change.

"I suspect your grandfather is snoring loud enough to peel the paint from the walls right about now. And your son is probably doing the same."

"Graysons do not snore," she responded with an indignant little sniff. "Now let me up."

Declan grinned at her. She was adorable when she wore that mutinous pout, as if she'd like nothing better than to see him walk the plank. He lowered his head and brushed his lips across hers. Wooing her, he prolonged the kiss, nibbling at her mouth until she surrendered completely.

When at last he drew away, he was pleased to see the starstruck gaze had returned to her eyes. He bent to kiss her again and she blinked, then pursed her lips as she squirmed, warning him that their time for pillow talk had ended.

"Stay long enough to share a glass of wine with me. I bought you something today," he said, hoping to keep her beneath him a moment longer.

Her mouth opened in surprise. "For me? Why?"

He teased her lips again, feasting on their sweetness. "Let's call it a celebratory gift," he finally answered. "Come have a drink and you can open it."

Libby pushed at his chest, and this time Declan rolled to his side. She stood and tugged the top sheet off the bed, then regally turned her back and wrapped herself togalike in the fabric. The idea that she believed it proper for him, but not her, to lie here naked as the day he was born, was comically endearing.

Wearing the cloth like a shroud, she picked up her trousers and hopped on one foot, then the other, as she struggled to get the pant legs up and under the voluminous sheet. Not only was she modest as a nun, she had to be a master contortionist if she thought she could dress in the dark while trussed up like a mummy.

He heard the rasp of a zipper, then her satisfied-sounding

sigh. Finished with the trousers, she pulled her hair around the back of her neck and scanned the floor. "I don't have time for small talk or presents. Besides, we hardly know each other," she muttered.

Declan hid his chuckle behind a muffled cough. *Hardly knew each other?* The woman had matched him kiss for kiss. She'd stroked and fondled his manly parts until he'd been driven mad with desire. Didn't Libby realize he'd seen and felt every bountiful inch of her? And what he hadn't admired or touched, he had tasted?

She dropped to the tiles and he stretched to the edge of the bed, curious to see how she planned to finish dressing. He found her scrambling on her hands and knees for the rest of her things. Clumsily, she stood and pulled the T-shirt over her head. Still clutching the sheet, she stuck one arm into a sleeve, then the other. Smoothing the shirt over her chest, she let the sheet fall to the floor at the same time she finished tugging the top into place. After staring at the scrap of lace she'd called a "front loader," she stuffed it in a pocket.

"Libby, wait. At least let me see you to your—"

Her expression triumphant, she threw back her shoulders and headed for the door. "I know the way, O'Shae. There's no need for you to bother."

He shot from the bed like a musket ball, grabbed her in his arms, and raised her up until his eyes were level with her breasts.

"Put me down!" She smacked her hands onto his shoulders. "I have to get out of here."

Declan leaned forward and nuzzled the hardened nubs taunting him through the thin cotton. Libby moaned a protest and he bit gently, circling his tongue over a beaded tip until her shirt turned damp. When he'd tasted his fill, he cupped her bottom in his hands and let her slide down his front, inch by agonizing inch.

The friction of her clothed body raking his naked skin set his blood to thrumming. By the time her feet hit the floor, Libby's arms were threaded through his hair and she was arching her hips into his blossoming erection. Fitting against him like glove to hand, her aroused nipples burned his chest as her pelvis thrust against his aching member.

The erotic kiss seemed to last a lifetime, until she tore her mouth away and settled into him with a defeated sigh. "Damn it, O'Shae, you don't play fair."

He drew back and ran his thumb over her kiss-swollen lips. "The saying is an old one, but I believe 'All's fair in love and war' fits this situation perfectly."

Her shoulders sagged and she stepped away. Glancing around the room, she spied the time illuminated on the bedside clock. "All right. I'll stay for a drink, but don't expect anything fancy for breakfast in the morning." Her gaze darted to his chest. "You're wearing the amulet," she said softly. "I thought I felt it when you were . . . we were . . ." Clearly flummoxed, she bent down and retrieved her sandals. "Maybe you should put on some clothes."

Declan nodded, pleased to learn that his body stirred her. He'd climbed his share of rigging and loaded enough cargo to know he wasn't a puny man. Especially where it counted most.

He stood proudly, just to show her he had nothing to be ashamed of. "Give me a minute and I'll meet you in the galley."

Libby padded off while he searched frantically for his trousers. She said she would stay, but for how long? And what was it about the medallion that had her so bothered? Shirtless, he paced to the front of the cottage, where he found her putting on her shoes.

He flipped the light switch over the sink, grabbed the bottle of red wine and opened it, then poured them each a drink. Taking the gold foil box tied with thin gold string from the refrigerator, he carried everything to the round glass-topped table in a corner of the room. When she stood, he offered her the gift.

Libby held the box in both hands while she read the name inscribed on the lid. *Godiva.* How could Declan have known that the extravagant chocolates were her one guilty pleasure? Brett had given her a box of Godiva for their first Valentine's Day together, but he'd never given her a present without a good reason. Come to think of it, the next year he'd told her that she needed to lose weight and bought her flowers instead. After his snide remark, she'd never felt comfortable when she splurged on the calories.

Were all Irishmen this thoughtful? If so, maybe American women needed to take a little trip abroad; it would do wonders for their self-esteem. She bit at her lower lip. "You bought me chocolates?"

"Aye." Declan smiled boyishly. "The store's proprietor told me this brand was the finest available."

Blowing out a breath of longing, she set the box on the table. "I can't accept this. It's too expensive, and I know you don't make much money."

"Frank and Mary pay me well enough. I eat all my meals with you, and this cabin is free until after the fair. I have little else on which to spend my wages." Declan raised a glass and offered it to her. "Let's drink a toast to us, and the first of our many nights together."

The glass felt cool against her clammy palm. Libby took a sip and the ruby red liquid slid smoothly down her throat. Even though she'd been surrounded by alcohol most of her life, she'd never learned to enjoy the taste of the stuff, but Declan seemed to think this was the kind of thing people did after having . . .

Her face burned at the memory of what they had just done and she took another swallow. Lifting her head, she met his penetrating gaze as it followed the wine's path, stroked down her neck to her breasts and belly. Heat pooled between her legs, snaked up inside of her, and met the wine with a sudden flare of desire.

He picked up the box and untied the string, chose a heart-shaped chocolate and held it to her lips. Giving in to temptation, Libby bit the candy in half and let the dark, rich taste melt on her tongue as he popped the remainder into his own mouth.

"Sweet," he whispered, finishing the treat. "But not as sweet as this."

He took her wine and set it down on the table. Cradling her face in his hands, he slanted his head and fused his mouth to hers. When he licked at her lips, Libby was positive the candy had been laced with something potent enough to destroy her willpower. Opening to him, she let herself drown in the taste of the chocolate as it melded with the sinful flavor she was coming to recognize as Declan's alone.

Her knees buckled and he caught her in his arms. His rock-hard erection pressed against her thigh.

"The night can last until the dawn if we let it," he murmured, kissing the curve of her neck.

His seductive words slid over her like warm butterscotch. She sucked in a ragged breath and fought to stay in control. What the heck was happening to her? Yes, sex with the caveman had been incredible, but how could something that was supposed to be simple and uncomplicated short-circuit her brain cells? After believing Brett's lies, she'd sworn she would never let herself be swayed by pretty phrases, and here she was, longing to go to bed with Declan all over again.

She never should have come here. She couldn't trust herself to be objective . . . to see things as they were and not as she wished them to be.

"I have to go home." Libby pulled from his embrace, positive distance was just what she needed to put the mind-numbing incident in perspective. Morning would be here all too soon, and with it the reality of what they—what *she* had done.

She backed away from him, opened the screen door, and stepped onto the porch. "I'll see you at breakfast. Good night."

* * *

Declan climbed down from the ladder and gave a satisfied nod. The job had been grueling, but the roof of the Pink Pelican was finished. Truth be told, he was exhausted, but in the best way possible. His first night of passion with Libby Grayson had been all he'd hoped for and then some. Next to finding his treasure, their second intimate encounter was foremost in his mind.

He felt a tug at his pocket and glanced down at J.P. The tadpole had stayed by his side all morning, bringing him water and happily managing the slave work.

"Are we done?" J.P. asked.

He placed a hand on the boy's shoulder and squeezed. "Aye, lad. Now we have to clean the porch and put away the ladder and tools. Are you ready for it?"

"Yes, sir." He started picking up the ragged bits of thatch scattered about the landing. Once his arms were full, he asked, "Where does this stuff go?"

"In the trash bin behind the kitchen door. Then get the broom. I'll sweep while you hold the dustpan. Hurry now, or we'll miss lunch."

Declan watched him scamper away. A tantalizing smell wafted from the kitchen, and his stomach growled in anticipation. Libby's breakfast had been passable, but there hadn't been enough of it to keep a grown man doing hard physical labor content for the entire morning. True to her word, all she'd offered him was a bowl of cereal covered with slices of banana, toasted bread with jam, and coffee. He'd eaten enough to be polite, while J.P. had cheerfully downed two bowls of the colorful Lucky Charms. He could tell from the aroma filling the air that Tito's lunch would be much more to his liking.

J.P. returned, and they stacked the tools and cleaned up the porch together; then the boy ran inside to eat. Though his belly gave another angry growl, Declan propped himself against the railing, knowing Libby would be here soon to wait on the lunch crowd.

His mind wandered, and it occurred to him that he might at this very moment be standing over his treasure. Striding down the steps, he backed up and appraised the weather-beaten building. It seemed sturdy enough to survive a normal gale, but how did the roof and walls manage to hold firm in the kind of storm he now knew struck the Keys regularly—the same kind of storm he figured had attacked his ship—a hurricane? He'd tacked the thatch down tight and repaired the shutters, but would the Pink Pelican truly remain intact if they had another of those disastrous gales?

The building sat a mere foot above the ground on thick pilings over dirt mixed with sand and dotted with tufts of grass. The pilings seemed firm, but wood often rotted in heavy humidity, or became infested with insects from the inside out, which could compromise the strength of the footings.

He scratched the back of his neck, looked right and left, then got down on all fours. Peering into the shadows, he scanned the ground, hoping to recognize something that might tell him if he'd buried his treasure there.

Crawling farther, he wedged his body halfway under the porch and saw a triangle of bumps. A rush of breath escaped his lungs. Could those rounded projections be the tops of the three boulders he'd used to mark his spot? If so, they looked worn smooth by time and well-covered by sand and dirt. That meant the strongbox he'd hidden at their base would be buried deep, too deep to unearth without the use of a full-sized shovel and the muscle of a strong back. It would take days of lying on his belly, digging with a—

"What are you doing?"

Declan started. His head smacked the underside of the building so hard that a flash of light burst behind his eyelids. Muttering a flustered oath, he backed out and slowly rose to his feet. Damn if the woman hadn't managed to make him see stars again, and not from shared passion.

Still stunned, he kept his gaze trained on Libby's feet and the one sandal that tapped impatiently on the ground as he brushed at the sand clinging to his pants. Finally, he looked up and gave her what he hoped was a dazzling smile.

"Libby. Here to handle the lunch crowd already?" He made a production out of checking the time. "I had no idea the hour was so late."

She gave him a glare that would have sent a lesser man running. Crossing her arms beneath her magnificent breasts, she bent forward and angled her head to get a better view of the underside of the building. "What were you doing just now, crawling under the porch like that?"

Tread carefully, me boy-o, Declan reminded himself, *you promised not to lie.* "Looking for something I lost. I thought it might somehow have landed down there."

She raised a brow, her expression filled with disbelief. "Really? What was it?"

He climbed the steps and began straightening the already aligned pile of tools.

"Declan? I asked what it was that you lost."

"Um . . . money. Coins, actually." He rubbed at the raised knot decorating the back of his head, then tossed her another teasing grin. Surely the O'Shae charm would rescue him from further prevarication.

"How much money? And how in the world do you think it got under there?"

"I can't be sure. By the way, have I told you how fetching you look today? That color suits you," he said, complimenting her bright yellow blouse and navy blue skirt. "Will you be joining us for lunch?"

A crowd of tourists took that moment to climb the stairs and follow the porch to the front of the building. Seeing as Libby was a stickler for duty, Declan prayed the diversion would work to his advantage. And it did—for a half second.

"Looks like I'll have to eat after the rush." With her arms still folded, she squatted and focused past the pilings.

"J.P. is small. He could probably crawl under there and take a look for you. Was it a lot of money?"

Declan groaned inwardly. The woman made a better barrister than she did a serving wench. He needed to get her onto another topic with all due haste. "Tell me, are you missing anything?" He sidled to the ladder, still propped against the wall.

Bending down, he picked up the bag she'd left in his bedroom and held it out to her. "Last night, in your hurry to escape, you forgot this. I thought you might need it, so I brought it with me."

Libby rushed up the stairs onto the porch, whipped the purse from his fingers and opened it. Pink spots of color dotted her cheeks as she dug through the bag, then closed it and hoisted the strap over her shoulder. "Thank you. I . . . I didn't realize I'd left it at the cottage."

The idea that she still mistrusted him started Declan's temper to simmering. Surely Libby didn't think him scurrilous enough to steal from a woman he'd taken to his bed? "I can assure you, the contents are all there. Except for the condoms."

Her cheeks flushed red as she glanced quickly around the porch. "Sshhh. Someone might hear you."

"I was merely thinking of you. It could be awkward if J.P. were to root inside and find them. Since we'll be meeting at my cottage, I thought it more convenient to keep them there."

Libby stared at her shoes, picking at the bag's braided leather strap. "Look, about last night . . . I still don't think it was a good idea. I'm not sure we should continue to carry on the way we did."

"Carry on?"

"You know, meet there and . . . fool around."

"You mean, have sex?"

"Will you be quiet!" She swiveled her head, then smiled tentatively at a second group of tourists ascending the stairs.

"Welcome to the Pink Pelican. Make yourselves comfortable. I'll be right in to take your order."

Declan gave himself an invisible pat on the back. He'd managed to get her off track about why he was searching under the restaurant and remind her of their amazing evening all at the same time. He waited until the patrons disappeared before saying, "I thought we had a bargain."

Glaring, she stuck out her chin. "Don't you have any shame? The last thing we need is for people to know we're having an—that we're involved. It's just not a good idea."

She tried to push past him, but he caught her elbow and spun her around. "I've done as you requested and stayed away from you in public. I have no intention of letting you renege on our agreement. To think so is foolish."

Squaring her shoulders, Libby pulled away. "That's my point. After last night, I'm not sure I can be held to my word. Now, please, let me pass."

Declan knew he'd pleasured her in bed. No way could Libby have pretended her melting response to his touch, the trembling in her body when she'd cried out her release, or the incredible tremors they'd experienced together afterward. There had to be something else causing her to feel this way. But what? The book he'd purchased the other day spoke of men and women and their many differences. Talking things out, the book had said, was sometimes all a woman needed.

Resisting the impulse to take her in his arms, he stuck his hands in his pockets. "This bears further discussion. If you won't speak with me now or come to the cottage tonight, we can stay in the bar after it closes or meet at the cove. But I aim to find out what's happened to make you change your mind."

Her face paled to a blank mask. "Later. Right now I have to get to my job."

She turned and walked away without a backward glance.

* * *

Libby busied herself behind the bar, straightening liquor bottles and taking inventory as she listened to the members of the fair's planning committee. The men had worked efficiently at tackling each item on Frank's list. Hazel had accepted the first load of supplies that afternoon, and tomorrow would be day one of the construction. While Bob Grisham supervised the building of the booths, Declan himself had volunteered to assemble the gazebo on the grassy patch of land that stood as the town square.

When the committee began to discuss odds and ends, Libby's mind wandered. Soon, her grandfather would be shooing her out and closing up the Pink Pelican. It would be time to meet with Declan privately at the Dream Cove or at his cottage, the place where they had first been intimate. Right now, neither destination held any appeal.

Dream Cove was isolated and quiet, a romantic spot filled with special memories Libby wasn't sure she wanted to share. But Declan's cabin was small and personal and held memories of another sort. Steamy memories of hot, searching kisses, arousing touches and mind-altering passion.

She'd be alone with him no matter which spot she chose, vulnerable to his charms and her own body's weakness. She still had no idea whether it was his potently male pheromones or her own hormones running amok that made her unable to resist him, but either way she was going to be in big trouble if she allowed herself to meet with him privately again.

Distracted, she didn't hear Declan close the meeting until she glanced up and found him standing across from her. Though she knew it was impossible, his dark-eyed appraisal turned her insides to Jell-O. How could she feel the warmth of his hand caressing her from three feet away?

"Are you through here?" he asked, his face all carved planes and angles in the muted overhead light.

She tapped at the list she'd set on the bar. "I won't be free for quite a while. I still have to write up a liquor order and figure out how we're going to pay for it. Then I have to—"

"I already took care of the order and called it in. You run along home now," suggested Jack, who'd sauntered over to join them. "T and I can take care of things here."

Ignoring Declan's smug smile, she untied her apron and set it on top of the pile of linens she'd collected for the wash, then gave her grandfather a glare of his own. "Oh? And how did you plan on paying for it? Do you have a hidden stash of cash I'm not aware of?"

Jack raised a bushy brow and smiled sweetly, as if he'd just one-upped her. "I have yesterday and today's receipts. Guess you haven't noticed, but business has picked up a bit, what with our advertising for the fair. Folks have stopped in to talk about it and stayed to eat and drink. Just ask T, if you don't believe me."

Libby realized what he said was true. She'd worked her tail off the past few days. She just hadn't equated the surge in customers with the upcoming festival. Probably because she'd spent most of the time mooning over the caveman and the dozen or so ways he was impairing her mental capacities.

"Hazel says she has big plans for another advertisement. Maybe I should put a help-wanted sign in the window and place our own ad for another waitress in the weekly paper." A second server would give her an excuse to spend more time with J.P. She could even stay home on slow nights and give Ruth a break with the baby-sitting.

"Sure, go ahead and try," Jack said agreeably. "More help means better service, and that means more business. Maybe with the tips, it'll be enough to lure another body to Sunset."

He searched his back pockets and handed her two envelopes. "Got a few more contributions tonight. You can go into Marathon tomorrow and place the ad, then put this cash in the bank."

Libby stuffed the envelopes in her bag and headed around the bar. "Good idea. J.P. needs new sneakers, and Wednesdays are usually slow. If you and Uncle T can handle the lunch crowd, maybe he and I can have some quality time together. I haven't been a very good parent lately, spending every minute here or working on the books at home.''

Jack slapped a hand on Declan's back. "Nonsense. A boy can't spend all his time with his mother. He needs a man's influence every now and then. He goes fishin' with me, and Declan here's been takin' the boy under his wing just fine. J.P. doesn't even miss you.''

Well, isn't that just dandy, Libby thought. She'd been so busy worrying about herself and how to handle the caveman, she hadn't noticed how much her own son had started to depend on him. That was one more thing they needed to discuss, after they settled their intimacy issues.

"He's only five years old. He stills needs his mother.''

"Of course he does.'' Declan paced to her side. "Jack just means that J.P. enjoys the normal things men do, and he can't do them if he's always with you. If it's any consolation, he talks about you constantly while we're together.''

Libby opened her mouth to tell him that she didn't need or want his opinion of her and J.P.'s relationship, but Declan hustled her out the door before she could say a word. She heard the sound of her grandfather's laughter as the door shut behind them.

Wrenching her arm free, she made tracks toward the house, ticked to see the caveman matching her step for hurried step. When she got to the front porch, she called a loud, "Thank you for walking me home,'' over her shoulder, then charged up the stairs, opened the door, and made polite small talk with Ruth, waiting until the older woman shrugged into her sweater.

Alone at last, Libby closed the door, rested her backside against it and heaved a sigh. She heard Ruth's tinny laughter and Declan's lilting voice, then the blessed sound of silence. Relieved she'd avoided a confrontation, she waited for her heart rate and her temper to return to normal.

Three rapid taps at her back had her skittering like a drop

of water on a hot skillet. She turned and stared at the door. He wouldn't dare—would he?

"Who is it?"

"Open the door, Libby."

Was that laughter she heard tinting his demanding tone?

Maybe if she glared hard enough, her gaze would burn a hole through the wood and skewer the caveman where he stood.

She groaned when the knob turned and the door opened. Next time she'd remember to lock it.

"What do you want?"

Declan's lips twitched in amusement as he propped himself against the door frame. He gave her the same calculating stare he'd used when they'd first met—the one that made her feel like a butterfly he wanted to pin to a board.

"It's really quite simple, dear lady. I want you."

Chapter Thirteen

Libby opened and closed her mouth. She'd been stared at in bars, leered at on the subway, even whistled at on the sidewalks of New York, just like a lot of well-dressed, halfway attractive women usually were. Then again, most construction workers and flashers in the Big Apple considered any woman who wasn't pushing a shopping cart and mumbling to herself fair game.

But Declan's gaze was different, so intense she thought he could see through her flesh right into her very soul. She couldn't remember any man ever staring at her with such complete command of ownership. The idea that he might be thinking of her as a possession unnerved her. She wanted to be furious but had to admit that deep down inside, a tiny part of her was flattered.

"Well, you can't have me," she lied. The second he'd opened the door and scoured her with that all-encompassing gaze she knew she was lost. Declan O'Shac could have her any time and any place he wanted.

His raised eyebrows told her that he'd heard what she said but didn't believe a word of it. "Then it seems we're at a standoff. Perhaps we should flip a coin to see who wins?''

Libby inhaled a breath, shoring up the wall she'd erected around her heart. "I'm not some kind of prize to be won or lost. I'm a grown woman with a mind of her own, and as I told you, I've changed it."

He ambled into the foyer so smoothly she didn't realize he'd moved until he stood two feet away from her. "We had an implied agreement, Libby. You and I are testing the waters of a—how did you put it?—sexually compatible, no-strings arrangement. I'm merely giving you the opportunity to back out of it gracefully. But God knows why you would want to after what we shared."

She sidled toward the stairway, prepared to make a quick getaway. "That's just your testosterone talking. What we *shared* was a case of lust. I hadn't been with Brett in a while and you . . ." Libby wasn't sure when Declan had last made love to a woman and suddenly realized she didn't want to know. "Well, it's common knowledge men are always ready for a good time. I'm sure if you went into Marathon some night, you'd find another woman willing to help you feel the same."

He took a step closer and cupped her cheek with his palm. "You're trembling. Is it me you're afraid of, or what happened between us that has you so upset?"

She was afraid, all right, but in typical male fashion he'd missed the mark on what it was that terrified her. She'd given her heart away once, and the man had taken her gift, spit on it, and tossed it back at her so many times she'd lost count. She'd promised herself she would never give anyone that kind of power over her again, and here she was, very close to breaking that promise.

He stroked the curve of her neck, his fingertips leaving a wake of goose bumps as they trailed down her arm. "How about a swim to clear the air and settle your fears? Come to Dream Cove and we'll talk. Only that, if it's all you want to do. If you won't visit my cabin tonight, I'll need a good dunking.'' He took her palm in his. ''Meet me halfway, at least.''

A swim in the moonlight . . . under a canopy of stars . . . with Declan O'Shae. She had to be insane to even consider—

He smiled and tugged at her hand.

Her heart stuttered with an almost painful longing.

''Please?''

Dumb, dumb, dumb. She closed her eyes. ''Let me change into a suit. And we have to wait for Jack. I don't want to leave J.P. alone.''

Libby raced up the stairs, her incredible legs flashing at him through the rails. God, she was a sight to make a blind man see. And he was a fool. He needed to find his treasure and leave this place, before he said or did something he would regret. Right now, they were a man and a woman playing a heady game, enjoying the exhilaration of a sensual chase. Soon they would discover the joy of knowing one another thoroughly, reveling in the release of tension their nightly trysts would bring. But how long before they grew tired of one another, argued or hurt each other and ended the affair? Unhappy with those possibilities, he tucked them aside and set his mind on the evening to come.

He heard footsteps on the porch and turned to see Jack Grayson pushing through the door.

''Declan. You're here late. Are you waiting for me?''

Declan walked to the landing and sat on the stairway. ''Libby decided to accompany me on a midnight swim. We weren't going to leave until you arrived and agreed to watch J.P.''

Jack's brown-eyed gaze turned sharp. Looking as suspicious as a bandy-legged rooster with a fox in his henhouse, he folded his arms across his chest. ''You and Libby been seein' quite a bit of each other, ain't ya?''

Declan sat back and lounged on the steps. ''I enjoy your granddaughter's company and I think she enjoys mine.''

Jack skewered him with a glare. ''You know, it came to me a while ago that folks around here don't know much about you. Are you plannin' on staying around after the fair?''

"I'm not sure," Declan answered. He'd never promised to tell Jack Grayson the truth, as he'd done with Libby, and besides, he had to find his treasure before he left. The search could take longer than the fair's end. Without money to make his way in the world, he might have to remain in Sunset for a time. The idea of his staying wasn't impossible. He just hadn't given it any thought.

Jack cleared his throat with a cough. "There's going to be plenty of work around town if the festival is a success. Could be we'll be needin' a permanent coordinator. Think you'd be interested in the job?''

"I'd have to hear the offer first. And I doubt seeing to the fair would be interesting enough to keep me going the entire year. I'm not used to sitting idle. There would have to be more for me to do in Sunset, an incentive to stay."

Jack's disdainful snort echoed in the hallway. "Seems to me you found incentive all on your own; you just ain't realized it yet. Libby's a good girl, but she's got a soft heart. She's been hurt bad, and I don't want to see her gettin' hurt again. I have to ask you, just exactly what are your intentions toward my granddaughter?''

Before Declan could answer, Libby trotted down the stairs wearing a pair of khaki shorts and a gauzy white shirt over her plain black swimsuit. "I'm ready. I brought towels and one of Gram's quilts so we could sit and—Grandpa Jack, I didn't hear you come in.''

Declan watched the old man stare up at his granddaughter as if seeing her for the first time. With her amber eyes aglow and her cheeks a soft, petal pink in the pale foyer light, she resembled more a maid of seventeen than a woman with a son. Jack narrowed his eyes, but his smile widened as Libby's golden gaze darted from man to man and back again.

"Did something happen at the Pink Pelican?''

"Nope. Everything's fine. I'm in for the night, and Declan tells me the two of you are goin' for a swim.''

Libby held the quilt tighter to her chest as she walked sedately down the steps. "I just checked and J.P.'s sound asleep. You don't have to do anything but be here in case he wakes up. I won't be out late."

"That boy sleeps like the dead most every night. I can take care of J.P. just fine," Jack said, his gaze holding Declan's for a bit too long. "Maybe you ought to stay home and turn in early."

She stopped and gave him a quick kiss on the cheek. "Thanks for worrying about me, but I'll be fine."

Declan held the door open and took the quilt and towels from her arms. Nodding to Jack, he followed Libby out the door, but not before he said, "Good night. And I'll give proper thought to what you said."

"What the heck was that all about?" Libby kept a few steps ahead of Declan on the gravel path, knowing her voice would carry in the still night air. She couldn't imagine why he and Jack had reminded her of first-graders ready to go at one another on a playground when she'd come down the stairs, but she was fairly certain she hadn't imagined the tension arcing between them.

When Declan didn't answer, she stopped short, only to have him bump into her backside and pull her against the wall of his chest. He nuzzled at a particularly sensitive spot he'd found behind her left ear.

"To what exactly are you referring?"

A jolt of electricity sizzled from her head to her toes. Her knees wobbled and her pulse danced a jitterbug of desire as he wrapped his arms around her waist and cupped her breasts from behind. God, the man knew just how to touch her to make her weak.

"You and Ja-ack. I got the idea . . ." He slipped his fingers into the top of her suit and plucked at her nipples. ". . . you two were having . . ." His lips found her earlobe, his breath tickled her ear. ". . . a serious dis-cussion."

Dropping the quilt and towels, Declan turned her in his arms. "It was nothing we couldn't work out. Now, do I have to carry you to the beach, or can you make the trip under your own power?"

Delighted by the impossible suggestion, Libby framed his jaw with her palms. "You are a nutcase. I must weigh . . . um . . . well, never mind what I weigh. I just don't understand why you keep treating me as if I were this delicate little female, when it's plain to see I'm capable of getting where I have to be on my own."

His teeth flashed white in the moonlight. "I beg to differ. You *are* a female; therefore it is my duty to see you taken care of. As to how much you weigh . . . well, since you're exceptionally well-packaged, the amount doesn't matter. You fit against me perfectly and that's what counts."

He kissed her long and slow and sweet, and Libby lost herself in the magic of his mouth and tongue. Sliding her hands over his shoulders, she couldn't help but notice his strength as muscles tightened and flexed beneath her palms, or how sheltered and safe she felt in the circle of his embrace. Okay, so the man had the body of a Greek god and the silver tongue of a devil. What harm could come of letting herself enjoy this strangely old-fashioned adoration a little while longer? He was right when he said they'd knocked each other's socks off in bed. She was an adult with a sensible head on her shoulders—she could live for the moment and still be responsible, couldn't she?

Declan freed her lips and she sighed. Sighing right back at her, he rested his chin against her forehead. "Let me make love to you, Libby. Why deny the two of us what we both want and need, simply because of propriety or convention?"

"Are you sure you weren't a politician or maybe a lawyer in an earlier life?"

Amusement laced his voice when he answered. "I was many things in my former lifetime, but none of them so proper as what you suggest." He grasped her hands and took a step back. "Now, shall we continue to the cove?"

Still not quite sure she was doing the right thing, Libby nodded. He picked up the linens and slung them over one arm, then wrapped his other arm around her waist, and together they walked to Dream Cove.

Though he knew he'd won the battle, there was little elation in Declan's heart. He might have lured Libby to his bed, but he'd done so with logic and persistence instead of his manly charms. In his day, people preached of high moral standards in public while enjoying promiscuity in private. After watching the saucy actions of some of the tourists and viewing an enlightening selection of television shows, it looked like most men and women of this time practiced the same.

He now knew for certain that Libby was not a woman of loose virtue, even if she'd borne a child out of wedlock. Her reticence to continue the affair told him she'd come to his bed only after a great deal of soul-searching. He was no better than the pirate so many had accused him of being because of the way he'd had to practically blackmail her into becoming his lover. Her suggestion that he look elsewhere for a more willing woman would have been a good one, if a woman was all he wanted.

But nothing could be further from the truth. From the moment Libby Grayson had alternately awakened him and knocked him senseless in the cave, she'd danced in his mind and thrummed in his blood as if no other female would do. And from as far back as he could remember, she was the only woman to ever make him forget about his treasure.

They arrived at the cove in silence. Declan shook out the quilt and laid it gently on the sand. Dropping the towels, he folded his arms to keep from stripping her naked himself and gave her the time to tug off her shorts and blouse. Then he pulled his T-shirt over his head and removed his jeans, unashamed to show her the extent of his arousal.

Libby covered her face with her hands and peeked through

splayed fingers. He'd been hard as a plank since he'd bumped into her on the path. The thrill of watching her watch him made his member throb and lengthen at the same time.

"Good golly, O'Shae. Don't you own a bathing suit?"

"There's no one here but the two of us, woman, and you've already seen me in this condition." He slipped her an easy grin. "You could do the same with that contraption you're wearing."

"Me? Skinny-dip? I don't think so."

"We're alone, Libby. And I enjoy looking at you as much as you enjoy looking at me."

She brought her palms to her cheeks again, and he imagined her face, pink and warm under his lips. He waited, his breath a prisoner in his lungs until, slowly, she peeled the swimsuit to her waist, over her hips and down her legs. Air rushed from his open mouth as if he'd been slit throat to gullet. Standing before him, she was a miracle in the moonlight, a goddess for his eyes alone.

She smiled shyly and he took her hand. They waded into the surf until the water reached their chests. Bobbing together, they dove in tandem, swimming to the ocean floor and kicking to the surface like a pair of seal pups at play. When he stayed deep in the water and tugged at her ankles, Libby treaded away until he came up for air, then swooped forward to dunk him in return.

He found his bearings and captured her in his arms. She laughed out loud as she shook the sea from her hair. Liquid diamonds showered over them, scattering in the air and rolling down her lashes and cheeks to shimmer across her lips.

Declan drank from her mouth, tasting her salty sweetness until they were breathless. Warm silky-wet skin met his chest, her jutting nipples twin points of fire that seared him to his core. Grabbing her about the waist, he lifted her up. "Wrap yourself around me so I can feel you," he whispered, nipping at a rosy bud.

She looped her hands around his neck and let the water

buoy her against him as she scissored her legs to his back. Settling his engorged shaft between her woman's cleft, he rocked them both with the ebb and flow of the ocean, until she dug her fingers into him and gave a ragged moan.

Hoisting her up, he walked from the water while she clung to his chest, her head nestled under his chin. He dropped to his knees and carefully laid her down, then reached for his trousers and the foil packet he'd tucked in the pocket.

Libby's arms opened wide, offering him safe harbor. He moved into her damp slippery heat, teased with the tip of his shaft, thrust forward and drew back until she arched against him and pulled him to her breasts.

Pumping with swift, powerful strokes, he matched her frantic rhythm until they moved as one being. She clutched his shoulders and he caught a pebbled nipple in his mouth, suckling until she shuddered in his arms and cried out her climax.

Trembling, Libby opened her eyes to a sky full of stars. Declan continued to rock steadily over her, sending another burst of shock waves zinging through her system. Their gazes locked and he rasped out a breath. Rising to his knees, he drew her up with him until she was sitting on his muscle-corded thighs, her legs still locked around his waist.

He arced into her and she felt her orgasm build all over again. Riding the incredible wave of sensation, she was amazed to find the stars still there in her eyes long after she closed them and found her release.

Libby cracked eggs into a bowl, added milk, and beat the mixture with a wire whisk. She'd slept like a stone after her midnight swim with the caveman and missed getting up to make breakfast. Luckily, Jack had risen at dawn and taken care of both his and Declan's morning meal. J.P. had slept late as well, but he'd been up early enough to chat with Declan before the man left for his daily chores. At the moment, he was regaling his mother with their conversation.

"Declan says I can help him today," J.P. chattered, reaching for a slice of toast. "He said to tell you he expected a really big lunch because you weren't here to make him breakfast."

"Oh, does he, now?" Libby poured the eggs into a skillet and stirred them with the spatula. "And did he give you his order, by any chance? Filet mignon, or maybe duck l'orange?"

Her sarcasm was lost on the five-year-old as he shook his head and continued to chew the toast. "Nu-uh. He just said it had better be good. If he has time later, he says he's gonna take me to see the kittens."

Libby scraped at the fry pan as the eggs simmered, her mind a short walk away on the sands of Dream Cove. The memory of her and Declan's playful swim and its heated afterburn was still as fresh as the coffee she'd just brewed. She was glad she'd slept late. No way could she have faced him over breakfast with any semblance of normalcy. Much as she hated to admit it, the man was getting to her. The intimacy they shared was an eleven on the climax meter and, after last night, she doubted she'd be able to resist his next sexual onslaught.

Worse, he'd started her thinking of things that could never be: sharing cozy breakfasts or sitting side by side in front of a blazing fire, taking long walks on a moonlit beach or making slow steamy love in her bedroom upstairs.

The realistic part of her brain told her that Declan O'Shae wasn't the kind of man who would want to settle down and do any of those warm, homey things. For lack of a better word, he was a drifter who'd as much as confessed he was in town only until the end of the festival. Though it didn't seem likely, he might even have a sweetheart or wife back in Ireland. Until she knew more about him, she just couldn't accept that he was the kind of man she could depend on.

"Mo-om, I'm starvin'. Are my eggs ready?"

Libby blinked back to the present, scooped scrambled eggs onto two plates, and carried them to the table. Sitting next to J.P., she tucked his napkin more tightly under his chin. "You really like Declan, don't you?"

"Yep, and he likes me. He's gonna let me help him build the za-ge-bow, and after that him and me are gonna look for his treasure."

"I think you mean gazebo, honey." Libby held her forkful of eggs in midair. "And what kind of treasure are you talking about?"

"Um . . . Declan's treasure. He said he lost it and he came here to look for it."

"Then he's already asked you to crawl under the Pink Pelican and help him search?"

J.P. raised a shoulder as he tucked into his eggs. "He didn't zackly say where he lost it."

She blew out a breath, thinking how irresponsible it was for the caveman to call a few coins a treasure and then get her son to buy into the story. The next thing she knew, J.P. would be pestering her to take the metal detector onto the beach, and then Jack would start to fill the boy's head with all kinds of nonsense again and—

Tiny fingers tapped at her wrist. "I asked if it was okay if I helped him look? Can I? Please?"

Lifting her coffee cup, Libby rested her elbows on the table. "Honey, I don't want you to get your hopes up about some lost pennies Declan's started referring to as a treasure. The way I understood it, he didn't lose much and he'll probably never find it. If I say yes, I want you to promise you'll keep things in perspective and not think about the money as if it were a million dollars or anything, okay?"

"What's *sper-pek-tive* mean?"

She set down her mug and tugged at his chin. "It's perspective, and it means keeping a sensible head on your shoulders. Men like Declan O'Shae don't have treasures, honey. Right now, the man's lucky he has a job."

J.P. downed the last of his milk in one swallow, then swiped his lips across the sleeve of his T-shirt. "Is it okay if I go see the kittens with him, at least?"

"To tell you the truth, I had another idea for this afternoon. I thought maybe you and I could go into town and have lunch, just the two of us, like we used to do when we lived in the city. You need new sneakers, sport, and a few new T-shirts might be nice."

J.P. hopped down from his chair. "Can Declan come with us?"

"Do you want him to?" asked Libby, already positive what his answer would be.

J.P.'s eyes grew bright. "Yeah."

She sighed as she smoothed the dark brown curls off his forehead. "Okay, go find him and see what he says, but no pester—"

Before Libby could finish, J.P. ran out the back door. Jack wandered in a half second later, his face grim. "Where's that boy goin' in such an all-fired hurry? He 'bout knocked me off the porch as he blew by. Didn't even say excuse me."

Libby sighed. "He's going to help Declan. By the way, thanks for taking care of breakfast this morning. I guess I needed the sleep."

Jack walked to the counter and poured himself a cup of coffee, then made a great production of filling Libby's mug as well. After returning the pot to the warmer, he took a seat at the table and cleared his throat. "Stayed out kind'a late last night, didn't ya?"

Libby swallowed the near scalding liquid in a surprised gulp. It had been years since she'd had to explain to anyone how she spent her private time. She and Brett had given each other one night a week to do whatever either of them pleased, no explanations or curfews required. She'd usually gone to a movie or a bookstore, or met a girlfriend for dinner, but she was fairly certain Brett had caroused with a group of men he'd hung out with in college. From the sound of it, she was still a sixteen-year-old in her grandfather's eyes.

"Late enough," she finally said, tapping a finger against

the side of the mug. "I've been working hard, and the peace and quiet was nice."

Jack peered at her from under bushy brows. "I know you work hard, little girl. Ain't like you don't deserve some fun once in awhile." He sipped at the coffee. "I just want you to look before you leap is all."

"Who said anything about leaping?" Libby scowled into her cup. "I never leap."

"Ya used to," Jack reminded her. "When you were little, I spent half my time rescuin' you from one adventure or another. Remember the time you climbed up the palm tree in front of Olivia's shop 'cause you wanted coconut milk for breakfast?"

"I remember," she said with an embarrassed smile. She'd been seven years old, without a brain in her head and with absolutely no sense of fear. "You were my white knight that day, climbing up to catch me just before my arms gave out and I was forced to let go. I thought you were bigger than life from that moment on."

Red-faced, Jack stared down at the table. "Aw, it weren't such a big deal. Your dad was afraid of heights, so I couldn't very well expect him to do it."

"Daddy got seasick, too," Libby said, reaching out to take his hand. "That's why you and I went fishing without him. He never could sail a boat like you could, Grandpa Jack. He just didn't have the stomach for it."

Jack rubbed two fingers under his nose. "Your dad was a good parent, Libby. So was your mom. And they left you to me and Martha in their will. I tried my best, but I guess I didn't do so good after Martha died. I always meant to tell you I was sorry about that."

"Don't be ridiculous." Libby fought back the lump rising in her throat. "You did just fine. And what you didn't handle, Uncle T did. Between the two of you, I had the best parents a girl could ask for."

Jack laid his gnarled hand over the one she'd placed on

his fist. "But I wasn't much help with that jackass Brett Ritter, now was I?"

"I knew my own mind. At the time, I doubt I would have listened to anyone, even Grandma Martha. Brett Ritter was my mistake, not yours."

Blinking, Jack patted her hand, then pushed away from the table. "You're doing a fine job raising your son, Libby."

"I had an excellent role model."

"If we pull this festival thing off, it'll be thanks to you. Not a one of us would'a thought to take a chance at turning things around without you forcing us to face facts the way you did."

Declan had been the clever one, then he'd dived right in and taken charge, a fact that still rankled. No way did she deserve the credit. "I just brought up the subject. Declan had the idea and the leadership skills to take charge."

Jack rinsed his cup under the tap, then turned and leaned against the counter. "Funny, ain't it, how everybody just went right along with whatever he said. Since day one, it's like he was meant to be here."

Funny? That wasn't exactly the way she would describe it. Finding him in that cave had been downright spooky, especially after Uncle T's weird magic man predictions. "I don't know about that, but I'm okay with the way he's handled things so far."

"Just about the way he's handled things concerning the festival?"

Libby sighed. She'd been seventeen the last time Jack had quizzed her about a member of the opposite sex. She hadn't told him much then and she wasn't about to start now.

"I'm almost thirty, Gramps. Too old to be spilling secrets about my personal life to anyone. And you need to get a life of your own. Olivia's always been very open about her feelings, as has Hazel. Which one are you going to sit with when it comes time to watch the fireworks after the fair?"

Jack snapped to attention and raised his wrist to his face.

"Holy fish cakes and fried bananas, will you look at the time?" Racing out the door as if his feet were on fire, he said, "I got to go help T serve lunch so you can take J.P. to town. I'll see you later. And in case you're feeling proud of yourself," he called back over his shoulder, "this conversation is far from over."

Chapter Fourteen

Libby and J.P. finished their shopping and were enjoying a leisurely meal before heading back to Sunset. The Cracked Conch was crowded with tourists and locals, all happy to be devouring lunch in the quaint roadside diner, a restaurant that always received positive write-ups in the vacation magazines and guidebooks circulating through the Keys.

Declan had declined J.P.'s invitation to join them, saying he had to work on things concerning the fair, which disappointed J.P. but had Libby breathing a sigh of relief. She didn't want to spend her lunch hour explaining to her son why her face was red, especially if she had to do it in front of Declan O'Shae.

J.P. picked at his burger while Libby gazed through the window at the various birds, mostly gulls, pelicans and egrets traversing the sky as if they were flying above open marshland. After ten years of living in the big city, she'd finally come home. No matter how nice it might be to travel, this was the place she wanted to raise her son. Even the idea of running the Pink Pelican appealed to her, especially if the festival was a success and she and Jack could make the bar profitable again. Lost in her daydream, she didn't notice Nelda McKey until the woman stood right next to their table.

"Libby? Libby Grayson?" Nelda's severe-looking face softened with her smile. "As I live and breathe, it *is* you."

"Hi, Nelda," Libby responded in an equally pleasant manner. "How are you and Pete doing?"

"We're good, though Grandpa's legs are done for. Uses a wheelchair full time now, but his mind is sharp as a tack, so he passes his days tormenting me. Turning ninety-six will do that to a body, I guess."

Libby knew Pete McKey had resided on the Keys since before Grandpa Jack. Legend had it his ancestors were the first white men to populate these islands, but ninety-six?

"I'm sorry to hear it, but at least he's fine mentally. You've got to be grateful for the little victories, I suppose."

Nelda nodded and turned her sharp-eyed gaze to J.P. "This must be your son. I heard you became a mama a few years back. Hello there," she said to the boy as she stuck out her hand. "I'm Nelda McKey. What's your name?"

J.P. swung his legs under the table as he took her fingers and gave them a shake. "John Patrick Grayson, the same as my great-grandpa. But everybody calls me J.P. 'cause Mom doesn't want people to get us confused."

"I doubt that would happen, young fella." She turned to Libby. "Is Jack doing okay?"

"Fine. Did you hear, Sunset is planning a two day festival to celebrate the Fourth of July."

"I heard. Hazel asked if I'd put a sign in the window of the Lucky Buccaneer and I said sure. I'm glad I ran into you, because I was going to come see you as it got closer to July. I need a favor."

Libby pulled over a chair from a nearby table and Nelda took a seat. The woman was old enough to be her mother, and Libby and Nelda had always been on friendly terms. "Sure, if I can do it. What is it you need?"

"It's about Pete. I heard you were planning entertainment

for the kids coming to the fair—puppet shows, face painting, and such—and I was wondering if you'd like a story hour.''

The question zinged straight to Libby's heart when she realized the direction in which Nelda's favor was heading. Along with most of the locals, she'd sat at Pete's knee many times to lose herself in his stories. When she was growing up, she'd thought the old man's mind a library of wonder, filled with tales of pirates, the Keys first white settlers, and how they'd interacted with the Caloosa Indians. His tales were always so animated, Libby'd thought she was sitting right alongside the fascinating characters who peppered his sagas.

''You're asking because of Pete? He wants to tell his stories at our fair?''

Nelda set her elbows on the table and *hmphed.* ''He doesn't know a thing about it. If you say yes, I'm not even gonna tell him until we show up in Sunset. He'd probably get so excited over the idea of spinning those yarns in public, his ticker'd give out. Then where would I be?''

''So you don't want me to announce it'll be Pete heading up the story hour? Just put up the times on the chalkboard and let it be a surprise?''

''If it's all right with you. Pete'll probably like it that way, too,'' said Nelda. ''Seeing as there isn't much left in life to surprise him anymore.''

Libby didn't have to ask anyone for permission to make the decision. The committee had put her in charge of scheduling the entertainment, and she couldn't think of one person who would object to Pete McKey.

''Sure, I mean, great. Pete's the most wonderful storyteller I've ever heard.'' *Though I know of a charming Irishman who could give him a run for his money.* ''But is he up to it? I wouldn't want to tire him out or anything, and ninety-six is kind of ancient to be onstage speaking for more than a few minutes, don't you think?''

Nelda gave an indelicate snort. ''That old walrus could talk a cormorant from a telephone pole if I let him. Since no one ever stops by to hear him anymore, he's bored, which gets him to thinking, which makes him come up with things guaranteed to drive me nuts. Besides, the talkin' will stir up his memory and keep his mind fresh. I'd welcome the diversion, and so would he.''

Libby sipped her iced tea, thinking how Jack would probably enjoy doing the same thing if he ever reached such an impressive age. "I'm positive it can be arranged. We're building a gazebo on the town square, and I hope to assemble the children there for the group activities. It would be the perfect spot for Pete to park himself and tell his tales.''

'' 'Fraid I'm gonna need another favor.'' Nelda toyed with a paper napkin. "I'd like to video this talk for posterity's sake, if you know what I mean. Pete's great-grandson— you remember my sister Ruby's oldest boy—well, he's not shown a lick of interest in carrying on the family tradition. We're all worried that after Pete goes—''

"Those wonderful stories will be lost forever." Stunned, Libby sat back in her chair. "You mean no one has ever written them down?''

Nelda shook her head. "Never. It's always been a given that the youngest Pete who's alive when the oldest Pete gets ready to pass would just naturally latch on to the tales and take up the task. Young Pete—Ruby's son, I mean—doesn't want any part of the process, so she and I thought we could record everything. When the boy comes to his senses and recognizes his duty, the videos will be waiting for him.''

"I never gave a thought as to how your family managed to get those sagas to survive for as long as they have. I guess it's taken a lot of work on everyone's part, huh?'' Libby nodded at J.P. "I'd hate for my son to miss out on hearing them, so yes, let's record them. I'm sure young Pete will do his duty eventually, or you could just save them for the next Pete. He might really get into it.''

Nelda's pinched face relaxed a bit. "I'll supply the video camera and tapes, of course. You just need to make sure Grandpa has a comfortable spot with some shade, and maybe a glass of water and a fan to keep him cool while he talks. Ruby and I, we'd really appreciate it. Just let us know the time. Once we're there, I'll give him the good news, then have him divide the stories into two parts, so he won't have to rattle on too long each day.'' Standing, she heaved a sigh. ''The family owes you one, Libby. Thanks.''

After Nelda left, Libby paid the check and scooted J.P. out the door. ''You ready to go home, sport? It's close to three, and I know where there are some kittens who could use a little human companionship.''

J.P. took her hand and led her to Jack's rusty red truck on racing feet. ''Yeah, me, too. When do you think I can pick one out for my own and bring it home?''

She opened the door and buckled his seat belt as she thought about his question. ''Another week or so, I guess. We don't want whichever kitten you choose to miss its mama too much, and we definitely want to be sure the little fellow is trained to do its business in a litter box.''

His eyes full of mischief, J.P. grinned at her. ''Once, at my day care in the city, Suzy Franks told everybody how her cat pooped in her shoe and her mom had to buy her new ones. And Teddy Bishop had a dog that piddled on his pant leg. One morning, he came in all smelly and Mrs. Lymon sent him home. It was cool.''

''Seems to me I remember those gross stories,'' said Libby, tossing him a teasing frown. ''We certainly do not want the kitten you choose doing its duty in your shoes or anywhere else in the house. That's why we have to make certain the little thing knows how to take care of itself.'' She eased onto the highway and headed for home. ''By the way, have you made up your mind yet which one you want?''

J.P. turned in his seat, his voice filled with hope. ''I want all of them to come live with us.''

Libby only needed to raise a brow to give him her answer.

Rubbing his nose, he said, ''But I guess that won't work. Maybe Declan could help me decide between Bridget and Black Pete.''

"As long as it's only one," she said, catching on quickly to his game.

"Okay, but it's gonna be really hard to choose. And I been wondering, what's gonna happen to the rest of 'em? If we don't take them, where will the other kittens go?"

Uh-oh, thought Libby; the last thing she needed was for J.P. to start thinking about loss again. "Not to worry. We can help Mary find homes for them with the folks in town, or people who visit the fair. How does that sound?"

Unfortunately, J.P. didn't seem convinced of her brilliant plan. "But what if no one wants them? Will Miss Betty keep her babies, or will she make them leave? 'Cause I know sometimes babies have to leave their mommies and daddies, even if they love them, right?"

Okay, so how was she expected to answer that one? Loving parents were supposed to always want to be with their children, but Brett had left. Did J.P. think his father hadn't loved him? Suddenly overwhelmed by the pointed question, Libby said the first thing she thought made sense.

"Oh, honey, sometimes people, or in this case animals, just don't have a choice. You have to remember, just because a mommy or a daddy leaves doesn't mean the love goes away. Love between parents and their children is forever."

From the corner of her eye, Libby saw J.P. nod, but the pensive expression on his face said he didn't quite believe her oversimplified theory.

Declan wiped his brow with his forearm, cursing silently at the muggy Florida heat. He didn't remember this stifling humidity when he'd traveled here in the past. Of course, no one had used atomic bombs or Freon gas or jet-propelled engines two hundred years ago, either. And all of those modern inventions had, according to what he'd read in his history book and the newspapers, caused global warming, which led to something called the greenhouse effect, which made the polar ice caps melt and brought about all manner of dangerous atmospheric conditions.

When he first realized he was in a new century, he'd thought the modern era better than the one in which he'd been born. After studying this time, Declan was no longer so sure. He'd come from a simpler age, where the land was untouched, the air sweet and clean, and no one ever worried about pollution or the HIV virus or mad cow disease.

Things today were more complex, the people sometimes too smart for their own good. The science of cloning, for instance, made him leery, as did outer space exploration and nuclear weapons. The world had grown larger, yet so much smaller at the same time.

Take a simple thing like building, for example. He glanced down at the array of wood, shingles and power tools scattered at his feet. In his day, a man would purchase lumber and lay out a house; then his neighbors would help hammer it together straight and true by the sweat of their brow. Today, he was going to construct a gazebo delivered from a store, precut and ready to assemble, using a paper that detailed the placement of every nail. It would be simple to build, once he figured out which end was up on the directions and how to work all the newfangled gadgets required to put the pieces together.

In the distance came the whine of saws and a din of male voices. Bob Grisham and the building crew had started the construction of the booths on the dock of the marina. Declan had been the one to volunteer for gazebo duty, insisting he could handle it alone. He'd borrowed an electric drill and a power cord from Bob and plugged it into an outlet inside the Pink Pelican. He'd found two different sizes of hammer in the restaurant's storage room, along with a level and some screwdrivers. According to the directions, he was ready to begin.

Thank Poseidon he'd encouraged J.P. to spend the afternoon with his mother. The last thing he needed was to make a fool of himself in front of the boy or Libby, never mind the rest of the town. What kind of man was he, that he couldn't read the plans for what was touted as an "easy to assemble" building that didn't even have solid walls?

As had all his brothers, he'd attended the finest school in Dublin until he was sixteen, then trained under his father in the craft of shipbuilding. He was not a stupid man. Yet this pile of construction paraphernalia had him sweating.

Squatting down, he set the diagram on the grass and studied it. A shadow fell across the page and he turned to find Tito staring, his teeth a crescent of white in his coffee-colored face.

"You havin' a problem?" T asked, trying to sound serious.

"Nothing I can't handle," muttered Declan, coming to his feet.

"Seems to me a smart man like yourself would be hammerin' away by now. Instead, you're lookin' at those directions as if the words were in Swahili."

T snatched the paper from his hand. "Lunch is over and Jack's inside tendin' bar. Guess I can give you a hand for a while. Let's see . . ." He pointed to a pile of wood. "Those there are what's called part one-o-one on this list. I'll give you the rest of the part numbers and you can find 'em and stack 'em. Once that's done, you won't have a problem."

Declan had always been able to take orders when he knew the man giving them to be in the right. After an hour of working companionably alongside T, he was ready to begin the actual task of assembly. Not surprisingly, the huge islander pitched in as if he belonged there, and soon they had the base of the gazebo, a raised octagonal structure about fifteen feet in diameter, securely in place. During the day, it would be used as a meeting place for the children. At night, a band would play here, while people danced on the grassy square.

"Mm-mm-mm," said T proudly. "So far, we done a mighty fine job." As if conducting an inspection, he turned and ran his gaze over Declan from head to toe. "Sure is nice to know I haven't lost my touch with them bones."

Declan raised a brow. "I once crewed with a man who read the bones," he said, remembering the black men he'd met in his past and their myriad superstitions. "And I was treated to a bit of the same in Ireland. My granny used to cast the runes each month on the night of the full moon. Most of the time her predictions came true in one form or another." He rocked back on his heels as he fingered the broken medallion in his pocket. "So you're into magic, then?"

T swiped at his forehead with the towel he kept tied to his belt. "Powerful magic, learned from my mama, and hers before that." He pulled at a chain hanging from his neck and brought out a small leather pouch. Opening it, he poured the contents onto his palm. "This here got passed down to me. It's a rare day when the bones tell me wrong."

"Granny used to say the same thing," Declan agreed. "I once met an old gypsy woman who reminded me of her, but it was a long time ago . . ."

T gathered the bits of bone and feathers back into the pouch and tucked it away. Narrowing his gaze, he pointed to Declan's chest. "Care to tell me what you is wearin', hidden there like it always is?"

Since Libby had already seen the amulet, Declan felt there was no harm in revealing the charm and a bit of its history. Some nights, when he mulled over all that had taken place, he thought about how coincidental it had been that she'd found the missing half at the mouth of the cave and, though frightened enough to want to brain him, had made it whole. Aware of how Tito viewed magic, he was certain the man wouldn't laugh if he heard some of the story.

He pulled the leather thong out from under his shirt. "I got this from a gypsy woman, before my last voyage. She told me it would keep me safe and lead me to my destiny. I believe its part of the reason I came to be here. Have you ever seen another like it?"

Tito touched the semicircle with his forefinger, squinting into the sunlight arcing off the broken disk. "Hmm. Looks like a woman's profile stamped in the center." Without taking his eyes from the amulet, he asked, "What happened to the other half?"

Declan dug in his back pocket, brought out the piece Libby had found, and set it on his palm. "I have it. I only wish there was a way to put it back together again."

Still prodding the medallion, T said, "*Pssh*. That's easy enough. Someday, when I got the right equipment, I'll take care of it for you."

Declan nodded and slipped each piece back in its proper place. He borrowed T's rag and wiped the sweat from his face, then clapped the cook on his back. "I think we've done enough for today. What say we visit Jack and convince him we deserve a pint of ale, on the house?"

T reattached the towel to his belt, and together they headed to the Pink Pelican.

"Miss, excuse me. Miss?"

Libby snapped up her head and blinked at the well-dressed, middle-aged man who was smiling hesitantly from across the bar. "Um . . . sorry. Can I help you with something?"

He set two barely touched drinks onto the shining oak. "My wife and I asked for gin and tonics. I'm fairly sure this is straight gin. Taste it if you don't believe me," he said in a clipped British accent.

Picking up the glasses, she gave an apologetic nod. *Good going, Libby. This is your third screwup of the night.* "No, no, I believe you. I'll take care of it and bring the correct order to you right away."

She watched the tall, gray-haired man amble to a table in the corner, where he joined an attractive woman wearing a form-fitting white sheath. The bar's clientele was definitely on the upswing, she noted. Jack had been right. Now that advertisements for the fair were circulating, people were stopping by to check out the town and decide if they wanted to attend.

With everyone working so hard to make the festival a success, it was no wonder she was distracted. If the town wasted this chance to shine, they wouldn't get another. Logically, she knew failure would not be her fault, but in her heart Libby felt responsible for everything. She was the one who had called the meeting and insisted the townspeople do something to pull themselves out of debt.

She was the one who had found Declan O'Shae.

Carefully measuring the liquor for new drinks, she silently cursed the caveman, the festival, and anything else she could think of that had flustered her today. She delivered fresh glasses to the couple's table, her head still ringing with the echo of hammers, saws and shouts. Now that the building for the fair had started in earnest, she supposed there wouldn't be a day of peace and quiet until the end of the July holiday.

Sighing, she checked her watch. It was close to seven. Declan and a few of the fishermen would be in any minute to eat their evening meal. If she kept acting as if she'd left her mind at Dream Cove, it wouldn't take long before someone noticed her bungling. Couple that with the way she blushed whenever the caveman looked at her and people would make the connection. Everyone would know they were *involved*.

After taking a round of dinner orders from new arrivals, Libby headed toward the kitchen, annoyed that her mind kept wandering. Bits and pieces of the conversation she'd had with Grandpa Jack were itching at her brain. Jack had been correct when he'd said that the townsfolk trusted Declan O'Shae. Though no one in Sunset knew what he'd done before he arrived, the older citizens had naturally gravitated toward him, as if he were their unofficial leader. He seemed to bask in an aura of command, as if leading men came to him as easily as taking a breath. Like a Pied Piper, he'd used his charming personality and lilting voice to earn their trust and loyalty.

In order to get her into his bed, he'd used the same, except he'd thrown in a drop of blackmail and a healthy dose of sexual attraction for good measure.

Had she done the right thing in not telling them where she'd first met the caveman? To date, he hadn't done any harm and had, in fact, given the people of Sunset renewed hope—not a bad thing, when she thought about it sensibly. The problem was, these days she had a difficult time thinking rationally at all where Declan O'Shae was concerned. And when she did have a clear enough head to question him, he always managed to evade her.

Then again, being a member of something as covert as the IRA could cause anyone to long for anonymity. But he had never actually said yes or no when she'd mentioned the IRA. In fact, Declan had never given her a straight answer to any of her questions.

She pushed through the swinging door and found T at the stove, humming some island tune as he flipped food in a cast-iron skillet. After turning on the overhead fans, she sidled up to him and waited until he set the pan back on the flame. "It's hot in here. I turned on the fans."

"I see that. Thank you."

Okay, so it hadn't been the most clever way to start a discussion about the caveman. Steeling herself, Libby tried again. "Jack told me you did double-duty today, helping Declan with the gazebo and all."

"That I did." Tito poked a long handled fork into a pot of boiling potatoes, turned off the burner, and carried the pot to the sink. Steam billowed as he drained the potatoes and set them aside.

"Did you two talk about anything . . . important?"

T took his time, filled a glass with water, and drank it in one long swallow. Then he set his hands on his hips and faced her, his cheeks damp from the heat of simmering pots and pans. "You got somethin' specific on your mind, little girl, or are you gonna take that order to table three?"

"I . . . um . . . nothing," she stammered, following his gaze to the warming lights, where a quartet of dinners waited to be served.

T chuckled as he wiped his brow. "If you're wonderin' whether or not I done changed my mind about Declan O'Shae, the answer is no." Shuffling past her, he returned to the stove.

Feeling foolish, Libby checked the order, then juggled the plates. Subtlety had never been T's strong suit. She might have known she couldn't put anything past him. And while he'd answered her unspoken question, she didn't feel any more secure where the caveman was concerned.

She gave T a final glance, only to find him still grinning. "I hate it when you do that," she muttered as his laughter followed her out of the stifling room.

Trying to finish the night without a hitch, Libby delivered the food and took another order. Still analyzing her feelings for the caveman, she raised her gaze just as he, Bob Grisham, and a group of fishermen sauntered in. Taking a table near the bar, the men joked loudly to Jack about their day, and Jack, who enjoyed their lively banter, hurried over with a round of beers.

All business, she walked to them and managed to jot down their orders without making eye contact with Declan. The night passed quickly, and before she knew it, the festival committee members were the only people left in the bar.

Libby busied herself at the sink while she listened to the various reports. Bob Grisham's sons would be arriving in a day or two to help with the construction. Olivia's niece and sister would be here soon to organize the children's activities, and a few other townspeople had relatives coming in as well. Things were shaping up nicely, as far as she could tell.

Lost in thought, she didn't see T until he was standing

beside her. "So, you ready to talk to Mr. O'Shae himself about what's on your mind?"

Libby rinsed the last of the dirty glasses, snapped open a clean terry-cloth towel and picked up a beer mug. "I have no intention of speaking to him about anything, and I'd appreciate it if you'd stop meddling in my life. I'm a grown woman with a son. I can—"

"No, you can't. Leastways not until you stop moonin' over the man and get your questions answered," he said smugly.

Not wanting to call attention to their discussion, Libby kept her voice low. "You are impossible. And I am not mooning over him."

"I know you like the man. And that bothers you a lot more than it should. You worry about the influence he's havin' on J.P. and what kind'a things he's done in his past. Seems to me you need to put your mind at ease so you can start enjoyin' life a little. The only way to do that is by gettin' some answers, and the only way to do that is to ask the man yourself."

Libby rubbed at an invisible spot on one of the glasses. "I've tried. All I get is double-talk."

Tito threw her another exasperating grin. "You're a fine-lookin' woman, Liberty Grayson. And a smart one. Didn't you learn anything about men up there in the big city?"

She set down the glass and folded her arms, shocked by his suggestion. "You mean I should bat my eyelashes and simper like some kind of empty-headed tease? Use my feminine wiles to get him to talk?"

"I didn't say that, 'zackly. But women have a secret weapon when it comes to men. I 'spect by now you know how to wield it."

Good grief! Did T meant *sex?* She'd never used sex as a weapon with Brett. Relationships were supposed to be built on honesty and trust and . . . Great, now she was putting herself and the caveman in a relationship. So much for promising they would have a simple, no-strings affair.

"I don't operate that way and you know it. In fact, right about now I'm thinking I should just demand he leave town. The fair is organized enough that we don't need him anymore, and he's made so much money from the folks around here he can consider himself paid. If he says no, I think I'm just going to tell everybody where I found him and—"

"Does where you found the man really mean that much?" T's simple statement came out more like a comment than a question.

She furrowed her brow. Jeez, the way he was grilling her, it sounded as if he thought she was the interloper. And what did he know about where she'd found Declan O'Shae? What had the caveman told him?

Taken aback by Tito's observations, she made up her mind. "Yes, it does, and unless I get answers, he's outta here."

His smile wide, T fixed his impudent gaze over her shoulder. "Hm-mm. Well then, I guess it's time you started askin' your questions again."

Libby didn't need to turn around to know who he was grinning at. Declan's breath warmed the nape of her neck, sending a sizzle of heat to her belly.

Standing so close she could smell his distinctive scent of the open sea, he said, "I'd give you answers, sweet Libby, if I thought you would believe them."

Chapter Fifteen

Declan followed Libby to Dream Cove, her grandmother's quilt draped over one arm. They'd left T and Jack in the Graysons' kitchen, sparring over the menu Tito had compiled for the fair. Luckily, Jack was so concerned over the cook's culinary plans, he hadn't bothered to give her even a glance when Libby announced they were going to spend some time together.

Libby walked quickly, sure-footed on the worn path, as if she had a singular purpose in mind. And she did, Declan realized, with more than a niggle of worry. She was finally going to receive answers to questions she'd pestered him with for the past several weeks.

Dream Cove, he thought, would be a fitting place to tell his tale. He'd found refuge there after his ship sank, and it was the spot where they'd first met. After he'd overheard her and T arguing at the Pink Pelican, he knew the time had come to explain his past. Libby was trustworthy, and she was the only one who'd seen him sleeping in the cave. Besides Tito, she would be the most logical person to believe him.

But there were risks. The people in this town respected her and listened to her advice. If he couldn't convince her that he was telling the truth, she might brand him a liar and end their liaison. Worse, she could get him tossed out of Sunset before he had time to find his treasure. If that happened, he would lose his life's work.

Knowing it was a possibility, Declan decided to confess everything—except the part about his buried strongbox. A man needed a few secrets, after all. Libby might be as honest as a nun, but J.P. had made him well aware of what his mother thought of hidden treasure and those who sought it.

Once he convinced her that he'd slept in that cave for over two hundred years, he would tell her the rest. When he found the damned gold, it would prove he spoke the truth.

They reached the beach, where Libby turned to him and said, "This is as good a spot as any for the quilt." Folding her arms under her bosom, she waited while he laid the coverlet flat on the sand.

The moon hung low in the starry sky, giving a Cheshire cat smile of approval. A balmy breeze cooled the air, sweeping the humidity out to sea. Libby sat and stretched her shapely legs, then leaned back and stared at the sky. Taking her actions as an invitation, Declan did the same.

She gave an embarrassed-sounding laugh as she continued to peruse the heavens. "Some nights when I come here and it's quiet like this, I swear I can feel my parents and grandmother watching over me from those stars. It sounds silly, but this is the one place I know I'm truly close to the three of them."

He took hold of one of her hands and clasped it tight. "It isn't silly. People need dreams, if only to have a reason for living."

Snatching her hand free, she used it to straighten a corner of the quilt. "I thought we agreed there would be no touching tonight," she admonished. "We're here because you promised to give me the truth."

"Correction: I promised I would never lie to you. You have to decide whether or not I'm telling the truth."

"Yeah, well, that just sounds like a lot more of your double-talk. Dreams are not reality, O'Shae, and reality is all that counts in today's world."

Oh, Libby, he thought, *how wrong you are.* "So a man with a dream holds no worth in your eyes?"

She *tsked,* openly showing her impatience. "Don't put words in my mouth. I had dreams of my own once, and nothing good came of them. I had to learn the hard way about reality, and I know you can't have it both ways."

"What about your son? Have you told J.P. he isn't allowed to dream? If so, then what does the lad have to look forward to in life?" Her startled expression confirmed that he'd hit her a low blow. But he was desperate. If Libby didn't accept the fact that dreams could exist, he had little chance of getting her to believe him.

"Leave J.P. out of this," she snapped. "And I'd appreciate it if you'd stop talking to him about finding lost treasure. The little guy is having a hard enough time adjusting to the real world without you filling his head with nonsense."

"Nonsense, is it? Then may I suggest you leave now? If you don't intend to be receptive, there's no use in us having this conversation."

She whipped her head to face him, her expression clouded with doubt. "I said I was willing to listen, didn't I? Go ahead, start talking."

Declan nodded, determined to do his best. Emulating a storyteller he'd once heard in the West Indies, he folded his legs in front of him and gazed over the open sea. There had been other times when he'd tried to recall the events that had led him to the cave, but he'd never had any success. Shoring up his resolve, he settled into the meditative pose and mentally forced himself back in time, back to that sun-filled, almost enchanted afternoon.

Determined to recall the day, he cleared his throat and began the only way he knew how. "Once upon a time—"

Libby sniggered, and he raised a brow. "Don't all stories start that way?" he asked, offended that she still wasn't taking him seriously.

"The fairy tales do. You're supposed to be telling the truth."

Declan wasn't sure whether he should laugh out loud or pound his chest in frustration. Libby Grayson was the most contrary, exasperating, obstinate woman he'd ever met. And the most compelling. If he didn't find a way to shut her up so he could think . . .

Leaning toward her, he grasped her by the shoulders and captured her lips with his. Libby moaned, just a tiny quiver of surrender, and heat flooded his loins. Suddenly, the desire to have her believe his tale, *to believe in him,* seemed infinitely more important than unearthing a trove of buried coins. Drugged by her response, he deepened the kiss, until she pulled away.

With her eyes flashing annoyance, Libby heaved a breath. "I said no touching . . . and . . . and no kissing, either. No hanky-panky of any kind. That was the deal we struck before I agreed to come here, and I'd thank you to stick to it."

He smothered a grin, pleased to see her flustered. Awash in a wave of hope, he closed his eyes and concentrated on the sounds and scents he could remember from that long-ago afternoon. As if watching a play taking place in his mind, he saw himself pacing the dock in Charleston. The *Lady Liberty*'s mast bobbed in the distance, her sparkling white canvas dancing against a crystalline blue sky. The call of vendors hawking their wares echoed in the air. His nostrils twitched at the smell of roasting meats and warming pastries, while the sound of Black Pete's cackle when the crusty old mate had first spied the amulet rang in his ears.

"Once upon a time, there was a young man from Dublin who longed to see the world. On his twenty-fifth birthday his father, one of the finest shipbuilders in all of Ireland, gifted him with a ship, and the young man decided to make his dream come true. After hiring a crew, he set sail for America, a land he'd heard was filled with opportunity.

"Shortly after his arrival, his new country became embroiled in war. He had no choice but to lead his men into battle, doing all he could to help them defeat the enemy. After a time, the war was won, and it became safe for them to sail freely. On the day he was to leave Charleston, the captain met a gypsy woman on the dock. He'd never seen her there before, but she seemed to know him and what he was about. After much discussion, the crone insisted he accept an amulet for his protection. Believing it to be harmless, he acquiesced, chose a token, and placed it about his neck. It was, I think, the true beginning of his adventure."

Libby clenched her fists on her thighs. She'd demanded to know the truth about Declan's past, and instead he had the nerve to sit there and make like the Brothers Grimm. What the heck did he think he was doing?

"The United States hasn't been involved in a sea battle since World War Two, O'Shae. Unless you've found the fountain of youth down here in Florida, you can't possibly be old enough to have fought in that war." Frowning, she cocked her head. "How old are you, anyway?"

A corner of his mouth lifted as he said wryly, "I'm afraid I'll need a bit of help sorting that out, after I've explained, of course. May I continue?"

Libby swallowed a sigh. His evasion of such a simple question gave her one more reason to insist he leave town. And this time she'd inform Jack and everyone else of her suspicions. "Sure, go ahead. I haven't been this entertained since I read J.P. a pirate story a few nights ago."

Casting her a doleful glare, Declan furrowed long fingers through his hair. "You would do well to hear the entire tale before you pass judgment."

Libby swiveled on her bottom until her body faced his. "Sorry; go ahead," she said, stifling a snort.

He cleared his throat. "Thank you. Now, where was I?"

"The ship's captain in your story has just been given an amulet for his protection."

"Aye, the amulet." Declan closed his eyes, then opened them slowly. His jaw clenched and he swallowed. "The captain wore the amulet from that point on, until the feel of it against his chest came as naturally as drawing a breath. It soothed him to sleep at night, just as it woke him in the morning, pulsing to the beat of his heart, as if it were a physical part of him."

"What did it look like, this ... um ... amulet?" Libby asked, suddenly remembering the broken medallion he kept under his shirt.

Ignoring her question, he continued. "They began their journey southward toward this very inlet, for it was here the captain and his crew planned to rest and decide what to do with their lives. But before they reached land, the devil's own breath blew up a terrible storm. The sky grew black. Rain streamed in blinding sheets and the wind howled like a banshee, tossing the boat as if it were a child's toy. In seconds, the ocean turned to blood before their eyes."

He stopped abruptly, then dropped his voice to a whisper. "Never before nor since had the captain seen anything like it."

Libby's breath caught in her throat. Declan was describing a hurricane, a force of nature so fierce that it destroyed everything in its path. To her knowledge, Andrew was the last storm of any magnitude to hit the Keys. She'd been a junior in college then, but she could still remember how worried she'd been about Jack and the people of Sunset.

"You were here when Andrew hit?" she asked, unable to believe he'd lived in Florida then. "That was back in Ninety-two. I thought you'd never been to Sunset before."

"This storm had no name, although I've learned that scientists now christen these deadly hurricanes. I think it curious anyone would want to humanize such a tool of the devil."

Libby sighed. There he was again, using antiquated language and an outdated thought process to complicate the issue. "It's a weather phenomenon, not a tool of the devil. Science is simple, once you understand it."

Declan turned to her, his face a grim mask. "I'll never accept the fact that such mass destruction is a whim of nature. Not when it destroys so many lives. Fate raised her hand and killed good men that day, changing my . . . changing the captain's life forever."

Resting her elbows on her knees, she blew out a breath. As a child, Grandma Martha had taught her to be open-minded and willing to accept all kinds of belief systems and points of view, but this was getting too fantastic for words. After Brett left for good, Libby feared there might be something inside her, some hidden character flaw that caused her to attract only deceitful men. Now she was starting to reel in the ones who needed a straitjacket.

"Are you trying to tell me that you're the captain in this story? That *you* led men into battle on a ship and later survived a hurricane?"

Stone-faced, Declan cut his gaze back to the sea. Staring up at the stars, he rubbed his palms on his thighs and took a deep breath. "The captain lashed himself to the wheel in hopes of saving his ship, but it was no use. The mizzen mast snapped in two as the vessel rose out of the water and split apart with a thunderous crack. He was forced to untie the ropes and jump overboard. To this day I wonder what would have happened if he'd remained bound to the wheel."

His desolate-sounding voice reached deep into Libby's heart, mesmerizing her with its sadness and desperation. It had taken her a few minutes, but she realized that no matter what she thought, Declan believed he was telling the truth.

"His body battered by planks of splintered wood, he tried to find his men, but the churning water pulled him under again and again, until all he could do was swim for his life. When he reached land the wind tossed him back into the sea, but he fought the waves and kept heading for shore.

Finally, he found the strength to crawl across the sand and drag his body to a small opening he'd spied in the rocks."

"The rocks? You mean a cave?" Libby glanced over her shoulder at the pile of boulders where she'd found him. "My cave?"

"Once inside, the captain managed to heave himself onto a ledge—a safe spot above the high-water mark. It was there he fell to rest, exhausted but sheltered from the storm. And there he slept . . . for a long, long time."

His plaintive sigh sent a chill through her heart. "Um . . . how long is long, O'Shae?"

"Very long."

Libby couldn't stop her voice from shaking. "Are we talking hours here? Or days, or what?"

Declan stared through hollow eyes, his expression shrouded in shadow. "Years. Many, many years."

"Years?" She swallowed hard against the lump in her throat. "Um . . . how many, exactly?"

This time, when Declan took her hands in his, she left them there. "Over two hundred, by my calculation."

"Two hundred?" Libby's common sense stood at attention. "You expect me to believe you slept in that cave for over two centuries?"

"Aye," he answered. "It was the year seventeen eighty-three. Two hundred and nineteen years had passed before you found your way inside and woke me with your touch. And I don't remember a second of it."

Libby sat at the kitchen table, her head resting in her hands. It was a clear and beautiful Sunday morning. She'd fed J.P. and Jack a hearty breakfast, then shooed them off to help with the building for the fair. Declan had yet to show, and she doubted he would after his incredible revelation.

Though she'd stewed over it most of the night, she couldn't deny the fact that Declan O'Shae had been gifted at birth. Along with natural leadership capabilities, a charming personality, and fantastic looks, he'd been blessed with a completely hypnotic way of relating a story.

He'd also kissed the Blarney stone. Several times. Or maybe he'd swallowed it whole.

But he'd kept his word. After he finished his tale, he hadn't begged her to believe him or swore he told the truth. He'd simply waited to hear what she had to say. And for all she knew, he was waiting still.

Because she, the woman who never shied away from confrontation, had risen to her feet and, like a coward, left him sitting on her grandmother's quilt gazing out to sea.

Exhausted, Libby swiped at her eyes, then glanced down at the pile of expenditure receipts she'd collected from the fair. Thanks to the caveman and his incredible story, she'd gotten very little sleep last night. Right now, the column of numbers in her ledger was swimming across the page like a school of drunken minnows.

She heard a knock on the door and raised her head. Before she could tell whoever it was to go away, Tito walked in, poured a cup of coffee, and took a seat at the table.

"You look like somethin' I wouldn't hang from the end of my fishin' line," he said a bit too happily. "Must be you got a few answers from Declan O'Shae last night."

Libby placed fingers to her temples and rubbed at the throbbing in her head. "I got answers, all right. Let's just say they were not what I wanted to hear."

T's snort echoed off the white enameled appliances. "Shoot, Liberty, they might not'a been what you wanted to hear, but they sure was what you needed. I hope you were smart enough to believe the man."

Her hands shading her eyes, she slid him a questioning gaze. "What did you do last night? Spy on us?"

"Don't need to spy to know what's true." He shot her a wounded look, then took a long swallow of coffee. "Declan O'Shae wouldn't know the truth if it jumped up and bit him on the—Well, you know where."

"What makes you say that?"

"He expects me to believe something so amazing . . . so crazy, it isn't even possible. It can't be."

T set his empty cup on the table and crossed his arms over his massive chest. "Let me ask you somethin', little girl. Do you believe in heaven?"

Resting her chin on her palm, Libby answered automatically. "Heaven? Of course I believe in heaven."

"And hell? What about hell?"

"The jury's still out on that one, but I like to think the Lord is forgiving. After all, there's atonement . . . and there's *atonement.*"

"Hm-mm. But you never seen either place, now have you?"

"Not yet." She quirked a brow. "What are you getting at?"

"Oh, nothin', less'n you want to explain to me how you can be so sure about places you ain't never seen, places no one you know has ever seen, and yet you can be so disbe-lievin' of a real, live flesh-and-blood man, tellin' you somethin' he knows to be true. How come you can believe in one and not the other?"

"Good question," Libby admitted, giving a wimpy shrug.

"What is it you got against this man? The fact that he showed up here without warnin'? 'Cause that ain't true. I done told you he was a'comin, now didn't I?"

Oh, great. How come whenever they had this argument it all looped back around to T's ominous predictions and his hoodoo magic? "But you don't know what he told me . . . or where he said he was from. He says he's—"

"You know what?" T interrupted. "I don't want to hear it. The man could be from outer space and I'd still feel the same way 'bout him."

She could only sigh in response. Her surrogate uncle was on a roll, and she didn't have the energy to stop him.

Tito drummed his fingers on the table. "You're punishin' Declan for another man's sins, Liberty, an' that ain't fair.

Since he's been here, O'Shae ain't never done one thing to give you a reason not to trust him.''

"I know.''

Stretching his mouth into a grin, T slammed the brakes on his tirade. "Well, now, there you go. Nice to know you're finally seein' reason.''

Libby dropped her forehead on the ledger. She was so confused she hurt, and not just in her head. The expression on Declan's face, so wistful yet tormented, the way he had scanned the ocean as if reliving the hurricane all over again, rose to her mind. And when he'd gazed at her so plaintively, asking her to believe with his eyes alone . . .

Her chest gave a painful lurch. She wanted to run, but there was no place left to go for comfort or protection. Oh, hell, she'd gone and done it again.

She'd fallen in love with another fast-talking man who had charmed his way into her life.

The revelation took her by surprise. She'd warned herself nothing good would happen if they became intimate, but this was far more than she'd expected. The man had talked to her as if he was an escapee from an insane asylum. He might even be dangerous. If she had half a brain, she'd curtail the time he spent with her child and never find herself alone with him again.

Especially after she'd sworn the next man she loved would be upstanding and forthright—and so honest *his* face should be etched on a penny instead of Lincoln's.

She sniffed back a tear and felt T's hand on her shoulder.

"There ain't no reason to cry, little girl. Bein' in love is a wonderful thing.''

Libby lifted her head and brushed at her cheek, but the tears continued to fall. "I'm not in love with him,'' she lied. "I can't be.''

"Hm-hmm.''

"You don't understand, T. If I love him, I have to believe him. And I don't know if I can do that.''

Tito handed her a paper napkin and waited until she blew

her nose. " 'Course you can. Just give it time. Everything's gonna work out fine. I got me a mojo workin', remember? And Declan O'Shae be a magic man.''

There were more people in the bar than usual for a Sunday night, and Libby guessed it was because of the fair. Two of Bob Grisham's sons and their families had arrived, as had Olivia's niece and sister. The older couple whose drink order she'd screwed up Saturday evening was there as well, busily chatting with guests at another table. A CD of Grandma Martha's Celtic music played in the background, while Jack tended bar and Libby served appetizers to the crowd.

Declan had managed to steer clear of the Pink Pelican the entire day, though J.P. shared with her over dinner everything the two of them had accomplished during the afternoon. From the sound of it, T had been off base. Instead of calling Declan a magic man, he should have used the word *super,* because Libby had grown tired just listening to her son recite a litany of their completed chores.

J.P. had helped Declan raise the posts on the gazebo.

Declan had inspected the booths, while J.P. held his clipboard; then they stored the final delivery of lumber inside the boathouse.

J.P. and Declan had played with the kittens, after which they had swept the garage bays and helped Frank unload cases of canned goods.

And last but not least, Declan and Frank had accepted a truckload of prizes for the booths, counted them out, and stacked them in the garage.

J.P. had come home so overtired, she'd had to tuck him in bed early so he wouldn't torture Ruth. The only way she could calm him down was to agree to join him tomorrow afternoon, when he accompanied Declan on a sail. Hazel had insisted Declan take the afternoon off as a thank-you for all his hard work. The caveman had accepted her offer and invited J.P. to come along.

Libby had actually promised she would pack a lunch.

She'd thought over and over again about the story Declan had told her last night, then ran the conversation she'd had with T through her mind a dozen more times. Logically, she knew there could be only one answer. But her heart kept inserting its own two cents, until all her thoughts funneled in another direction. Thanks to the caveman, J.P. seemed back on the road to becoming a trusting, happy little boy. That alone would cause a mother to have kind feelings toward a body.

Unfortunately, being in love with the man opened up an entirely different can of worms.

The front door swung open and Declan sauntered in. His brilliant blue gaze scanned the restaurant and locked on her like a tracking beam. When he nodded in her direction, his face set in a questioning but congenial expression, she knew exactly what he wanted.

"Hey, O'Shae, sing us one of them Irish songs, would'ya?" called Bob, oblivious to the electricity arcing across the room. "I been tellin' my boys how you should be makin' records and they want to hear."

A few people clapped, and Declan held up his hands. "In a minute. First I need to wet my whistle."

The customers laughed, several offering to buy him a beer. Olivia made space for him at her table and he sat down. Jack drew a frosty mug and ambled to his side. And through the fanfare, Declan continued to stare, until Libby felt her cheeks burn and her stomach tie itself into a knot.

Finally, he nodded a thank-you to Jack and raised the mug, drinking half the beer in one long swallow. After wiping his mouth with his hand, he cocked his head, and the crowd grew quiet. Music trilled through the hushed room, and she turned to find T at the CD player, his hand on the volume control.

Declan closed his eyes, waiting for the right note, and finally let his voice soar. Libby didn't think for a moment that anyone in the bar understood a word of the ancient

Celtic song, but it didn't matter. Bright and sweet, his tenor filled the room and her heart with its plaintive, piercing sound. The female customers grew teary-eyed, while many of the men ran hands over their faces or discreetly cleared their throats.

Not a shuffle or sneeze or comment was made until he hit the song's final note and slowly opened his eyes. After a full five seconds of quiet, the room echoed with applause. Declan grinned and lifted his glass, toasting their boisterous approval.

T turned down the music a notch and sidled over to her. "Ain't no way a man can have a voice like that and be a liar, Liberty."

She stared down at her fingers, clenching the towel she'd been using to scrub the bar. Now there was logic for you: The man could sing, therefore he was incapable of telling a lie. Too tired to explain to Uncle T the flaw in his thinking, she raised her gaze to find the British couple and Declan involved in what looked to be a serious discussion. Good, maybe if he made some new friends he'd leave her alone for the night. She carried a tray of dishes into the kitchen. When she returned, Declan was waiting for her.

"The festival committee isn't meeting tonight. Families have arrived, so we're turning in early. Jack said he would close the bar. Will you come home with me, just for a short while?"

Gazing into his eyes, she remembered to breathe. "I . . . um . . . I guess so. But I should warn you, I haven't made up my mind yet . . . about things."

"I know. And it doesn't matter. I just need to be with you. There's time enough for you to believe."

Chapter Sixteen

Libby welcomed the short trip to Declan's cottage. It was strange comfort, knowing she could hide a while longer under cover of the night. After everything he'd told her, she was amazed it felt so right to be walking at his side like this, with his hand sitting low on her back as they made their way across the empty street. Even more incredible was the fact that his touch still made her tremble like a freshman on a first date.

Once inside his dimly lit cabin, an almost palpable aura of calm filled the sultry air, as if she'd left the outside world and entered a place of peace and safety. Instead of being frightened, she was soothed.

Declan seemed to feel it, too, this need for each of them to have private thoughts. When he closed the front door and threw the bolt, he didn't rush to take her into his arms. He turned on the ceiling fans to stir the air, then came to her slowly, stopping just close enough for her to catch the drugging scent of the wind and sea on his body. If he could find a way to bottle the invigorating outdoor aroma, he'd have women flocking to him like—

"Would you care for something to drink? A glass of wine, perhaps, or water?" Declan asked, interrupting her wayward thoughts.

"I don't think so, but thank you anyway," Libby answered, taking a step back. "I want to get this over with."

His boyish smile gleamed in the faint light coming through the kitchen window. "By *this* I take it you mean my execution. I suppose I should ask you to be merciful and make it quick."

She paced to the sofa and slumped onto the cushions. How could he joke about something so serious? "It's not an execution, you dope."

"Ah," Declan said, his voice tinged with amusement. "That's a worry off my mind." The sofa rocked with his body weight as he settled down beside her. "If not my execution, then why did you agree to come here so readily? Most of the time you put up a fight before I get you to myself."

Libby made an unladylike noise deep in her throat. "But it never does much good, does it? You always seem to get your way and we end up sleeping together. Guess I'm just another woeful example of a weak-willed NOW dropout. It must make you feel great."

"Though we've shared a bed, to my knowledge we've done very little sleeping. And the idea that you come to me only because you feel threatened certainly doesn't make me 'feel great.' You must realize by now that I would never do anything to harm you, or jeopardize the way you appear in the eyes of your son or the people of this town."

Libby inched away from the brush of his thigh pressing intimately against her own. It was hard enough to think when they were together in the same room; she couldn't remember her own name when they were touching.

"Since we say we're telling one another the truth, I have to confess I've been a coward. I should have acknowledged the . . . um . . . attraction I've felt for you and acted like an adult about it."

"Attraction?" His dark brows rose to question marks. "Then you *do* want me in your bed? You admit you've been coming to me willingly?"

The force of her sigh lifted her shoulders. She plucked at the hem of her shorts. "Yes, I've been having sex with you willingly. At least, I have until last night."

"Ah, yes. Last night. The night of my revelation."

"It was more than a revelation, O'Shae. How can you expect me to swallow that story—unless you forgot to mention the part about your being an escapee from an insane asylum."

Reaching out, his finger traced the line of her jaw. "I was afraid you might say something like that—or worse. I'm not insane, but I'm not going to beg you to believe me. In my time, everyone knew I was a man of honor. And I've already promised to always tell you the truth."

Libby leaned forward. Resting her elbows on her knees, she stared at the floor. "In your time . . . you mean the eighteenth century, during the War for Independence?"

"Aye. Seventeen eighty-three."

She raised her hands to her forehead; the outlandish statement made her head throb. "God, don't you realize what you're asking of me? What you expect me to accept is not only physically impossible, it's—"

"Preposterous? The ravings of a madman?"

She sighed as she turned to look at him. "Exactly."

"And there's not a chance in hell you'll ever believe me?"

Placing her palms flat on her thighs, Libby straightened her back. She was too confused to answer. The words Tito had used in Declan's defense thrummed in her brain, battering what little common sense she managed to muster.

If I love him, I have to believe him.

But how could she tell the caveman she loved him when she wasn't used to the idea herself yet? Love was supposed to make you elated, dazzled . . . happy. Never had she heard that being in love would cause such a painful burning in her heart. Then again, not many normal women fell in love with nutcases. Maybe this weird reaction only happened to equally insane females.

Loving Declan O'Shae, she realized, was tantamount to being the victim of an earthquake or a volcanic eruption. Like an uncontrollable force of nature, the disaster lasted for scant moments, leaving nothing but destruction in its wake.

Could she rise above the destruction and continue with her life if—no—*when* he left? More importantly, could her son?

"I want to believe you, O'Shae, for nothing else than J.P.'s sake. If I truly thought you were a raving lunatic, I'd be wrong not to protect him. But the things you told me are so overwhelming ... I need more time," she said on a whisper. "I need to think."

Declan grasped her chin with cupped fingers. His breath tickled her ear, turning the tingle in her stomach to a tremor.

When his mouth nuzzled her throat, a shock wave of longing vibrated through her system.

"Take all the time you need to think on what I've revealed, then open your mind to the possibilities. For tonight, it will have to be enough."

Her breasts grew warm, then hot, as he traced a line of kisses from her ear to her jaw. Catching her breath between his parted lips, he found her breast and thumbed a budding nipple, sending her into a spasm of need.

His gentle seduction made her feel as if she was the most desirable woman in the world. She could almost believe what he told her ... could almost believe in *him*. Surrendering to the kiss, she leaned back against the sofa and tangled her hands in his hair.

Declan inhaled Libby's womanly scent. Hearing her soft sighs and tasting her tremulous kisses, he wanted nothing more than to bury himself inside her and forget where he'd come from or how he'd arrived. All he wanted was the here and now, with her pliant and quivering beneath him.

When Libby melted into his chest, he slid an arm under her thighs and another against her back, then rose to his feet and headed for the bedroom. With their gazes locked, he set her onto the mattress. After tugging his T-shirt over his head, he undid the metal snap and zipper of his trousers and pushed the pile of clothes and shoes out of the way, until he stood before her fully aroused, offering all he had to give.

It seemed an eternity before she undid the buttons of her blouse and the clasp of her bra. Slipping the garments off her shoulders, she stood and dropped her shorts and underwear to the floor, then sat back on the bed.

When she reached out to stroke his throbbing flesh, every muscle in Declan's body drew taut as a bowstring. Exercising control, he clenched and unclenched his hands. "Don't make me beg, Libby. Invite me to lay with you—give me that much at least."

Her expression turned resigned as she studied him. "I'm a grown woman, O'Shae. I can handle whatever happens between us. Just promise me one thing—as long as you're in Sunset, you won't hurt my son. If you can do that, I won't call you a liar or tell people I think you're crazy."

In silent agreement, he retrieved a condom from his nightstand and held it out to her. She took the foil packet and opened it, then rolled the sheath down and over his rigid shaft. If not for the fact that her sigh tore at his heart, Declan would have shouted with joy.

He knelt beside her on the bed. "You're a tough one, Libby Grayson, but I'll agree to your terms. Only remember this: one day I'll have proof of what I say. And when I do, I want to hear from your lips that you believe me."

In answer, she stretched out her arms in a gesture of welcome. Molding to her side, Declan traced the contours of her ear with his tongue, then set his hand at the apex of her thighs and delved into her sweetness. She moaned, and he plied slow nibbling kisses down her neck to her breast, until he found a tightened bud and began to suck.

Libby writhed against his searching mouth, clutching him to her breast. Like a match to tinder, he touched the secret place that ignited her desire. Her eyes widened as she arched from the mattress. Her body uncoiled with the force of her climax and she came apart in his hands.

Declan rose to his knees and settled between her thighs. With their fingers entwined overhead, he entered her swift and true. Riding the crest of her passion, he rocked to the pulsing of her aftershocks as he emptied himself inside her.

Finally, exhausted and content, he drew her close and held her until she fell asleep in his arms.

Humming a nameless tune about pirates sailing the high seas, J.P. marched soldierlike ahead of Libby to the dock. If she didn't know better, she'd swear the caveman had told her son the story he'd concocted about his past. It would be just like Declan to fill the boy's head with more fairytale nonsense. But he had sworn to her that he wouldn't tell J.P. any more tall tales.

If she loved him, she had to believe him.

Last night had been as frustrating as it was incredible. Declan hadn't pushed her into making love but had let her make the choice. And just as he'd promised, he hadn't badgered her to accept his story. All he'd done was love her. They'd spent the night in each other's arms. He'd awakened her just before dawn and walked her home, then kissed her tenderly at her front door. Not only had the intimate encounter reinforced the love Libby knew was growing for him in her heart, it had also cemented their differences.

Declan truly believed he was some kind of Revolutionary War–era Rip Van Winkle who had slept away two hundred years of his life. Even Brett hadn't been that much of a dreamer. Just her lousy luck to have gone back on her promise to herself and fallen in love with a man who belonged in a fairy tale, or maybe an episode of ''The

Twilight Zone.'' If she wasn't so miffed that she'd done such a stupid thing, she might be laughing right now.

But today was for J.P. She'd spent so much time on preparations for the fair, she'd been neglecting him. As the date drew near, her duties for the festival would probably double, which meant today might be the last afternoon they could enjoy together for quite a while, even if they had to share it with Declan O'Shae.

J.P. had chattered all morning about their planned outing; he'd even helped Tito make sandwiches and bag cookies for their lunch. When one of Bob Grisham's daughters-in-law offered to take the noon shift at the Pink Pelican, Libby no longer had a reason to disappoint her son.

Gripping the handles of the soft-sided cooler, she hoisted it in her arms, regretting the fact that she'd packed enough food for an army. Besides the sandwiches and cookies, the cooler held ice, a container of lemonade, a bowl of fruit salad, and all they needed in the way of utensils. When Tito asked her if she wanted to take along her own refrigerator, she hadn't given him the satisfaction of a smile.

She heard the clamoring sounds of construction well before they reached the dock. Mingled with the buzzing of saws and the whine of electric drills were the blaring notes of a band at practice ... or a chorus of serenading alley cats. Screaming Mean and their instruments had arrived.

It didn't take long to locate the quartet of raggedly dressed boys crowded under a yellow-striped tent in the marina parking lot. Before she could stop him, J.P. ran toward the fledgling rock band as if an invisible line reeled him into their presence.

Mesmerized, he stared up at the musicians, then back at her, jumping like a sunfish on a hot skillet. "Way cool, Mom. Can we stay and listen for a while?"

Once my fillings stop vibrating, Libby thought, gritting her teeth. Ducking down, she shouted, "I don't think so, honey. We have a date to go sailing, remember?"

The racket was so loud, she didn't notice the caveman

until he appeared at their side. With his mouth agape, he ogled the band, then stuck a finger in his ear and jiggled it in exaggeration.

J.P. giggled happily as he said, "Hey, Declan, Mom made us lunch, just like she said she would." He pointed to the compact disk tucked in the waistband of Declan's cutoffs. "What's that thing?"

After handing the young man at the mike the CD, he cupped a hand around his mouth and shouted, "Something the boys said they would work on for me. Are you ready to go?"

"Yeah, I guess so." Dragging the toe of his sneaker in the grass, he gave a final yell. "But if they're still here when we come back, I want to watch . . . if Mom let's me."

Libby knocked the heel of her palm against her temple and nodded toward the dock. Laughing out loud, Declan ruffled J.P.'s windblown hair. When her son placed his small hand into the caveman's larger one, a knot of tears threatened to choke off her air supply. Declan grabbed the cooler with his other hand and headed for the far end of the marina, giving her no choice but to keep up or stay behind and lose her hearing.

The day was warm, but a brisk breeze blew through the cloudless blue sky—perfect sailing weather. They walked past ramshackle fishing trawlers, huge pleasure boats, sleek catamarans and delicate sailboats designed for two, before they came to Hazel's pride and joy, a single-masted, twenty-foot sloop named *The Home Free*.

Agile as a panther, Declan jumped the three feet into the boat. After placing their lunch to the side of the ladder, he plucked J.P. from the top rung and set him down lightly next to the cooler. Holding out a hand, he guided Libby down the ladder and onto the deck.

"I'm glad you decided to join us," he said when her sneakers hit the wood.

Adjusting her sunglasses, she took in the polished teak, gleaming brass, and snow-white canvas draped across the boom. "It's been a while since I've been sailing. I'm afraid I won't be much help."

Declan's grin broadened to a full-blown smile. "Not as long as it's been for me, I'd wager. But you needn't worry; I can handle this wee bit of a ship with one hand tied behind my back."

J.P. tugged at the hem of Declan's shorts. "I'm going to help, right? You said I could help."

"Aye, lad, that I did. But first, how about you and your mother go below and stow lunch while I see what I can do about launching us out to sea?"

He swaggered away with the rolling gait of a sailor, and Libby quickly rejected the idea of how well he fit the bill of a ship's captain. Determined to make the day a good one for J.P., she took the stairs to the galley. She stored the cooler in the bottom of the refrigerator while J.P. found the head, and beyond that the bunk-lined room that slept four. After explaining a little of what she understood of the ship's layout to him, Libby felt the tremble of an engine and realized they were motoring from the dock.

Before she could say a word, J.P. scrambled up the ladder. By the time she joined them, Declan was manning the wheel with one hand while helping J.P. into a life jacket with the other. She took over, strapping the bright orange canvas bubble tightly to his little-boy chest, while Declan guided them out of the marina and into the open sea.

Declan ordered J.P. to take a seat on the far side of the boat. Libby wanted to sit beside him but knew her son wouldn't approve of the idea, so she continued to play the part of an invited guest ... until the heat from the near-blinding sun poured over her, and she remembered the sunscreen she'd tucked in her bag.

Jumping from her bench seat, she went back to the galley. When she returned with the lotion, Declan had the sail unfurled and J.P. was standing in front of him with his hand on the wheel.

"I wondered what happened to you," Declan said with an easy grin. "Not seasick, I hope."

Trying to stay upright against the lean of the boat, Libby shook her head as she tottered back to her seat. J.P. beamed up at her, his face wreathed in a smile. His tiny fingers barely fit around the wheel, but that didn't stop him from holding on tight.

"Declan's letting me steer."

"I see, honey, and I hate to cut your fun short, but you need to wear sunblock or you'll get a nasty burn. Come over here so I can grease you up. It'll only take a minute."

"Aw, Mom, I already got a tan." He held out a thin arm for her inspection. "See?"

"Having a tan doesn't mean you won't burn, young man."

J.P. craned his head to stare up at Declan. "Obey your mother, lad. And when she's through, I'll ask her to do the same for me."

Libby bit back a retort regarding the way her son looked to Declan for approval and set to her task. It only took a few minutes to cover J.P.'s pouting face and any body part not protected by clothing with the lotion. When finished, he scooted back to his place at the wheel and set his hands next to Declan's, then braced his sneakers a shoulder's width apart, a caveman in miniature.

Libby slathered the creamy liquid onto her legs, then took off her sunglasses and skimmed her palms across her face, neck and arms. She looked up to find Declan staring with one dark brow cocked jauntily.

"I thought you were a compassionate woman. Surely you don't want to see me burned to a cinder," he prodded in a teasing voice.

"Stow it, O'Shae. You're tan enough to handle it." She sat the sunglasses back firmly on her nose, hoping he wouldn't see the trepidation in her eyes.

"But you just told me havin' a tan didn't mean I wouldn't burn," piped J.P. "You got to do Declan, too."

Caught in a web of her own making, Libby avoided the

caveman's superior gaze and stood beside him at the wheel. After squirting a dollop of lotion onto her palm, she set down the bottle and rubbed her hands together. All business, she gingerly applied the sunblock, smoothing it over a corded biceps, down a hardened forearm to his wrists and the back of his hand. Without raising her eyes, she sidled to the other side and repeated the action.

When she tried to scoot behind him to get to the back of his neck, the big dolt made the magnanimous gesture of moving all of three inches to make room. Pressed up against his backside, she laid the flat of her hands on his shirt, tightening inside when she felt his muscles do that impossible rippling thing under her palm.

Glancing over his shoulder, he waggled his brows. "Perhaps you'd like me to remove my shirt."

"You're fine as is," she muttered. The frustrating man knew very well what touching him was doing to her insides, and he was determined to enjoy it.

She set her lips in a thin line and gave him a sharp shove, but it was like pushing against a boulder. The rumble of his silent laughter vibrated under her fingers. Annoyed at the idea that he knew exactly what she was feeling, she grabbed one earlobe and gave a serious tug.

"Jay-sus, woman, you damn near pulled me ear off!" Declan shouted, wincing under the pinch.

"Watch your language, O'Shae," Libby said smugly, sliding out from behind him. "And watch where you're going." She pointed to a fast-growing dot in the distance. "We're heading straight for that island. If you're not careful, we'll run aground."

"I've checked the tide. We should be fine. Besides, I know this channel well." Squaring his shoulders, he steered toward the spot of land, one of many unnamed keys that dotted the area's waterways.

Libby took a seat and watched as he expertly guided the boat toward the shore. After giving J.P. the order to hold steady, he hopped across the deck and dropped sail, then returned to the stern and started the small engine used to guide the boat. They motored so close, she was certain they'd end up on a sandbar or scrape bottom on a coral reef, but it didn't happen. The boat rocked from side to side as Declan dropped anchor and shoved his shoes into a canvas bag he'd slung over his shoulder. After stripping down to red cotton swim trunks, he climbed over the side.

In water up to his waist, he reached out his arms to J.P. "Jump, lad. I'll catch you and take you to shore."

Libby stood, ready to protest, but her son had no qualms. Quick as a monkey, he tugged off his shoes, then scuttled to the rail and took a flying leap, landing securely against Declan's broad chest.

"Gather our lunch. I'll be back shortly," the caveman called as he waded to shore.

"Well," Libby said to herself with a disgruntled *hmph*. It was bad enough J.P. obeyed Declan's every command; now the man was expecting her to do the same. Stomping to the galley, she decided to give him a piece of her mind. Nowhere in their agreement did it say she had to take orders, even if he was doing a fairly good job of playing captain.

Libby was dragging the cooler out of the fridge when she felt the boat rock beneath her. She turned, ready to bite Declan's head off, but the words stuck like peanut butter to the roof of her mouth. Bare-chested, he stood with his hands on his narrow hips, his swimsuit molded to his muscular thighs. Drops of water sparkled on his hair and face, bathing his cheeks and lips in a shimmer of diamonds.

"A woman who follows orders. Just what I'd hoped to find."

Swallowing hard, she wiped her damp hands on her shorts. "Yeah, well, don't get too comfortable with it."

One long step brought him so close that if she wanted, she could run her fingers through the swirling dark hair on his finely sculpted chest. Exercising self-control, she raised her gaze and found herself entranced by the sparkling drops clinging to his spiky lashes.

"So, what made you choose this key?" she asked, pacing backward. "I didn't think you knew the islands that well."

He sidled closer, until she hit her bottom on the small Formica rectangle that served as a table. Caging her between his arms, he reached around and grabbed the cooler handles. "If you say so."

It was her turn to raise a brow. "Have you been here before?"

"I have. Would you like to know the year?" One corner of his mouth twitched upward.

She rolled her eyes. "Wait, don't tell me—let me guess. Seventeen eighty-three?"

"Seventeen seventy-eight. But you're catching on." He lifted the cooler over her head and marched up the steps. "Come along, madam. There are two hungry men waiting to be fed."

Libby shook her head. What the idiot lacked in brains, he certainly made up for with imagination. She arrived on deck to find him hanging off the edge of the boat, waiting for her.

"Shall I carry you?" he asked, a sly smile on his lips.

She ignored his offer, took off her shoes, and tossed them onto the deck. Swinging a leg over the side, she waved at J.P., who was calling to her from the shore, and slipped into the water. Admiring the easy way he carried the cooler, she asked wryly, "What did men do in the seventeen hundreds? Spend all their time lifting cannonballs and kegs of ale?"

"Not all their time. But it was different back then." He waded beside her, the cooler balanced on his shoulder as if it weighed no more than a feather. "I enjoyed working beside my men. That's why I'm satisfied doing physical labor. I couldn't imagine sitting at a computer all day, as so many people do now."

"Brett never lifted anything heavier than a paper clip," she said, concentrating on making her way to her son. "He wasn't very physical."

"You mean he never carried you to bed, or swung you in his arms, just for the joy of it?"

"Not unless he wanted a hernia, he didn't. Besides, it doesn't matter anymore. He's out of my—our life for good."

They reached the shore in silence. J.P. raced into the water to his knees and Declan scooped him up and tossed him over his other shoulder, then ran with him onto the beach. While she unpacked lunch, the two played at tossing a Frisbee that Declan had whipped from his canvas sack much like a magician pulling a rabbit from his hat.

Their hearty male laughter filled the beach, reminding her of how long it had been since her son had played full out, like any normal, carefree little boy. It had been weeks since he'd talked of death or made a comment about losing someone he cared about.

Just her luck to owe the amazing transformation to a man she loved, but really didn't know.

Chapter Seventeen

"This is important work, huh, Declan? My mom says we're buildin' a brandstand. It's the place the kids are gonna go to hear stories and do face painting and stuff. And at night the screamers are gonna play music here, too."

Declan shuddered at the idea of defining anything Screaming Mean played as music, but such was the way of the twenty-first century. Besides, the townsfolk had requested he sing on both nights of the fair, just before the closing fireworks display. When Bob Grisham asked if his son's band could make an attempt at replicating the ancient Celtic melodies and accompany him, Declan hadn't the heart to say no. Now he was stuck rehearsing daily with a bunch of cocky, tone-deaf wags barely dry behind their ears.

"I believe the word is grandstand, lad. And yes, it's going to be an important place," he finally acknowledged.

He raised the ladder and got ready to climb onto the roof. The gazebo would indeed be the hub of the fair, and it was up to him to see to its construction, including the roof, which he'd hoped to finish today.

It was unfortunate that he wouldn't be around to celebrate

future Independence Days with the people of Sunset, but yesterday's outing had left its mark. He hadn't realized how much he missed the freedom of the open sea until he'd ridden the waves again. Once he found his treasure, he was going to buy a boat and catch up with the world, sail to all the places he'd missed in his former life and—

Declan felt a tug on his belt and looked down to see J.P. staring at him. "What'cha doing?"

"Thinking," he said with a sigh.

" 'Bout what?"

"Too many things to mention," he answered, not wanting to worry the boy. At times, J.P.'s puppy-dog adoration weighed heavy on his mind. It would be hard saying good-bye to the little fellow when he left.

"Are you worryin' about your treasure?" J.P. asked in a whisper. " 'Cause Mom told me you don't have one."

Declan raised a brow. "Did she, now?"

"Uh-huh. She said you were makin' up a fairy story when you told me about it. She says you're a dreamer, just like my dad, and I shouldn't take anything you say as god-spell."

Grinding his molars, Declan held back a frown. How dare the woman compare him to that blackguard who'd left her and her son, when he'd been nothing but honest with her about where he'd come from? He'd—

J.P. gave his belt another jerk. "You want to know somethin'?"

"I suppose so," he muttered, gathering a handful of shingles. Setting a foot on the bottom rung of the ladder, he waited for the boy's pronouncement.

"I believe you anyway."

Like a popped balloon, the breath left Declan's lungs in a quick burst of air. Of late, he'd been walking a fine line between mother and son. It wouldn't be proper for him to undermine Libby's parenting skills, but his current predicament was proof positive of the impossible. If he agreed with J.P., he'd be calling Libby a liar; if he told the boy he'd concocted the story, he would lose face. Either way, he would be no better than the man who'd abandoned his own child.

Luckily, he didn't have to take a stand, as Libby was bearing down on them like a clipper ship under full sail. He set down the shingles and waited, admiring the way her long gauzy skirt molded to her legs and lushly rounded hips as she made her way down the sidewalk from the Pink Pelican.

"J.P.," she said sharply, ignoring Declan, "aren't you supposed to be helping Ruth in her garden right now? I thought that was the deal you two worked out this morning, after you broke her kitchen window."

J.P. hung his head. "I forgot."

"And you." She gave Declan a mutinous glare. "Why are you letting him shirk his duty?"

Declan placed a hand on J.P.'s shoulder. "I had no idea the lad was being disciplined." Hunkering down, he caught the boy's chin with his fingers. "Is it true you have another place to be right now, and a promise to keep?"

J.P. rubbed a fist in his eye. "I didn't mean to crack Ruth's window, honest. I was just playin' with the Frisbee you gave me and it sort of slipped."

Declan choked down his rising guilt. He'd made J.P. a gift of the simple plastic disk after they'd tossed it on the beach. It was his fault the boy was in trouble.

He stood and faced Libby. "Does Ruth have replacement glass? Has she made arrangements to have the window fixed?"

"I'm not sure. But it doesn't make any difference. John Patrick is supposed to work off his lack of good judgment by pulling weeds in her garden. It's his responsibility to—"

"I gave him the toy, so I'll help him take care of it." Pushing on J.P.'s back, he guided the boy ahead of him down the sidewalk. "If anyone asks, they can find us at Ruth's bungalow."

Libby watched her son and Declan march away. Feeling like the school principal every student hates, she sat on the steps of the gazebo and set her chin on her palm. Okay, so she'd come on a little strong, but the sight of J.P. hanging around the caveman when he should have been taking care of business had driven her to the edge of her patience.

She'd been on her way to the bank to make a deposit in the festival fund and visit their suppliers when she'd stopped by Ruth's to see if there was anything the older woman needed. When she walked around to the backyard, she'd been shocked to find her weeding the garden alone, with no knowledge of J.P.'s whereabouts. It had taken Libby only a moment to figure out what her son was doing. The idea that J.P. had bonded so strongly with the caveman that he dared to disobey a direct order really rankled.

Sighing, she stood and reached into her bag for her keys. Just then, the same pair of tourists who'd shown up on and off at the Pink Pelican for the last weeks sauntered her way. Apparently her drink mixup hadn't bothered them a bit.

"Hello. We were hoping you'd be free. If you have some time, my wife and I would like to speak with you," said the man. His clipped accent and smartly tailored resort clothes reinforced Libby's original assumption—the pair had money and came from somewhere in the British Isles.

"Sure, I have a minute. Do you want to talk here or in the Pink Pelican?" During the course of the conversation she might even be able to find out why they were still hanging around Sunset, when the town had no more than an afternoon's worth of sightseeing to its name.

"Right here is fine. By the way, I don't believe we've been properly introduced," said the woman. "I'm Virginia Applewaithe and this is my husband, Clive."

After shaking hands with them, Libby asked how she could be of help.

"To be honest, we've fallen in love with your charming little village," gushed Mrs. Applewaithe. "Since you seem to be someone on whom the residents depend, we were wondering if you might be willing to discuss a mutually beneficial idea we've had concerning the town."

Libby smiled warily. "I'm not sure if it's good or bad—

that the town depends on me, I mean. Though I was raised here, I've only recently returned. I might be able to answer a few questions, but I—"

"You are the treasurer of the upcoming festival, are you not?" asked Clive. "And one of its main organizers?"

"Yes, with the help of Mr. O'Shae."

"Wonderful." Virginia pressed folded hands against the front of her lime green silk blouse. "Since it's the festival and Mr. O'Shae we want to speak to you about."

Libby frowned at the bizarre turn the conversation had taken. "I can probably help if it's fair business, but I'm not Mr. O'Shae's keeper. I suggest you speak with him yourself."

"We've tried," Virginia continued with a sigh. "But the second we mention his singing, he refuses to talk to us. He's very stubborn."

"His singing? You want to talk about Declan's voice?"

Clive pulled a business card from the back pocket of his ivory-colored linen slacks and handed it to Libby as his wife continued talking. "Back home, Clive is president of a small recording company called Sounds of Time. Nothing fancy or grand, you understand, but well-respected in classical music circles. We cater to a more eclectic listener, one who enjoys the finer works and older, forgotten folk tunes. It's uncanny the way Mr. O'Shae has managed to capture the essence of such ancient melodies. We'd like to offer him a recording contract, but the contrary man won't even listen to our terms."

"You want to offer Declan a contract to make records . . . um . . . CDs?" asked Libby, dumbfounded.

Clive nodded. "And a whole lot more."

Later that evening, the festival committee met in the Pink Pelican. With less than three days left until the fair, Libby's head was spinning. Thanks to Bob Grisham and the construction crew, the booths were up and ready on the dock. Olivia,

Mary, and the ladies of the town planned to spend every second of their spare time sewing red, white and blue bunting and hanging it on the booths as well as the signs that had been erected around town. Tito and Jack, along with Phil and Don, had filled the Queen of the Sea's walk-in refrigerators with food and drink. The perishables were scheduled for early morning delivery on the day of the fair, which was also when a few of the nearby eating establishments would arrive to man the specialty food booths.

After he'd repaired Ruth's kitchen window, Declan had finished the gazebo roof, but he hadn't stopped by for any of his scheduled meals. According to a report from her son, Libby learned that the caveman had plans to practice with Screaming Mean every afternoon from now until opening day in one of Hazel's empty storage buildings. J.P. also reported that the band was actually starting to sound "really good."

Now, as the committee members assembled, she kept her eye on the door. After the Applewaithes' surprising revelation, she'd invited them to attend tonight's meeting. Besides the contract they were prepared to offer Declan, their magnanimous plan to aid Sunset was so startling that there was no way she could accept or reject it on her own.

When Declan finally sauntered into the bar, looking drawn and badly in need of a shave, an unexpected wave of tenderness swelled inside her. Libby had the crazy urge to rush over with a cold beer and a plate of hot food . . . then take him home, where she could give him a consoling backrub, or a—

The too-intimate thought caused her stomach to roll. Her scalp prickled and she raised her head to find Declan regarding her through eyes crinkling with boyish mischief, almost as if he could read her mind. Definitely not a good sign. Hoisting the tray of drinks, she walked to a table and began to serve her guests.

"Hey, Libby, did you hear about Riley Jones? Smashed his thumb this mornin' hammerin' together one of the booths.

His wife had to run him over to the medical center to get it taken care of,'' said Frank, caught up in his favorite pastime of spreading gossip.

A few of the others commented on the incident, and before she knew it the room echoed with stories of one near catastrophe after another. Velma Gibson had fainted from the heat yesterday afternoon while washing the front windows of her what-not shop. Orin Thatcher took a tumble from his boat when he tried to anchor a new flag on the prow. The list of accidents was so long, it was all she could do not to rush to a phone, call the closest rescue squad, and ask them to stand by from now until the end of the fair.

''That's nothing,'' one of the fisherman added as a finale. ''My Janie was hangin' bunting this mornin' and the darn step stool she was standin' on collapsed right out from under her. Thought she'd broke her ankle for sure, but it's just a sprain. She's plannin' on spending the next few days in bed.''

Someone made a risqué comment about the pair of seventy-year-olds spending time together in the sack, and the crowd hooted with laughter. Libby glanced toward the bar in time to see her grandfather wink, only the teasing gesture wasn't directed at her but at Olivia, who returned Jack's wink as if they were two hormone-riddled teenagers at a high school mixer. Holy moly, they were flirting!

Scanning one wrinkled but happy face after another, it dawned on her that not only were the senior citizens having an enjoyable time adjusting to the rigors of a full workload—they were reveling in it. Before she could process the information, the door opened and the room grew quiet as Clive and Virginia Applewaithe strolled into the bar.

''Mr. and Mrs. Applewaithe,'' said Libby, hoping to put them at ease, ''I'm glad you could join us.''

Clive showed a mouthful of perfectly capped teeth as he took her hand and pumped it vigorously. ''It's Clive and Ginnie, and please, don't let us intrude on your meeting. Just tell us when we can speak.''

A raft of whispered comments filled the air, and Libby had a fairly good idea what they were about. The Applewaithes were strangers and this gathering was private. Why had she invited them?

She caught Declan glowering, straightened her shoulders, and headed toward the bar. If the caveman didn't want a recording career, that was his business, but it was up to the people of Sunset to decide the rest. Once the townsfolk heard what the music mogul had to say, they would thank her instead of acting like a group of geriatric gang members defending home turf at a nursing home.

But before she could hide behind the counter, Declan jumped from his chair, took off across the room, and grabbed her arm on the way. "Grandpa Jack, have Frank and Bob give their reports," she hissed as he propelled her toward the kitchen.

Tito shook his head as they continued through the cooking area, out the rear door and onto the porch. Once in the open air, Libby wrenched her elbow free and spun on her heels.

"Do not manhandle me," she said with false bravado. "I'm not some weak-minded female you can push around at will."

A muscle twitched in Declan's cheek and he began to pace pantherlike on the aged wood. Libby waited, wondering why he had a problem with the idea of recording a CD. Clive had mentioned a respectable advance, plus royalties on the finished product, and Sounds of Time was willing to pay all his travel expenses, as well as put him up in a classy hotel.

She settled into a corner of the porch, rested her bottom against the railing, and folded her arms. If he'd just stand still long enough, maybe she'd be able to figure out what was bothering him.

Declan furrowed his fingers through his hair. His chest rose and fell with the force of his breathing as he propped himself directly across from her against the restaurant wall.

Teeth clenched, he said, "What are those people doing here?"

She met his frown with a tight-lipped smile. "They're here in good faith with an offer of assistance. I, for one, find it wonderful."

"So, you've already accepted their ridiculous proposition?"

Libby stiffened. "Of course not. I wouldn't do that without consulting the rest of the committee."

He peered at her through the dim glow of a lone lightbulb. "I suppose you know what they want from me?"

"A recording contract. And I don't understand why you won't listen to their offer. It sounded pretty darn good to me."

He ran a hand over his jaw, his eyes hidden in shadow. "They want me to go with them to London. That's where the studio is."

"I guessed as much," she answered. She'd always figured he would leave, so why not use the excuse of fame and fortune? At least that might make sense to J.P. How could the kid think he'd been abandoned if he knew Declan had a real job to go to and an important reason for leaving? "As far as I can tell, you don't exactly have a career, so what's the big deal? It's the chance of a lifetime."

Gathering his thoughts, Declan stepped to her side of the porch and leaned into the railing. He'd known it would come to this eventually. He'd read plenty about what was expected of modern-day travelers, and knew well the myriad requirements needed to fly or drive. That was the second reason he'd planned to sail around the world instead of taking an airplane or learning to drive one of those devilish automobiles.

Docking at smaller ports didn't require any identification. He'd seen people tie up at Hewitt's, walk into the marina, and plunk down cash for the dock space without Hazel asking for a thing.

"Think on it, madam, and remember how you found me.

I have no passport or driver's license—not even a birth certificate to prove who I am. There is no way I can enter the Applewaithes' country without at least one of those documents. After tossing me in jail, the authorities would ask dozens of questions. How would I explain myself?''

Libby half turned to face him, her expression as cheerful as a gravedigger at midnight and twice as suspicious. "Oh, yeah, that's right. You're the man from the eighteenth century. Guess they didn't have passports back then, did they?''

Her recalcitrant attitude tried his patience. "No, they didn't. And I doubt I could write Dublin and ask them to delve into their records and search for a two-hundred-and-fifty-year-old birth certificate, even if it still existed.''

Libby leaned back against the railing. "You're bound and determined to stick to that story, aren't you? Even if it means you have to throw away a bundle of money.''

"Sadly, I do not have a choice.''

"Hah!'' she shouted triumphantly. "I was right about you. You *are* on the lam from the IRA. There's probably a reward for your capture and everything.''

Declan damped back a growl. "If it would help to convince you of my story, I encourage you to call the Irish authorities and give them the name of Declan James O'Shae, date of birth July twenty-first, seventeen hundred and fifty-one. I'd be interested in hearing what they have to say.''

Libby chewed on her lower lip. Damn if the contrary woman wasn't giving his challenge serious consideration. Finally, her shoulders drooped in defeat. "All right. I'll admit to the fact that you don't have any papers, at least not any I remember seeing in that cave. But that means you're an illegal alien. If anyone caught on, you could be deported.''

Before he could answer, Tito stuck his head out the back door. "If you two is done flappin' your gums, the committee would like you to come inside. They don't want them *apple* people talkin' lessen both of you're there to hear what they have to say.''

* * *

The pale half-moon danced lightly across the ocean, painting a sparkling path from the horizon to the shore. The prevailing breeze carried a night bird's plaintive song out to sea, leaving an echo of sadness in its wake.

Lost in thought, Libby tried to focus on everything that had happened since she'd arrived home. But each memory dimmed in comparison to the one she held of that singular afternoon when she'd crawled inside the cave, which she knew lay directly beneath her, and awakened Declan O'Shae.

Thinking back, she couldn't remember the tide ever being as low as it had been the day she'd found him asleep on the ledge. If, as Declan kept insisting, it was a part of the magic that had occurred, it would explain the reason why her life had changed from that moment forward. And no matter what took place from here on out, it would never be the same.

Unfortunately, life was full of *if*s and *maybe*s. And empty promises and broken dreams. All kinds of ugly things she'd told herself she would never let happen to her or her son again.

Tonight, after the Applewaithes had made their pitch to the festival committee, she'd left the Pink Pelican to check on J.P. When Jack and Uncle T finally arrived home, she'd taken one of Grandma Martha's quilts and headed here to wait.

She didn't need to turn around to know who owned the muffled footsteps now accompanying the slapping of the waves. She kept her eyes trained on the moon as Declan climbed the boulders and sat quietly beside her. From the corner of her eye she saw that he'd showered and put on fresh clothes. The soap he'd used mingled with the smell of the wind and the sea, filling her senses with his familiar scent.

Sitting cross-legged, Declan rested his elbows on his knees and sighed, as if he automatically expected her to understand what his heavy exhalation of breath implied.

"Why did you leave tonight, before things were settled?" he asked in a weary-sounding voice.

"I thought everyone would talk more freely if I wasn't around to influence them. Besides, Ruth has enough to do without sleeping on our couch six nights a week, waiting for me to take care of my child."

"Did Jack tell you what happened?"

Libby shrugged. "He just said you walked out. The committee listened to a few more of the Applewaithes' ideas and decided to table the rest of the discussion until they could get you to give them your opinion."

"Did he tell you exactly what Clive and Ginnie wanted in return for their generous offer?"

She rubbed her damp palms on her thighs. "They already explained their plan to me. This year they're willing to absorb all the costs of the fair plus let us have any profits, provided we allow them to promote the festival for years two through five as an international event to which they will bring and showcase their artists. During that time, they'll take fifty percent of the profits. In year five we'll renegotiate the contract whichever way will satisfy both parties. If we can't see eye-to-eye, they'll leave us free and clear. They get to introduce their recording company to the States, and we don't lose any money. It's a win-win situation, no matter how you look at it."

Declan continued to gaze at the moon, his body leaning forward as if he wished he could sail away on the shaft of light streaking across the water. "It might be win-win for them, but not for me."

"What do you mean, not for you? I don't see what you have to do with it. You've already decided not to record for them."

He heaved another sigh. "You left before you heard what they called the 'deal breaker.' I thought Jack might have told you what it was they really wanted."

Libby scooted on her fanny until she faced him. "Will

you please tell me what you're talking about? I don't see how—"

"They want me." He ran a hand through his damp hair. "If I don't agree to record for them, they won't invest a dime in the town. Without a signed contract from me, there will be no assistance with the fair."

Libby's heart lurched in her chest. She'd known all along that her friends were risking everything on this project; that was why the Applewaithes' offer had sounded so perfect. Sunset would get the money it needed to guarantee the festival, Sounds of Time would get a showcase for their artists, and, if the festival took off, a decent profit. The town would have had only a few weeks of work a year to earn enough cash to stay afloat, draw tourists, and bring new life to Sunset's aging citizens.

And it all hinged on Declan O'Shae, a man who was either a clever liar or an escapee from a mental institution. She couldn't begin to think of him as a privateer who'd slept away the last two hundred years. Right now, she was too tired to think at all.

"I see." She brushed a tear from her eye.

"Libby." He placed a hand on her arm. "Try to understand. If I agree to sign that contract, I'll be opening myself up to the same questions you asked. And all I'll have are the same answers." Coming to his knees, he turned to her. "The ones you have yet to accept."

When Declan pulled her to her knees, she couldn't resist. Focusing on the neckline of his T-shirt and the dark curling hair at the base of his throat, she struggled for breath. He was asking her to have enough faith in what they'd begun to build here that, together, they could pull it off without the Applewaithes' money. He was asking her to believe in him.

"I . . . um . . ." She rested her forehead against his chin. "Jeez, you just don't know when to quit, do you?"

He cupped her jaw in his hands and brushed his lips lightly across hers. "I promise you that I can prove what I say. I just need time. When I find my—what I've been looking for, I'll even leave the town a little something to remember me by.''

Libby clasped his wrists and Declan kissed her a second time, drawing her into the circle of his arms. He fit against her like a second skin, his hard chest molding to the curve of her breasts and thighs. Heat pooled in her belly and raced to her knees and she trembled against him.

He ground his hips against hers. His hands found her bottom and he ran wayward fingers up and down her cleft. Dizzy with desire, she swayed into him. Damn but the man made her weak.

''It's your life and your right to turn the Applewaithes down. You don't need to bring me or the town into it. These people will understand if you refuse the offer; I know they will.''

''The citizens of Sunset have been good to me. They've given me purpose and a sense of belonging. I don't want to ruin this town. I want to leave it better than I found it.''

Of course he was going to leave. Whether she believed his outrageous tale or not, he would be gone after the fair. She came from a long line of fishermen. Would it be so terrible to play along and tell him that she'd finally swallowed his outrageous story hook, line and sinker? After all, he'd been the one to tell her that whopper about coming from a different century in the first place. What was the difference between the two lies? Sunset needed this fair and Declan O'Shae's presence to survive.

''I believe you,'' she whispered, shocked at how easily the falsehood slipped out.

''You do?''

She nodded against his chest. ''I do. And I'll help keep the Applewaithes off your back. Just promise me one thing?''

He smiled down at her, his face overcome with amazement. ''Anything.''

''Promise me you'll do your damnedest to see to it the

fair is a success. And when you're ready to leave, you'll let me be the one to tell J.P.''

His eyes focused on hers, until Libby thought he might be reading her soul instead of her mind. Finally, he nodded.

"I promise."

Chapter Eighteen

J.P. stood at her side as Libby squatted down next to the dilapidated playpen sitting on the floor of the Spitzers' garage. She'd been on her knees so long they ached from resting on the worn concrete. In her usual practical manner, Mary had rigged a two-foot-high edge of cardboard around the base of the mesh, so Miss Betty's kittens couldn't climb out. With a litter pan in the far corner and a variety of toys strewn over the plastic bottom, the six fuzzy residents were living in their very own kitty motel.

The kittens were more than old enough for adoption, and Mary planned to give them away tomorrow at the fair. This was J.P.'s moment of reckoning; the day he had to decide which baby cat he would keep.

Libby stood and placed a hand on her son's shoulder. "J.P., I have to get to the bar to work the lunch shift. Then we're closed until after the fair. I can only give you another minute to make up your mind. Please choose a kitten, or at least narrow it down to two. You can sleep on your choices and let Mary know in the morning. How does that sound?"

He shuffled from foot to foot, scuffing the sides of his

new sneakers. Libby felt his body tense and wished there was some way she could make this easier, but ever since he'd been old enough to talk, she'd given J.P. a say in what happened with his life. It was a basic tenet of her mother's creed to turn him into a responsible adult. She let him pick the clothes he wore each morning. Most times, she let him decide on the movie they saw and where they went to dinner afterward. Choosing a pet was an important occasion for a child, and she wasn't about to ruin it.

Besides, it would be just her luck if the kitten *she* suggested ran away or got hit by a car, or worse. No way was she going to take the blame if he made a bad choice, even though she'd be there to pick up the pieces if a disaster occurred.

J.P. rubbed a hand under his nose, then reached down and gathered up Black Pete, snuggling the green-eyed cat to his chest.

"Is that the one you want?" Libby asked, ready to breathe a sigh of relief.

Sniffling, he put the kitten back in the playpen and picked up Bridget, or maybe it was Bilge Water, now called Bilgey for short. "I do-don't know," he said with a little sob. "I want them all."

While her heart ached for him, Libby's practical side shifted into overdrive, thinking of a way to make things better. "Have you asked Uncle Tito if he wants a cat?"

"N-no. Why?"

She hunkered down again, wincing when her knees creaked. "Because he might be willing to adopt your second choice. If he did, you could bring kitten number one to his house to play every day. It would be almost as good as having both, don't you think?"

She crossed her fingers and waited.

"I . . . guess so," J.P. said pensively.

Suddenly, he gazed up at her, his eyes turning bright as polished amber. Libby's heart soared. She'd sunk another three pointer from center court in the name of single moms everywhere. It took all her self-control to keep from doing the happy dance and high-fiving the air.

"And Declan, too," J.P. said in a rush. "He could keep one of 'em at the cottage. That way I could have three—"

Libby's mental mambo suddenly developed two left feet. So much for her brilliant idea. If J.P. approached Declan about taking a kitten, the caveman, whom she'd come to believe was an honorable but crazy man, would refuse. When J.P. asked why, he'd find out his buddy was leaving. Yes, he was going to learn about it anyway, but she'd hoped to ease her son into the loss.

"I'm not sure that's such a good idea, sweetie. Declan's got a lot on his mind right now, what with the fair and all. In the meantime, we can ask Uncle T and hear what he has to say. Okay?"

J.P. shrugged, but he didn't say no. Leaning over the playpen, he put the gray kitten back and gave the black one a pat on its head. "Can we go find Uncle T right now?"

"I don't see why not. He should be in the kitchen putting the finishing touches on food for the fair. But if he's busy, we can't pester him. We have to wait until he gets his work done." Libby took his hand and they left the squirming balls of fur climbing on top of one another, all trying to escape their first-class accommodations.

They walked through town on the way to the Pink Pelican. Just about every shopkeeper was outside, hanging Old Glory or some type of decorative flag, sprucing up their business in one festive way or another. The sidewalks had been scrubbed, the wooden benches painted a sunny yellow, and clay pots overflowing with flowers decorated the doorways. Olivia Martinez's shop had a huge SUMMER SALE banner in the window and a NO VACANCY sign plastered over the advertisement for her cottages. Libby had heard from several sources that anyone who owned a spare room had rented it out, either to tourists or people working the fair. She couldn't remember the last time she'd seen Sunset so busy . . . or so alive.

It was exactly what she'd hoped would happen to the town and its residents. So why did she feel so on edge? Telling herself she was just being silly, Libby concentrated on all the things she had yet to do this afternoon. She needed to make a bank run, sign purchase orders for food deliveries, write a check to the company setting up the Ferris wheel and merry-go-round. Then there was the—

Before she knew it, J.P. took off at a run. "Declan! Hey, Declan!" he shouted at the top of his lungs.

She shaded her eyes against the mid-morning sun. Her heart caught in her throat at the sight of a bare-chested Declan O'Shae standing on the gazebo roof as he attached a weathervane to the bandstand's imposing cupola. The bright copper dolphin arcing across the billowing waves sculpted on top of the weather vane had an almost human smile etched into its face, as if overjoyed to be the unofficial mascot of the town.

Had it really only been weeks since she'd wished that magnificent body would take a slow roll off the bar roof? Had she truly wanted him gone from Sunset . . . gone from her life?

She watched as Declan waved at J.P. and threw him a genuine smile. Stepping carefully, he edged his way to the ladder and turned, planting his feet firmly on the top rung. He called out an order and J.P. held on to the ladder's side rails, absorbed in the important task he'd been give by his hero.

Declan's broad back glistened bronze in the sun. A light sheen of moisture polished his well-honed muscles to perfection. Snug cutoff jeans molded his taut rear; his thighs and calves flexed impressively as he tread lightly down the rungs. In a burst of clarity, Libby could see him scaling the rigging of a clipper ship as if he'd been born to ride the waves on an old-fashioned vessel of yore.

She shook away the impossible idea. Okay, so he wasn't as nefarious as she'd first believed. In fact, he'd proven himself to be a really nice man. Of course, she never could have fallen for a not-so-nice guy. She was way more sensible than that. But she still believed he was a wanderer and a dreamer, and a hell of a good storyteller. And none of those traits would give her the family she longed for and the father J.P. deserved, even if she did love the man.

She made it to the gazebo as Declan's feet touched the ground. "I've a powerful hunger, lad. How about you?" she heard him ask.

"Me too," chimed in J.P. "We were visiting the kittens."

"Hello," Libby said, deftly steering them to a safer topic. She put her hand on J.P.'s curly hair. "We're heading for the Pink Pelican and lunch. Will you be joining us today?"

Declan wiped his damp chest with the rag tied around his belt, then grabbed a faded blue T-shirt from the gazebo railing and slipped it over his head. "I'm looking forward to it."

J.P. danced from side to side, displaying his usual never-ending energy. "Let's race. Bet I can beat both of you to the bar," he taunted, jumping up and down.

"Oh, you do, do you?" Declan tossed Libby a teasing smile. "What say you, madam? Shall we take the lad on?"

"Gee, I don't know. I'm wearing a skirt," she said, her expression somber. "But I could give it a try."

Taking both men by surprise, Libby shot down the path. By the time they caught up with her, she was standing on the porch of the bar, giggling and gasping for breath.

There was no town meeting that night. Everyone was at Hewitt's Marina, putting finishing touches on the booths or setting up the sound system in the gazebo, while Grandpa Jack and Tito were checking on the food at Phil and Don's. J.P. had gone to Ruth's to have dinner with a few of the visiting children, watch a video, and stay out from underfoot.

Libby had made her bank run for change and bought dozens of rolls of tickets, which the attendees would trade in for the planned games, rides and food. Then she'd checked

with the local fire department to confirm her request for a
rescue squad vehicle and skeleton crew to be on site through
both days of the fair. She'd just left a training session with
the people manning the ticket booths, her final task of the
evening.

Now, with no job in particular, her only chore was to
meander from booth to booth, giving compliments or calling
out advice. Restless and edgy, she wished it was morning
and the festival was underway. The sooner she could put
the fair behind her, the sooner she and J.P. could get on
with their lives. They had survived Brett's loss; they could
survive without the caveman.

In the distance, she heard the whine of guitars and the
clamor of drums, then a soulful, delicate melody, not quite
modern in tone but not exactly classical either. From the
sound of it, Screaming Mean had a pretty good handle on
Declan's Celtic songs. She had yet to hear him and the band
together but imagined the performance would be interesting.

Lifting her face to the brisk easterly breeze, she spied a
billow of angry-looking clouds scuttling across the face of
the moon. The day had been about as muggy as a July
afternoon in the Keys could get. Tito had warned her since
yesterday that a storm was brewing. She only hoped the bad
weather would cooperate and hold off for another forty-eight
hours, because rain would ruin everything. If the tourists and
their money stayed away . . .

"Hi-ho," came a lilting voice from the shadows.

She turned to find Clive Applewaithe propped against a
cluster of pilings, well-positioned to observe but out of the
way of bustling workers.

"Hello." She walked to his side. "I'm happy to see you're
staying for the festival, even though I know we disappointed
you."

His patrician face creased into a grin. "We're looking
forward to it. Ginnie and I are confident we and the citizens
of Sunset will work things out eventually. I still plan on
bringing my artists here next year, you know. The committee

gave their permission for that at least. We're willing to pay a fee for the privilege, even if we didn't arrive at a mutually satisfactory agreement.''

Jack had already told Libby some of what the town had agreed to do for the Applewaithes. ''I assumed that would be the case, but only if we decide to hold the festival again. Last I heard, that point was up for debate.''

''Based on whether or not you show a profit this year, I gather. Still, Ginnie and I have high hopes.'' He scanned the dock until he spotted Declan unloading aluminum kegs from the back of a pickup truck and setting them in huge tubs of ice. ''We have high hopes for Mr. O'Shae, as well.''

Libby joined him in leaning against the pilings and followed his gaze, admiring once again the flex and play of muscles on a well-built man. ''Oh? I wasn't aware you and Declan had another talk.''

''We didn't,'' Clive confessed. ''But the word *no* isn't listed in my personal dictionary. I plan to keep sweetening the offer until we reach an accord.''

''I hate to burst your bubble, but I don't think he can be persuaded once he's made up his mind.''

''Nonsense, my dear. Every man has his price ... or weakness. Once I find O'Shae's Achilles heel, I intend to use it to my advantage.''

If Clive was planning to wage war on Declan, Libby wasn't going to be party to it. She'd promised the caveman she would keep the Applewaithes off his case and she was a woman of her word. ''He's going to leave as soon as the festival is over,'' she said, fairly certain she was telling the truth.

''Ah, but he hasn't heard my next offer. Besides, I feel there's more to your Mr. O'Shae than meets the eye.''

I wish, Libby thought, then gave herself a mental slap upside the head. ''Declan doesn't belong to anyone but himself. I'm sorry he doesn't want to record for your company, Clive, but I don't think he'll change his mind.''

The Englishman took one of her hands in his and gave

it a comforting shake. "There's no doubt he would be a great asset to Sounds of Time. Ginnie and I can be very convincing when the need arises. We haven't given up yet."

"I promised Declan I would stand by him in this, and respect his wishes. I can't push him into something he doesn't feel comfortable with. You understand, don't you?"

Clive patted her hand in a fatherly gesture. "It's a woman's duty to support the man she loves. I admire you for it."

"Oh, but I don't—I mean, we—" Libby sputtered. The heat she felt zinging to her cheeks had probably turned them bright as one of the potted geraniums lining the wharf.

"Oh, dear. There's Ginnie waving at me from the quilting booth. If I don't get over there and grab the purse strings, she'll buy up all the crafts before the tourists arrive and put me in the poorhouse to boot. Ta."

Before Libby could catch her breath, Clive Applewaithe was strutting down the dock. She rubbed at the knot of nerves throbbing at the base of her neck. Maybe this was a good time to take a couple of aspirin, then check on the kids and see if Ruth needed a hand. Someone called her name and she raised her head in time to see Jeff Spitzer trotting over from the rides area.

Jeff had flown in from Chicago earlier that day to help with the fair. He'd been two years behind Libby in school, and Mary loved to brag about his brilliance. At twenty-eight he was finishing a doctoral thesis in world history while he taught at Northwestern. Libby had been so wrapped up in seeing to the festival, she'd forgotten all about him until this minute.

"Hey! You look fantastic," Jeff said, catching her in his arms and spinning them both around. "I hear you're home for good."

Libby took a step back, her smile welcoming. Though he'd grown a few inches and wore thick horn-rimmed glasses, Jeff's face was still boyish. He'd filled out some since they'd last talked, and matured into an attractive, studious-looking guy. "Probably. And what about you? How long are you here for?"

"Just long enough to get through the fair and help with the breakdown. Mom and Dad are getting up there in years, and I figured they'd need me these next few days. It's really great, what you're trying to do for them ... hell, for the whole town. Makes me feel like a rat jumping ship."

"Don't feel guilty about going off to school. I did the same thing," she said, still holding on to his hands. "And I don't regret a minute of it. It was only recently that I realized Sunset was my home. I want to raise my son here."

"I heard about the little guy. J.P., is it? Mom can't say enough about what a great kid he is."

Libby bounced on her toes, always thrilled to hear compliments about her son. "You'll have to meet him while you're here. You can tell him about all the not-so-great things we did growing up. I know he'd get a charge out of it."

Jeff pulled her closer and draped an arm over her shoulder, then steered her back to her seat on the pilings. "I'll be glad to, after you fill me in on something that has me concerned."

"I know. The money. But I'm sure we'll break even, and—"

He shook his head. "It's not the money, Libby. From the look of it, this fair is going to do just fine. I met the new man in town a little while ago, and I want to hear your take on why you think a guy like Declan O'Shae would end up here, in this almost invisible key in the middle of nowhere."

Libby hugged her arms across her chest. If Jeff knew the story from beginning to end, he'd think both she and the caveman were nuts. "I'm not sure," she told him, forgiving herself for the white lie. "He just appeared one day and made himself at home. Why?"

" 'Cause Mom and Dad think the world of him, and so, I gather, do most of Sunset's citizens. Seems he strolled into town wearing nothing but a 'Will work for food' sign and tattered clothes. To hear Dad tell it, since then, he's earned a Superman cape and a halo." Jeff scanned the dock, squinting into the darkness. "And from the look of it, our super-hero is loaded for bear."

Libby followed his brown-eyed gaze until she spied Declan walking deliberately toward them with a keg balanced on one brawny shoulder.

"Good evening," Declan said, frowning at Jeff and the arm he still had roped casually around Libby's shoulders. "Seems to me you could find better use for those busy fingers, Mr. Spitzer. If you're here to help, you might as well do something productive."

With that, he shoved the cask against Jeff's chest. Taken by surprise, Jeff raised his hands and jerked backward. Arms circling like a windmill in a gale, the young man tottered precariously until his back and bottom hung over the edge of the pilings. Libby reacted on instinct and grabbed him before disaster struck.

Declan watched the two of them teeter until they found solid footing. Just as he'd suspected, the man was but a pup, a youngster unable to put muscle behind his actions. Nodding smartly, he set down the cask between them and folded his arms across his chest. Surely Libby could see Jeff Spitzer was a boy instead of a man.

Catching Declan's challenging glare, Jeff barked out a laugh. Glancing first at Libby, then back at Declan, he said, "Okay, I get it. You've staked your claim and there's no poaching allowed." After brushing at his shirtfront, he pecked Libby's cheek. "We'll talk later, after you explain to Mr. O'Shae who I am. Oh, yeah, and remember to save me a dance tomorrow night." Cocking his head toward Declan, he added, "If that's all right with you."

Declan watched Jeff stride away. Beside the fact that Libby had been acting entirely too friendly with the man, the idea that she had the power to put his world here in jeopardy had him worried. He'd spent time researching the things they'd talked about last night, and read up on all the definitions of an *alien*. He hadn't arrived in Sunset from a distant planet, but he might just as well have. Libby had been correct in saying he could be deported if word got around that he was in this country illegally. The question was, where would they send him if they threw him out?

The force of Libby's stare burned a hole in his back and he turned slowly to face her. Standing under the glow of the lights lining the wharf, she looked very young and exceptionally pretty. But no man in his right mind would mistake her for a child. For the first time since he'd met her, she'd piled her chestnut-colored hair on top of her head in a riot of cascading curls. A scoop-necked, pale yellow shirt caressed her full breasts. Black, form-fitting shorts molded to her shapely thighs and showed off her long legs and sandaled feet. Even her toes were spectacular, with an erotic splash of bright pink on each perfectly shaped nail.

"Was that necessary?" she asked, tapping one of those dainty feet like a jackhammer.

For one intense second, Declan found it impossible to take his eyes off her toes. "No, but it was enjoyable." He snapped up his head. "Pity you were agile enough to keep the lad from falling in the drink."

Steely-eyed, Libby stalked him. Walking around the keg until she forced his back to the water, she stopped a foot from his chest. "You're acting like a child. Jeff Spitzer and I grew up together. We're just friends."

Declan raised a brow. "That's not what it looked like to me. And you certainly can't use that excuse for your behavior with Clive Applewaithe."

Libby opened and closed her mouth. "You thought that I—and Clive Applewaithe—Oh, for Pete's sake, the Applewaithes are respectable businesspeople. We were talking about the fair."

"The man is a menace to my safety. And I didn't like the way he and Jeff touched you," Declan answered through clenched teeth.

"You're being ridiculous. Clive Applewaithe is a happily married man. Besides, he's old enough to be my father."

"Maybe so, but in my day many a man, young or old,

could be led astray by a tempting, buxom wench. Beside the fact that you were smiling at Applewaithe in a decidedly improper manner, you were practically plastered to the Spitzer lad's chest.''

''I was not!'' she shouted, close enough that he could see the golden glint in her eyes. ''And who are you calling a wench?''

Declan thumped his forehead with the heel of his palm. ''May the saints forgive me for being so blind. It must have been Ruth I saw ogling that damned Englishman. And maybe it was Olivia flirting with Jeff Spitzer.''

Libby thrust a finger against his chest and poked hard. ''I was not ogling Clive Applewaithe. And how dare you accuse me of flirting with—''

''I'll dare whatever I choose. You've had me dancing to your tune long enough, bedding you in secret and sneaking around as if we had something to be ashamed of. And I'm tired of it.'' He cupped her jaw and pulled her close. '' 'Tis time to say you're mine and be done with it.''

Planting his lips firmly against her open mouth, Declan kissed her with a fierce burst of passion. He didn't lose his temper often, but seeing Libby tonight as she flitted from one man to the next had set his stomach churning. Since the moment they'd met in that damned cave, he'd thought of her as his. It was about time she admitted the same.

Libby struggled, and he caged her in his arms, just tight enough to prove ownership. A second passed before her body softened against him and she returned the kiss. The warmth of her lips filled him to overflowing with an unfamiliar feeling of tenderness, and suddenly he was disgusted by his boorish actions.

He heard a distant catcall, then a few rousing whistles. The dock began to vibrate and he tore his mouth from hers. All around him the townsfolk were applauding and stamping their feet.

''All right, Declan!''

''Way to go.''

" 'Bout time, if ya ask me.''

Rife with embarrassment, he stepped away and ran a hand across the back of his neck. Damn if he wasn't a ham-handed lout for putting the both of them on display like this. Then he saw Libby's half-closed eyes and melting expression, and it did him proud to know he'd just set the woman to reeling.

As if waking from a dream, Libby blinked, her eyes wide as she scanned the crowd. Even the men who'd arrived to set up the rides were watching. Locking her gaze with his, she arched a winged brow.

He smiled and gave a courtly bow, a bit surprised at her demure reaction.

Her lips curved in invitation. Taking a step back, she curtsied, exactly as had the ladies of his day.

Declan straightened his shoulders and perused the wharf, grateful to find most of the citizens ambling back to work. Thinking he might get away with planting another kiss on Libby's come-hither lips, he took a step forward.

Still smiling, she set her palms on his chest and heaved a mighty shove.

He staggered back, tripping over his own feet. Striding toward him like a lioness on the prowl, Libby gave a second forceful push. One that sent him flailing into the warm summer air, directly into the cooling swell of the ocean.

"Damn idiot woman," Declan muttered, wiping his face on a towel. Scowling into the mirror over the sink, he plucked a piece of seaweed from his hair. After Tito had helped fish him from the drink, he'd followed the man to the Pink Pelican to get cleaned up. At least he knew where he stood with the cook.

Tito thrust a black arm thick as a tree trunk through the open doorway of the half bath and dangled a clean white T-shirt. Declan snatched it up and put it on, then slipped into the gray sweatpants that came through the door next.

Bundling his wet clothes into a pile, he walked into the kitchen and stomped to the table.

T set a tumbler of neat Scotch in front of him, and Declan swallowed it down in one annoyed gulp.

"What are you staring at?" he ground out when Tito pulled out a chair and sat down.

The islander shook his head. "Why, I just ain't never seen a talkin' jackass before. Guess I'm shocked, is all."

He slammed his glass on the table. "Well, this jackass not only talks, he drinks when he's been made a fool of, so fill it up again, if you please."

Chuckling, the cook did as he was told. This time, Declan lifted the drink in salute before he guzzled it down.

"You best be careful how much o' that stuff you swallow," Tito warned. "Tomorrow's the big day and you got a lot of folks dependin' on you. 'Specially Libby."

Declan's breath hitched into a snort. "The woman is a termagant. I've been nothing but kind to her and her boy, and all I've received for it are suspicious accusations and a dunking." He gave a quick shake of his head for emphasis. "She's ashamed of me."

Tito sipped at his own drink. "Now, you and I both know that ain't rightly so. You two ain't fooled anyone with your secret midnight meetings and moonlight trips to Dream Cove." He spoke slowly, measuring his words. "If Libby was ashamed of you, those moments done never would'a happened."

Fisting a hand on the table, Declan shrugged his shoulders. It was all he could do to not tell Tito the entire story. Right about now he needed a bit of sympathy and understanding for his lack of discretion.

"The entire town knows about us?" he asked, though T had just said as much.

Tito merely nodded.

Declan clenched long fingers around the empty glass. "I had no idea. So much for the promise I made, telling her I wouldn't ruin her reputation. After tonight . . ."

Sighing, he rested his forehead in his hand. "For what it's worth, I was the one who did the chasing. Truth be told, I had to practically blackmail Libby to get her in my bed. It was never her idea to sleep with me."

"Hm-hmm," T hummed sagely. "Whatever you say."

"I haven't had to convince a woman to have sex with me since I was seventeen," he groused. "Damned daunting to a man's ego."

T sat back, propped an arm across his chest, and tugged at his chin. "Let me see if I got this straight: You chased after Libby from the moment you met her—did your best to finagle her into your evil clutches, even though she kept tellin' you to back off."

Declan winced inwardly. Tito's explanation made him sound like a seducer of innocents or worse. "Yes."

"Now you think she's ashamed of you, but you want to be with her anyway, even if she don't want to be with you."

He blew out a breath. "So it seems."

"And tonight, when you saw her with the Apple man and Jeff? You wanted to tear the men in two?"

"With my bare hands," Declan muttered. "I thought I showed remarkable restraint." He sighed. "Something comes over me when she's near. Being a part of her life has become a hunger in my gut, such a powerful need I'm at a loss to explain it."

"Hmm." Tito raised a brow. "Manipulation. Lust. Anger. Desire. Jealousy—"

"I was not jealous," he snapped.

"Wantin' to break a man in two sure fits my definition of the word," Tito pronounced. He leaned into the table, his voice hushed. "And the private parts with Libby? Were they good?"

"The best of my li—" Declan frowned. "Just what are you getting at here?"

"I think it's plain as the nose on your face. You're in love with the woman. Have been from the start, if I'm hearin' you right."

"Love?" Declan fairly shouted the word. "That's ridiculous. No, wait—it's more than ridiculous. It's ludicrous." He slammed a hand on the table. "Besides, love is not for men like me."

"Oh, really?" Tito asked, all innocence. "So you're sayin' it's impossible for a man such as yourself, one who's honorable, hardworkin', kind to chil'rens and old folks, to be in love."

"Yes. No." He swiped a hand over his jaw. "Yes." Thinking hard, he stared down at the table. "Saints and sinners and all that's holy," he whispered.

Tito began to whistle a tuneless ditty purposely, Declan knew, to irritate him. He inched up his chin. "So how do I make it up to her? Wear a hair shirt, perhaps, or confess my sins in the town square tomorrow and prepare for a public flogging?"

Tito's smile slashed white across his broad face. "Nothin' so dramatic. A simple apology would work the same, I'd bet. Then you got's to tell her how you feel."

Stretching his legs out in front of him, Declan shook his head. A piece of seaweed fell onto the table and he crushed it in his hand. "I'm well and truly hooked, aren't I? I just wish I knew why."

Lost in thought, neither man spoke. The kitchen fan thrummed overhead. In the distance, the sounds of Screaming Mean mingled with people's laughter. Suddenly, Tito rapped his knuckles on the table and jumped to his feet. "I almost forgot to show you somethin'."

He walked to the counter and opened a drawer, then pulled out the amulet Declan had given him earlier in the day. "This afternoon, after I got through weldin' them side bars for my food stall, I soldered the pieces together like you asked. I think you might want to take a good look at your medallion."

The golden disk, now one smooth circle of metal, still hung from its leather thong. Tossing the seaweed aside, Declan grasped it tight. When it pulsed against his palm, he pressed it between his hands and let the warmth of the talisman flow through him in a single humming current of energy, just as it had the first time he'd looped it around his neck.

His gaze slid to T's, and the black man nodded. "Go on. It ain't gonna bite. But it sure do explain a lot."

Declan heaved a breath and set the medallion on the table, directly under the glow of the hanging lamp. It had been so long since he'd seen the disk whole, he could hardly recall what the figure looked like.

A flash of awareness ripped through him as the profile came to life before his eyes. The delicate etching was still that of a beautiful woman with a crown of curls piled high on her finely shaped head. Her slightly aquiline nose, strong stubborn chin, and slender elegant neck were the same as he remembered.

Only this time, the woman had a name.

Chapter Nineteen

"Mom! Mom! Mom! It's time to get up!"

J.P. bounced, jolting the bed with every word. Libby rolled to her side, and he jumped over her quick as a bunny. She groaned and he giggled. Slowly, she stuck the top of her head out from under her pillow and raised an eyelid. Her son had interrupted a very real and emotionally satisfying dream. One in which she was a female pirate and Declan O'Shae was just about to walk the plank.

"You, young man, will be on kitchen duty for a week if you don't stop rocking this boat . . . I mean bed."

"But it's morning."

She turned her head in the direction of the scant ray of pinkish light edging its way through the curtains. J.P. sat back on his heels and flung an arm toward the same window. "See. Today's fair day. You got to get up."

Snaking a hand out from under the sheet, Libby groped for her alarm clock and eyed it blearily. Five-thirty A.M. was not fair day. It wasn't any kind of *day* at all.

"Come on, Mom," the boy insisted. "Declan and

Grandpa and me already had breakfast. They said to tell you it's time."

She pulled the pillow back over her face to stifle words no five-year-old should ever have to hear. Heaving a sigh, she mustered the patience to force her voice through the fluffy goose feathers. "It's barely dawn, J.P. And who made breakfast?"

"Declan did. At least for him and me. Grandpa Jack ate cereal, but Declan made the two of us toad in the hole. He said he ate it as a special treat when they were aboard his ship."

Try as she might, Libby couldn't recycle toad in the hole into any kind of edible food substance. Then again, with J.P.'s knack for twisting words and phrases, he could have eaten just about anything. Maybe it was a breakfast dish from Ireland. If it was a seafaring term for a particular kind of meal, she'd never heard of it.

"Was it good?"

"Dee-lish-e-us! He said he'd teach you how to make it, so I could have it whenever I wanted."

"Great." *And how nice for me,* she thought, grateful the pillow would hide her frown. After last night's dunking, the caveman probably had lots of things to show her, like a ferocious scowl or a raging roar. Quite possibly, his broad back as he hotfooted it out of town.

"So where did everybody go?" she asked, clearing the cobwebs from her brain.

She felt the mattress sway, then heard the muffled thud of sneakered feet, and figured J.P.'d had enough of wasting time with his uncooperative mother. "To the dock. Grandpa Jack had to help Uncle Tito meet the food people. An' Declan's helpin' the screamers wire the za-ge-bow for the insta-mints."

Libby raised the pillow and flashed her son a weak grin. No way did she have the strength to correct him, not when he sounded so eager. He'd done a fine job of dressing himself this morning, she noted. A clean yellow T-shirt, freshly pressed navy blue shorts, navy socks, sneakers and something . . . something gold and flashy hanging from a leather thong around his neck all the way down to his waist.

She jerked to a sitting position and threw her legs over the side of the bed. "What are you wearing?"

J.P. stared down at his shoes. "My new stuff. Why?"

"Not that, honey. Come here."

He took a step closer and she reached for the medallion draped over his chest. "Doesn't this belong to Declan?"

"Yeah. He gave it to me to wear. But just for today and tomorrow. He said it had special powers and it would keep me safe. I have to give it back after they shoot off the fireworks two times."

To keep him safe? Libby staved off the rising panic by tugging her son to her chest. J.P. stood still for a few seconds before he squirmed to get away.

"Not so tight, Mom. You're squeezin' too hard."

Holding him at arm's length, she struggled to remain calm. "What did he mean by safe, sweetie? Did Declan tell you there would be some kind of danger? Tell me exactly what he said."

J.P. shook his head, his expression befuddled. "He was smilin' when he said it, so I don't think he meant it. 'Sides, there's no danger here, not like in the city, where you told me I shouldn't go anywhere with a stranger or cross the street by myself. Nobody would hurt me in Sunset."

Libby bent her head and took a deep breath. When she caught up with the caveman she was going to kill him. First because it sounded like he'd been telling her son bits and pieces of his so-called past, second because what he'd said to J.P. had just frightened fifty years off her life.

Pasting a smile on her face, she smoothed the boy's shirt, then hefted the amulet and checked out the back. Last time she'd seen it, the disk had been in two jagged pieces. Someone had taken the time to solder it together, and done a darn fine job of it. Turning it over, she stared at the profile etched in the metal. She couldn't even see a damage line.

J.P. jumped up and down. "Can I go now? Please? Declan's waiting for me."

"Hang on a second." She tried to focus on the disk, but J.P.'s impatient dance had the profile jiggling up, down and sideways. Whatever it was she thought she'd seen there was now a jumble.

Dropping the medallion, she pushed the tangle of curls off her son's forehead. "How about brushing your teeth and combing your hair before you go outside?"

"Aw, Mom—"

"After that, you can go to the gazebo, but no farther. If Declan's not around, wait for me. You can watch the band set up the speakers and instruments, but don't get underfoot or touch anything."

"Okay," J.P. said, shrugging his shoulders. "Then can we go see the kittens?"

Libby stood and started to make her bed. "We can. Mary will need help rounding them up. Has Uncle Tito decided to take you up on your offer?"

J.P. skipped from the room as he called over his shoulder, "Not yet, but I just know he's gonna want one."

Sighing, Libby headed for her closet. Picking through the rack, she decided to wear her pink-flowered cotton dress and sandals. By the time she was dressed, J.P. had thudded down the stairs and slammed the back door. She walked into the bathroom and applied astringent, sunscreen and a hint of mascara. The air was humid with the possibility of an approaching storm, but a rousing breeze ruffled the curtains, telling her that the day might be bearable. Still, she'd be wilted by noon if she didn't do something practical to stay cool.

Usually, she wore her hair down, simply because the heavy fall of curls never wanted to stay put. Last night she'd tried an upsweep, kind of like the old Gibson Girl look. It had taken a raft of bobby pins and hairspray, but she'd finally gotten the hang of it, and the do had held. When she'd inspected Declan's amulet, the style on the profile had seemed the same. Maybe that was what had caught her attention and tugged at her brain this morning, just a similar hairdo.

Five minutes later, her hair was arranged in a tidy bun with a few wayward tendrils curling around her face. Impressed, she turned her head from side to side, examining herself from several angles. "Nah," she whispered out loud. "It couldn't be."

She heard the off-key warble of a guitar in the distance, then the nails-on-blackboard screech of a sound system in protest. By now, J.P. was probably standing reverently in front of the bandstand, totally enthralled with the racket, mostly because it sounded exactly like he did when the boy tried to carry a tune.

Coffee. She needed coffee and maybe a piece of toast to start her day. Then she had to find Declan. After last night's embarrassing confrontation, he was sure to be ready for round two. But he'd had it coming, the arrogant jerk, acting as if she was some kind of possession. He'd been rude to one of her oldest friends, and certainly owed Jeff an apology as well. Who did he think he was, trying to dictate who she could and couldn't talk to? If she didn't know better, she'd think the caveman was jealous. Which was a totally preposterous idea.

Still, she had to hear for herself what Declan meant by his "It will keep you safe" comment. After that, she intended to ignore him for the rest of the day. There were suppliers to pay, booths to organize, and a program of events she needed to transfer to the blackboard.

Once the fair was underway, she'd have a huge amount of money to keep track of. She'd be so busy she wouldn't have a single free second to worry about the medallion or anything else that had to do with Declan O'Shae.

Declan watched the young men who made up the band called Screaming Mean fiddle with their instruments. Earsplitting vibrations and raucous squawks interspersed with the twang of an electric guitar had been erupting from the boxes placed around the outside of the gazebo for the past thirty minutes. From the way everyone was scurrying about taking care of business, it looked as if he was the only one bothered by the mind-numbing racket. Even J.P., who had arrived a few seconds earlier, seemed in awe.

Finally, Bob Jr. strummed his fingers across the guitar strings, and a ripple of notes trilled in the air at a respectable pitch. Nodding at Declan, he started to play, signaling that the bandstand was wired and ready for the upcoming festivities.

Declan stood next to J.P., and the boy automatically took his hand. "They play really good, don't they?"

"If you say so," he intoned, not wanting to burst the boy's bubble or bore him with an outdated opinion on acceptable music. Squatting down until they were at eye level, he inspected J.P.'s neatly groomed hair and clothes. "You look a fine figure of a man this morning. Ready to begin work, are you?"

J.P. held up the medallion. "Yep. I got your magic charm to keep me safe, so I can do anything you can do."

Declan kept his voice low as he tucked the golden circle under the boy's shirt. Earlier at breakfast, an unexplainable inner sense had compelled him to give the lad the token, but he hadn't meant for J.P. to show it to the world. "Did your mother see you wearing it?"

"Uh-huh. And she wasn't too happy about it. I think she wants to talk to you."

"Fine," Declan answered, his expression neutral. "Did you tell her it was only on loan?"

"Yep."

"Well, then. Good." Standing, he headed toward the docks. If Libby wanted to confront him about the medallion, she'd have to find him first. After last night's dunking, he wasn't ready to face her just yet. But his and Libby's rash actions on the dock, coupled with the profile on the amulet, had brought him to a singular conclusion. One that had him up and pacing until dawn.

He was in love with Libby Grayson.

When Tito first suggested the outlandish idea, he'd thought the man insane. Love was for men who wanted permanence, a family and a home on dry land, not for the likes of him. But a heartfelt and logical examination of his emotions had led him to no other explanation for the way he—the way they had both—behaved. The only thing left was to convince Libby she was in love with him as well, and get her to admit it.

Had she gazed long and hard enough at the medallion to recognize herself imprinted there? If so, the likeness was sure to aid him in his crusade. Even she would have to agree it went a long way in proving he'd been telling the truth. His only obstacle in fulfilling both their destinies was getting her to face the fact that they belonged together.

After the fair, he told himself. They could set everything to rights after the fair.

He and J.P. headed to the Spitzers' garage, where they helped Frank load prizes onto a truck and deliver them to the waiting booths. The men in charge of operating the rides pitched in, and soon the task was done. Now close to ten A.M., the workers started the merry-go-round and Ferris wheel for a final check of the equipment. In fine humor, one of the men offered J.P. a seat on the carousel. The boy scrambled onto a brightly painted horse and Declan strapped his safety belt, then jumped off just as the magical machine began to spin.

"Is it safe? Did you use the belt to buckle him on?"

Declan knew even before she spoke that Libby was near. Every nerve ending in his body shot to attention. Her familiar flowery scent filled his senses, just as her voice thrummed in his veins. Love, he quickly decided, was not such a bad state of being after all.

"Aye. I strapped him on myself." Turning, he trapped her with a look, hoping to find an echo of his own feelings in her eyes. "I'd never let anything harm your son, madam. Surely you know that by now."

She raised her chin to meet his penetrating gaze. "Yeah, I do," she said on a defeated sounding sigh. "But don't think he didn't tell me about that medallion-as-protection nonsense. I thought we agreed you weren't going to fill his head with any more fairy tales."

"God's blood," Declan hissed, his jaw clenched. "You are the most stubborn woman ever created. I thought you said you believed me. Did you even bother to take a good look at the amulet? Surely you recognized the profile. Hasn't it helped convince you of anything?"

J.P. flew by, calling out a frantic, "Mom. Watch me, Mom." Libby didn't answer, but Declan caught the tremor of her hand as she waved, saw the rosy glow suffuse her cheeks and the sheepish way she refused to meet his eyes. It was then that he realized she'd been lying the other night when she'd said she accepted his story. Libby knew what he was talking about, all right, and he was going to move heaven and earth to get her to admit it.

Grasping her upper arms, he turned her to face him. "How can you ignore the truth when it's staring you in the face? I don't know why you lied to me, but prevarication does not become you."

"I'm not—I wasn't—" She gave another halfhearted wave at J.P., then focused on Declan's chest. "It's just that I didn't get a chance to study the thing. Besides, lots of women look the same from the side. It could be a profile of anyone."

"It wasn't of just anyone, Libby," he said with a growl. "It's an exact depiction of you. And the medallion was given to me in seventeen eighty-three. Don't you realize what happened in that cave? *You* found the broken half. *You* carried it to my chest. *You* aligned the pieces and pushed them together. It wasn't until then that I awoke."

"No . . . you're wrong. One thing had nothing to do with

the other. It couldn't have—'' She raised her head to meet his questioning gaze. "Could it?"

Before he could answer, the carousel ground to a halt. J.P. hailed his mother. Bob Grisham called Declan's name over the loudspeaker, asking him to report to the construction shed. The spell was broken.

"Take the day to think on it. There'll be time to talk after the fair." With that, Declan marched toward the far end of the dock, his stride determined.

Libby shook her head. The caveman had to be mistaken. No medallion made over two centuries ago could have her profile etched on the front. This was just another one of his ploys to win her over and get her to believe his crazy story.

"Hey, Mom. Did'ja see? I was riding on that horse just like a cowboy. Where did Declan go? I waved, but he didn't wave back." J.P. grabbed at her dress. "Mom. Mom, where'd Declan go?"

"Hmm ... oh ... he had to help Mr. Grisham with something. We'll find him later." She spied an empty bench and led him there to sit. "Honey, are you still wearing the medallion?"

Nodding, J.P. laid a hand at his waist. "Uh-huh. But I don't think Declan wants me to show it to anyone."

"Do you think I could look at it again? One more time?"

"You're not gonna yell at him, are you? 'Cause I already told him you weren't happy he gave it to me."

Libby shook her head. "No yelling," she added, making a cross sign over her heart.

"Okay." J.P. tugged at the leather strip, then set the disk in her hand.

Squinting against the sun's reflection as it bounced off the shining metal, Libby held her breath. The woman's hairstyle looked exactly the way she'd worn it last night and today, and there was that same turned-up nose and strong chin Brett had always said mirrored her defiance. She traced the line of her jaw, then ran a trembling finger down her throat, so similar to the one on the profile. It was one of the physical traits she'd been most proud of, that long graceful arch that Jack had told her was just like her grandmother's. Brett had said it reminded him of Audrey Hepburn, the way her neck curved so delicately up from her shoulders. She'd always laughed at the description, because it had to be the only *delicate* thing on her entire body.

Libby gazed a bit longer, finishing her appraisal. Suddenly, her heart began to beat double-time in her chest.

"Mom. You okay? You're awful quiet," said J.P.

In a smooth but calculated move, she tucked the amulet down the front of his shirt and gave it a pat. "I'm fine, honey. What say we go find Mary and help her bring the kittens down to one of the booths? Would you like that?"

"Maybe Mary will let me carry one of 'em," he said, scrambling to his feet.

J.P. raced ahead while she slipped on her sunglasses. In the distance she could hear the joyous calliope-style music of the carousel. The aroma of food smoking in the barbeque pits Tito had set up last night wafted through the air. Up ahead, the Spitzers' gas station parking lot was beginning to fill with cars, as was the lot for the Queen of the Sea. The street was packed with tourists, all making a beeline for the dock.

Fearful that if she breathed too deeply she might hyperventilate, Libby took a few shallow gulps of air. The memory of the profile on the medallion was eerie enough. What Declan had failed to mention, because there was no way he could have known it, was the significance of the phrase etched along the perimeter of the disk. If he'd truly fought in the War for Independence, he'd think the words nothing more than poetically patriotic.

In the flurry of the fair, she and everyone else had forgotten her birthday. She'd been born on the Fourth of July, so her parents in their clever whimsy had named her in honor of the holiday. The word was one a freedom fighter would treasure, but the way it was used on the medallion meant

something else entirely to her, a woman named Liberty
Elizabeth.

*Through all time I search for Liberty, for she is mine unto
eternity.*

The day continued hot and muggy, but a brisk wind kept
the air moving enough that no one seemed to mind. Tourists
and locals from the mainland descended on Sunset in waves
of summer abandon. Libby was unsure whether it was the
energy of the holiday or the sheer draw of the fair, but
business was brisk. Attendees filled the Ferris wheel to
capacity, while a gaggle of children waited in line to ride
the merry-go-round. The ladies manning the quilting booth
were running out of merchandise, as was Ruth's antiques
stand and Olivia's trinket booth.

Libby'd already made two trips to the ticket kiosks to
collect money and driven into Marathon to make a deposit.
Lucky for her this was the day *before* the holiday and the
bank was open. She had no idea where she was going to
keep the profits tomorrow.

Right now, she was standing in front of the gazebo, watching Nelda McKey and her sister get their grandfather situated
in front of the video camera. Children and adults alike stood
at attention, waiting to hear the old man speak. Pete, dressed
in garb from a bygone era, looked alert and excited as he
sat on his wheelchair throne.

Nelda trotted down the steps and walked to Libby's side.
"Pete's as ready as he'll ever be, I guess," she said with
cheerful enthusiasm. "Maybe you could make a final
announcement over the speakers. Give 'em five minutes and
then he can get started."

Libby did as the woman asked, then sidled over to the
elderly man. "We're so happy you decided to join us, Pete.
Your story hour will be the highlight of the fair."

Pete gave a dry chuckle. The breeze from a stand-up fan
ruffled the few hairs left on his sun-browned head. "Haven't

been this excited since . . . hell, I can't remember when. And I'm gonna be on tape, so's the youngsters can see me again and again. How do ya like that?''

"I like it just fine," Libby answered, placing a hand on his bony shoulder. "I can't tell you how pleased I am that J.P. will get to hear you in person. I told the crowd you were going to choose a group of kids to sit at your feet and be in the film. You ready to do that?''

"Guess so. Just wheel me over to the edge there and I'll have me a look.''

Libby had gathered the children around the gazebo steps and announced that some of them were in for a special treat. Pete McKey was going to pick twelve youngsters to be in the video. Afterward, Olivia's sister would paint their faces free of charge in any style they liked.

About forty kids crowded the steps, each one bright-eyed and hopeful. Most had their hand raised; some jumped in place and shouted for attention. J.P. was in the second row, his hands clenched around Declan's medallion as if in prayer. Libby had kept an eye on him all day, observing his reaction to so many unfamiliar children. He'd be attending kindergarten in the fall, but he hadn't played with a single child since they'd arrived here weeks ago.

Pete gazed over the crush of boys and girls through rheumy gray eyes. Raising a gnarled hand he pointed a finger, first at a little girl Libby guessed to be about four. Dressed in pink with a cap of blond curls, she resembled a fluff of cotton candy. The youngster climbed the steps shyly, and Pete indicated she should crawl onto his lap, which she did. Then, one by one, he chose the victors: an older boy in typical baggy shorts and an oversized T-shirt, two girls who looked to be sisters, three boys who raced up to the stage whooping like Indians. Finally, there was one spot left.

Libby gnawed on her lower lip. J.P. hadn't moved so much as a pinkie finger. She imagined him holding his breath, much as she'd been doing. Pete scanned the crowd, then gave a cackle. "How about you, young fella?"

J.P. looked around to be certain he had it straight.

"You, there. The little guy with the big shiny medal on his chest. Come on up here, less'n you're afraid."

Tears stung her eyes as Libby watched her son's face light up like a Roman candle. He scrambled to the stage, and her heart filled with pride as J.P. stood in front of Pete. Pointing to a spot near his left side, he said, "Right there, son. That's the place for you."

J.P. complied, his grin even wider than the one he'd worn the day she told him that he could have a kitten. Almost as one, the crowd settled down. Some people sat on blankets, others opened lawn chairs, and a few dropped directly to the grass. Libby wended her way through the masses and found a spot in the shade of a palm tree at the edge of the square. Pete waited a few seconds, then cleared his throat.

"Howdy. I'm honored to be here, as this is prob'ly my first and last appearance in such a public place." He set one hand on cotton-candy girl, another on J.P.'s head. "These here children are the future, but they need to hear about the past. All a you do, seein' as what happened here hundreds of years ago affects us today.

"Now, I'm gonna tell it straight, like it was told to me by my father and his before that, and his before that. It's all true. Mostly, anyways." The crowd tittered, and so did Pete. "So you just sit back and listen.

"Once upon a time, there was a young man came from Dublin; that's in Ireland, in case you don't know. His name don't matter none, and nobody remembers it anyway, but the story begins with him. He was a privateer, but some called him a pirate, just the same. And when he sailed his ship to America, he brought with him the first of my ancestors, Black Pete Mackelvy. Black Pete was a first mate on the ship, so he knew what was what. And he remembered it all and told it to his children, making them promise to keep his story alive.

"It was right after the War for Independence, 'bout seventeen eighty-three, I'd say, that Pete and his captain and crew sailed down to the Keys to unearth their treasure. What they found instead still haunts these islands today.

"They began their journey southward toward an inlet not far from here, but before they reached land the devil's own breath blew up a terrible storm. The sky grew black. Rain streamed in blinding sheets and the wind howled like a banshee, tossing the boat as if it were a bathtub toy. In seconds, the ocean turned to blood before their eyes." Pete's voice dropped ominously. "Never before had they seen anything like it."

Libby's breath hitched in her throat as the year jumped out at her. It had been forever since she'd heard this tale. Why didn't she remember Pete mentioning that exact date in his earlier stories? Why hadn't the words sounded familiar when Declan had spoken them a week ago? Frantically, she searched the crowd, looking for the caveman. It would be just like him to have gotten to Pete somehow and convinced the old man to adapt his story.

"The captain lashed himself to the wheel in hopes of saving his ship. Black Pete Mackelvy did his job as first mate and battened the hatches, but it was no use. The mizzen mast snapped in two as the vessel rose out of the water and split apart with a thunderous crack. He and the crew jumped overboard, just as the captain untied his ropes and hurled himself into the sea."

Each word, every sentence burned itself into Libby's brain. Despite her shock, she continued to scan the audience. Heads bobbed in agreement with Pete's colorful description. They all knew the old man was describing a hurricane, but back then that type of storm had no name. Standing on tiptoe, she squinted into the sun. Where was Declan? Why wasn't he here, listening to Pete tell his story?

"Now, Pete was a strong swimmer, and he made it to shore. Dragged himself to the mangroves and waited out the storm. But he never saw hide nor hair of any of his shipmates or his captain again. They'd all perished in the gale and found their rest in Poseidon's graveyard. It was Pete who picked himself up and headed inland. He made friends with a small band of renegade Caloosa Indians and founded a settlement down the road, over on Windley Key. It's his descendants that spread throughout these islands and began to build what we have today.''

Pete droned on, holding the crowd in the palm of his hand, like a true showman. He had about an hour left to speak before his time was up. If people wanted to hear the second half, the part on local lore and animal legend, they would have to return tomorrow. Nelda's idea about breaking Pete's tale into two acts had inadvertently guaranteed Sunset that at least some of the tourists would return.

Mary appeared at her side and put her arm around Libby's shoulder. ''Hey now, you're pale as a ghost. Is something wrong?''

Libby gave a weak smile. ''I'm tired and I need to go home for a little while. Can you watch J.P. for me when story hour is over?''

''No problem. And I'll get Frank to collect the next round of money from the ticket-takers. How's that sound?''

''It sounds great. Thanks.''

Mary threaded her way through the crowd to wait for J.P. Relieved that she didn't have to worry about her son for a while, Libby set a hand to her heart and sagged against the rough palm bark. Closing her eyes, she massaged the knot of nerves that always sprang up over the bridge of her nose when she was at a loss. She had to take a walk and find a quiet place to gather her thoughts. She'd been wrong about Declan O'Shae.

Wrong about everything.

Chapter Twenty

The hair on the back of Declan's neck stood on end. It was just past sunset and he was about to perform with the band when a gust of wind blew across the town square, rattled the gazebo where he stood, and rudely pushed its way into their midst.

He looked to the west and spied a mountain of greenish black clouds moving furiously in his direction. Fear settled like a cannon ball in the pit of his stomach. The last time he'd seen those clouds the devil had walked the earth, and life as he'd known it had changed. He swallowed as he glanced over the unsuspecting crowd.

Tito barreled through the revelers just as the first wave of rain hit the square. Racing up the grandstand steps, his face sported a massive frown. "We's in big trouble, O'Shae. That storm I said was comin'—well, it's here. I already tol' the men workin' the rides to shut down. Folks is startin' to gather up the games and prizes and such, but I'm afraid it's gonna be too late."

Declan turned to Bob Jr. and grabbed the boy's guitar. "Turn off the instruments, lad, and start packing. If you can, unhook the power supply. There's a storm coming, and it looks to be a bad one.''

People finally began to react to the force of the rain, clutching at loved ones as they raced to their cars. Jack appeared at the foot of the stairs, heaving and out of breath. ''I got the dock cleared, but we have to find shelter for these folks. Now! There's no time to get them off the key.''

Flashlights in hand, Phil and Don shoved their way through the crowd, followed by a group of fishermen. Locking gazes with Declan and Jack, they shouted, ''There's room at the restaurant. Have them follow us!''

In silent agreement, Declan and Tito nodded. The Queen of the Sea was the best place to hole up. Larger and more modern than most of the buildings, it was protected on both sides and had an emergency generator, just for this type of emergency. After a quick exchange of ideas, they decided to send the overflow to the Spitzers' garage. If that filled up, they would use Olivia's shop.

With Phil and Don in the lead, the fishermen marshaled the mob. ''Everybody follow us to the Queen of the Sea! Take it slow and easy. No need to panic.''

Rain washed down in sheets, subduing the masses as they fought against the driving water. Slowly, folks began to move toward the restaurant. Jack fought a head wind to stay at Declan's side and shouted into his ear, but the unruly breeze tossed his words away.

Declan grabbed the older man's arms and held him in place. ''What! I didn't hear you. What did you say?''

Jostled from all sides, Jack tottered in his grip. ''It's J.P. and Libby. The boy's disappeared, and I haven't seen her for hours. We have to find them.''

The fear in Declan's gut swelled to mammoth proportions. ''I'll do it. You help Tito with the women and children. Head to the Queen of the Sea.''

Jack's lips opened and closed. Declan turned the man away and pushed hard. ''Go!''

Libby. J.P. Sweet Jesus, where had they gone? He prayed

they were together somewhere safe, but why hadn't he looked for them earlier, instead of sitting in that cursed dunking booth. Buffeted by the wind, Declan grabbed at the gazebo railing. A woman carrying a baby stumbled by and he broke his hold, hustling her to the rear of a line of stragglers. Scanning the now deserted square, he saw the street lamps flicker and wink out. He floundered to the middle of the road at the same time that a figure in a flowered dress staggered toward him from the direction of the Pink Pelican.

"Libby!" A wall of rain slammed the ragged cry back in his face. With arms pumping pistonlike, he raced to meet her. Libby saw him and ran faster.

"Declan! Thank God!" She swayed into his arms, gasping for breath. "I lost track of the time. I didn't realize—" She grabbed at his shirt and kissed him hard on his lips. "I have to tell you. You have to know—"

Even through the driving rain, he found the wherewithal to grin. "I do know. Now tell me, where is your son?"

Her face washed pale. "Isn't he with Mary or Jack?"

He shook his head. "Where was he when you saw him last?"

"At Pete's story hour." Libby's gaze darted across the square, her face a mask of terror. "Oh, God, we've got to find him."

Fearful that if he allowed Libby to search, he might never see her again, Declan held her in place. She was having a hard time just keeping her footing against the force of the storm. The wind had risen to an unholy roar. Water streamed down so hard, he thought he might be drowning on land. The sky was black as pitch, and there was no electricity to light the way. He'd slept through centuries to find her, by God. He wasn't about to lose her now.

Hoisting her up, he tossed her over his shoulder and headed toward the Queen of the Sea. Bucking and kicking, Libby shrieked like a banshee, pummeling at his back with her fists. He ignored her fury and pushed through the door to the restaurant, where he passed her off to Tito.

"See to it she stays put. I'm going to find J.P."

Libby struggled in the islander's arms. Her expression turned to defeat as Tito shook her from behind. "Here now, there be none a that goin' on. We got frightened chil'ens to care for. 'Sides, one of you runnin' around in this storm is enough. You be a grown-up and stay here to help."

Libby hung like a rag doll. She raised her head, and Declan read the silent plea in her eyes. "I'll find J.P. and keep him safe." Reaching out, he stroked her cheek. "That's a promise."

Charging out the door, Declan forged into the darkness. Trudging toward the dock, he fought his way through the opposing wall of rain. Bits of trash and vegetation grazed his head and struck at his chest. The wharf shook under his feet as waves crashed over the boards, raking the booths and pounding at the rides.

"J.P! J.P., are ya here, lad?"

He inspected every booth, shouted into the gusting wind, but received no answer to his calls. Retracing his steps to the town square, a hurricane shutter came out of nowhere and slammed into his shoulder, almost tearing his arm from its socket.

Blinded by the pain, Declan sucked in a mouthful of water. Roofing thatch and shingles pelted him from all sides. He clutched his injured arm to his chest and bit back a curse. He had yet to check the bar. The boy could have gone to the Pink Pelican, looking for his mother or Jack.

Staggering up the steps, he raced through the kitchen door. The bar swayed on it pilings, moaning in the wind. Groping along the counter, he found a towel and made a sling, then stuffed his useless arm through the cloth, ignoring the stab of pain.

"J.P.! Are ya in here, son?" He jolted into the bar and stumbled against a round of tables and chairs.

"Declan!"

The pathetic cry came from somewhere beneath his feet. *I'm going mad,* he thought, staring at the floor.

"Declan, I'm here!"

"J.P.? Where are you?"

The little boy's voice grew louder. "Here! I'm under here!"

Sweet Mary and all the saints. J.P. was *under* the building!

"Stay where you are, lad. I'm coming!"

Fumbling back through the bar, he made his way to the half bath and dug into one of the boxes in the closet Tito had once told him held emergency supplies. He raised the flashlight and flicked the switch, grunting in approval when it shot to life. Bolting from the bathroom, he dived out the rear door and slid down the steps, smashing his wounded arm on the stair newel.

The roar of the storm intensified, shutting out everything except the wail of the wind and the beating of the rain. Dropping to his knees, Declan scuttled under the edge of the porch, thrust the flashlight in front of him and searched for his quarry. There, sitting dead center under the bar, was J.P. huddled over a tattered cardboard box.

He scooted forward a few inches, but the logistics failed him. He was too big a man to fit under the building, and he only had one good arm. There was no way he could hold the flashlight and drag himself forward at the same time.

"Declan." J.P.'s face was dirty, his shirt torn, but his smile said he was unharmed. "Are you here to save us?"

Us? Something big and hard hit him in the backside and slammed him forward. Declan's forehead rammed into a board and he saw stars as his injured arm met the ground. Shaking his head, he took a slow, deep breath. "Aye, lad, that I am. Can you come to me? Are you well enough to crawl?"

J.P. stared down into the box. His eyes wide, he shouted, "I can't leave 'em here. They might die."

"They?" Declan yelled back. "What they?"

"The kittens. I got the last three. One for Tito, one for me, an' one for you."

The kittens. Declan closed his eyes and muttered an oath. His injured arm throbbed in rhythm to the pulsing in his brain. He might have known the lad would be off rescuing his precious cats instead of worrying about himself. Grinning feebly, he arced the flashlight toward the center of the ground. The boy was all heart, and smart, too. He'd picked a spot that would protect them. Flying debris had little chance of finding its way under the floor of the bar.

Perhaps this was the best place for them both to be. Even if J.P. got brave and agreed to crawl out, there was no way he could carry the boy with his arm in such a sorry state.

"Are you comin'?" J.P.'s voice trembled above the sound of the wind.

Inching under the porch, Declan rolled to his wounded side and hefted the flashlight in his good hand. "I'm going to throw you the light, boy, and I want you to catch it. If you miss, just move nice and slow until you have it. Do you understand, lad? Did you hear what I asked you to do?"

"Uh-huh." J.P. shoved the box away and crouched, readying his hands.

Declan drew a long deep breath. Raising his good arm, he threw with a quick jerk. The flashlight hit the ground a foot in front of the box and rolled in a slow circle.

J.P. dove forward and clutched at the light. "I got it!"

"There's my lad," he called, masking the pain in his voice. "Now shine it toward me so that I can see where you are. Give me a minute, and I'll be at your side."

He rolled again, until the pressure was off his injured arm, then dropped back to his belly. Gritting his teeth, he began the twenty-foot, one-armed drag-and-slither needed to get to John Patrick.

Huddled against a front window of the restaurant, Libby stared out into the darkness. Damn the caveman for bringing her here, and Tito's logic for keeping her inside. Every muscle and joint ached, her lower back was tied in a knot, and her feet felt the size of snowshoes. It had to be near dawn. The rain had stopped an hour earlier. Birds were twittering, and she could hear the brisk aftermath of a breeze blowing across the key.

Last night, after she'd calmed down, she'd given T her word she would wait at the Queen of the Keys for Declan's return. Common sense told her it would do no good to race around in the dark while the wind tore the island apart. Tito was right when he reminded her that she had to be here if J.P. managed to find his way to the only lighted building in town. But that didn't stop her from pacing away the hours, staring out the window into the eye of the storm as it battered the restaurant and ravaged her world.

Robotlike, she'd thrown herself into the job of comforting the tourists. She'd made hot tea, served soup, quieted fussy children, and turned tablecloths into blankets. But her heart hadn't been in the effort. All she could think about were the two most important people in her life, trapped in the gale.

Had J.P. spent the night alone and frightened, crying for her to rescue him? Had Declan gotten caught up in the storm and been injured? Had he found her son and gotten them to safety? Where was Declan? And where was J.P.?

Propping her back against the door, she furrowed her fingers through her hair as she gazed over a sea of bodies. Most were still sleeping in clustered groups under the tables, while others lay between or on top. A few people were talking in whispers. She spied a light in the kitchen, heard the hum of voices. If Tito and Phil were making breakfast, it had to be near morning. No one would notice if she slipped out to start her search.

Grabbing a flashlight from the windowsill, she slid her feet back into her damp shoes. Making a mental list of the places she was going to search, she threw the bolt on the door and crossed the threshold, where she ran smack into her own personal gift from heaven, J.P. with his hand poised to knock.

Libby's heart two-stepped into a victory dance. His hair stood up in spiky curls and his face was streaked with mud, but her child was definitely unharmed. Sobbing, she swooped down and grabbed him, alternately hugging him to her breast and patting him down for broken bones. "Honey, are you okay? Where have you been? Where's Declan? Did he find you?" She smothered him in her arms. "Where have you been?" she babbled again. "Are you all right?"

She felt a hand on her shoulder and gazed up at Tito. "Let Jack know he's safe, okay?"

Turning back to her son, she found him regarding her through solemn eyes. "Honey, do you know where Declan is?"

J.P. nodded, then grasped at her skirt and tugged her toward the stairs. "He found me last night, but now somethin's wrong. Declan's with the kittens and he won't wake up. You got to come help."

Libby stood in the pale dawn light, hands over her mouth in shock. All that was left of the Pink Pelican were the pilings and floorboards, plus the kitchen area, with its sink, stove, and refrigerator. Huge sections of wall, thatch and shingles lay scattered across the green or in the street. The chairs and tables, the bottles of liquor, even the beautiful oak bar, had simply disappeared.

Thank God J.P. had had the good sense to crawl under the bar to hide instead of going inside. Thank God the floor had held. And thank God Declan had found him.

With her heart beating frantically, she dropped to her hands and knees in the mud and peered under the ragged remains of the porch while J.P. crouched beside her. Declan was about twenty feet away, lying still as a corpse. J.P. said he'd been that way most of the night. At first he'd thought

Declan was asleep, but this morning when he hadn't moved J.P. knew he had to get help.

"Mom, is Declan gonna die?" he sniffed. " 'Cause if he does, it'll be all my fault."

Libby swung around to hug him tight. "Not if I can help it, honey. You did everything right. You were a very clever boy to hide under there when you didn't see anyone you knew. By finding me this morning, you probably saved Declan's life."

J.P. nodded, but the look of disbelief in his eyes shot straight to her mother's heart. This wasn't the time to lecture him because he'd disobeyed Mary and put himself in danger to save a few kittens. If Declan died, she would find the strength to go on, but her son would be traumatized for life. There had to be something—

"J.P., do you still have the medallion?"

"Uh-huh." He pulled the amulet up and out of his shirt. "It per-tek-ed me all night. I tried to give it back to Declan, but he said it was important I keep it."

"Well, now that you're safe, I think this might be a good time to talk him into accepting it. What do you say?"

Whipping the disk from around his neck, he handed it to Libby. "But who's gonna give it to him?"

She kissed his forehead, then tucked the glittering token in the front pocket of her dress. "I am, silly. And while I'm doing that, I want you to run to the Queen of the Sea and go straight to Uncle Tito. Tell him Declan's hurt and we have to get the rescue squad back here on the double. Okay?"

J.P. took off at a run. Inhaling a deep breath, Libby ordered herself to be strong. Lowering herself to her elbows and dropping to her belly, she half-crawled, half-dragged herself toward her target. Declan lay on his back, one arm cocked awkwardly, the other flung out from his side. He looked to be asleep, but his breathing was shallow. She set the back of her hand on his cheek and found him cold to the touch. Curling into him, she placed her palm on his chest, where she felt the slow but steady beat of his heart.

"Hey, O'Shae. You awake? Come on, big guy, talk to me."

Declan lay still as stone, just as he had that day she'd found him in the cave. Biting back tears, she groped for the medallion and set it on his shirt, then draped the leather thong around his neck. The disk had brought Declan to her, then called him awake. Maybe there was enough magic left to work one more miracle.

Slowly, his eyelids flickered. In awe, she gave a silent prayer of thanks, still not certain of what had just happened.

"Umph." He rolled his head toward her. Licking at his lips, he asked in a raspy voice, "J.P.?"

"He's safe. The little stinker." *And it's all because of you.* She smoothed the tangle of hair off his forehead, wincing at the bloody three-inch gash she found. "But you don't look so good. How do you feel?"

This time, when his lashes fluttered, Declan's lids remained open. "Like I was rammed head-on by a frigate. This century is damned dangerous to a man's skull."

"Lucky for you you're such a hardheaded Irishman, huh?" She smiled through a sheen of tears. God, how she loved him. "Tell me what hurts."

Declan frowned, moving his upper body. "My shoulder and my arm. Afraid something is . . . broken." One corner of his mouth twitched as he tried to focus. "And there are two of you."

Libby knew the signs of a concussion and guessed Declan's was a doozy. But he was breathing and coherent and definitely alive. And he had risked his life to save her son. "I'm going to stay with you until we figure a way out of here. The sun's up, so it shouldn't take long. Hang tight, okay?"

He turned to face her and the breath hissed from between his clenched teeth. "I'll be fine," he groaned. "In another hundred years or so."

From overhead came the sound of footsteps and voices. She turned to see Jack peering from under the porch. "Liberty? Liberty Elizabeth, is everything all right? Did you find him?''

"Liberty? Did Jack just call you Liberty?" Declan asked, taking a gulp of air.

She laid a hand on the medallion and felt it pulse against her palm. In a heartbeat, all her fears and doubts vanished and she was enfolded in a blanket of calm. With one long sigh of happiness, she saw the past, the present and the blessed future there in Declan's eyes. It didn't matter if he left Sunset, because she would follow him to the ends of the earth, sleep by his side, live with him, die with him . . . as long as she could be *with him*.

"It's a long story, but something tells me you'll understand." Declan squeezed her fingers. Swallowing a sob, she called to her grandfather, "Declan's fine. But he's going to need the rescue squad. We have to get him out of here."

Precious seconds passed while she listened to the men argue above them. A few of their ideas were frightening, especially the one where Frank wanted to get his tow truck and winch Declan out from under like a stalled Buick. When Bob Grisham arrived, she knew it would only be a matter of time before they were freed safely.

Finally Jack was back at the edge of the porch, his sun-browned face wreathed in a smile. "Lie still and don't worry. Bob's got everything under control. Oh, and Libby, cover your head, if you can. Declan's, too. This might get dicey."

Declan managed a strangled-sounding laugh. "I've heard more comforting words in my lifetime."

Libby silently agreed as she searched and found the remains of the box she guessed J.P. had used to carry the kittens. They, unlike the caveman, had managed to crawl out on their own. With a bit of agile maneuvering, she laid the flattened cardboard over their heads.

"You ready down there?" called Bob.

"Ready," she shouted. Turning, she again placed her hand on the medallion and snuggled close. "Once we get you out of here, everything's going to be fine."

"Is that a promise, madam?" Declan asked, eyeing her under the cardboard shield.

Libby nodded, then remembered there was something she'd forgotten to do. "I think this might be a good time to tell you I love you."

Grinning, he raised a brow. "And?"

"And I believe you . . . about everything."

"Everything?"

"Every word."

Declan met her halfway in a kiss that was sweet and fierce and filled his heart with hope. The medallion flashed a wave of heat across his chest, and he knew in that instant his destiny had been fulfilled. If he never spent another moment on earth, the journey he'd made to find Liberty Grayson had been worth the risk.

He turned his head toward the boulders that marked his treasure, useless rock hiding useless gold. In the beginning, he'd thought it was the reason he'd been brought to this time. Since he'd lost his heart to Libby, he'd become a much wiser man. His love for her, the woman who was his destiny, had drawn him to this time. The medallion knew the truth. Like Tito, it was never wrong.

Something creaked above them as falling debris rained down on the cardboard. Libby smiled from the shadows. "I think the cavalry has arrived."

Content, Declan dropped a swift kiss on her nose. "By the way, I love you, too, and that boy of yours. You should know I intend to spend the rest of my life showing you both how much."

A lone tear trickled across her hope-filled face. "Sounds to me like you're planning to hang around for a while."

"For eternity, if you'll have me." He placed his lips on the salty-sweet drop. "And you know I'm a man of my word."

Epilogue

Declan stared at the group of boulders that marked his buried treasure. Two weeks had passed since Sunset had been hit by the strangely mystical storm. Thanks to Tito's healing potions and Libby's careful nursing, his separated shoulder and concussion were almost a memory. The joy of having J.P. sit on his bed, entertaining him with games and stories while he recuperated, had been a balm to Declan's soul.

Having Libby hover over him while he mended, hearing her tell him every day how much she loved him, had been just short of heaven on earth.

It had been clever of Bob to cut that four-foot square in the floorboards and haul them up from under. After what happened to the Pink Pelican, everyone thought a hole in the floor would be the least of Jack's worries. Libby, of course, had been the person most upset about the demise of the bar, until the old man informed her that he'd had the good sense to keep up his insurance payments.

The only other damage to the town had been lost thatch and shingles, a few broken shutters, and the disappearance of the laughing dolphin from the gazebo's cupola. Oddly enough, the storm had turned back out to sea after it passed through Sunset.

Once he realized the destruction of the Pink Pelican was the hand of Fate giving him a shove, Declan had contemplated long and hard about whether or not to dig up his loot. The townsfolk could use the money, but he wasn't sure he wanted the burden. He'd signed a lucrative contract to record for Sounds of Time, Clive had assured him that they could obtain a birth certificate and the papers necessary to make him legal, and Libby believed in him unconditionally.

The gold was a symbol of his past. He had a new life with the woman of his heart, and a son who thought he walked on water—all treasures worth a hundred times more than a strongbox full of doubloons.

Crossing the street, he settled in a deck chair under the shade of a palm tree to think. Did he truly need more riches in his life? In a few moments Jack and Tito would be here to clear the last of the debris before cement trucks arrived to pour the new foundation. If they handled the bulk of the work themselves, the money Jack had received from the insurance company would stretch far enough for the rebuilding. With help from the locals, the new Pink Pelican Bar and Grill would be up and running in time for the tourist season. After that, nothing short of an earthquake would bring the gold to light.

"Hey, Declan." J.P. trotted from the direction of Frank Spitzer's garage, a small spade in his hand and three kittens scrambling at his heels. "Grandpa Jack is comin'. We're gonna dig for buried treasure."

"Are you, now?" asked Declan, puzzled by the sudden niggling in his gut. He set a hand to his chest and found the medallion warm under his fingers. "And where exactly might that be?"

"There." J.P. pointed. "By those boulders. Grandpa Jack said he wanted to dig 'em up when he first built the bar, but Grandma Martha talked him out of it. He says this time, when he builds the new Pink Pelican, he's gonna do it right.''

Declan almost jumped from his chair. Damn if the amulet wasn't about to set his chest hairs on fire. "And who said anything about finding treasure there?"

"Uncle Tito did. He rolled the bones and said the goddess was smilin' on us."

Shaking his head, Declan heaved a sigh of resignation. No matter what he decided, it seemed Fate and the medallion would have their due. Black Pete crouched, then sailed into his lap for a stroking. "And what of your mother? What does she have to say about the idea?"

J.P. shrugged, patting the kitten's head. "I don't think she knows. Grandpa Jack said we have to prove to her it's there." Fidgeting in place, he whooped at the sight of Jack and Tito ambling toward them, shovels and pickaxes in hand.

"Declan," said Jack, drawing near. "Fine mornin' for a treasure hunt, ain't it?"

"So I heard. Would you like some help?"

Tito set a hand on Declan's shoulder. "Jack and me can handle it. Don't want you doin' nothin' to mess up that shoulder." He raised his gaze and frowned. "Uh-oh. Here comes trouble."

Jack, J.P. and Declan turned as one to see Libby, dressed in jeans and an oversized red T-shirt, charging toward them, a shovel hoisted over her shoulder. "Is everybody ready?" she asked, her eyes shining golden in the early morning light.

"Ready?" Jack's weathered face turned pale. "For what?"

Libby fisted a hand on her hip. "Don't think you can fool me, Jack Grayson. I heard you and T whispering in the kitchen last night, and there's no way I'm not getting in on this. If you're going to find buried treasure, I want to be with you when you do."

T boomed out a laugh. "Well, well, well, you is just full

of surprises. Come on, boy, we'd better get started, less'n your momma beats us to the loot.''

Black Pete bounded to the ground and followed his siblings, J.P., and Tito across the street. Jack ran a shaky hand over his eyes, then stepped to Libby's side and gave her a hug. ''I'm glad you decided to be my little girl again, Liberty. I really missed you.'' Winking away a tear, he walked with a sprightly step to the boulders.

Libby set down her shovel, plopped onto Declan's knee, and rested her head in the crook of his neck. Pulling her close, he kissed her soundly, reveling in the way she melted in his arms. She was a perfect fit, this woman who was his destiny. And after their wedding next weekend, she would be his forever.

Breaking the kiss, she snuggled against him while they watched the crowd gathering across the way. ''So,'' Declan began, waiting for the fun to start, ''it sounds like you believe they'll find buried treasure.''

Libby's unladylike snort ended on a laugh. ''I know, I'm being foolish. It's just that so many wonderful things have happened since we found each other. My son is a happy, well-adjusted little boy again, you and the Applewaithes have come to an agreement, and Sounds of Time is sponsoring next year's fair—who am I to spoil the fun by saying there isn't another miracle waiting in the wings?''

''I see,'' Declan answered, trying his best not to grin. ''And what if I told you it was there?''

She jerked up her head and stared, her eyes wide. ''That what was there?''

''A treasure.''

''A treasure?'' Libby frowned. ''Buried under the Pink Pelican?'' Seconds passed before a glimmer of understanding washed over her pale face.

He raised a brow in encouragement.

''The treasure you were looking for that day I caught you crawling under the bar? The one J.P. kept saying he wanted to help you find?''

Declan nodded.

"The one Pete McKey mentioned in his story?"

"Undoubtedly."

"Oh, my God." She pursed her lips and blew out a breath. "I—I—I'm speechless."

"That's good," Declan murmured. Leaning down, he kissed her again—until J.P.'s shouts and Jack's hysterical cackle drew them apart.

Libby shot to her feet. Bouncing on her toes, she tried to see over the small crowd gathered around the boulders. Dancing a jig, Jack was pointing at the ground; Tito high-fived J.P., then swung him in a circle. She pulled Declan from the chair, then took off at a run. Jostling her way through the gaping group of seniors, she dropped to her knees and gazed into the hole they'd dug.

J.P. skidded to her side, his eyes big as gold doubloons. Scrabbling in the earth, he scooped out the rusty metal box and thrust it at her. "Treasure! We found treasure!"

Libby's breath caught in her throat. She swiped her T-shirt over the lid and gasped. "DJO," she whispered, reading the initials scratched in the tin. "Seventeen seventy-eight."

She locked eyes with Declan. The man was grinning like a fool.

"Open it, Mom," J.P. demanded. His fingers danced in the air. "Go on. Open it."

Jack squatted beside her. "It's okay, Liberty. Even if it's empty, the joy was always in the believin'."

Tears welled behind her eyelids. Standing, she held out the box to Declan.

He shook his head. His eyes told her that he already knew what they would find. " 'Tis yours, madam, yours and the boy's to do with what you will. I've already found the only treasure I'll ever need."

Libby smiled through her tears. Turning, she placed the box in her grandfather's trembling hands. Stepping to Declan's side, she took his hand, and together they walked through the crowd and across the street to his chair under the palm tree.

She heard shouts and cries of wonder, and knew Jack had opened the box. But it didn't matter what was inside. She, too, had found a treasure. And for now and eternity, she had her very own happily-ever-after.

Free Public Library of Monroe Township
306 S. Main Street
Williamstown, NJ 08094-1727

Please turn the page for an exciting
preview of Judi McCoy's
next contemporary romance
HEAVEN IN YOUR EYES.
A May 2003 paperback release from Zebra Books.

Tom glanced up from his post at the desktop TV. The doughboy wasn't kidding when he said his idea was a radical one. "Let me see if I've got this plan of yours straight. I'm supposed to return to earth and enter the body of another human being, someone who can get close enough to Annie to push her in the direction needed to find happiness. And my only choice is one of those three exemplary subjects on the view screen."

"That's it exactly," said Milton.

"Well, gee, let's just review the lucky contenders. Behind door number one we have Annie's sixteen-year-old paperboy—an oversexed, acne-prone, dope-smoking adolescent who's been peeking in her window at night to watch her undress—"

Milton stared down at Warren Beavers, six feet of gangly, testosterone-laden teenager. To say he had the IQ of a chimpanzee would be too kind. "Warren's body is young and malleable. If you're able to get it off drugs, you'd have a long life span; you could relive your teen years, go to college again, be or do anything you wanted."

"Swell. I could go through the agony of drug withdrawal, the uncertainty of getting into a good college, the misery of trying to get laid, the difficulty of choosing the right career—all the good stuff that makes kids want to grow up fast—all over again." Tom ran a hand over his jaw. "Just what every man wants to hear at my age."

Milton *tsked*. "You make adolescence sound like hell on earth. It isn't that difficult. Besides, you've already committed your share of mistakes. You know what works and what doesn't.''

''And I don't want to do it over again. My life may not have been one you approved of, but I worked hard to get where I was. I had a good job, money in the bank, a happy mar—''

''Tom.''

''Whatever. Let's get back to my choices, pathetic though they are.''

''All right.'' Milton sighed. ''Take a look at panel number two—Esther Rabinowitz. She lives in Annie's building. If you picked Esther, you wouldn't have to do much more than find the right man for Annie. You'd be back up here in no time.''

Tom studied the cranky-faced, gray-haired woman sitting in a wheelchair. She was leaning out a window with a rifle of some sort in her hand and looked mean enough to eat rattlesnake for breakfast. ''What's she doing?''

''Oh, she's just keeping occupied,'' the doughboy muttered. Esther pulled the trigger and the recoil slammed her backward in her seat. ''Shooting at the rats that scavenge the alley behind the apartment building.''

Tom shuddered. ''Great, a senior psycho. What would I do, wing some homeless guy scrounging in the Dumpsters and tell Annie to go out back and bag her man?''

''There's no need to be flippant. She is your first available. If you don't choose her, Mrs. Rabinowitz won't be with us past today.''

Tom made a rude noise in the back of his throat as he peered into the desktop. ''And choice number three is that— that criminal. A man so devoid of decency, his only thought is to save his own hide. A mobster-turned-informant who, if he does manage to survive long enough to testify, will probably disappear to another state.''

''I agree that Dominic Viglioni is a long shot, but he's closest to her right now, and Annie's supposed to be on this job for a while. Besides, he might need an agent to accompany him to his new life. That agent could be her.''

Tom bit back a snort of laughter. Right about now, the *other* place was looking darned good.

''You don't mean that,'' snapped Milton. ''No one in their right mind wants to go there, even for a visit.''

''Okay, okay. I was just thinking.'' Tom rubbed at his chin. ''So, I have to become one of these three people to get a second chance at heaven. Somehow, through them, I'm supposed to insinuate myself into Annie's life and help her find a husband. Do I have it right?''

Milton sniffed. ''Not just a husband, the perfect husband. One who will make her truly happy.''

''And after she's happily married, I'd get the chance to live out my life in one of those bodies, then get sent back up here. Only I'd go straight to the *good* place.''

''Not automatically,'' Milton clarified. ''There would still be rules to follow. The remainder of your life would have to be exemplary. You couldn't go out and commit mayhem just because you helped Annie find happiness.''

Mayhem? What the hell was mayhem anyway? Tom wondered, staring at the blue-and-white expanse of ceiling above him. ''And if I say no way, no how, no thank you to this mind-boggling offer? Then what?''

Milton puckered his lips. ''Then it will be the *other place* for you.''

''Hell?'' Tom's eyes shot open wide. ''I'm going to hell just because I was a failure as a husband? Jeez, I think there are a whole lot of men down there who deserve to be informed of that little news flash, don't you? Once word gets out that being a lousy spouse is a one-way ticket to eternal damnation, it's going to change the face of marriage around the world.''

''Not that place,'' the angel said with a *tsk*. ''The *other* other place—where you were before you came here. And I guarantee you'll be in a holding pattern for a lot longer than six years.'' Milton bounced on the balls of his feet. ''Trust me, one of those three humans is your best ticket for getting into heaven within a reasonable amount of time.''

Tom wanted to scream. He wanted to stomp and shout and curse at the top of his lungs. Why hadn't someone informed him of the rules while he still had a heartbeat? The only tenet he'd ever learned was the one that said life wasn't fair. Whoever had coined that little gem had obviously never talked to a heavenly being.

Milton stared at him as if he were a first-grader cheating on an exam. ''Don't be childish. You knew very well what the rules were. I believe He sent the human race a raft of men and women who listed them quite clearly. You simply chose to ignore them, as do so many of your brethren. Next thing you'll be telling me is that you didn't know there was life on other planets.''

ABOUT THE AUTHOR

JUDI MCCOY considers herself one of the world's luckiest women. She has a wonderful husband, a loving family and two lapdogs to keep her company while she writes. Besides accomplishing her dream of becoming a published author of romantic fiction, she is an elite-level women's gymnastic judge. She has lived in Illinois, New Jersey, Texas, and Maryland. In the fall of 2002 she'll be moving to a new house at the tip of the Delmarva Peninsula in Cape Charles, Virginia. Please visit her website at *www.judimccoy.com* or send a note to her at *judi1022@AOL.com*. She loves to hear from her fans, and promises to answer every e-mail.